Mary Pepperrell Sparhawk Jarvis Cutts

The Life and Times of Honored William Jarvis of Weathersfield

Mary Pepperrell Sparhawk Jarvis Cutts

The Life and Times of Honored William Jarvis of Weathersfield

ISBN/EAN: 9783337337063

Printed in Europe, USA, Canada, Australia, Japan

Cover: Foto ©Raphael Reischuk / pixelio.de

More available books at **www.hansebooks.com**

THE

LIFE AND TIMES

OF

HON. WILLIAM JARVIS,

OF WEATHERSFIELD, VERMONT.

BY HIS DAUGHTER,

MARY PEPPERRELL SPARHAWK CUTTS.

NEW YORK:

PUBLISHED BY HURD AND HOUGHTON.

Cambridge: Riberside Press.

1869.

RIVERSIDE, CAMBRIDGE:

PRINTED BY H. O. HOUGHTON AND COMPANY.

DEDICATION.

To my dear Mother, Sisters, Children, and Grandchildren, Nephews and Nieces, this memoir of my revered Father is dedicated.

The love and gratitude that I have cherished toward him from earliest childhood, has led me to endeavor to record the various incidents of his eventful life — and to preserve the memory of his noble character, — so remarkable for benevolence, hospitality, strict integrity, disinterested patriotism, and for wisdom and prescience in advocating measures, promotive of the welfare and prosperity of his country.

How inadequate has been my ability to do justice to this undertaking, none can so sensibly realize as myself; and I can only hope that the motives that have actuated me, may induce you to throw the mantle of charity over its imperfections. M. P. S. C.

PREFACE.

THE friends of Mr. Jarvis had often requested him to write his autobiography, and two near relatives sent each a son to Weathersfield, offering their services as amanuenses. But he made light of their solicitation, saying that while such a man as Thomas Jefferson and others, wiser and better than himself, had no record of their lives, it was not worth while towrte his.

Finding that he was persistent in his refusal, my wish to preserve the memory of his life became so strong, that I determined to attempt it. During a long convalescence, that followed a dangerous illness, I spent much time at my father's, which favored my design, as I commenced taking notes of conversations, in which I led him to relate the incidents of his early life; his uncommonly retentive memory enabling him to recall the various scenes, and depict them with vivacity and pleasure. Afterwards I took occasion to ask him questions about the same event, and by collating the two, have endeavored to make the relation perfectly accurate, a great labor, but affording me much happiness.

Eight or ten months before my father's death, an article appeared in the "Christian Register," entitled LIVING WORTHIES, giving "an outline of the life and character of William Jarvis."[1]

Not long afterwards, on a visit at the paternal mansion, my mother inquired if I knew who wrote this article, which had attracted their attention. With some diffidence I acknowledged it, and my father, much gratified, dictated a more detailed account of his public services in Lisbon. Thus improved, it was published in the "Montpelier Watchman." In answer to my mother's inquiries, I then confessed that I had been endeavoring to write his life. My secret was now revealed, and as he did not seem displeased, I begged him to allow me to read it to him, as I happened to have the manuscript with me. He made the same remark that he had done when requested to write an autobiography; but to my great joy, finally consented.

He soon became deeply interested, and as we proceeded, corrected some parts, and dictated others anew, especially the account of his being stranded near Ocracoke Inlet, and the disastrous voyage in the leaky ship.

---

[1] It had been preceded by one giving a sketch of several Bostonians, his friends and contemporaries.

It removed a weight of responsibility, and made me unspeakably thankful, that he sanctioned, and even corrected the difficult task, upon which I had labored in secret for nearly two years.

He heard as far as his appointment as Consul, when I was obliged to go home, confidently hoping to return in a week or two, and read the remainder to him. But this hope was never realized.

A few days afterwards, he had a slight paralytic shock, and was never able to hear more.

Since his death, I have had access to all his correspondence while in Lisbon, which has been a great assistance, enabling me to correct my notes from his letters, so that I feel assured that this is an authentic narrative.

Numerous domestic avocations have frequently, for months together, prevented my devoting any time to this work, and many parts have been rewritten several times, owing to my finding papers, that enabled me to give a more perfect account of the subject ; as, for instance, the life of his father, Dr. C. Jarvis, the chapter on merino sheep, and his official services in Lisbon, etc., etc.

My late venerable friend, William C. Bradley, did me the favor to read my manuscript some years ago, as far as I had then written, *i. e.*, to the termination of the Consulate in Lisbon.

He made some valuable suggestions in the chapter on Boston in the Eighteenth Century, and greatly cheered and encouraged me in my undertaking by his commendation. He honored me by the following note in reply to my saying that some of my friends thought I had given too many particulars : —

"BRATTLEBORO', SATURDAY MORNING, *April* 26, 1862.

"DEAR MADAM, — I am hardly able to advise you, being myself in the sere and yellow leaf, but as there are two ways of writing personal history, one as if aiming at a high literary standard, and the other simple and natural, telling a plain story (Robinson Crusoe fashion), as if hardly thinking of the reader, I think I may well say you have chosen the proper one. The only danger is that those of a different taste may lead you to alter it, not in any little verbal matters, but in its structure. I am sorry to tell a lady I do not agree with her friends, but must say that I look upon the little details as one of the charms of your work. . . . .

"Thanking you for the perusal of your manuscript, I remain

"Very sincerely yours,

"WILLIAM C. BRADLEY."

This note, from so great a scholar, was extremely gratifying.

BRATTLEBORO', VT., *November*, 1868.

CONTENTS.

PART I.

CHAPTER I.

PAGE

HIS ANCESTORS 1

CHAPTER II.

HIS CHILDHOOD AND EARLY SCHOOL-DAYS 9

CHAPTER III.

BOSTON IN THE LATTER PART OF THE EIGHTEENTH CENTURY . 13

CHAPTER IV.

BORDENTOWN ACADEMY. — SCHOOL AT PHILADELPHIA . . 24

CHAPTER V.

LIFE IN VIRGINIA 32

CHAPTER VI.

A MERCHANT IN BOSTON 43

CHAPTER VII.

HIS FAILURE 53

PART II.

CHAPTER VIII.

HIS VOYAGES 59

PART III.

CHAPTER IX.

PAGE

HIS APPOINTMENT AS CONSUL-GENERAL FOR PORTUGAL AND
    CHARGE D'AFFAIRES AT LISBON   128

CHAPTER X.

CHARGE D'AFFAIRES AND CONSUL-GENERAL FOR PORTUGAL   . 138

CHAPTER XI.

PRESENTATION AT COURT. — ROYAL CHRISTENING   .   .   . 160

CHAPTER XII.

MANNERS AND CUSTOMS OF THE PORTUGUESE. — FRUITS AND
    FLOWERS 168

CHAPTER XIII.

HIS PRIVATE COMMERCIAL AFFAIRS   175

CHAPTER XIV.

QUARANTINE   178

CHAPTER XV.

EVIL REPORTS   194

CHAPTER XVI.

A NEW HOUSE. — AN EARTHQUAKE   199

CHAPTER XVII.

IMPRESSMENT OF AMERICAN SEAMEN   204

CHAPTER XVIII.

IMPAIRED HEALTH. — GUNNING ON THE KING'S HUNTING-
    GROUNDS 209

CHAPTER XIX.

A ROBBERY   215

CHAPTER XX.

CATALINI 223

CHAPTER XXI.

PAGE

M. MARCELLINO R. SILVA, VICE-CONSUL AT LISBON. — AT FARO. — HIS IMPRISONMENT. — A SHIPWRECK 225

CHAPTER XXII.

LORD ST. VINCENT AND HIS SQUADRON. — THE "CONSTITUTION." — COMMODORE CAMPBELL. — A BALL ON BOARD THE "CONSTITUTION" 230

CHAPTER XXIII.

GENERAL JUNOT. — EMBARKATION OF THE ROYAL FAMILY. — THE FRENCH ARMY SUPPLIED WITH FLOUR. — JUNOT'S CAPITULATION 236

CHAPTER XXIV.

HIS MARRIAGE 252

CHAPTER XXV.

MERINO SHEEP 270

CHAPTER XXVI.

MASSENA'S INVASION OF PORTUGAL. — WELLINGTON'S DEFENSES. — TORRES VEDRAS. — REMARKS ON NAPOLEON'S INVASION OF SPAIN AND PORTUGAL 292

CHAPTER XXVII.

RETURN TO THE UNITED STATES. — FAREWELL TO LISBON. — ARRIVAL IN BOSTON. — SENHOR PEREIRA. — LETTER FROM MR. JEFFERSON. — INTERVIEW WITH MR. MADISON . . 297

CHAPTER XXVIII.

MRS. JARVIS REMOVES TO HAVERHILL. — BIRTH OF THEIR SECOND DAUGHTER. — MRS. JARVIS' SICKNESS AND DEATH . 305

CHAPTER XXIX.

PURCHASE OF REAL ESTATE AT WEATHERSFIELD, VERMONT. — HIS REMOVAL THERE, ETC., ETC. 312

CHAPTER XXX.

PAGE

RETURN TO LISBON. — MUTINY ON SHIPBOARD. — BRITISH FRIG-
ATES. — VOYAGE HOME 319

CHAPTER XXXI.

DEATH OF MR. B. JARVIS. — DANGEROUS SICKNESS OF THE CON-
SUL. — SARATOGA. — FAILURE OF CROPS. — HIS MARRIAGE.
— DEATH OF MR. SAMUEL G. JARVIS. — HIS COUSINS. —
IMPAIRED EYE-SIGHT. — HIS CHILDREN 337

CHAPTER XXXII.

PECUNIARY TROUBLES OF THE FARMERS, AND THE CONSUL'S
READY ASSISTANCE. — HIS UNWEARIED EFFORTS FOR THE
ENCOURAGEMENT AND PROTECTION OF AGRICULTURE AND
MANUFACTURES 351

CHAPTER XXXIII.

HIS CHILDREN; BIRTHS, DEATHS, MARRIAGES, ETC., ETC. . . 373

CHAPTER XXXIV.

THANKSGIVING DAY 391

CHAPTER XXXV.

CONCLUSION 394

BIOGRAPHICAL SKETCH OF MAJOR C. JARVIS 397

DEATH OF MRS. ANN BAILEY JARVIS 415

APPENDIX 418

PART I.

— ⋆ —

CHAPTER I.

WILLIAM JARVIS was born in State Street, Boston, February 4, 1770, one month and one day before the " Boston Massacre," — that first shedding of American blood by British troops. He was the only son of Dr. Charles Jarvis, an able and scientific physician, and a distinguished patriot and orator.

" The first of the name who settled in this country was Captain Nathaniel Jarvis, who was born in Wales, and had been master for several years of a large trading-ship from Bristol to Jamaica, in which place he married the widow of a rich planter, gave up his nautical career, came to Boston in 1668 with his wife, settled there as a merchant, and became a citizen of much consideration. Not long afterwards his two brothers came out from England, and it appears, traditionally, that one went to Hartford, Conn., and there settled with his family; and the other to Concord, Mass.[1] From the first settlement of the family in Bos-

---

[1] Dr. Jarvis, an Episcopal clergyman of much celebrity, belonged to the Connecticut branch; Dr. George O. Jarvis, a distinguished physician

1

ton, in 1668,[1] there were two or three generations of respectable merchants prior to the Revolution. The son, or grandson of Captain Jarvis, who was also named Nathaniel, married Elizabeth Peabody, of the 'District of Maine.'[2] Leonard, their eldest son, was born in 1715, and married Sarah Church, daughter of Sheriff Charles Church, of the Old Colony; and granddaughter to Colonel Benjamin Church, distinguished as a captain in our early Indian wars, who captured King Philip. She possessed an excellent understanding, and had received one of the best educations the country afforded in the time of her youth. Colonel Jarvis, her husband, was also a man of taste and sense, and was well informed by an extensive range of miscellaneous reading." He was remarkable for firmness, decision, and uprightness, which is exemplified by the following anecdote:

Not long before the Revolution, a mob had collected in King (now State) Street. Colonel Jarvis was ordered to call out the militia, and suppress it. He was very unwilling to wound or kill the citizens of Boston, yet determined to do his duty. He drew up his men on the opposite side of the street, and hoping to induce them to disperse without bloodshed by reasoning with them, said he had been ordered to call out the military, but should be very sorry to be compelled

in Portland, Maine; Mr. Leonard Jarvis, a merchant of eminence of Baltimore; and Dr. Edward Jarvis, of Dorchester, Mass., the learned physiologist, are descended from the Concord branch.

[1] Some traditions state that he came over in 1654.

[2] The remains of the ancient members of the family still rest in the "Copps' Hill burying-ground," then the most respectable part of the town.

to fire upon his townsmen, though he must do so, unless they immediately separated and returned to their
homes.

They did not stir!

He then sternly told them that unless they dispersed
in fifteen minutes he should fire, and gave orders for
the soldiers to load their guns with balls; with private directions to let them rattle as much as possible in
dropping, that they might know the guns really were
loaded with ball. This greatly frightened the mob,
who were unarmed, and they quickly disappeared.

"He was commissary of supplies to the British
troops, and the first Colonel of the 'Cadet Corps,'
which was originally called the 'King's Guards,' and
was then incorporated as the 'Cadet Corps,' of which
he was elected Colonel, and remained so during his
life. The uniform was then red, faced with yellow. It
is the same corps now known as the 'Independent
Cadets.' There is in the family of his grandson, William Jarvis, a fine portrait of him, taken in his uniform, which was the last painting executed by Copley
before he went to England. Colonel Jarvis was highly
loyal to his king, and his hospitable mansion was the
resort of all the English officers, and of all strangers
of distinction that visited Boston."

He had eight children who survived him: Leonard,
Samuel, Gardiner, Charles, Nathaniel, Sarah, Mary,
Benjamin, and Philip.

"At an early age, Charles displayed singular marks
of genius and strength of mind, and his parents determined to fit him for a learned profession. He
graduated at Harvard College, at eighteen, in 1766;

and finally decided to study medicine, with the approbation of his parents. He commenced with Dr. Perkins, a learned and distinguished physician, who shortly afterwards going to England, the pupil finished his studies with Dr. Joseph Gardiner. After Charles had completed the usual course of study, he went to England, where he was thoroughly prepared for his vocation by lectures, and practical courses in physic and surgery in the hospitals. On his return he commenced the practice of his profession in his native town, and perhaps no young man of his time was better fitted for it. Not contented with pursuing the usual routine of collegiate and professional studies, his taste for reading and love of knowledge had led him to devote most of his spare time to science and literature.

" He was affable and elegant in his manners; frank, sincere, and engaging; his conversation developed his extensive and varied resources, and the brilliancy of his wit and repartee.

" In his practice he was particularly attentive to investigate the remote as well as proximate causes of his patients' complaints; and in discerning their peculiar habits and diatheses.

" His prescriptions were generally simple, preferring medicines that had been tested by long experience.

" He performed the most difficult operations in surgery with uncommon dexterity and success.

" With such qualifications and endowments, he immediately entered into a highly respectable and successful practice, and could early number among his patients some of the most fashionable and opulent families in town.

"He was appointed by Mr. Jefferson physician and surgeon to the Marine Hospital at Charlestown, which was complimentary to the Doctor, as it had never directly or indirectly been sought.

"His natural benevolence was always exhibited in the performance of official duty. To the seamen who came under his care, he was attentive and kind; and whatever he did for them was marked by the same degree of zeal and skill which he displayed at the bedside of a friend or fellow-citizen."[1]

"At an early period the Doctor took a lively interest in the political affairs of his country; attaching himself to the principles, and to the leaders of the Revolution; his pen, his purse, and his person were uniformly exerted to promote the sacred cause. His political principles were decidedly republican, and these he supported with that zeal which conscious rectitude inspires.

"He believed that the people had the power and the discernment to manage their own affairs; and that they ought, and should be trusted with their political concerns. The establishment of schools and seminaries of learning; the promotion of knowledge and information, as tending to help the public taste, and discipline the public mind, by cultivating and improving it; and the free exercise and enjoyment of the rights of conscience in matters of religion, were favorite principles with him. Men of letters courted him for their companion; the proscribed patriots, Hancock and Adams, took him for their confidant and friend.

1 From a biography of Dr. Jarvis, by his nephew, William C. Jarvis, Esq., of Pittsfield, Mass., which was never published.

His native town with one voice invited him to take the highest places of trust and responsibility in all interesting crises of their affairs; and he was repeatedly chosen to represent the town in the legislature.

" In 1786, when the voice of discord, like the distant thunder, murmured in the western part of the State, and portended some dread convulsion, the zeal and talents of Dr. Jarvis were displayed in that soothing policy, which, under Providence, dissipated the clouds, and restored peace and harmony to the Commonwealth." [1] This sedition of the settlers in Western Massachusetts, is generally known as "The Shayes' Insurrection." In concert with his friends, Hancock and Adams, he exerted himself to obtain a pardon for the malcontents, and finally succeeded, with the exception of Shayes and two others.

" Benevolence and philanthropy were the reigning virtues of his heart.

" From this period he became so popular with the people, and his hold upon the good-will and admiration of his fellow-citizens was so great, that he and his friends were steadily elected to the legislature from 1787 to 1795; when the Hon. Stephen Higginson, who stood high among the Federalists in Boston, recommended to his party to nominate Dr. Jarvis to head the Federal ticket that year, and to put in six Federalists with him, urging as a reason for this step, that Dr. Jarvis was so popular in Boston, that no ticket could be carried unless his name headed it. The Federalists refused to comply with his views, and nominated the

---

[1] Extracts from an obituary notice, written by a gentleman who had been a witness of his character, his eloquence, and his deeds.

strongest ticket that their party afforded. The result was that they were beaten about the ratio of three to two.

"In 1796 Mr. Higginson again recommended the same course; and his party suffered so severely under their last year's defeat that they wisely adopted it, and both Republican and Federal nominations appeared with the name of Dr. Charles Jarvis as the first candidate. But Dr. Jarvis was sick at the time, and not wishing to enter the legislature, thought it would be a good time to decline with honor to himself; and he did decline both nominations, and thus enabled the Federalists to carry their ticket. Dr. Jarvis was held in high estimation throughout the State; and so great was the confidence in his integrity and talents, that he told his son he never lost but one question during the seven years that he was a member of the legislature, and that was a local one.

"He was about five feet ten inches in height, of just proportions; with a fine commanding figure; handsome, well-chiseled features, and a finely shaped head, that might have served as a model for a sculptor. He was of an ardent temperament, regulated by prudence and moderation; and his sensibility and feelings were of that fine, discriminating character, that made him fully alive to the wrongs of others, and led him to refrain from pressing any measure, which, in his judgment, had a tendency to injure the many for the benefit of the few.

"His eloquence was of the highest order. His voice was clear, well-toned, and sonorous; and so perfectly modulated, that all his passions or feelings were made sensible to his hearers; and with talismanic influence those feelings met with a response throughout Faneuil Hall when it was filled to overflowing; for his fine voice reached every part of the audience through that large building. He was truly an able and an honest man, and such men must prove a blessing to every country that has the benefit of their influence.

"Mr. Benjamin Russell, so long editor of 'The Centinel,' although a political opponent, was a personal friend of Dr. Jarvis and of his son. On some occasion, having accompanied the latter to Faneuil Hall, to listen to a speech of Daniel Webster, he remarked, 'O! he has not your father's silvery tones.'"[1]

---

[1] Part of this account of Dr. Jarvis and his family is taken from a letter written by his son (Hon. Wm. Jarvis), in January, 1858, to a gentleman who had sought some information regarding the family, — Lemuel G. Olmstead, Esq., of New York.

CHAPTER II.

HIS CHILDHOOD AND EARLY SCHOOL-DAYS.

On account of revolutionary disturbances in Boston, Dr. Jarvis' infant son William was nursed by a respectable and worthy woman at what was then called Little Cambridge, but is now Brighton.

A Mrs. Wood and her daughter taught him to read in Dillworth's spelling-book, and in the *famed* " New England *Primer.*"

When five years old, he was placed at the school of Master Hunt, who had kept one of the best Latin schools in Boston, in what is now called School Street; which street, indeed, derived its name from the circumstance of the Latin school-house having been erected there. The Revolution had caused his removal to Brighton. Little William advanced in reading and spelling with Master Hunt, who was a strict disciplinarian.

In after-life, he remembered going to Brookline Heights, in the spring of 1776, when six years old, to witness the bombardment of Boston, by General Washington's forces; and of seeing with great distinctness the sparks from the fuse, as the bomb-shells passed through the air.

After the evacuation of Boston by the British, he

returned thither.   One of the first events that was
there impressed upon his mind was hearing the Declaration of Independence read by Sheriff Henderson,
who was dressed in a red coat, yellow small-clothes,
and a cocked hat, and stood at the east end of the balcony of the State House, which position commanded a
full view of State Street to the end of Long Wharf;
and some years afterwards he heard the Declaration of
Peace read by the same person, from the same spot.

Very few, if any, at that time could realize the
momentous consequences that were to result from the
Declaration of Independence; but a great crowd assembled to hear it publicly read.

When about seven years of age he was sent to the
school of a stern master named Griffiths, a tall, mus-
cular man of six feet, whose principle of government
was borrowed from Solomon, "Spare the rod, and spoil
the child."   But though strict, he was a good master.
Spelling, reading, writing, and arithmetic were taught
in his school.   The boys were thoroughly drilled in
spelling; first the column of words was put out in
course, then skipping, and finally they were required
to recite the whole column from memory; the poor
boy who should miss a word was kept in an hour after
school.   The result was that William became an excellent speller, and was never at a loss as to the orthog-
raphy of any word during his after-life.   At ten he
left Mr. Griffiths and went to Master Carter's school,
who was long celebrated for writing and arithmetic.

The dark day, which occurred in 1780, made a strong
impression upon Master William's mind.   He distinctly
remembered seeing a young girl in the neighborhood

of his father's house rush into the street, wringing her hands and crying bitterly, " The end of the world has come, and I am only eighteen."

The darkness was so great that candles were placed upon the dinner-table, which appeared so singular an occurrence, that William sportively blew them out, leaving the company in the dark, for which he was chastised by his mother. Many people were apprehensive that the earth's last great change had arrived. It must have been a startling and wonderful phenomenon, and have produced a great sensation upon the whole community, as it seemed at first inexplicable and supernatural. But whether correctly or not, it was afterwards supposed by many, to have been caused by a vast mass of smoke that had collected over the burning wilderness in Maine, which was blown in the direction of Boston, and was so dense as to obscure the sun's rays. It was then considered by the *multitude* a chastisement upon the world for the ladies' enormous hoops, high head-dresses, and extravagant style of dress. Although this appears almost incredible at this day, yet it is related that a popular divine preached an eloquent sermon upon the text, " *Top-knot, come down,*" hurling denunciations upon their pride and vanity in so highly adorning themselves ; for wearing their " farthingales," " head-gear," and especially the " top-knots," worn on the summit of the other head adornments. But upon searching for the text, it proved to be, " Let those who are on the house *top not come down.*"

At about twelve years of age, William was placed at Master Holbrook's, a select private school, kept in

Quaker Lane, now Congress Street. There was then a Quaker meeting-house in that lane, from which it derived its name. Master Holbrook had formerly kept a public school near the Common; but the building having been burned, he had opened a private school.

He instructed chiefly in writing, arithmetic, grammar, and geography, which latter branch was a great accomplishment in those days; astronomy and algebra were never taught.

He was noted for his chirography, and it was to Master Holbrook that Mr. Jarvis was indebted for that plain, round hand so easily read, and so manly and handsome, for which he was ever remarkable. The course of reading in the schools at that time was from the spelling-book to the Psalter; from the Psalter to the New Testament, and from that to the Old Testament. They were also taught the Catechism, which they recited to the minister. When a boy could read, write, and spell, knew a little arithmetic, had read through the Bible, and learned the Catechism, he was considered a finished scholar, and nineteen twentieths of the boys were taught nothing else.

At Master Holbrook's William finished his Boston school education, and at fourteen was sent to Bordentown Academy; but ere he leaves his native town we will take a few notes from his reminiscences of that now great city.

CHAPTER III.

BOSTON IN THE LATTER PART OF THE EIGHTEENTH
CENTURY.

THE beautiful Common, now the ornament of Boston, was then a cow-pasture. One large tree, once "the pride of the forest," was its only attractive feature. The land had been left to the town of Boston for that purpose, by a Mr. Hughes, after the English custom in large villages.

The cows went in the morning of themselves, and sometimes returned to their owners at night, without being sent for. In the centre was a frog-pond, where the boys skated in winter. The old elm was then very large, and the ample shade of its wide-spreading branches formed a fine play-ground for the children. The Hughes family, formerly quite wealthy, had then not much property, — only one house opposite the Old South Church, — and would have been very glad to have had the Common revert to them. The lot was to be forfeited to the heirs if applied to any other purpose than pasturing cows; therefore they were tolerated till the early part of the present century, when the penalty was evaded, and the difficulty overcome, by a law forbidding the citizens of Boston to keep cows. Rows of trees were then set out, and it was inclosed, first with a wooden fence, and then with an iron one. About this period, it was called the "Mall."

In 1777 Mr. Jarvis (then seven years old) remembered to have seen the "fortification gates" on the Neck; the wall was a landmark about one mile from the old State House; it was very massive, being built of hewn stone, thirty feet wide at the base, ten on the top, and was erected across the "Neck" as a defense against the Indians. The gates were very heavy. During the Revolution an unusually high tide, which overflowed Long Wharf, materially injured this wall.

Just beyond it was the gallows, as if to warn every one ere they entered the town, that all villainy would terminate *there*.

There was a whipping-post in State Street, and also stocks for minor offenders. There were no houses on Fort Hill at this time, only the old fort, with a few cannon to be pointed against the British when *required*.

There were three rope-walks where now is Pearl Street; one of which was owned by Mr. John Codman. The first house in this street was built by Mr. James Lovell, known to the young people of the middle of the nineteenth century as the grandfather of Mrs. Mary Ware.[1]

Two other houses were soon afterwards erected. State Street, Summer Street, and Winter Street were then fashionable places of residence. Most of the shops in what is now a part of Washington Street, then Main Street, had dwelling-houses over them. There were only three or four stores in Hanover

---

[1] He was a member of the First Congress, and General Washington gave him an office in the Custom House. When Ethan Allen was prisoner at Halifax, Mr. Lovell was commissary for the prisoners there.

Street, then called Middle Street, a neat and respectable one, principally occupied by mechanics and captains of vessels. Federal Street was Long Lane, in which some of the first families resided.

After the Revocation of the, "Edict of Nantes," Peter Faneuil, a Huguenot, came over to America. He was very wealthy, built Faneuil Hall, and presented this handsome building to the citizens of Boston, by whom it was named, at a later period, the "Cradle of Liberty."

Mr. Bethune, also a Huguenot, married his only daughter, and built a spacious and elegant house at the corner of Winter and Washington Streets. In this mansion Dr. Jarvis spent his last years. It had a front yard, carriage-drive, and large barn. Three stores now occupy the spot.

The "King's Chapel" was erected, in consequence of a complaint being made by the Episcopalians to the Mother Church in England that they were forced to hold their services in a Presbyterian meeting-house. It was afterwards called the "Chapel Church," and then the Stone Chapel. Dr. Freeman, after the Revolution, altered the services in some respects, in accordance with Unitarian views. Hon. P. Morton and other gentlemen were instrumental in this change.

When a boy, Mr. Jarvis usually attended this church with his mother, but sometimes accompanied his friend, Edward Davis, who was connected with the Vassalls, to Trinity Church, in which Bishop Parker preached ; he favored the British side in the Revolution, and received many attentions and favors from the British officers.

Beacon Hill, the highest land in Boston, derived its name from the fact that, in case of impending dangers, a large light was displayed there as a signal to alarm the neighboring towns. In the time of the Revolution there were no buildings upon it, and it was a favorite resort with boys for coasting in winter. The prospect was very extensive, commanding a fine view of Dorchester, Brookline, etc., as well as the harbor and shipping.

Governor Hancock's house was considered a very splendid one, and was then unequaled. There was but one house beyond it, and only two between it and Charles Street. Afterwards William and Thomas Vassall built elegant residences on Pemberton Hill, second only to the Governor's, but more in the Grecian style. The elevation above the street was considerable, and they were approached by long flights of steps leading through handsome front yards. Behind the houses were fine gardens, much in the fashion of modern villas in the country.

Being a very aristocratic family they espoused the English side in the Revolution. Both went to England, and both were banished by the Massachusetts Assembly in 1778.

John Vassall built a noble mansion in Cambridge, where he lived in princely style; he strove, but in vain, to uphold the royal cause, and finally went with his family to England, having large estates in Jamaica. His house became Washington's head-quarters, 1775–1776.[1] Mrs. Haley, a rich English lady, related to

---

[1] Longfellow now resides in it, and has displayed his taste and patriotism by its preservation, as far as possible, as it was when occupied by the "Father of his Country."

the celebrated Wilkes, bought William Vassall's house. She afterwards married Patrick Jeffrey, uncle of Francis and John Jeffrey (so long connected with the "Edinburgh Review"), and removed to Brookline, or Roxbury, and Deacon Philips bought her house for his son, Governor Philips.   T. Vassall's house was sold to Gardiner Green.   A Mr. Pemberton had lived on Pemberton Hill, and owned it.   That part of the city where the Revere House now stands was Dr. Bulfinch's cow-pasture, with a board fence all round it. On one side of what is now Bowdoin Square, were four houses: Dr. Bulfinch's, Governor Sullivan's, Mr. Parkman's, and Mr. Gore's.

Mr. Leonard Jarvis, a brother of Dr. Charles Jarvis, a man of sound understanding and much energy, purchased a large landed property at what is now Cambridgeport.   He became very active in efforts for the erection of the bridge now called Cambridge Bridge, which was built about 1794, and Cragie's a few years later.   Charlestown Bridge was erected in 1786. There was a great festival on its completion in June of that year.[1]

Before the erection of these bridges Boston was entered by land over the Neck, or over Charlestown or Winnisimmet Ferry.   Boats passed and repassed Charlestown Ferry continually, carrying two chaises at · a time.

There were six distinguished physicians in Boston at this time, all eminent men.

Dr. James Lloyd had bought the Pemberton estate,

[1] The bridge at Bellows Falls, Vt., called "Hale's Bridge," was the next large bridge erected after the one at Charlestown, Mass.

on Pemberton Hill, and lived in the house which adjoined the mansion and estate of Thomas Vassall. Dr. Lloyd had the care of this property, being a relative of the Vassalls, and rented it (when Lord Howe was in Boston) to Sir William and Earl Percy. It was afterwards sold to Gardiner Green. Dr. Lloyd was one of the first and oldest physicians in Boston; he was greatly respected as a man of high moral character, and as a physician. He was for a time opposed to a separation from the mother country; and in 1785, protested against the alteration of the Liturgy at King's Chapel. He completed his studies in Paris, and commenced practice in Boston in 1752, and died there, "full of years and honors," in 1810.

Dr. Danforth lived on Pemberton Hill, near Dr. Lloyd. Dr. Warren was a contemporary of Dr. Charles Jarvis. He was a brother of General Warren. His father had given him every advantage in his profession, keeping him two years in London and one in Paris to visit the hospitals, and to obtain all the medical knowledge that could be acquired. In the time of the Revolutionary War, he assisted and was present at a great many operations. He was celebrated for his surgical talents. Dr. Bulfinch lived in Bowdoin Square. Dr. Rand resided near the church on Copps' Hill, and had all the practice in that vicinity. The North End was first settled, and was originally the most respectable part of the town.

Dr. Charles Jarvis has already been noticed. After the Revolution he lived in a very large house near the Old South Church, that had a spacious hall and staircase, and an office attached. In 1791 he took a

house owned by Dr. Gardiner, corner of Winter and
Tremont Streets, the garden of which extended some
distance back into Winter Street. In 1795–96 he
removed to the Bethune House, in which he died
very suddenly, November, 1807.

There were four distinguished deacons during the
latter part of the eighteenth century : Deacons Tyng,
Torrey, Salisbury, and Tuckerman. Deacon Salisbury kept a hardware store ; and Deacon Tuckerman,
during the Revolution, always had bread and flour,
even when others were out. Sometimes he would sell
only six biscuit to one person, but always had a little
for each customer. These men were all looked up to
with great respect and consideration. Mr. Jarvis
distinctly remembered them, and the reverence and
awe with which he gazed at them when a boy.

He had also a vivid recollection of those great
patriots — Samuel Adams and John Hancock. Samuel
Adams — born 1722, and graduated at Harvard 1740
— was five feet eight or nine inches in height, very
erect ; a gentleman of the Old School ; grave, thoughtful, dignified, with dark hair and keen black eyes ;
somewhat antiquated in dress, but neat and precise.
A true Puritan — with such firmness in his religious
principles, that his passions were kept under strict
subjection, and he was never severe or passionate, but
honest, sincere, benevolent, and upright. " He was
one of the most unwearied, efficient, and disinterested
assertors of American freedom and independence."
Possessed of talents and eloquence, he was the prime
leader and moving spirit of the Revolution. There
was a strong sympathy between Mr. Adams and

Dr. Jarvis on political subjects, and they were on the most friendly terms.

Being frequently at Dr. Jarvis' house, his son William attracted his attention, and became quite a favorite with Mr. Adams, who manifested his approbation by patting the boy's head, and predicting that he would become a patriot, and defend the rights and promote the welfare of his countrymen ; and when they met in the street, the good statesman greeted him with a paternal smile and a few kind words.

John Hancock presented a striking contrast to Samuel Adams in his personal appearance and deportment ; yet with one heart and purpose they joined hand in hand in the accomplishment of the freedom of their country. While Adams was simple, unostentatious, and rather reserved, Hancock was polished, graceful, and affable, courtly in manners, and fashionable in dress, with blue eyes and brown hair ; and appeared as if educated at St. James' or the Tuileries. He was very hospitable and popular, and entertained a great deal of company at his house. On election days, he invited the minister who preached the election sermon to dine with him, and all strangers to whom honor was due ; he thus became noted for his election-day dinners, which were abundant and handsome.

Dr. Jarvis, who was his intimate friend, used to say that he was the most elegant and gentlemanly man that he had ever seen. This was a great compliment, for Dr. Jarvis had associated with families of high standing in London ; had mingled with the best society in Boston, and met many Englishmen and other foreigners of distinction at the house of his father, Colonel Jarvis.

In the early part of the Revolution, Hancock and Adams, happening to be at Lexington together, it became known to the British, and hoping to take these *noted rebels,* and also to seize some ammunition lodged there, they formed the plan of marching up to accomplish both these objects. When their intention became known, a party of Bostonians, headed by Paul Revere, hurried to Lexington, apprised Hancock and Adams of their danger, saved part of the ammunition at Concord, and concealing themselves behind fences, fired upon the British soldiers and sorely harassed them.

At the time of the " Boston Massacre," Samuel Adams displayed his characteristic courage, independence, and ability.

" The soldiers of the Twenty-ninth Regiment had behaved with great insolence, and committed many abuses upon the inhabitants of the town ; but the immediate introduction to the massacre was a quarrel between some of these soldiers and certain rope-makers at the rope-walk of a Mr. Gray.

" In the contest, the soldiers were worsted, and this reflecting, as they thought, on the honor of the regiment, there was a combination among them to take vengeance on the town indiscriminately. Of such a combination there is satisfactory proof; in consequence there was, on the evening of the 5th March, a great number of abuses committed by the soldiers on the inhabitants in various parts of the town ; and being carried to such excess by one party, a bell at the head of King Street (now State Street) was rung as for fire, which brought the neighboring inhabitants into the street, and as

King Street was the last scene of that party's exploits, a number of people collected there; about which time the sentry at the custom-house, on pretense of having been insulted, knocked at the door of said house, and speaking with somebody that came out, there went from thence two persons to the main guard, opposite the court-house, and procured Captain Preston, with a party of soldiers, to go to the sentry. Captain Preston, therefore, went from the guard-house with a party of seven or eight men, who passed roughly through the people, and pushed some with their bayonets, till they were posted near the custom-house. This was resented by some of the people by throwing snow-balls. Soon after which the armed party fired, not all together, but in succession; by which means eleven persons were killed and wounded." [1]

This bloodshed was highly resented, and Samuel Adams was appointed by the town authorities to visit the British commander, and inform him that the soldiers could no longer be tolerated by the citizens of Boston.

When Mr. Adams delivered the message, his hand shook a little with palsy, which the commander observing, attributed to fear, and paid little attention to what he said. When Mr. Adams perceived this, the powerful energy of his mind enabled him to overcome this infirmity, and standing firm and erect before the commander, he said with dignity and determination, "Sir, if the soldiers are not removed from town before to-morrow morning, not one of them will be left alive, for the people will rise in a mass for their expulsion."

[1] From a letter of the Council, signed by S. Danforth (senior member of the Board), to the agent of the province in England.

He then bowed and took his leave. The strong intellect conquered; for the commander, convinced that he uttered the sentiments of a people whose endurance had been taxed to the utmost, removed his quarters to Castle William. This occurred 6th March, 1770.

Directly opposite the spot where the "massacre" took place, in King Street, lived Madame Clapham, Mr. Jarvis' maternal grandmother, a lady of fortune, in the Governor Shirley house, a spacious mansion of the olden time. On its site a handsome bank has been erected.

Mr. Jarvis knew Paul Revere, who, dressed as a Mohawk Indian, was the leader of the party who threw the tea overboard. His ancestors were Huguenots.

The "Continental money," which was issued about the time of the Revolution, depreciated so much, that when a boy Mr. Jarvis once offered forty dollars for a pint of chestnuts, which was refused.

CHAPTER IV.

BORDENTOWN ACADEMY. SCHOOL AT PHILADELPHIA.

HAVING improved all the advantages to be derived from the best schools in Boston, Mr. Jarvis at fourteen was sent to the Bordentown Academy in New Jersey, as we have already stated, and placed under the care of the principal, Rev. Burgess Alison. He went from Boston to New York by land in a stage-coach, which occupied five days. At New York he crossed in a ferry-boat to the Jersey shore. Before the discovery of steam a row boat was used, and when the wind was fair a sail was hoisted. New York in 1784 contained not over 30,000 inhabitants; what is now the fashionable part of the city was then mere pasture land. Where Greenwich Street now is, was a pasture. There was not a row of houses between Broadway and the river, and only a drinking-house at the ferry. It was a great day's journey to Princeton. In the vicinity of Philadelphia he met a rope-ferry working on pulleys, like the modern wire ferries — an improvement then unknown in New England.

Mr. Alison, the principal of the Bordentown Academy, was a Baptist minister, — a pious, sensible, intelligent man, and a benevolent and judicious teacher. His memory was wonderful, and he preached extemporaneously. In later years he was at one time Chaplain of the House of Representatives. In this seminary instruction was given in most of the branches taught in our modern academies. The students read aloud in the " Tatler " and " Spectator," and words from these works were put out for spelling.

The fare here was rather hard at first to a youth accustomed to a generous gentleman's table ; being beef and boiled pork, potatoes and a hard boiled Indian pudding, with molasses and bread, six days in the week. On Sunday the boys were favored with roast meat of some kind, and a nicer pudding of flour or rice. In summer the boys rose at half-past four o'clock ; dressed, washed, and were in the school-room at five ; breakfasted at half-past seven ; returned to the school-room at eight. From twelve to two was given them for dinner and recreation. They were dismissed for the day at half-past four, except in winter, when three evenings were devoted to study. Saturday afternoon they had to themselves, and Sunday, excepting attendance at church.

William's social and cheerful disposition soon won the friendship of the boys, with whom he became a favorite; and also with Mr. Alison, from his good conduct and diligence in study. It was Mr. Alison who first awakened the embryo love of reading in his youthful mind. Probably perceiving that he was an intelligent, observing boy, he distinguished him above his schoolmates by frequently inviting him into his library, which was a large one, and inquiring if he had read various books; to all which queries he was obliged to reply in the negative. At last, ashamed of his ignorance of books, he requested his preceptor to lend him one. Mr. Alison selected a well-written novel, wisely judging that the interest it excited would induce him to go through with it and arouse a love for more substantial reading, and a curiosity to acquire useful knowledge. He set about the task of reading to gratify his kind master; but as soon as the plot began to unravel he read with interest until his candle failed. Securing an extra piece for the next day, he finished the first volume that night, and the day following requested Mr. Alison to lend him the second. Mr. Alison was most happy to do so, but in order to ascertain if his pupil understood and remembered what he had read, he asked him various questions, to which he received most satisfactory replies. The second volume was eagerly perused, and from that time he became a constant applicant for books, the perusal of which afforded him real pleasure. The taste for reading and love of knowledge then acquired, attended him through life, and proved a never-failing resource and recreation in the various changes of his eventful career. At fifteen he left Bordentown, and was one of the three who stood highest in the school at the time of his departure. A year's residence with Mr. Alison had awakened a warm respect and attachment for him. He was now placed under the tuition of William Waring, a Quaker of Philadelphia, whose school was considered the best for mathematical instruction in that city, perhaps in the United States. Philadelphia at this period was the metropolis of the Union. It was the seat of Government, and Congress held its sessions there. Its population was 30,000, while Boston contained but about 10,000. It was a

neat and handsome city, laid out with great regularity.
Mr. Waring's school-house was a large brick building
between 5th and 6th Streets. He was so scrupulously
plain in his dress as to conceal the buttons of his coat
with a lappet.

During his residence in Philadelphia young Jarvis
became intimate with the family of a Mr. Scott, an
engraver from Scotland, whose lady was a Bostonian.
It had been Mr. Alison's ambition to have his coat
of arms engraved for his study; and it occurred to
young Jarvis that if he could learn to engrave, he
might gratify his respected master's long cherished
wishes. He therefore begged Mr. Scott to be so kind
as to teach him the art, with which request he cheerfully complied. Most of the youth's leisure hours were
now assiduously devoted to its acquisition, and ere
long he could engrave tolerably well.

Mr. Scott told him, in reply to his inquiries, that he
thought he could execute the coat of arms. He therefore wrote to Mr. Alison, saying if he would please send
it, he thought he could get it engraved for him. Mr.
Alison, delighted with the proposal, immediately forwarded it. The ardor and diligence with which he
applied himself to the work, insured its successful execution. He took several copies, and then sent them
to Mr. Alison, with a handsome letter begging their
acceptance, as a slight testimony of his respect and
remembrance. It will readily be believed that his
preceptor was highly gratified — not only by the
work itself, but by the affection and talent displayed
by his pupil. It was indeed, a remarkable circumstance that a boy of fifteen should acquire the art of

engraving in his hours for recreation, with the single purpose of giving pleasure to his kind master, and manifests the strength and warmth of his attachments.

The friendship of George Dunn, one of his old schoolmates and friends at Bordentown, added much to his happiness while at Mr. Waring's school. They were both strangers in this city, and spent their leisure time together. George was the son of Captain Dunn of England, and had now entered the large book-store of his uncle, Major Dunn. George often invited his friend William to accompany him to church, and to dine in his uncle's family on Sunday. On one of these occasions the boys had repaired early to church, and were comfortably seated, when Mrs. Dunn and a fashionable young lady came up the broad aisle with stately dignity, in the full dress of that period — wide hoops, rich elegant brocades, flowing lace ruffles, high-heeled shoes, and elaborate head-dresses, making a goodly appearance. The boys were obliged to vacate the pew, as the two ladies and Major Dunn completely filled it — conclusively proving that the hoops of those days were more extensive than those of the present. The height of the head-dress was enormous, with its crape cushions, fly caps, stiff curls, and ostrich plumes. It is related of a fashionable lady that being in full costume, she was obliged to sit on the floor of the carriage, as her head-gear would not admit of her sitting on the seat, to the annoyance of the gentleman who was escorting her to a ball. [1]

[1] It may be a matter of curiosity to ladies of the present century, to learn how this head-dress was constructed: The hair was combed back on the top of the head over a cushion filled with horse-hair, and a row of stiff curls was arranged on each side, resembling sausages in shape, as some

As a great favor, young Dunn lent his friend Jarvis from the bookstore a new history of England, then considered a valuable work, who persevered in reading the eight volumes during the winter evenings, very much to his credit, for it was a dull, tedious history that never reached a second edition.

At the house in which Mr. Jarvis boarded in Philadelphia several gentlemen, also boarders, were one evening assembled in a parlor, playing whist. One of them, who was a physician, was called out. His partner said to young Jarvis, who was looking on, " Can you play ? "

" No, sir," he replied.

" Do you know one card from another ? "

" Yes, sir."

" Then sit down and take the Doctor's hand."

It so happened that this gentleman won. They had played for a bowl of punch, which was brought in, and in passing round offered to the youth. Being very sweet and rich, he was pleased with the flavor, and drank considerable. Another game was played, and again good fortune attended the partner of young Jarvis. It was now proposed to go to a neighboring oyster house, and have a supper of hot oysters. The gentleman invited his youthful partner to accompany them. He declined. They urged him. He said he had no money to spend in that way. They offered to pay his expenses. He thanked them very cordially for their politeness, but firmly refused ; and rising to go to bed

---

one has humorously observed. The hair was then powdered, and over it was worn a triangular piece of lace trimmed with ribbon, called a fly cap. Above which, for full dress were ostrich plumes or flowers.

found himself very dizzy. He had not until he rose felt any inconvenience from taking the punch, but his dizziness was so great, that it was with difficulty he reached his chamber, when he became so much nauseated, that he never afterwards could endure punch.

It was becoming very fashionable to smoke, and at the close of his school-days in Philadelphia, he was invited to join several young men in a walk ere his departure; but not content with the pleasures of social companionship in the open air, to prove themselves *fashionable*, they constantly smoked. It was a pleasant evening, and they promenaded up and down the river for two hours; in which time young Jarvis had smoked five cigars, to keep his associates company.

At eight, he suddenly recollected that he had an engagement to tea, with a small party at Mr. Scott's, and bidding the young men farewell, hastened to the house. He had been in the warm rooms but a short time, and was conversing with Mr. Scott's daughter, when in consequence of his indulgence, he became excessively sick, and was forced precipitately to leave the room. Mrs. Scott followed to learn the cause of his abrupt departure, and beg him to return. But he explained his situation, and too deeply mortified to do so, took leave of his kind hostess, requesting her to make some excuse for him to the young people, and returned to his lodgings. He suffered so severely in body and mind from this occurrence, that he *never smoked again*. And through his life, the smell of tobacco smoke was extremely offensive to him.

The next day he sailed for Norfolk. Mr. Waring was so excellent a man that he made a most favorable impression on the mind of his pupil regarding the character of Quakers. This was strengthened by after experience, for he often remarked that he never met with a *dishonest* Quaker — nor was he ever defrauded by one in all his business transactions.

CHAPTER V.

LIFE IN VIRGINIA.

HE was now sixteen, and, having made good proficiency in his studies, was considered thoroughly educated for mercantile life, which had been selected for his future business; and the South offered a good opening to enterprising young men. He reached Norfolk without accident, and in a few weeks found an eligible situation as clerk in the store of Christopher Gardiner & Co., which was situated on the fork of two roads — three miles above Great Bridge, and ten from Norfolk. Mr. Gardiner owned a large house and store in this place, and carried on an extensive business, employing four or five clerks.

One of the roads led to the Great Dismal Swamp, and great quantities of lumber were brought thence to Mr. Gardiner to be sent down the river; such as scantlings, boards, red-oak staves for barrels and kegs, shingles made of cypress and juniper, etc., etc., which were mostly shipped to the West Indies. The shingles contained so much rosin and pitch that they were very durable, and were in great demand in that hot climate. All the planters in the vicinity repaired to this store, exchanging their produce for groceries, cutlery, English goods, etc., etc. The elder partner in the firm —

Mr. C——, had retired from business, owned a fine place, and had a pleasant family, who were kind and attentive to young Jarvis. He was also frequently invited by the planters in the vicinity to their houses, and treated by them with much hospitality; and thus formed some very agreeable acquaintances.

The following incidents display the high estimation in which he was held by the people.

A Scotchman, who was frequently at the store on business, was taken sick, and thought himself dying. He had become acquainted with young Jarvis, and must have considered him superior in abilities and education to the other clerks, for though a comparative stranger, he sent for him to come and make his will. It was two miles to Mr. McGuire's house by the road; but there was a foot-path upon the edge of the swamp which was only half that distance, but impassable on horseback. As haste had been enjoined upon him, and it was early twilight, he chose the path; but he was detained till nearly midnight ere he could return. As he was pursuing his solitary way, by the light of the stars, in the solemn stillness of the night, with the dread, mysterious gloom of the forest in the swamp bounding his steps on one side, his attention was attracted by a white object on the ground, resembling a man stripped of his clothes, his head reclining on his arm. He recollected that reports had been in circulation that some negroes, who had run away from their masters, were secreted in this swamp; and the first idea that occurred to him was, that they had murdered and robbed a white man, and this was his dead body. Terrified by the spectacle, he turned quickly round, and ran with speed to a planter's house which he had passed about a quarter of a mile back.

Without stopping to consider, his first impulse was to flee from the frightful scene of bloodshed. But as he drew near to the planter's residence, he began to be a little ashamed of his fears, for he was a courageous lad, and picking up a stout club, determined to return and view the dreadful object more attentively, thinking that possibly the man might not be dead, and he could render him some assistance. With firmness he retraced his steps, and marched up to the *unfortunate victim;* when lo! he beheld an old *chincapin-tree,* stripped of its bark, which the wind had overthrown; and one branch lay in such a manner, that it bore a strong resemblance to a man's arm with his head upon it. The chincapin is a species of chestnut, and when it dies, the outer bark peels off. How many groundless fears might be dispelled, by a similar effort of bravery. With nerves a little discomposed by his fright, he resumed his homeward walk, when suddenly a terrific shriek arose near him. Again thoughts of violence came to his mind, and horror filled his soul. The stoutest heart might well tremble in such a situation! A repetition of the dreadful sound, and seeing a bird fly out from the tree above his head, disclosed to him that it was only the cry of the *screech-owl* that had thus alarmed him, and greatly relieved, he quickened his steps, and soon reached home.

On another occasion, a woman having died near Great Bridge, and there being no clergyman in the vicinity, some gentleman of the family, who had formed a high opinion of this young New Englander, invited

him to officiate at the funeral, — to read the church
service and a sermon. He modestly declined; but
the gentleman said it would confer a great favor on the
family, as there was no one else they could engage;
and urged it more strongly. It was impossible to
refuse; and on the appointed day he repaired to the
house, and read with propriety the solemn and impres-
sive Episcopal Service for the Burial of the Dead, till
he came to the place where it is left optional with the
minister to say " sister " or " brother," when unfortunately he said " *Brother*," as printed. Immediately
one of the relatives touched his arm and whispered
" *Sister*, sister." He rectified the mistake, and went
through the rest very well. Then read a long sermon
of forty pages that had been selected for him, with
much solemnity. His performance of the services was
highly complimented, especially his excellent reading
of the sermon.

Once or twice after this he was called upon to
officiate in the same way — certainly a strong proof of
their good opinion, that this youth of seventeen should
be selected to fill the place of a clergyman.

At this period many of the churches in Virginia
were closed, the clergy having gone to England.

" In 1696 each minister of a parish had been provided with an annual stipend of sixteen thousand
pounds of tobacco. The price of tobacco had long
been stationary, at sixteen shillings, eight pence per
hundred. They sometimes commuted it for money at
the market price. In 1755 the tobacco crop having
fallen short, the legislature passed an act to enable the
inhabitants of the colony to discharge their tobacco

debts in money, for one year."[1]   A second short crop,
in 1758, caused another similar act.   This gave rise
to a lawsuit between the clergy and planters.

It was in this trial, in December, 1763, that Patrick
Henry first displayed that wonderful and overpowering
eloquence, which gained the cause of the planters, and
so astonished and captivated his hearers.

By this decision of the court, the stipend of the
clergy was so much lessened, that many of them left
Virginia, and returned to England.

While at Great Bridge, young Jarvis' mother died.
He entertained for her a strong affection and respect;
and always spoke of her as possessing firmness, energy,
and talent.   It was to her that he was indebted for the
direction of his judicious education.   The rich brocade
dresses, etc., she left her son, and which he carefully
preserved amid the changes of his life, are still in the
possession of his family.

After remaining two years with Mr. Gardiner, with
his approbation, he obtained a more desirable situation
as book-keeper with Mr. Mackay, in Portsmouth, Va.
He was a native of Ireland; good-humored, social, and
kind-hearted, but occasionally a little hasty.   Mr.
Jarvis soon became a favorite with Mr. Mackay, who
reposed such entire trust in his capacity and fidelity,
that in a few months he gave up the business almost
wholly to him, only purchasing the goods himself.

At this store, the merchandise was as miscellaneous
as at Great Bridge, but cash only was received in
payment.

Mr. Jarvis occasionally visited his friends at Great

---

[1] Wirt's *Life of Patrick Henry*, p. 20.

Bridge and the vicinity ; and was also invited to various homes in Portsmouth, thus forming many pleasant acquaintances. Among these were the family of Mr. Bray, Mr. Mackay's partner. Agreeable in conversation, social in disposition, and gentlemanly in manners, young Jarvis was received with high favor by all, and was ever a welcome guest. At this period it was the universal fashion in Virginia to take egg-nog, mint-juleps, etc., in the morning. The effects of the punch drank in Philadelphia had caused such a disgust for rum, that it saved him from this dangerous practice. But during the Christmas holidays people drank to a great extent.

One morning at this season, Jarvis having been induced by his young companions to take other liquors very freely, met Mr. Mackay in the street, who informed him that he had just received a letter from a gentleman in Petersburg, who requested that his account might be made out, and forwarded by return post, and he must trouble Mr. Jarvis to do it.

Although it was a holiday, he cheerfully complied, and repaired immediately to the store. The account was a long one of two or three pages, but he assiduously set about the business. After completing the copy, he found that it was erroneously transcribed. He then made another, but found that he could not reckon. Suddenly the idea flashed upon him that he had indulged in liquor to excess. A sense of horror filled his soul. A cold sweat covered him all over ! Could it be possible that he had been so overcome ? He was sobered in a moment. He thought deeply, and made a solemn resolution that he would never again taste of any kind of liquor before dinner. In half an hour he became perfectly clear-headed, and returned to his account, which he cast up accurately, and presented to Mr. Mackay, who was quite pleased with his promptness and neatness of execution. He firmly and nobly adhered to this determination through the various temptations by which he was assailed in after-life.

In manhood he drank only light wine in moderation with his dinner, — never at any other time ; and he never tasted of rum, brandy, or any kind of ardent spirits, till it was recommended by a physician in his old age.

During the latter part of the last, and the early part of this century, drinking in the forenoon was an almost universal practice ; and it must have required great firmness, rectitude of purpose, and self-denial to stand alone in resisting the solicitations of good fellowship, both in America and Europe. When in Lisbon, at the semi-weekly dinners he gave to American gentlemen and sea-captains then in the city, he often found that they were disposed to drink more wine than was for his good, and to avoid intemperance, he ordered his servant to place a goblet of water by his side, and filled his glass with water, after he had drank a reasonable quantity ; while his guests, too busy to notice it, replenished theirs with wine.

In about two years Mr. Mackay died. Before this event, almost the whole management of his affairs had devolved upon Mr. Jarvis. Mr. B——, the senior partner in the firm, had a son who was a clerk in the store, a very intelligent and noble-hearted young man, but inclined to intemperance. Mr. Jarvis had established such a character for temperance and firm principles, that Mr. B —— thought he would exercise a beneficial restraint upon his son George, and therefore urged him to enter into a partnership, and keep up the establishment.

He acceded to this proposal, and for a year he perseveringly endeavored to effect a reformation ; but finding the young man's habits too firmly fixed, he told his father that he thought he would be exposed to fewer temptations on his plantation, and the partnership had better be dissolved.

Mr. B —— was convinced that he spoke justly, and sadly assented. The year's profits were divided, and their affairs settled.

Mr. Jarvis now determined to return to Boston. He took passage with Mr. Reynolds, who had been in business in Norfolk, and was about to return to Boston in his own vessel. While at sea, a storm arose, and they were drifted on Martha's Vineyard, at Holmes' Hole. The two gentlemen, glad to escape the perils of the voyage, were put ashore at Falmouth, leaving the brig in charge of Captain Luce. There being no other mode of conveyance to Boston, they went on horseback, and hired a boy to lead back . the horses. They reached Plymouth at the close of the first day. Active, vigorous, and at home in the saddle, young Jarvis performed the journey with ease ; but Mr. Reynolds, not accustomed to this exercise, and more sedentary in his habits, suffered severely, especially on the afternoon of the second day, when it com-

menced snowing, and they had to contend with a
violent northeast storm.   It was quite dark when they
reached Boston Neck, where they were exposed to the
whole fury of the wind, there being no buildings at
that time to shelter them ; and to cross it in the night
was a formidable undertaking, the snow being driven
into their hair, faces, and necks with pitiless' force.

At about eight o'clock they reached a tavern in
Boston with the sign of a white horse.   Here they had
their horses and boy provided for, when Mr. Reynolds
went to his brother's, and Mr. Jarvis to his father's.
Dr. Jarvis lived near the Old South Church, in Main
Street (now a part of Washington Street), which ran
from Fortification Gates on the Neck, to Winnisimmet
Ferry.   Cold, wet, and weary, he knocked at his
father's door about nine o'clock.

What an interesting meeting it must have been to
both father and son, after so long a separation !   The
youth had attained to manhood ; had passed through
a variety of scenes and trials, and in each had acquitted
himself with honor, and won the esteem and confidence
of his teachers and employers.

Dr. Jarvis had married Miss Mary Pepperrell Sparhawk, only daughter of Colonel and Elizabeth Sparhawk, of Kittery, Maine ; granddaughter of General
Sir William Pepperrell, the hero of Louisburg, and
sister of young Sir William Pepperrell,[1] who inherited

---

[1] Sir William Pepperrell, Bart., graduated at Harvard College in 1766,
and was for many years a member of the Council, in Massachusetts. He
married Elizabeth, daughter of Hon. Isaac Royall, of Medford. In the
Revolution he joined the Loyalists, or Tories, and went to England, taking
his personal property and plate. His lady died of small-pox at Halifax, on
the voyage. He was proscribed in 1778, and his vast domain confiscated

his grandfather's title and estate. In the early part of the century, from 1725 till his death in 1759, the elder Sir William P. had been one of the most wealthy and influential merchants in New England, owning an immense landed estate. Possessing great ability, enterprise, and rectitude, he was truly "a man whom the people delighted to honor." After the capture of Louisburg, honors were showered upon him, both in the mother country and in the colonies. On the death of his only son, Andrew, in 1751, he adopted his grandson, William Pepperrell Sparhawk, on condition that he should take the name of Pepperrell. Dr. Jarvis met Miss Sparhawk in Boston, where she was attending school, and was charmed with her. She was refined, lady-like, and talented; painted skillfully and beautifully in water-colors, and had much taste for literature; but she had been nurtured with so much care and tenderness, that her sensibilities were too acute to cope with life's severer duties and trials.

After Dr. Jarvis was betrothed to Miss Sparhawk, he went to Kittery, and met there her grandmother, Lady Mary Hirst Pepperrell, the relict of the old hero, then quite advanced. She was a woman of superior abilities, witty, highly cultivated, conversant with the best English authors of her day, and possessing much poetical genius, having written a

by the United States government. He died at his residence in Portman Square, London, in 1816, and the name became extinct. He left three daughters: Elizabeth Royall, who married Rev. Henry Hutton; Mary Hirst McIntosh, married Sir William Congreve; Harriet, married Sir Charles Thomas Palmer. Their descendants are numerous.

volume of poetry. He greatly admired this accomplished and elegant lady, and was surprised by the
merit of her poetry, though it was never published —
for some reason she destroyed it before her decease.
She was of the Old School, and devotedly attached to
her husband and children. Her figure was of medium
height, well-formed, and graceful. She had an intelligent countenance, fine eyes, and beautiful hands.
She lived to the age of eighty-eight, in the immediate
vicinage of her only daughter, Madam Sparhawk, her
husband and children, and of their respected and
learned pastor, Rev. Dr. Stevens; and died in 1789,
retaining her faculties to the last.[1]   Colonel Sparhawk
died in 1790, and Dr. Stevens, 1791. After which
Madam Sparhawk was persuaded by her daughter to
reside in Boston.

[1] See Appendix A : Pepperrell family and Sparhawk family.

CHAPTER VI.

A MERCHANT IN BOSTON.

MR. JARVIS was twenty-one when he established himself as a merchant in his native town. He entered into partnership with a young man of great promise, who was to reside in Virginia, and do the business of the firm at the South.[1]

Mr. Jarvis took a store on Long Wharf, next to Mr. Samuel Breck (Nos. 37 and 38), a gentleman of high standing, and possessing a handsome property. These were very old stores, belonging to Dr. Eckley, the Congregational minister who preached in the "Old South Church," and who had inherited a large fortune. They were found to be unsafe, and Mr. Jarvis proposed to Mr. Breck to go with him to Dr. Eckley, and beg him to repair them. After listening to their statements, Dr. Eckley said he was unwilling to expend much in repairs. Mr. Jarvis then respectfully inquired what he was willing to do. He said he would give them an answer in two days; when he told them they might rebuild the stores, and occupy them two years and a half free of rent. These terms

---

[1] It may be related here that this partnership was dissolved in two years, for this gifted partner also became a victim of intemperance, and his life was sacrificed at an early age to this seductive foe.

were accepted, and a good carpenter contracted to
build them for a sum a little less than the rent for this
period.   Dr. Eckley was highly pleased with the
buildings when completed, for they were three stories
high and well finished; and being so much more valuable than the old ones, it proved a most advantageous arrangement for him.   Mr. Breck removed to
Philadelphia soon after this, and Mr. Thomas H.
Perkins succeeded him as occupant of the new store.
He was a most kind and friendly neighbor during the
next five years, and numerous were the acts of
courtesy and accommodation exchanged between them.
Not long before the death of Mr. Perkins, this benevolent and excellent gentleman spoke of the pleasure
he had derived from the friendship and companionship
of Mr. Jarvis in those early days, and of the high
esteem in which he had always held him.

From the high standing and extensive connections
of Dr. Jarvis, his son soon became acquainted with
some of the first gentlemen in Boston; among these
were Dr. Warren, Dr. Danforth, Dr. John Howard,
Harrison G. Otis, David Sears, Dr. Lloyd, Jonathan
Mason, William Smith, and Isaac Winslow.   His
friendship with the last truly Christian gentleman
only terminated with his life.   He often in advanced
years spoke of Mr. William Smith in terms of great
respect.

Mr. Jarvis attended the assemblies,[1] and was invited
to private parties, where he met some of the best
society, and soon became a popular beau with the
ladies.   His residence at the South had made his

---

[1] These assemblies were held once a month, at Concert Hall.

address easy, and his fluency in conversation was rendered more pleasing by his polite and graceful deportment, to which were added the charms of a handsome person. He was five feet ten inches in height, erect and active; with fine, curly, dark brown hair (though dressed with powder); high, broad forehead, large white teeth, a pleasant mouth, and florid complexion.

He was also punctiliously attentive to his dress, which was then considered a distinguishing mark of the gentleman. It consisted of a blue or black broadcloth coat, white silk vest, black satin small-clothes, with silver knee-buckles, white silk stockings, and shoes with large silver buckles; a shirt with finest linen cambric ruffles on the bosom and wristbands, a white cravat, and cocked hat. This costume was " a la mode " from 1785 to 1800.

There were at this period three clubs in Boston — one of elderly, one of middle-aged gentlemen, and one of young men. Mr. Jarvis belonged to the last; the members of which were James Lloyd, son of Dr. Lloyd; Josiah Quincy, Dr. Isaac Rand, a student and assistant of Dr. Lloyd; Dr. John Howard, whose father was a minister in the North Church; Thomas and Benjamin Green, nephews of Gardiner Green; Sylvester, or (as he was familiarly called) Silver Gray, nephew of William Gray; two other Rands, one of whom came but seldom; Samuel Barton, and William Reed.

J. Q. Adams and T. H. Perkins belonged to the middle-aged club, as did also a brother of Dr. Jarvis — Benjamin Jarvis. J. Q. Adams was usually very silent, but some of his personal friends frequently made an effort to draw him out, and on these occasions his varied knowledge, extensive information, and rich eloquence, were a feast for all the members of the club. He had been much abroad, which had enlarged his sphere of observation; and being a deep thinker and diligent student, few equaled him in natural and acquired talent. The clubs were held in Concert Hall. There was a large ball-room, where the assemblies were held, and several smaller rooms, in which the clubs met. Mr. James Vilay kept the establishment, and provided suppers proverbially good. At the clubs they usually amused themselves with cards the early part of the evening, but gambling was strictly prohibited. At nine o'clock the cards were laid aside, and they had a hot beefsteak — or brants, in the season — and toast; when a great deal of agreeable conversation was sustained on literary and social subjects, intermingled with pleasantry and wit. Politics were interdicted, as party feeling then ran too high to render them a safe or agreeable topic of conversation in meetings designed to promote harmonious and friendly sentiments. There were twelve members in each club. Each member had the privilege of inviting a friend for one evening.

After residing three years in his father's family, Mr. Jarvis went to board with Mrs. Archibald, who kept one of the best boarding-houses in town, in Bowdoin Square. The house was built on an extensive scale, by Judge Sullivan, who still owned it. The apartments were large and pleasant, and gentlemen sought accommodations there, as they now do at the Tremont and Revere Houses, etc.

Mrs. Archibald and her daughters were admirably calculated to make their house a pleasant home for gentlemen, — possessing tact, good sense, and good-humor, and being excellent housekeepers.

General Jackson, a rich old bachelor, was a permanent boarder, and a large front chamber was appropriated to his use. General Knox and General Cobb, his particular friends, visited him once or twice a year, when " the three Harrys," as the young ladies facetiously called them, — these three companions in arms as well as in peace, — had a rich season of social enjoyment, occupying the same apartment, from which issued many a hearty laugh.

They had been intimate before the Revolution. At that period General Knox kept a large bookstore, and had formed a strong attachment for Miss Flucker, which was reciprocated. Her father,[1] who was one of the most aristocratic men in Boston, at first objected, on the score of family ; but at the outbreak of the Revolution, finding that his daughter's affections were deeply interested, he gave his consent to their marriage ; and shortly after this event, he went with his family to England, in company with the Boylstons, Royalls, Pepperrells, Sparhawks, Vassalls, Olivers, etc., etc., in consequence of their adhesion to the British side. Mrs. Knox had inherited a good deal of her father's pride, and it was generally believed that she had exerted her influence to induce her husband

[1] Thomas Flucker, Esq., married Miss Hannah Waldo, daughter of Gen. Samuel Waldo. She was engaged for two or three years to Andrew Pepperrell, only son of Sir William P. Owing to his long protracted illness, followed by heavy losses of property at sea, their marriage was delayed; and she finally broke the engagement, and married Mr. Flucker.

to leave his bookstore and enter the American army. His firm friends, Jackson and Cobb, followed his example. General Knox soon became a favorite of General Washington, for, in addition to his worth of character, his manners were very gentlemanly and urbane. At General Washington's table, he was frequently called upon to assist in doing its honors; and when the great head was absent, General Knox always presided.

Beside General Jackson, Messrs. Nicholas and Daniel Gilman, Mr. Elwyn, and several others were fellow-boarders with Mr. Jarvis, at Mrs. Archibald's. He became very intimate with the Gilmans, who were from Exeter, N. H., and brothers of Gov. John T. Gilman; they were merchants in Boston. Mr. N. Gilman had been a member of the old Congress. Mr. Elwyn was an English gentleman of literary attainments and fortune, who afterwards married Governor Langdon's only daughter, in Portsmouth, N. H.

Mr. Jarvis soon won the good-will and favor of the ladies, who were very attentive to his comfort. His father's family connections were at this time numerous. Five brothers and two sisters resided in Boston; and their society added much to the son's enjoyment.

Leonard, the eldest of the five, was a merchant of high standing. When the British government prohibited all trade with Boston, in 1774–75, he removed to New Bedford with his mother (the widow of Col. Nathaniel Jarvis), and his sisters, Mary and Sarah, and there entered into commercial business. While in New Bedford his sister Sarah married Mr. Joseph Russell, of a very respectable Quaker family. When the British forces evacuated Boston, Mr. Leonard Jarvis returned, with his mother and sisters, and established himself in that town under the firm of " Jarvis & Russell." After the adoption of the Constitution, and the passage of the Excise Law, he was appointed by President Washington Inspector of Revenue — the whole of the excise duties of that day being under the control of that office ; and he remained head of this department until the repeal of the act. He was methodical and energetic in his business habits, and remarkable for integrity, sound sense, and judgment. He married Miss Sarah Scott, of Newport, R. I., a lady greatly respected for her many virtues. They had a large family of children, and resided in Cambridge from 1790 to 1798. His sister Mary, who remained single, a lady of talents, wit, and uncommon attainments, became a member of their family, and found great pleasure in cultivating the youthful minds of her nieces and nephews.

Samuel Gardiner Jarvis, the Doctor's second brother, was also a merchant in Boston, genial, warm-hearted, and abounding with humor. In 1772, he married Miss Susannah Pierce, of Portsmouth, N. H., and they had several children, only two of whom, Leonard and Susan Pierce, lived to mature years. His wife died in 1782 ; and he married, in 1786, Miss Prudence Davis, of Newbern, N. C., a refined and lovely lady, who had three children, Mary Sparhawk, Russell, and Helen. His family was a very interesting and pleasant one.

Mrs. Russell was a model of neatness and order ; sensible, benevolent, intelligent, agreeable in conversation, and affable in manners. Her house and dinners

4

were much frequented by the family; and her nephew William was her especial favorite.

The two youngest brothers, Benjamin and Philip, were also merchants. Benjamin held an important office under the United States Government until 1812. He married a daughter of Mr. Hall of Dorchester, who had a fine old place, and several other daughters, — Mrs. Price, Mrs. Gibbs, and Mrs. Blagg were married, and lived in Boston. Benjamin was near the age of his nephew William. He was witty, intelligent, and remarkable for his colloquial powers, when drawn out by intimate friends. They were fond of each other's society, often walking and conversing together. Philip married Miss Head, and his oldest son was John, who was afterwards in Lisbon. Nathaniel had been a captain in the Revolutionary army, and had two children — William C. and Susan, both quite talented.[1]

In 1793 it was proposed to introduce theatrical entertainments into Boston. Dr. Jarvis was the open and bold advocate of their introduction, both in the town of Boston, and in the legislature; arguing that the representation of a well-selected play had a tendency to instruct the mind, improve the morals, and elevate the sentiments of the spectators, as well as amuse them; and our youth, by such a recreation, might be diverted from low pleasures and demoralizing amusements.

Samuel Adams, the Doctor's venerable friend, who was warmly attached to him, and coincided with him in opinion on all political questions, disagreed with him upon this subject, for he considered scenic representa-

---

[1] See Appendix C, — Jarvis Family.

tions irreligious and contrary to the spirit of the Puritan Fathers.

There were many others, both in town and country, who entertained the same aversion, and some who favored them secretly, but dared not express their sentiments openly. Dr. Jarvis at last succeeded in effecting their toleration, and the legislature granted a charter for a theatre, which was built in Federal Street, formerly Long Lane. Harrison G. Otis was much interested in obtaining a good set of actors from England.

Some dissatisfaction being felt about this theatre, another called the " Haymarket Theatre," was erected on what was afterwards " Colonnade Row," now Tremont Street, but then open ground. This was a high wooden structure, which was said to endanger the houses in the vicinity, and was finally pulled down.

Although he highly enjoyed social amusements, and the charms of cultivated society, in which he was so much esteemed and admired, yet Mr. Jarvis never permitted them to interfere with the strictest attention to his business. He uniformly practiced upon the motto, " Business first, and pleasure afterwards."

This application and industry, with scrupulous honesty, honorable dealing, and judicious management, resulted in a very prosperous state of his affairs.

In 1796 he was engaged to Miss Mary Pepperrell Sparhawk, a niece of Mrs. Dr. C. Jarvis, a young lady possessing a rare combination of virtues: beauty of person, unusual cultivation and strength of mind, and loveliness of disposition. Modest, unaffected, and affectionate, she was warmly beloved by her relatives and friends, and Mr. Jarvis was most happy in winning her love.

Now, his ship of life, fanned by favoring gales, sailed on the waters of prosperity, in bright sunshine; but too soon, alas, the sky was overcast; and suddenly the storms of adversity burst upon him!

CHAPTER VII.

HIS FAILURE.

MESSRS. CLARK & NIGHTINGALE of Providence, a most respectable house, — mutual friends of Mr. Jarvis, and the Murrays of New York, thinking they would benefit each other, recommended Mr. Jarvis to them as an active correspondent, for he stood in high credit as a merchant in Boston. Mr. Robert Murray of New York brought a letter of introduction from Messrs. Clark & Nightingale, to Mr. Jarvis, and in this way the acquaintance commenced. Mr. Robert Murray was in partnership with his brothers, one of whom resided in Paris, and they hazarded great risks in purchasing assignats, with small rational prospect of gain. In consequence of the recommendation of Messrs. Clark and Nightingale, Mr. Jarvis was induced to indorse at different times, to a large amount, for the Murrays.

They had speculated largely in breadstuffs and rice. A most prolific and abundant harvest in France caused a great depression in breadstuffs, and wheat fell from sixteen or eighteen francs, to three or four francs per bushel. The Murrays had paid thirty shillings per hundredweight for rice at the South, for which they only received enough to pay the freight. Whoever had been concerned in breadstuffs failed by this depression, and among others the Murrays. Mr. Jarvis, with the confiding generosity of youth, had yielded to Mr. Robert Murray's solicitations, on the assurance that he would soon free him from the obligation, and indorsed for them to the amount of $38,000.

When he heard of the failure of the Murrays he immediately determined to pay off every debt both small and great of his personal contraction. He had about six thousand dollars by him, and he rested not until he had paid all persons, principal and interest, from whom he had received property, to the full amount of their dues. When he was applied to on account of the Murrays, he said, " Gentlemen, I have paid all my own debts, you can take the remainder of my property."

With his high-minded integrity, he never dreamed of putting his property out of his hands, or any other equivocation of modern times, but manfully surrendered all that he possessed to the creditors of the New York house. Having pursued this honorable course of conduct, he was dining at Mrs. Archibald's, when he was informed that some one wished to speak to him at the door. It was the sheriff, sent to arrest him for his liabilities for the Murrays. He told him that he was at dinner, but he would go to the prison in the afternoon if he was willing to trust him. The sheriff replied that his word of honor was sufficient. After dinner Mr. Jarvis made some necessary arrangements, and then walked alone to the jail.

The jailer being engaged, as he was informed, he sat down and waited patiently for an hour or two, calm and firm ; yet seated thus in the precincts of a prison, this sad reverse of fortune must have filled his heart with most painful feelings, — disappointed hopes, and blasted prospects.

When the jailer came in, Mr. Jarvis remarked that he had kept him waiting a long time.

" Yes, sir," he replied, " but I have been busy, and was sure you would not attempt to go away." He told Mr. Jarvis that by giving bonds that he would appear at court at a certain time, he could be released from confinement.

" Will you accept my father as my bondsman ? "

" O yes, sir."

" Then will you please to send him word where I am, and request him to do me the favor to come to me ? "

Dr. Jarvis quickly obeyed the summons, signed the bond, and father and son went away together, wiser, if not happier men, and thankful for his speedy liberation.

The Murrays issued a paper stating the amount of their assets to be £250,000 ; they owed £300,000.

The houses in France and England that owed them large sums had stopped payment ; but it was thought they still possessed a large amount of property, and that they would eventually pay. There was $2,000 due the Murrays in Boston.

Mr. Jarvis went to Mr. Codman, the upright and judicious agent of the creditors, and told him that if they attempted to confine him, he should make no promises ; but if they would give him his liberty, and take his notes, he would pay seven and sixpence on the pound, in five annual installments; and give up all his claims upon the assets of Robert Murray & Co. to the creditors. Mr. Codman told Mr. Jarvis that these amounted to eighteen shillings on the pound, and were in good hands. They were estimated to be more than sufficient to pay principal, interest, and damage on the bills of exchange, and he begged him not to bind himself for so large a sum, but to wait the issue. He replied that he was not willing to involve his father in his difficulties, by being bound for him, and felt confident that if he were at liberty to use his faculties, he should eventually be able to clear himself.

His proposal was accepted, and he gave his notes for $14,500, payable in five annual installments. It was a large sum, and he knew that great exertion would be required; but he was determined, with God's blessing, to make it, if energy, enterprise, and untiring labors could enable him to do so.

He made a resolution — to which he steadily adhered through life — that he would never again *indorse* for any one.

He was now so much worse than *nothing* in point of property, but nobly did he rise above his misfortunes. With the poet he felt —

> " Be thou secure of soul, unbent by woes:
> The more thy fortune frowns, the more oppose."

It was a hard reverse for him, owing to no extravagance, idleness, or neglect of business, but solely to yielding to the solicitations and fair promises of a brother merchant, from a spirit of accommodation, in the generous confidence of youth.

He now decided to go out as supercargo of a vessel,

and chartered one for the voyage. He must bid adieu to relatives and friends, and exchanging his silk stockings and small-clothes, broadcloth coat and ruffles, for loose trousers and a pea-jacket, brave the perils of the ocean, and inure himself to the hardships of a sea-life.

Bereft of fortune, and about to enter upon an employment that involved so many risks, Mr. Jarvis, with his characteristic generosity and thoughtfulness for the welfare of others, begged Miss Sparhawk not to consider their engagement binding, but to feel free to form another, should her hand be solicited by a person agreeable to her.

She was very young, only about seventeen, and her fresh affections had been too deeply interested easily to forget. Her attachment was rather strengthened than weakened by his misfortunes; especially as they had elicited the strength, probity, and nobleness of his character.

With deep sympathy for her affianced, and a sad heart, she returned to the family of her respected uncle, Hon. Bailey Bartlett, of Haverhill, Mass., where she was tenderly loved as a daughter and sister by its amiable members.[1]

Not long before Mr. Jarvis sailed, he met at Mrs.

---

[1] Miss Sparhawk's mother was Elizabeth Bartlett, who married N. Sparhawk, Esq. She died two years after her marriage, which so much affected her only sister Catharine, that she soon followed her sister to an early grave. Mr. Bartlett was so deeply afflicted by the loss of both his lovely sisters, that he wished to adopt Mrs. Sparhawk's offspring as his own. The little orphan inherited some property from her mother and Aunt Katy; but her Uncle Bartlett's house was always her home until she was thirteen, when at the earnest request of her Aunt Jarvis, who had no children, she spent most of her time in Boston, attending the best schools.

Archibald's, her pastor, Rev. Dr. Clarke, for whom he entertained a high respect, and the excellent Doctor was much interested in him. At this, their last interview, he urged him, as he had often done before, to join a meeting of young men for religious instruction, at which he presided. Mr. Jarvis hesitated, then, pleading some other engagement, declined, though he afterwards regretted that he did so.

Subsequently the Doctor expressed a good deal of solicitude about him, saying he thought they should never meet again. Mrs. Archibald thought this a presentiment that Mr. Jarvis would perish at sea. The event proved otherwise, though the prediction was verified by the death of Dr. Clarke, who was suddenly seized with apoplexy in his pulpit, on the 1st April, 1798, and expired in less than twelve hours — the good and faithful servant called home to " joy unspeakable and full of glory."

> " Servant of God, well done!
> Rest from thy loved employ:
> The battle ceased, the victory won,
> Enter thy Master's joy."

PART II.

CHAPTER VIII.

HIS VOYAGES.

Iᴛ was late in the year 1796 that Mr. Jarvis made his first voyage to Corunna. During his two first voyages he studied navigation with close attention, and spent much of his time on deck, to acquire some practical knowledge of the management of a ship.

As they neared Corunna he noticed a vessel at a considerable distance ; and after scrutinizing her carefully through his spy-glass, he found that she was rapidly bearing down upon them. It soon became evident that she was a French privateer in full pursuit. All at once she changed her tack, and ran up through a narrow and difficult passage to Corunna. Mr. Jarvis ordered one of the men up the mast-head, to see what had caused this sudden diversion, who reported that there was a large ship heaving in sight in the offing, which he thought was English. As she drew nearer, she proved to be an English cruiser ; which explained why the French corvette abandoned her pursuit of the American brig. It was a Godsend for her.[1]

---

[1] After Jay's treaty with England, differences arose between France and the United States. The French captured our commercial marine, but the United States would not allow of retaliation.

After landing at Corunna, next morning, Mr. Jarvis called upon the French Consul, to whom he had a letter of introduction, and while they were conversing a naval officer entered. The Consul introduced Mr. Jarvis to him ; when the Captain, surveying him with close scrutiny, said in a gay, dashing manner, —

"Are you the commander of the brig that I chased yesterday in the Bay ? "

He replied affirmatively.

"Ah ! " said the Frenchman, with an air of nonchalance, "had it not been for that English frigate, I should certainly have made a ' bon prize ' of you ! "

"You would have found very little on board my ship, sir, to make it a desirable object."

"No matter, the brig is valuable ; and I should have captured you without fail."

He then turned to the Consul, and after half an hour's conversation, invited him to join a dinner-party on board his ship that afternoon ; and again addressing Mr. Jarvis in an easy off-hand way, said that he should be most happy if Monsieur Jarvie also would favor him with his company ; speaking with the familiarity of an old acquaintance.

He thanked him civilly, saying if he could conveniently, he would avail himself of his polite invitation ; but felt no inclination to visit an officer who boasted that he had so nearly captured him, and might still do so, should an opportunity offer.

There was no market for his corn, and he determined to escape from so dangerous an enemy. He returned directly to the brig, and told the Captain to have everything ready for sea, but to do it quietly, to avoid attracting attention — to loosen the sails, be ready to raise anchor, etc.

About two o'clock the company began to go in boats to the corvette; these boats plied to and fro for some time, then the ladies and gentlemen were seen promenading on the quarter-deck. After a while they all went below.

"Now, Captain," said Mr. Jarvis, "they have gone to dinner; this is our time."

It is sufficient to say that they escaped without molestation, and reached Lisbon in safety.

While in Corunna, and subsequently in other parts of Spain, Mr. Jarvis was struck by the manners and customs of the lower classes of Spaniards. When the peasants come in to market from the country, the poor women walk behind their "lords and masters," their babies on their backs, and fruit and vegetables on their heads; while the men, both proud and lazy, stalk before, a long staff in their hand, and their pantaloons and jacket adorned with numerous bell-shaped, silver or silver-plated, buttons.

On his return from the second voyage, in 1797, Mr. Jarvis was convinced that it would be more for his advantage to take the entire command of the vessel, being better qualified to cope with the officers of foreign ships of war, and to answer their various questions, than were most sea-captains. In company with his friends, Nicholas and Daniel Gilman, he purchased the brig Mary, of Mr. Coombs of Newburyport (a man of large self-acquired wealth), taking one third part of it.

At his request the Gilmans gave him a power of

attorney, authorizing him in all cases to act as he thought most judicious; leaving the cargoes he purchased, the ports he visited, etc., etc., entirely discretionary with himself. Mr. Jarvis knew that he should thus be enabled to make the voyages more profitable. On his third voyage Mr. Daniel Gilman, who was out of health, accompanied him.

One day, while walking the quarter-deck, Mr. Jarvis observed that the service was off the foretop-mast back-stay; whereupon he ordered one of the old sailors aloft to mend it. The old tar, who had been boatswain in the English service, suspecting that the Captain was not a very skillful seaman, and wishing to raise a laugh at his expense, by exposing his ignorance, replied, —

"Shall I put on the service with the sun, or against the sun, sir?"

Penetrating his design, Mr. Jarvis immediately said to him in a tone of surprise, —

"I thought I hired you as an *able seaman?*" [1]

"You did, sir."

"And don't you know how to mend the service on the back-stay? If you do not, go and ask the second mate," he said sternly.

The mortified sailor dropped his head, and went directly to perform the duty, with which he was perfectly familiar, and conducted himself with propriety and respect during the remainder of the voyage. His readiness of mind on this, and many other occasions, was a great benefit to him.

The vessel touched at Madeira, but as corn could

---

[1] A nautical term, meaning thoroughly trained or first-class.

be sold there only in exchange for Madeira wine, which was very low in New York and Boston, from the market being glutted, he would not dispose of it here.

Early next morning he observed a schooner which had come in during the night. It occurred to him that he might gain some desirable information from the captain, and taking a boat and two sailors, he ran alongside it. He questioned them thus :

" Where from ? "

" St. Michael."

" What nation ? "

" Portuguese."

" What is corn worth in St. Michael ? "

" It is very low ; they had a great crop ; there are 6,000 moyas." [1]

" Any vessels in from Lisbon ? "

" No.".

" Are you sure that there are no vessels in ? "

" Yes, very certain ? "

Mr. Jarvis returned to his vessel and said to Mr. Gilman, —

" Daniel, I have made up a new voyage."

" Ah ! " said Mr. Gilman, " what is it ? "

" To go as fast as possible to Lisbon ; sell this cargo of corn, then go to St. Michael and purchase another, which we will also sell in Portugal."

Mr. Gilman approved of the plan. A short voyage of eight days brought them to Lisbon. The cargo sold remarkably well, there being no corn in the market. He received $11,200 for it.

---

[1] A *moya* is 24 bushels.

Mr. Bulkley, an English merchant, who had assisted him in the sale of his cargo, became very curious to know what he was going to purchase to reload his vessel. Mr. Jarvis had made some inquiries, with apparent carelessness, to ascertain if any vessels had been cleared for St. Michael, and was informed that there had been none.

When he gave the order for salt, for ballast, Mr. Bulkley became very urgent that he should buy fruit and Lisbon wine of him. "At this season of the year," said he, "you will make a handsome profit on fruit."

"Yes, sir, that is true; but there is a possibility of my losing half of it by decay." Still Mr. Bulkley was not satisfied, and strove to pry into his plans. After two or three days, when Mr. Jarvis' arrangements were nearly made, he told Mr. Bulkley he wished to buy pistareens; who referred him to two Maltese brokers, of whom they were readily obtained. A pistareen is a silver coin, worth about twenty cents; current money of St. Michael, but not in Portugal.

He finally told Mr. Bulkley in confidence that he was going to St. Michael, without stating the object of his voyage.

Next day he had the vessel prepared for sea, intending to sail the following morning. Mr. Gilman and himself boarded at the house of a Mrs. Derbyshire, a very respectable English woman. At about nine o'clock in the evening, having just retired to rest, a loud knocking was heard at his door. A young man had called, who wished to deliver a message from Mr.

Bulkley. On being admitted, it proved to be his head clerk, who said that Mr. Bulkley had some information of importance which he wished to communicate to Mr. Jarvis in person.

"But I am very much fatigued, and do not like to rise."

"Mr. Bulkley said it would materially affect your interests, sir; and he is very desirous to see you."

"If it is a matter of so much consequence, I will be ready to accompany you in a few minutes."

On arriving at Mr. Bulkley's, Mr. Jarvis inquired the cause of his summons.

"The English Consul has just arrived from St. Michael, and says the island is full of corn."

"Yes, sir; I am aware of that."

"You had better leave here as soon as you can, as the news may spread about."

"I am all ready, and shall sail in the morning."

"Will you take this packet of letters, which some of my friends have handed to me, wishing me to send them to St. Michael?"

"But, Mr. Bulkley, when I told you I was going to St. Michael, it was in strict confidence, trusting to your honor to keep my secret. I am surprised that you should have spoken of it!"

O, his friends had requested him to inform them if he knew of a vessel going to St. Michael.

"But, sir, I cannot possibly take these letters; they are from merchants who will state the price of corn *here*, and this will immediately raise the price of corn *there*. I will not consent to take them."

Still Mr. Bulkley pertinaciously pleaded that his

5

friends would be greatly offended ; and he should esteem it a great favor, if Mr. Jarvis would be so obliging as to be their bearer.

"If I do, Mr. Bulkley, I shall not deliver them until after I have purchased my corn, as it would ruin my voyage."

The merchant was so earnest to have them sent, that he assented to this condition, and eagerly delivered them to Mr. Jarvis, who locked them up safely in his trunk and thought no more about them.

Mr. Gilman remained in Lisbon, hoping to derive benefit from the salubrious climate. During the voyage Mr. Jarvis strained his eyes in taking an observation of the sun ; and afterwards injured them still more by thoughtlessly reading the "Vicar of Wakefield," with the sun shining on the book.

The inflammation increased so much, that ere he reached St. Michael, he was forced to bandage them. On landing, he went directly to the house of the American Consul, Mr. Hickling ; who received him with great hospitality, and introduced him to his family. With the utmost kindness and sympathy they ministered to his wants, and immediately sent for a physician, who prescribed powerful medicines, which relieved him in a great degree.

When it was known that a vessel had arrived from Lisbon, boats were sent to inquire for letters. The mate said he knew of none, and the captain was on shore. It was ascertained that he was at Mr. Hickling's, and messengers were sent there to ask for letters.

Mr. Jarvis replied truthfully, that he was too ill to attend to any business.

He requested Mr. Hickling to purchase his cargo of corn, and to make writings that would secure it to him, even should the price rise. This Mr. Hickling did, and obtained the corn for a pistareen (or twenty cents) per bushel.

When this business was completed, on fresh inquiries being made for news from Lisbon, Mr. Jarvis sent his keys on board to his mate, wishing him to unlock his trunk, and look for a packet of letters, which were found and duly delivered.

Some dissatisfaction was occasioned by the delay; but as Mr. Jarvis was still confined to the house, there seemed to be an excuse for it, and the unpleasant feelings soon passed away.

He gave orders to have the corn put on board his vessel, but was not able to attend to it himself. The weakness of his eyes detained him a week or two in this social, agreeable family.

The youngest daughter, an interesting child of four or five years, became quite a favorite; for then, as in after-life, he was extremely fond of children. They had many frolics together, and he taught her the alphabet.

This little girl became an accomplished woman, and married Professor Webster. In his latter days she met Mr. Jarvis in Boston, and reminded him of the circumstance, which had entirely escaped his memory. Not so with the child upon whose mind his kind attentions had made an indelible impression. She was loved and respected by all who knew her for her many virtues, — a valued member of society, an excellent wife, a most devoted mother, educating her daughters almost wholly herself.

When his eyes were nearly well, Mr. Hickling and his lady, desirous of promoting his amusement, proposed an excursion to an old volcano about three miles distant.

He objected, fearing the sun and dust might prove prejudicial; but they consulted the physician, who, more desirous to please them than considerate for his patient, said there was no danger. Accordingly a very pleasant party, consisting of Mr. and Mrs. Hickling, and their two eldest daughters, a few friends, and Mr. Jarvis, were mounted on mules, and set out in fine spirits.[1]   On their arrival at the mountain, the intensity of the heat, the glare of the sun on the sand, and a north wind blowing the cinders and ashes of the extinct volcano into his eyes, renewed the inflammation and caused him much suffering. He begged Mr. and Mrs. Hickling to excuse him, and permit him to return, which they readily did, deeply regretting that their kind intentions had resulted so unfortunately.

It proved most disastrous to him, for his eyes became nearly as bad as on his first landing.

---

[1] The Azores belong to Portugal, and lie about 20° west of Lisbon. They are volcanic and mountainous, but well watered and fruitful, producing corn, wine, and various fruits. St. Michael, Terceira, Pico, and Fayal, are the principal islands of the group. Mr. Jarvis said the St. Michael oranges surpassed any he had ever tasted, being very sweet, juicy, and heavy, from the great quantity of juice and saccharine matter they contain, with a skin almost as thin as kid, and a delicate pulp. A lofty mountain, with its summit in the clouds, rises from St. Michael. There are remarkable boiling springs in a plateau on its side, some sulphuric, some impregnated with iron, continually bubbling up and emitting vapors. Here, between vast fissures in the rocks, the sea is seen surging below, at immense depths. "The Peak of Pico" is still higher, 7016 feet; rising in majesty from the ocean; its conical form visible at a great distance.

But it being of the utmost importance that he should hasten to Portugal, and dispose of his cargo ere the price fell, he was forced to take leave of his hospitable friends and embark in his present condition. The weakness of his eyes obliged him to bandage them again, and to trust to his mate to take observations of the sun, and manage the ship.

They were becalmed off Figuera for twelve days, in sight of the city, yet unable to enter the port. He had learned that two or three cargoes of corn had been carried into Lisbon, and thus having been anticipated, he determined to sell his in Figuera, where it continued high and scarce. At last, after this tedious detention, they landed. He immediately sought a comfortable lodging, and sent for a physician, who proved a very skillful one; he prescribed some gentle cooling medicine, a light diet, and a poultice for his eyes of sweet elder flowers, gently steeped in water. The effect of this remedy was wonderful. At night he had scarcely been able to see; in the morning he could use his eyes without pain. When the doctor called, he said he was doing well, but he must keep his room darkened, and renew the poultice. On the second morning he said Mr. Jarvis' eyes were out of danger; but he must keep a shade over them, not go into the glare of sunlight, persevere in the same regimen, and continue to exclude most of the light from his room. In the afternoon Mr. Jarvis found that he could look out on the shady side of his room without inconvenience. On the third day the medical man pronounced him well; but enjoined the utmost care, advising him not to walk in the sun, or use his eyes.

On the fifth day he was able to attend to the sale of his corn, which he disposed of very advantageously, clearing $6,000. This was most cheering and encouraging, after his extreme suffering. He had been absent from Portugal but six weeks.

These two fortunate voyages enabled him to pay for the ship and both cargoes, and placed a lever in his hands that gave him power to raise the heavy burden by which he was oppressed.

He felt throughout that his future independence and success depended entirely upon his own persistent efforts, and through the blessing of God, he overcame every misfortune and difficulty that beset his path, and came off victorious.

He wished to carry the silver, which he had received in payment, to Lisbon ; but as privateers were to be apprehended on the coast, he determined to send his vessel round to Lisbon in charge of his mate, and convey his silver by land.

He hired two mules, riding on one and packing the silver in strong panniers on the other, and employed a muleteer as guide and to drive the laden one, supplying himself with pistols, as a defense against robbers.

Figuera is ninety miles from Lisbon. At the close of the first day's journey, he put up at a private house; where a good supper, clean bed, and sound sleep greatly refreshed him. The muleteer and mules were also well cared for. The second day they struck the Coimbra road, which was macadamized with white limestone. It is one of the finest roads in Europe. There is also a similar one from Bilboa to Madrid, with fine trees set out on each side of the way. But the reflection of the sun from this white stone was very irritating to his eyes. As night drew on, the muleteer stopped before a hidalgo's house. Mr. Jarvis alighted, and was going up the steps, when the muleteer exclaimed in Portuguese, " O ! no, no ; you must not go in ; the house belongs to a nobleman."

" But I am wearied and exhausted ; I must have food and shelter for the night."

" Yes, sir, you can go up there ; " pointing to a flight of stairs, outside a miserable looking building, the lower part of which seemed to be a stable. On ascending the crazy steps, he entered a room which had been partially finished off for the accommodation of travellers, and might once have been tolerably comfortable ; but now the floor was worm-eaten and had cracks, through which he could see the mules below. Three rickety chairs and a table, composed the furniture. Miserable and comfortless as it was, he was forced to make the best of it, there being no alternative, and ordered the muleteer to bring up the panniers of silver. Much reduced in strength by his recent illness, he told Michael he must if possible get him some supper soon, for he was faint. Michael replied, " Si, Señor ; " disappeared, quickly returned with a clean white table-cloth ; and then, to Mr. Jarvis' surprise, brought up a very good supper of bread, fricasseed chicken, and weak wine.

Somewhat recruited by this refreshment, he asked the muleteer where he should lodge.

" O, here, sir," was the reply ; and in a few minutes a servant brought up a large mattress and some snow-white linen sheets ; swept a place on the dirty floor, which looked as if such an operation had not been performed for months, and then prepared the bed.

Mr. Jarvis immediately sought repose, but *fleas*, the common pest of the country in such situations, long precluded the possibility of sleep. The sun shining brightly, awoke him in the morning, but little refreshed by his disturbed slumbers.

Thinking that fresh eggs would be better for him, in his present condition, than the highly seasoned Portuguese dishes, in which garlic was so freely used, he wished to ask Michael to get him some, but could not recollect the Portuguese word for eggs. How should he make him understand? In this dilemma, he took a piece of charcoal and drew an egg on the table. But no, Michael was at a loss. He took him to the window and pointed to fowls in the yard below, and renewed his attempts.

" O, yes, he could have fowls."

No, that was not it. Just at this moment, a woman servant fortunately threw some egg-shells from the hidalgo's house (probably having been preparing an omelette). He pointed to them, and the muleteer's face lighted up, — " O, *ovas, ovas!* Si, Señor."

Ova then was the word ; he would not soon forget it. After a comfortable breakfast, he resumed his journey, and at night reached a caravanserai, around which were about twenty low, suspicious looking men.

As one of them was assisting the muleteer to unload the panniers, Mr. Jarvis heard him say, " This is very heavy ; it must contain silver."

It seemed a dangerous place to lodge in ; and taking the master of the house apart, he requested him to take charge of his money during the night, and put it in a place of security, which he did faithfully; and not a dollar was missing.

Mr. Jarvis had a good night's rest, and the next day they reached Lisbon, without molestation. During this journey, he passed the magnificent Convent of Batalha, and spent an hour in examining this noble specimen of architecture.

He found that his vessel had but just arrived in Lisbon. He purchased a load of salt for ballast, and taking his silver with him, sailed for Saffa, to obtain a cargo of wheat. This town, on the coast of Morocco, was then a place of considerable commerce, and many mercantile houses were established there.

Leaving his vessel in charge of his mate, he went ashore in a boat, which he sent back. He soon met a Jew, whom he requested to conduct him to an English house, to which he had letters. Soon several men and boys began to follow him, attracted by the novelty of a stranger; and by the time he reached the English merchant's, about forty were crowding about him.

This house was built in the Eastern manner on three sides of a hollow square; on the fourth was a wall with double gates. The outer gate was made of bars of iron, secured by a strong iron lock; the inner one, of wood. In this court were several persons, whom he addressed in English, saying he had letters from Lisbon. Presently one of them approached the gate, and took his letters through the iron bars with a pair of tongs. Mr. Jarvis thought this strange, but supposed it some form peculiar to the country; the letters were then dipped in a tub in the centre of the court, spread open and read, which appeared still more singular. Then the head of the house came forward, and said he must apologize for keeping a gentleman outside the gate so long, who had been so highly recommended; but the plague was raging in the city, and they held no intercourse with those without."

"Indeed, then I am in great danger, for I have been surrounded by every blackguard in your town."

The merchant said that the exportation of wheat had been prohibited; and it being impossible to obtain any, he thought Mr. Jarvis had better not come in, evidently afraid that he would convey the contagion.

But a young English physician now interceded for him, saying if he was thoroughly smoked, and then washed in "Four thieves' vinegar," there would be no danger of infection. His friendly arguments finally overcame their scruples; the great gate was unlocked, and he was admitted. A few shavings were thrown down, upon which sulphur was sprinkled, and then set on fire. Mr. Jarvis was smoked over the fumes, till he was nearly suffocated. He was now led to the tub containing "Four thieves' vinegar," [1] and requested to

---

[1] The history of the "Four thieves' vinegar," noted as a safeguard against the plague, is very curious. At the time the plague was raging in Marseilles four thieves were observed to go from house to house robbing with impunity, not only deserted habitations, but those in which the sufferers from the plague were yet alive. Yet they escaped the infection. At last they were all arrested, proved guilty, and condemned. But their preservation from the pestilence seemed so wonderful, that the magistrate promised their pardon, if they would explain the mystery, thinking it might benefit the community. Their secret was the free use of vinegar, wherein cloves, nutmegs, cinnamon, myrrh, and camphor had been steeped, in which they bathed their hands, faces, and wrists; and plugged their noses with cotton, dipped in it. It was afterwards extensively used.

wash his face, hands, and wrists in it ; after which he was sprinkled all over with a large sponge, until his clothes were well saturated ; when the head of the house ventured to approach, and shake hands with him, invited him into his house, and treated him with much hospitality.

Being very desirous to obtain a cargo of wheat to carry to Lisbon, Mr. Jarvis sent a messenger with a handsome present to the Governor, soliciting him to make an exception in his favor, and permit him to purchase it. He waited nearly a fortnight for an answer, and then received a refusal. A trying delay it was.

During this time, he became acquainted with the young English physician who had pleaded in his behalf, an interesting, intelligent young man, who had been sent out to cure the Governor of some disease ; but the patient's carelessness, and mode of living, rendered the doctor's skill unavailing; and finding his prescriptions and advice useless, he was anxious to return to England. Mr. Jarvis decided to go to Mogadore for a cargo of saltpetre, and offered him the best accommodations his cabin afforded, if he would accompany him ; but he declined, unless he would promise to land him at Madeira or Gibraltar, which he could not conveniently do.

The mate and sailors had become exceedingly alarmed about the fate of their Captain. A fortnight had elapsed, and yet no tidings of him had reached them. They feared that he had died, or been taken prisoner by the Arabs. The mate determined, if he did not come back in one or two days more, to lift anchor and return to the United States. When he saw a boat coming towards the ship from Saffa, which could be seen all the time, they feared an attack upon them; but as the boat drew nearer, the mate, who had been scanning it, cried out joyfully, "It is the Captain!" The sailors soon recognized him, and there were great rejoicings on board the ship. But when he recounted to them his exposure to the plague, they were somewhat dismayed; however, a kind Providence preserved him from this terrible disease, notwithstanding his dangerous exposure. A short voyage brought him to Mogadore, also a seaport of Morocco, situated on the Atlantic. The part inhabited by the Christians and Jews is on a high promontory, — a tongue of land, surrounded on three sides by the ocean, which renders it healthy; and the houses being built of white stone, give it a fine appearance. This is the chief commercial port in the kingdom. The exports are goatskins, oil, almonds, wax, wool, ostrich feathers, dates, pomegranates, morocco, saltpetre, and carpets, which are manufactured here. The population is about ten thousand. The Christian part of the city is separated from the Mohammedan by a wall and gates, which are always closed at night. The Mohammedan part, being on the main-land, is less healthy. The plague was now raging there, and the gates were kept shut all the time, thus cutting off all communication between different parts of the city. The Jews were the medium of communication between the Christians and Mohammedans.

There were but four days in the week on which business could be transacted, — the Mohammedans rigidly observing Friday as their Sabbath, the Jews Saturday, and the Christians Sunday, — which was very embarrassing to masters of vessels. Mr. Jarvis was obliged to remain here several days, though as many as thirty died daily in the Mohammedan part of the city.

He could stand upon the roof of the house where he boarded, and watch their funerals as they wound along the beach. There is always a walk on the tops of the houses, where the family go at eventide — a custom which is alluded to in Scripture.

Accompanied by an English gentleman, he called upon the Governor; they were introduced into his presence, and made the requisite number of salams. He was sitting on a carpet, in a very dirty dress, consisting of a large dingy-white muslin turban, full drawers gathered up below the knee, a short tunic, and a closely fitting jacket with sleeves, of a rich silk fabric, but greatly soiled. The Governor invited them to take mats and sit down. If they complied, by the customs of the country they would have been obliged to smoke and drink coffee with their host; and as they were not inclined to do this in so dirty a place, they excused themselves, and observing the requisite number of bows to his highness, left his presence, and returned to Mogadore.

Mr. Jarvis succeeded in obtaining a cargo of saltpetre, which is gathered in great abundance from old forsaken buildings and fences, from which it is scraped. It seems to be deposited from the atmosphere. He now sailed for Boston; had a pretty good passage; sold his cargo very well, and went to Norfolk, Virginia, for corn. He found that it was sixty-two cents per bushel in this place; but learning that it was very

low in North Carolina, he hired a horse and rode over
to Edenton, a distance of sixty or seventy miles, where
he ascertained that at Plymouth, near the mouth of the
Roanoke, it could be obtained for twenty cents per
bushel.   On his return to Norfolk, he took the south
side of the Great Dismal Swamp (having followed the
north route in going), with the intention of taking his
vessel round to Edenton as quickly as he could.   He
sailed early in December, 1799.   The weather had been
cloudy for several days, with a warm southerly wind.
When just off Cape Hatteras, he saw a strip of pale
blue sky in the northwest, in the form of a crescent,
which to the practiced and watchful eye of a nautical
man, presaged a gale.   Not a moment was to be lost.
He instantly gave orders to have the ship brought up
under a point of land, that would afford some shelter,
on a shoal about eighty fathoms deep, and there cast
anchor, having all the sails furled, and everything
made ready for a conflict with the elements.   Soon
the sea was white with foam; then a distant roaring
was heard, and the tempest came down upon them
from the northwest, with terrible power.   Two days
and two nights it continued to blow with unabated
fury, but the favorable position that he had taken
enabled them to bear up against it.   At last the wind
lulled.   They had weathered the storm, and were safe!
Thanks to Him who ruleth the winds and waves.

He passed over the shoals, which are about three
miles from the Cape, without accident.   When he
came to a place then called "Shell Castle," near
Ocracoke Inlet, he found General Dearborn, one of his
father's old friends, who had been superintending the

erection of a light-house, at Cape Hatteras, for the
United States Government, and had been waiting
several days to get a passage to Edenton, whence he
could return to Washington. Mr. Jarvis was very
happy to have the opportunity of obliging him ; and
he was rejoiced to quit these shoals. They sailed up
the difficult passage in Pamlico and Albermarle
Sounds, to Edenton. Here Mr. Jarvis took a boat,
and two men to cross the Chowan river, to Plymouth,
but the wind was very high, which caused a heavy
sea, and each moment he expected that his frail bark
would be engulfed. The water dashed over them,
nearly swamping the boat, which they as often bailed
out ; but with great difficulty at last they happily
gained the shore. He ascertained that there was
safe anchorage for his vessel at Plymouth, which is
the only port of discharge for all the corn sent down
the Roanoke. He had no trouble in recrossing to
Edenton, the wind having abated.

He now took his vessel to Plymouth ; and the following day hired a horse and gig and set out for Williamston, with three bags of silver, containing $3,000.
When within a few miles of Williamston, he came to
a causeway road, leading through a swamp, flooded
three feet deep with water. It was near night, and
the road seemed impassable in the darkness. He
stopped at a planter's house close by, and politely requested him to allow a black boy to take a torch and
light him across, offering to compensate him liberally.
But the surly planter refused, saying, there was no
danger ; that the tall trees on each side were a sufficient guide. As there seemed no alternative, he at-

tempted to keep the road, and cross over; but very soon found that his gig had lost its equilibrium, and that he was in imminent danger of being wholly overturned. He stopped his horse, stood up in the gig, and shouted for assistance.

Ere long the boy made his appearance with a torch, well mounted on horseback. By the aid of the torch, Mr. Jarvis discovered that one wheel had gone over the side of the causeway, but resting on an upturned tree prevented its upsetting. The water was too deep to extricate the wheel. What was to be done? He had great presence of mind in every emergency, and quick as thought, stepped upon the shaft, disengaged the horse from the carriage, mounted him, and told the boy to hand him the bags, which he placed in front of him, supporting them in part with his legs, which he was forced to draw up in a cramped position. With the other hand he gathered up the reins, and told the boy to guide him carefully, keeping about a rod ahead; to which he cheerily replied, "Yes, Massa." But his horse was fresh and spirited, while Mr. Jarvis' was wearied and worn, and ever and anon the torch-bearer would get far before, obliging Mr. Jarvis to recall him. This difficult passage was at last accomplished, and the dry land gained, without further mishaps. He then remunerated the boy generously, and dismissed him, proceeding on his journey alone. In disengaging the traces he had wet his arms to the shoulders, and his lower limbs were drenched with water. He grew very cold, and shivered all over; in addition to which the constrained posture in which he was obliged to sit, to support such a weight, must have greatly increased his suffering. It seemed an interminable distance to the public-house, to which he had been directed, — travelling in the darkness, through a strange country, in his present condition. His mental energy could not have sustained his physical powers much longer. But the long-looked for lights at last cheered his sight. He alighted at the door of the tavern, and gave orders for the special care of his way-worn horse. The necessity for care and exertion past, his overtaxed body and mind gave way, and he found his strength completely prostrated. He felt too ill to take charge of his money himself; and as the landlord seemed to be a respectable man, asked him if he could keep it in a place of safety till morning, to which he replied affirmatively, and relieved Mr. Jarvis of his three heavy bags of silver. He now requested the favor of a dry suit of clothes, to put on while his were drying. Perceiving that he was shivering with cold, they obligingly retired from the kitchen, which contained the only fire in the house, leaving an old colored man to assist him in taking off his wet garments. While he was thus employed, the landlord had ordered a large fire to be built in the parlor, in the genial heat and light of which Mr. Jarvis imbibed so much caloric, that he was well warmed and sufficiently recruited, by the time his hot supper was prepared, to partake of it with keen appetite. He was then conducted to a comfortable chamber and bed, and soon became oblivious of fatigue, cold, and hardships. The morning sun awoke him to the consciousness of being greatly refreshed by a night of sound sleep.

After dressing himself in his own clothes, which at

6

his request had been brought to his chamber, he made
inquiries for a man to go for his gig; and the offer of
liberal compensation induced a youth to undertake its
recovery.   By the time Mr. Jarvis had discussed a
pretty substantial breakfast, his vehicle stood at the
door.   The water had abated so much in the night,
that the task of disengaging it by daylight was com-
paratively an easy one.

The landlord now brought out the bags; for his
faithful care of which, and extra trouble, he was handsomely rewarded.   Mr. Jarvis then resumed his journey, following the Roanoke.

Almost every year this large river overflows its
banks, which irrigates the soil, rendering it very
fertile; and immense crops of corn are raised.   But
every few years, a freshet in August floods the meadows and destroys the crops, if the water stands upon
them three or four days.   When this disaster occurs,
the price of corn immediately rises to fifty or seventy-
five cents per bushel.   These flat lands are too unhealthy for residence; the owners select high, airy
situations, near pine woods, which are thought conducive to health.

The colored people plant and hoe the corn in the
spring; but in the summer months there is a miasma
so deleterious, that no human being ventures near.   In
October, after the frosts have purified the atmosphere,
the corn is harvested.   Two brothers, named Taylor,
resided near Hog Town, who owned large tracts of
this land.   William Taylor was a man of independent
fortune, and when Mr. Jarvis applied to him for a
large quantity of corn, he declined selling at the pres-

ent low prices, preferring to keep it for a year of scarcity. But Mr. Samuel Taylor had a large, expensive family, with less property than his brother, and to obtain ready money, was willing to sell at twenty cents per bushel, agreeing to send most of his corn down the river in boats to Plymouth, as soon as he could get it threshed. Trusting to his honesty, Mr. Jarvis paid for it in advance, in silver dollars. Mr. Taylor thought he should be able to forward it the latter part of December. He bought the remainder of his cargo of different planters on the river on his return, and at Williamstown, engaging it to be sent down the river as soon as threshed. Much to Mr. Taylor's and the other planters' credit, the corn arrived in good condition at Plymouth, punctually at the time agreed upon. He had his vessel loaded from the boats as they came down ; and finding that it was not full, purchased a quantity of rice in Edenton, where he engaged a black pilot named Dick, to steer the ship through the shoals, and set sail for Lisbon. Toward night, as he approached the dangerous shoals and islands that divide Albermarle from Pamlico Sound, the wind began to blow strong from the northwest, and in this difficult passage it was necessary to come to anchor.

" Dick," said Mr. Jarvis, " I think we shall have a hard blow to-night, and you had better let go the best bower. I don't believe that light one will hold."

" O yes, Massa," answered the pilot ; " this is three fathom hole ; there is a bed of blue clay here, which hold like the debil."

Yielding to what he supposed the better knowledge of the pilot, he suffered them to cast the light anchor, and when everything was made ready for the night, he retired to his berth — or in nautical phrase, " turned in " — about nine o'clock ; but in an hour he was awakened by the cry, " The ship's adrift ! " He hastened on deck, and found they were indeed drifting up on shore. Sorely did he regret that he had not followed the dictates of his judgment. He instantly had her course changed, and steered toward the Marshes, where he had the heavy anchor let go, and she lay there securely till morning. It was then found necessary to unload her, in order to get her off, the water was so shallow. Mr. Jarvis thought he could get some boats for this purpose at the Currituck Islands, that lay along the coast about nine miles distant.

Taking a boat and two sailors to row it, he set out about nine o'clock, A. M., for these islands. It was during the Christmas holidays, and the boatmen were drinking and carousing. Mr. Jarvis told them how he was situated, and begged them to come without delay with their boats, and relieve him by unloading the corn, which they readily promised ; and believing that they would keep their word, he left them about four o'clock on a cold winter's afternoon. The wind blew strong, and in order to regain the ship, they were forced to row against it, which was very hard work. As they toiled along, darkness overtook them. Mr. Jarvis had told his mate, if they did not return before night, to hang up a light at the mast-head ; but this signal could not be seen, and there was nothing to indicate to them where the ship lay. His only resource was in taking observations of the stars ; and holding up a large silk handkerchief, noticing in what direction it was blown by the wind, which was in the northwest; and he thus formed some idea of the points of compass, to guide their course. He looked anxiously for his beacon-light, but in vain; and began to fear that he had missed the direction, and that they should be lost in this waste of waters, for the waves ran very high, and any moment might break over and sink them. The suspense was fearful! At last, as they rose to the top of a high wave, the view became more commanding, and he thought he discerned a light. This was encouraging. He asked the sailors if they saw it. No, they had not. As they descended into the trough of the sea, it was lost to his sight; but on mounting another wave, was again so distinctly visible, that the sailors descried it, and convinced that it proceeded from the ship, were inspired with fresh vigor to ply their oars. Ere many minutes they were alongside, to the great joy of master and men, who experienced the satisfaction and gratitude those only can feel, who have been for hours in peril of their lives, with the attendants of cold, darkness, weariness, and hunger. Mr. Jarvis appointed a watch for the night, telling them that the boatmen might be expected ere long; and then, worn out by care, fatigue, and exposure, he sought rest. When he awoke in the morning he was informed, to his surprise, that the boats had not made their appearance. Telescope in hand, he watched for them hour after hour, to the great trial of his patience, till about noon, when he saw three boats put out from the islands, but it was nearly dark when they reached the ship.

He sternly asked them why they had failed to come

as they had promised, the night before, — keeping him waiting in this dangerous situation for twenty-four hours.

From their not very intelligible excuses, he gathered that they had been carousing all night, were tipsy in the morning, and only sufficiently sober to start about twelve o'clock.

They fastened their boats to the ship, and came on board; and then begged Mr. Jarvis to defer unloading the corn until morning, that they might get a night's sleep. This he positively refused, saying that there was danger of another storm; that they had already delayed him many hours, and he should insist on the immediate performance of the work. He hired his own sailors by extra pay to assist, which they cheerfully did. About four o'clock, A. M., he was told that the ship was afloat. He gave orders to have her hauled into deep water, and told the boatmen they might follow and fasten their boats to the ship. But no; they go deliberately back to their islands! Mr. Jarvis is indignant. His whole cargo is at their mercy. They may be honest; but could very easily take many bushels without detection. There is however no remedy, and he can only trust it to Providence. At daylight he hoisted sail and went down towards Ocracoke Inlet. The gale of the preceding days had carried away the poles that had been set up to mark the "Swash," a passage of the deepest water from the Sound, into Ocracoke Inlet; and as the wind continued to blow hard from the northwest, the pilot thought it the safest course to keep well to windward. Mr. Jarvis told him that according to his recollection, he was getting too far to windward.

" Better be too windward than too leeward, Massa," replied Dick.

This was true, and Mr. Jarvis acquiesced. But in a few minutes afterwards, the ship struck on the " Royal Shoal," and being by the head, the stern swung round higher upon the shoal. All the after sails were then pulled down, and only the forward sails kept standing. A swell coming from the sea, lifted her from the shoal, but in the hollow of the swell she again struck the shoal forward, and the stern swung round, notwithstanding she had all her forward sails set. This could not last long, for they were washing higher and higher on the sand, and would inevitably be dashed to pieces.

At this critical moment Mr. Jarvis recollected the thirty casks of rice that had been rolled into the forward part of her, to preserve an even keel, and ordered all hands down to roll the rice aft. The order was obeyed *with a will*, and the heavy casks were moved with that celerity with which men work, when their lives are in jeopardy. The effect was instantaneous. The next swell lifted her as before, but in the hollow of the sea she struck aft, and her head then turned toward the deep water, and continued in that direction till she got into three fathoms of water, when they made sail, and ran into Ocracoke Inlet.

Thus they were saved from shipwreck by Mr. Jarvis' quick perceptions and presence of mind, through the blessing of God. The day following, the Currituck boats came down with the corn, in good order, without apparent diminution, which was put on

board the ship ; but finding she leaked badly, Mr.
Jarvis gave orders to have her pumped, and after
pumping steadily for two hours, she was cleared. He
thought she must have knocked off some of her
sheathing in beating upon the shoal, which caused the
leakage. After waiting a day or two at Ocracoke
Inlet, he found the ship leaked about 400 strokes an
hour. He hesitated about venturing to sea in this
condition ; but should he return to Edenton, unload,
and have her repaired, he would completely lose the
voyage, as other vessels would precede him, and
lower the price of corn. It was " sink or swim "
with him then, and he finally determined to hazard
it. On the third day, the weather being fine, several
vessels went out to sea ; and he said to his boatswain,
a stout able seaman, —

" John, it won't do to let all these craft get out
before us."

" No, no, sir," was the prompt reply.

The cheerful bustle in getting under way, engrossed
their attention, until they had passed the Bar, and
once more emerged into the broad ocean.

But the voyage proved perilous and disastrous, to
an extreme.

Not many days afterwards a squall came on. Mr.
Jarvis had been watching by the helm some time,
only giving it up to one of the seamen, when he went
to supper. He had not been down more than ten
minutes when he felt the ship veering round. He ran
upon deck, and found that by some carelessness or
mismanagement, the seaman had suffered a sudden
gust of wind to strike the vessel from ahead, heav-

ing the sails all aback, causing her to veer round, and
the boom, which was forty feet long, and ten inches in
diameter, to swing from side to side, with the full
force of the wind, which quickly snapped it in three
pieces.

He soon got the vessel before the wind, and under
snug sail; and finally the pieces of the boom were got
in. By the use of spars and tackle the sail was made
useful to the end of the voyage, using it occasionally
when required.

Mr. Jarvis said that when he was on deck himself,
he never lost a spar, a mast, or a sail. In every instance of the kind, it was owing to the carelessness of
his sailors. Not long after this, his boatswain, — a
Dutchman, and very capable man, — one of his best
seamen, was at the helm in a gale of wind, when, as
he was pulling the tiller-rope, it broke, and precip-
itated him against a barrel of tar.

Mr. Jarvis saw the accident, and sprang to the helm
in time to save them from greater injury, calling a
sailor to his aid. But the wind was so high, that with
their united strength they could but just manage it,
until another rope could be supplied. He then went
to the assistance of the boatswain, who was groaning
in great pain; but the helm had demanded instant attention. He found the poor fellow had broken two of
his ribs. He had him carefully attended to, and made
as comfortable as possible. Thus his boatswain was
disabled.

Troubles never come alone. The cook, a colored
man, had placed a tea-kettle of boiling water rather
carelessly on the caboose, when, by the rolling of the

ship, it was upset, and one of his knees was badly
scalded.   He was assisted to his berth, and Mr.
Jarvis examined " Bucchan," and a nautical book on
medicines, for remedies; but although he tried every
cure that the medical faculty recommended, and that
his medicine-chest afforded, yet for three days it continued to be very sore and painful, and swelled badly.
At length the mate, who had been in a whaling-ship,
said that in cases of burns or scalds, they always used
scraped potatoes if they had them. Without much faith
in the remedy, but as a *dernier ressort*, on the third
night Mr. Jarvis applied it, and found that the knee
was highly inflamed. Next morning, to his amazement, he saw Tony with a cane hobbling about the
deck, and able to resume his usual duties. " Why
Tony! are you better to-day?" " O yes, Massa
Captain; I great deal better."   He examined his
limb, and of a truth, the inflammation had subsided,
and it seemed in a fair way of recovery. But still he
could not take his turn at the pump for more than a
week.   Then his first mate was laid up with a slow
fever, much to Mr. Jarvis' sorrow; and, as if to cap
the climax of mishaps, the second mate became disabled by a boil on his neck and shoulder. Thus a crew
of ten were reduced to six working men, including their
Captain, who had to take his turn at the pump with
the five sailors, in order to keep the vessel clear of
water.   He divided his hands into two watches of four
hours each : two at the pump, and one at the helm,
being obliged to pump fifteen minutes in every half
hour, in order to clear the vessel.
Beside the severe labor at the pump, the duties of

captain and mates now devolved upon him, being in
addition, nurse and physician to the disabled.

But the pump was worst of all, requiring great
strength and force to draw off the water. Not being
accustomed to such severe manual labor, he at last
wore a hole in the palm of one of his hands, and was
obliged to wear a thick glove to protect it. But
amidst these sufferings, they had the comfort of all
kinds of provisions in abundance, which Mr. Jarvis
had carefully laid in ere he sailed : tea, coffee, chocolate, sugar, rice, bread, beef, pork, and fowls, —
which he always carried to sea with him. They had
dry and comfortable berths ; their good food and
lodging were the means of sustaining their health and
spirits, amid almost unexampled perils and labors. He
had two men that were capable of taking charge of the
helm : one was put on each watch ; one into his, one
into the other watch, while two hands were pumping.
So many being disabled, he took down his top-gallant
masts and sails in order to keep the ship under as good
control as possible.

When he was two thirds across the Atlantic, his
morning watch having closed at four o'clock, he had
gone below for a cat-watch of two hours. At a quarter
past five o'clock the watch awakened him, and called
him to see a lunar rainbow. He hurried up and
beheld this wonderful phenomenon. A perfect rainbow spanning the heavens, as distinctly visible as a
solar rainbow, directly north of him ; the colors bright,
but of a paler hue than the solar bow. Beyond this
was a dark, heavy wall of clouds, bordered with a
fringe of white foam, resembling a cataract — which

steadily rose higher and higher, surely indicating a heavy gale.

He instantly ordered all the sails furled but the foresail and foretopsail, and then put the ship's head to the south. The wind had been light and southwesterly; the vessel rolling lazily along, making a creaking noise. But at 5.30 A. M., the ocean became perfectly white — one sheet of foam. When the wind struck the ship everything went crack, crack, crack, like nails in a severe frost. It seemed as if a strain came on every timber. She was thrown on her beamends, but soon righted. One of the men said the boltrope of the foresail had broken. Mr. Jarvis ordered the sail instantly furled. It was a perfectly new and very strong one; but the moment it was loosened, the wind took it, and with one mighty gust, slit it into ribbons, as if made of paper. He told two men to go up and save the remnants; but the wind came down upon them with such power, that it pinned them fast to the shrouds, and they were unable to move. Seeing their situation, he quickly recalled them, and as the ship descended the wave, they succeeded in getting down. Some pieces of the foresail twisted round the main yard, and were afterwards saved; others were torn from the bolt-rope and scattered away.

The topsail met a similar fate; the moment it was slightly loosened in order to furl it, there was a sudden cracking sound, and behold, that stout new sail was also torn in strips, and flew in tatters before the wind.

The ship was now put in the best possible state of resistance, and bore bravely up against the tempest.

Before noon the sea ran up into mountain waves, and Mr. Jarvis expected each moment that the ship would be swallowed up. But she was remarkably flat-bottomed, and seemed to slide down ere the comb of the wave broke over her. In the midst of this terrible conflict with the furious elements, he was at the pump with one of his sailors, who suddenly cried out, "Save yourself!" clinging, himself, to the mainmast. But before Mr. Jarvis, whose back was to the sea, could catch at anything, he found himself floating off in the wave that had broken over the ship. He said to himself, "Well, it is all over with me now!" certain that he should be lost in the raging ocean. But no! God had otherwise ordered it. In a moment he found his feet striking the fore shrouds. With desperate energy he threw himself sideways, and caught hold of the long boat, which he grasped like a vice. The water soon ran off the deck, he still holding on to the boat, until the deck was free from water, when he ran aft. We can imagine his feelings of thanksgiving, for this narrow escape from so sudden a death. Under the circumstances, his preservation seemed almost miraculous. He calmly went to the cabin, put on dry clothes, and returned to his post of duty at the pump, but took the precaution to wind a rope securely round his body, with which he lashed himself to the mast. There were two pumps in the vessel: one by constant use had become cracked, the other in the midst of the hurricane would not draw. The danger of sinking being added to the terrors of the tempest, made their destruction seem almost inevitable. They drew the boxes, and by a sounding-rod, finally worked the corn loose that had washed into the pump; but this delay occasioned much pumping ere she would suck again. In this awful hour of suspense, one of the sailors below called out to the man at the pump, and asked if she sucked. In a very droll manner he answered, " No, confound her; she is too *old* to *suck*."

But happily for all on board she *sucked* not long afterwards.

The wind continued to blow with unabated fury until about 3.30 A. M., when it began to lull. At five it became still more calm and clear; and at ten o'clock died wholly away; then it changed into the southwest, and so continued until they arrived in Lisbon. Mr. Jarvis said this was the most terrific storm that he ever experienced. It lasted twenty-four hours. In later years he read with intense interest Cooper's " Pilot," saying that its graphic descriptions of storms at sea, and navigating amidst shoals, brought back most vividly to his mind his own perils and hairbreadth escapes, insomuch that he awaited the issue of Cooper's scenes with almost breathless interest.

When the weather became fine, the boatswain, being the only good sail-maker on board, and much improved in his condition, was placed in an easy, reclining posture, and set to mending the old foresail, which they had on board, with the pieces saved from the new one; and this was used to the end of the voyage. In ten days they entered the smooth harbor of Lisbon, one of the finest and most capacious havens in the world. Lisbon is ten miles from the mouth of the Tagus, which widens to nine miles as it approaches the city, forming this noble harbor. And what a landscape met their delighted eyes as they sailed up this beautiful broad river, bordered on each side by verdant fields of grain, in all the freshness of spring, though early in February! Its hills covered with the vine, the olive, the fig-tree, and the laurel, clothed in rich, luxuriant, dark green foliage; the ever-blooming orange and lemon groves, filling the balmy air with sweet perfumes; the white " *Munhas*," or windmills, crowning the summit of each fruit-clad hill; the convents, churches, and palaces, seen through the medium of bright sunshine, and a warm, soft atmosphere, formed altogether a most picturesque and lovely scene. And when contrasted with bleak, snowy December in the United States, and the recent horrors of the ocean, appeared to these tempest-tossed mariners like an earthly paradise. After all their perils, disasters, storms, and sufferings, what joy and relief must have filled their hearts, to find themselves safely anchored in this haven! In the words of the song we might say, —

> " And O what rapture filled each breast
> Of the hopeless crew of the ship distressed!
> When landed safe, what joy to tell
> Of all the dangers there befell! "

What a land in which to refresh the weather-beaten crew who had been saved from such imminent risks of life !

Mr. Jarvis' courage, perseverance, and fortitude were well rewarded by the profits on his cargo. He sold the corn for three times what he gave for it, and the rice for double ; clearing seven or eight thousand dollars.

He often dwelt upon this voyage as the turning-point of his fortune.   As if Providence had taxed his faith and endurance to the utmost, ere crowning his labors with success.   And when we consider that all this was suffered, not for the attainment of wealth for himself, or to liquidate his own debts, but to free himself from responsibilities incurred by another's failure, and from that noble independence of mind that shrunk from involving his father in his difficulties, his conduct appears truly heroic.

To his surprise, the leak in his ship stopped in forty-eight hours after their arrival, satisfying him that she had beaten off several streaks of sheathing when she struck the shoal, and the mud of the Tagus had stopped up the nail holes, cracks, etc.

He took in a cargo of salt, wine, and fruit, and set sail for Chesapeake Bay for one of tobacco.   The return voyage was the very opposite of the one out, for owing to constant calms and light winds, they had ninety-four days' passage ! — most wearisome of itself; but to add to their troubles, in sixty days their water was almost exhausted, and they were reduced to half a pint per day, and this not of a good quality, being ropy.   They had an abundant supply of provisions, — beef, pork, bread, and fowls, but of what avail was food, when they were choking for water !   They dared eat but very little meat, for fear of increasing their thirst, and the bread began to grow short.

We hardly consider how essential water is to life, until we are deprived of it — that common blessing, which God bestows so freely on all, second only to the air we breathe !

Mr. Jarvis says, it is only by personal experience we realise the suffering that want of water produces. Thirsty and choking, the very idea that they could have but this small allowance aggravated the desire for more. They could only moisten their parched mouths by a swallow at a time.

This state of things had reached its acme, when, just off the Banks of Newfoundland, a shower came up very suddenly. The scuppers were immediately stopped, and as it was a copious rain, they caught about half a hogshead. But it was so dirty, that it would have been intolerable to any but men suffering with a dreadful thirst; for the fowls ran upon the deck, and the sailors threw their tobacco juice about without ceremony. But after it was put in a barrel and settled, they used it for coffee, which was to them a treat, and a great relief. On the next appearance of a squall, the deck was washed down, and the scuppers stopped; and when the shower came, they caught nearly a hogshead, which was most grateful, being only a little flavored with tar and salt water. They could drink it as it was, however, and this was a greater luxury. Finding it was a season of showers, Mr. Jarvis contrived a mode of catching water, without its coming in contact with the deck. He had a large barrel placed on deck; into this he put a tunnel, and had a sail so arranged as to strain the falling water into it. Sometimes water was caught in this way; at others, the wind was too high; but they succeeded in saving a barrel of pure water, which was an unspeakable comfort, and lasted until they reached Virginia. He put into James River and anchored at City

7

Point. The crew, having fulfilled their time of service, were impatient to be discharged and go home, after these disastrous voyages; and Mr. Jarvis was left alone with the ship.

He thought it prudent to have her graved before another voyage, and for this purpose was obliged to heave her down, hiring some colored men to effect this object. He now saw the cause of her excessive leaking, for as he had conjectured, several streaks of her sheathing were off, and he had no doubt that it was done when she was stranded near Ocracoke Inlet.

After much difficulty he succeeded in obtaining a ship-carpenter and caulker; but the former knew so little of his trade that Mr. Jarvis was obliged to plan all his work, and to stand by the side of the vessel, on a mud-scow (kept for repairing), overseeing and assisting in putting on the sheathing. He rose before the sun, breakfasted, and with the exception of half an hour for dinner, continued his labors till sun down.

It was a damp, unhealthy situation, and his exposure to the heat of the sun for so many hours in August was very dangerous in this climate; as he was liable to an attack of bilious or intermittent fever, etc., etc. Some precaution seemed necessary, and he was so fortunate as to find, at a store, a box of old port wine, which he used as a beverage with water when thirsty, for a safeguard, being exactly the thing he required; and while the necessity for exertion lasted he felt no ill effects from this great exposure.

The caulker, a colored man, did his work tolerably well; the seams of the new sheathing were at last caulked, and Mr. Jarvis' diligence and perseverance

were rewarded by the vessel's being put in fine order
for sea. The tobacco was sent down the Appomattox
River in boats from Petersburg to City Point, where
the ship lay. He now wished to engage a crew, and
just at this time, most opportunely, a ship happened to
come in, the hands of which being discharged, four
of them wished to get a passage to New York. These
four he hired to go with him to Martha's Vineyard,
where he expected to get seamen; and would pay
their passage from thence to New York. The tobacco
was put on board, and they sailed. The following
day a storm came on, and Mr. Jarvis was obliged to
keep on deck all night, exposed to a cold "north-
easter." This abated in the morning, but its effects
upon him were long felt. Towards night he was
attacked with chills, followed by fever;—and fever
and ague shook his frame for many weeks, being as
usual attended with debility. Doubtless the seeds of
this disease were sown during his exposure on the James
River, which the cold, taken during the storm, merely
developed. He took all the cinchona or Peruvian
bark that he had, which was very little. On arriving
at Martha's Vineyard, he purchased all the bark he
could obtain, which was only two or three ounces.
He succeeded in engaging a good crew — two capable mates, and five sailors — and then sailed for St.
Sebastian. He was feeble during the voyage, but
found the first mate a most efficient assistant; and
happily encountered no storms, until they reached the
bay of St. Sebastian, where, as he lay at anchor, a
violent gale arose, and his anchor not being heavy
enough to hold his ship, he was obliged to send ashore

for a larger one and a cable, which rendered them secure.

He was now compelled to undergo a tedious quarantine of forty-eight days. The Spanish authorities have a great dread of yellow fever; and their knowledge of geography is so limited, that they do not discriminate between those ports of the United States which are liable to this disease and those that are not, but condemn, alike, every vessel coming from America, whether she cleared from Boston or New Orleans. The ground where the quarantine was performed was a small island in the bay of St. Sebastian, about two miles long and wide, upon which there was some elevated land. Those subjected to this vexatious detention could here amuse themselves by playing ball and other games. The quarantine officers, with their usual short-sightedness, put the crews arriving to-day with those that came a month ago. They were in full view of the city, and boats passed to and fro every day — another instance of their inconsistency. When time was of so much importance to him for the transaction of business, it was exceedingly annoying to be thus detained, without the slightest reason. However, his overtaxed and diseased body greatly needed this rest; and it proved a merciful respite from care and labor. He could obtain plenty of bark, and all the comforts and luxuries that he required, and ere the quarantine ended he was completely cured of the ague, with which he was never again visited.

Owing to differences between France and the United States, Mr. Jarvis had been obliged to give bonds at the custom-house, before he left America,

not to go with his vessel into any port of France.
Soon after he was cleared from the quarantine, the
tidings arrived that the variances between the two
countries had been adjusted, and peace restored.
This news caused great uneasiness among the Americans there, who believed that it would cause a great
fall in tobacco. Several persons who had cargoes from
the United States, wished to sell even at the present
reduced price. Mr. Jarvis, on the reverse, argued that
they had all bought their tobacco at the very low price
of three dollars seventy-five cents per cwt., and were
absolutely certain, if they waited awhile until the
depression of the market was over, to obtain enough
over the cost to pay them a handsome profit. The
news of peace would immediately raise the price of
tobacco to six dollars in America, and as tobacco
shippers were usually men of property, they would
not probably sell in France for less than the cost
and charges of freight. And if they could obtain
this price, the difference between the first cost of theirs,
and that of Mr. Jarvis and others in port with him,
would give the latter gentlemen a very handsome
profit. Learning about the same time that England
was at war with the Danes, Swedes, and Northern
Powers, and ascertaining that a cargo of rosin, pitch,
and tar, could be obtained in Bayonne, he determined
to send down his tobacco to Bayonne in "chasse-
marées"; [1] and on their return to freight the boats with
these commodities.

As soon as his quarantine ended, he presented his

---

[1] A sort of decked boat employed in the coasting trade, and for the conveyance of fish, rendered literally *Chase the tide.*

letters of introduction to the widow Birmingham.
Her father was long the head of a most respectable
house, which at his decease was assumed by her husband, who was Irish by birth. After his death,
which occurred in a few years, his widow had conducted the business herself, wisely and prosperously,
taking her two sons into partnership. On being presented to this lady, Mr. Jarvis was much struck by
her noble and dignified deportment. Her dark
Spanish complexion was lighted up by her intelligent
countenance, and keen, sparkling, black eyes.

At this, and all subsequent visits, a servant presented
a cup of delicious spiced chocolate, and two or three
delicate little spongy cakes, on a silver salver, — this
being a Spanish custom when they wish to treat a
guest with particular attention.

The house of Birmingham gave him letters of introduction to two houses in Bayonne, who would be likely
to take his tobacco on commission, and advance money
upon it to purchase tar and other naval stores.

Mr. Jarvis took the land route to Bayonne, which
crosses the Bidosoa (a small river, dividing this part of
Spain from France), and a spur of the Pyrenees. His
mode of travelling on this occasion, was called " *en
cacolet,*" which may require an explanation to the un-
initiated. A large pack-saddle covered with green
baize was placed on a strong mule, upon which two
wooden frames or chairs were firmly strapped, in one of
which sits the guide, in the other the traveller ; the
former in this instance, was a trig, demure Spanish
damsel.

The country through which he passed was rocky,

thickly covered with underbrush, with only a foot-path for the mule in many places. It was a day's journey to Bayonne, but the weather was fine, the scenery novel and grand, and the ride proved a very pleasant one.

The first house in Bayonne to which Mr. Jarvis presented his letters, demurred about taking his tobacco ; one partner being very civil and wishing to oblige him ; the other, the very opposite, making objections. After some discussion, he resolved not to have anything to do with them, and went to Messrs. L———c & D———e, the other house to whom he had letters. They were polite, and readily agreed to take the tobacco on commission, and advance sufficient money to purchase a cargo of naval stores, recommending a Jew who would obtain them at a reasonable price. Mr. Jarvis now had his tobacco transported in chasse-marées, which on their return took back the naval stores, without insurance. The two signal-towns on the route, Port Passage and St. Jean de Luse, would give timely notice to the boats should danger threaten them, when they could take shelter in these ports.

The passage to and from Bayonne had been safely performed, and the vessel was nearly loaded and ready for sea, when the French Consul at St. Sebastian called on the Collector, and said he had been informed that a vessel in port was loading with naval stores, and he suspected they were destined for England. Knowing that Mr. Jarvis' vessel was consigned to the house of Birmingham, and being very friendly to the family, the Collector called upon the elder brother and repeated to him the suspicions of the con-

sul.   Mr. Birmingham told him that the ship was
bound to Hamburg (for so the papers had been made
out, in case of being overhauled) ; but this answer did
not seem quite satisfactory.

Mr. Birmingham hastened to Mr. Jarvis, informed
him, and advised his immediate departure; who replied,
that he thought he should be able to sail in the morning.

St. Sebastian was enclosed by very high walls,
being one of the ancient fortresses of Spain. The dock
was outside the walls, and the gates between the dock
and city were shut and locked at sundown, which
would prevent observation of what was passing on
the dock from the town. There were two or three
American vessels in port, and Mr. Jarvis begged the
captains to allow him to hire their sailors to work in
the night, to which they cheerfully assented, and as
soon as the gates were closed, about twenty men came
to assist his crew in putting the remaining naval stores,
which still lay in two chasse-marées, on board his
brig.

They were all stowed away before daylight, and
having the previous afternoon given the requisite sig-
nals to the castle, he warped his vessel out before sunrise, and pushed off as fast as the sails would carry
them towards London.   .

When off Holyhead they encountered the sloop-of-
war "Savage," of twenty-four guns, which immediately sent a boat alongside to reconnoitre, which
hailed him with —

"Where from ? "

Mr. Jarvis replied, "St. Sebastian."

" Where bound ? "

" To Hamburg."

" What nation ? "

" American."

" What is your cargo ? "

" Tar, pitch, and rosin."

" Will you please to come on board and see the captain ? "

" Yes sir."

Mr. Jarvis' costume at this time was anything but appropriate for a presentation to a British naval officer. An old beaver hat, once white, the under side of the brim green, had seen such hard service as nearly to have lost its original form, and was tied to his button-hole by a rope-yarn to prevent its being blown away. His coat was a coarse pea-jacket. His vest, a relic of his beauish days in Boston, had been a very handsome striped velvet, but was now worn threadbare; a shirt not over nice; coarse seaman's trousers, blue yarn stockings, and shoes that had been so thoroughly drenched in sea-water as to have assumed a reddish hue, were tied up with rope yarn, — making a *tout ensemble* very unfavorable to him. Judging from outward appearances, he would much more readily have been taken for a sailor, than a master of a vessel and a gentleman.

The officer in the boat stared at him as he entered it ; but there had been no time allowed for making his toilet. Very soon he was on board the man-of-war, and standing before the captain, who eyed him from head to foot with keen scrutiny, and in a stern, imperative voice, commenced his examination.

" Are you the master of that vessel? " he said, as if he doubted it.

" Yes sir."

" Where are you from ? "

" St. Sebastian."

" Where bound ? "

" To Hamburg."

" What is your cargo ? "

" Tar, pitch, and rosin."

" To what nation do you belong ? "

" I am an American, from Boston, Massachusetts, United States."

" Please to walk down into my cabin."

" Yes sir."

When there, he said, " Please to sit down."

This was a compliment not often extended to masters of vessels — an evidence that beneath the rough exterior he had discovered the language and deportment of a gentleman.   The captain then called his secretary.

" Mr. Secretary, get your writing materials, and write out the answers made to my questions."

" Yes sir."

He then repeated his queries, and to each answer he said to the secretary, " Write that down."   When this was done, he said to Mr. Jarvis, —

" Have you any English sailors on board your vessel ? "

" No sir."

" You are an Englishman yourself ! "

" No sir."

" But I never heard an American pronounce as you do."

" I cannot help that, sir. I never set foot on English ground in my life. I am a native of Boston."

" Did you get tar, pitch, and rosin in St. Sebastian ? "

" You know, sir, the country about the Pyrenees is full of pine-trees."

" Aye, aye."

This was a ruse, which the captain's geographical knowledge did not enable him to detect. The country on the French side of the Pyrenees is indeed full of pine-trees, for twenty miles north of Bayonne ; but it is not so on the Spanish side.

" Are you sure that you are not going to France ? " said the captain.

" To prove, sir, that I am not, and to be very frank with you, I will show you a letter I have to Mr. Braddick, a merchant in London ; and acknowledge that I purchased my cargo to sell in London ; supposing that naval stores would be very acceptable at this time for his majesty's service." He then showed the letter addressed to Mr. Braddick, to the captain, who still but half convinced, said —

" Very good, very well ; but you will need a pilot to pilot you into the Downs."

" Yes sir, I shall," Mr. Jarvis very cordially replied.

" I will provide you with one."

" Thank you, sir."

The pilot accompanying him back to his ship, the sloop-of-war cruised off towards France, and was soon out of sight, while Mr. Jarvis very unsuspiciously steered on towards the Downs, where it was customary to take in a river pilot, for London.

He mentioned this to the pilot whom the English captain had sent on board, and proposed to him to put him on shore, and hoist a signal for a river pilot.

"For the love of God, don't do so," said the pilot.

"Why not?"

"If you do I shall be suspected and punished for having left your vessel."

"Are you prize-master, then?"

"I was sent on board to watch your movements; the captain has gone over to the French coast, and will soon be back, and will send for me. You are in no danger now; pray consider my situation, and await the return of the English vessel."

Mr. Jarvis now saw through the captain's polite offer of a pilot. Suspecting that he was bound for France, he had gone over to the French coast to keep a sharp look-out, and would undoubtedly, had it been so, have made a prize of his cargo, which he would have been very glad to have done, dividing the spoils with his crew.

Mr. Jarvis had written to London for a license to admit him with a cargo of naval stores from St. Sebastian; but had there been any miscarriage of the letter, a very serious loss would have been sustained, both by detention and by the probable fall in the price of his naval stores. All these circumstances made it of the greatest importance to get clear from the gripe of the British officer, and he was strongly tempted to put the pilot ashore notwithstanding his remonstrances. He impatiently watched for the "Savage," but in vain. At last he sent a man aloft to look out, who said a vessel had just made its appearance in the southeast, which proved the English sloop-of-war. As soon as it was within hailing distance, Mr. Jarvis asked the captain if he had any further commands. He answered in the negative, and said he might send his pilot aboard, which was immediately done; a signal hoisted for a river pilot, who soon came; and that night Mr. Jarvis anchored safely in London.

Here a new political disappointment followed him, for soon after his arrival, news was received of the battle of Copenhagen, and of the peace that had been made with the Danes. This diminished the value of his naval stores considerably. He immediately presented his letters to Mr. Braddick, who gave him every possible assistance in the sale of his cargo, which he finally effected for about four hundred pounds sterling, profit; and invested the proceeds in Caraccas cocoa, then in demand in Spain. Mr. Braddick's experienced eye aided him essentially in selecting the cocoa, the quality of which is not always as good as its outward appearance.

Mr. Jarvis' acquaintance with Mr. Braddick ripened into friendship, for the benevolence and strict integrity of that worthy Quaker merchant deserved and won perfect confidence. A correspondence was kept up between them for many years.

One day as he was walking in the street he met a Mr. Monkhouse, a London merchant, who for a time boarded with him at Mrs. Archibald's in Boston. Monkhouse expressed much pleasure at the meeting, and very hospitably invited him to dine with him at the house of his partner, Mr. Bowerbanks.

Mr. Jarvis accepted the invitation, and, at the hour

appointed, went to the house, which was a plain, respectable one, without any pretension; and in its furniture and appointments, was free from all show or ostentation. Mr. Bowerbanks received him very politely, and introduced him to the company, which consisted of three or four American merchants, and a tall Yorkshire squire, six feet high, very stiff, ceremonious, and self-important. He was a school-mate and early friend of Mr. Bowerbanks, who seemed to wish to pay him particular attention. The company were soon invited from the drawing-room to dinner, which consisted of a fine boiled salmon, a large roasted leg of South Down mutton, a boiled flour or batter pudding, and two glasses of port wine — an excellent dinner, but plain compared with those which Mr. Jarvis had been accustomed to see prepared for a company of five or six invited guests in America, where a variety of dishes was considered indispensable. When the gentlemen had finished their second glass, Mr. Bowerbanks remarked that the ladies of his family were in the country, and he wished to join them. He then rose, and his guests departed. He was reputed very wealthy. Afterwards Mr. Jarvis dined *en famille* with other London merchants, when the dinner usually was boiled or roast mutton, vegetables, a pudding, and port wine — simple, comfortable, and sufficient, without much variety or superfluity, which led him to conclude that they lived more plainly and economically than the merchants in the Southern States and in Boston.

After his long continued hardships and privations, he felt that the success which had attended his exer-

tions warranted his indulgence in the pleasure of seeing the various structures and works of art in this
great metropolis, which had been so much celebrated.
For in his early life many Americans cherished affection for the mother country, and were proud of her
grandeur. Accompanied by Mr. Braddick, he first
went to see St. Paul's Cathedral, which from his boy-
hood he had heard spoken of as the world's wonder.
But unfortunately he approached the vast building
through a narrow lane, which being a most unfavorable point of view, his first impression was great disappointment. Its proportions were certainly immense,
but it appeared to him that the style of architecture
was neither Grecian, Gothic, nor Morisco ; and it was
destitute of any ornament to relieve the plainness or
gratify the eye. The interior was but little more
satisfactory. Some of the chapels he thought very
handsome ; but as a whole, he was more impressed
by its magnitude than by its beauty. He had seen
the magnificent Convent of Batalha, and the Church
of San Roque in Portugal, and other noble edifices,
which led him to expect more elaborate finish and
elegance.

He expressed his ideas to Mr. Braddick, who, in
answer to his remarks, showed him a plan of the
building, as it was designed originally by Sir Christopher Wren, but which had not been carried out,
owing to the prevailing opinions and prejudices of the
age — the pillars and ornamental parts having been
rejected, from religious scruples, on the ground that
they were an imitation of the Grecian *heathen* temples.

His beau ideal of the Tower was much more nearly realized. He gazed with deep interest on this ancient building, — fraught with so many historical associations, — its massive grandeur and antique appearance ; and examined with eager curiosity the arms and armor of past ages.

He next visited " Vauxhall Gardens," and after walking about some time, enjoying the novelties of the place and the music, he called for some refreshment, when a cup of coffee and a sandwich were brought. The bacon was shaved so extremely thin, that ever afterwards, " thin as a Vauxhall slice," was a favorite comparison with him ; and the charge being half a guinea, he thought, in the words of Dr. Franklin, that he had " *Paid too dear for his whistle.*"

The celebrated Mrs. Siddons was at this time a star of the first magnitude, and wishing to see her, he attended the theatre, but to his disappointment she did not make her appearance, owing to indisposition.

As a still greater indulgence, he hired a horse and rode about forty miles out of the city on horseback, to see something of the interior of the mother country. The high hedges at first intercepted the view, but on attaining an eminence, he was delighted with the landscape spread out before him. The fine residences of the nobility and gentry, with their gardens, parks, and highly cultivated fields, rendered it picturesque and beautiful, and gave him a very favorable idea of the agriculture, taste, and wealth of England. He often, in after years, spoke of these as " the *only solitary* instances " in which he had allowed himself any amusements, since the loss of his property.

While in London he chartered his vessel to bring back a cargo of cognac brandy from Charente in France, after delivering the cocoa in St. Sebastian. For this charter he received five·guineas per ton, and five guineas a day demurrage.

His cocoa sold remarkably well at St. Sebastian, for it was in great demand, and was of a superior quality. He purchased it for five guineas per English gross hundred weight (116 lbs.), and sold it for fifty-four dollars per 100 lbs. (the Spanish weight), clearing twenty-nine dollars on every hundred.

Immediately after it was delivered, he sent his mate to Charente with his vessel, and gave him directions to write to the house, of whom he was to receive the brandy, as soon as he arrived, and inform them that he was ready for it.

Mr. Jarvis followed by land in about a week. The road to Charente was through Bayonne, and to this city he rode *en cacolet*, as before ; but unlike the former journey, this proved a very unpleasant one, for it began to rain ere he had proceeded far, and when he reached the Bidosoa, it actually poured.

In crossing the Pyrenees by a narrow foot-path, he was exposed to the whole force of the storm. The sleet penetrated into his neck and garments, chilling him extremely, and severely taxing his powers of endurance. Wet, cold, and stiff, with pains in every limb, he felt really sick when he arrived at Bayonne in the evening. On entering the hotel, whom should he meet, to his great surprise, but his old friend Peter Gilman, the elder brother of his partners, who had been for some time a resident of Bordeaux, and had come to

8

Bayonne on business.   After a cordial greeting — both experiencing the pleasure of unexpectedly meeting a friend in a land of strangers, — Mr. Gilman invited him to sup with him.   He thanked him, but said he was sick, and must retire without delay.

" What is the matter with you ? "

" I ache in every limb, and am exhausted by cold and fatigue."

" If that is all, I can easily cure you."

" In what way ? "

" By taking you to the baths."

Mr. Jarvis replied that he felt unable to go out again in the storm.   But Mr. Gilman urged that he could order a close carriage, which he did, and very kindly accompanied him.   The temperature of the bath was at about 100° (Fahrenheit).   Mr. Jarvis remained in it until he began to feel faint; when he rose, and instantly two men threw hot towels over him, and commenced rubbing him with a friction of no gentle character.   When this ordeal was over, he felt like a new man — refreshed, and free from pain.

On their return to the hotel, he partook of the fine supper his friend had ordered with a good appetite, passing a social and pleasant evening with him.   The next morning he was as fresh as if he had not been exposed the day before, and ready to pursue his business.

He saw the merchants who had his tobacco, and arranged matters satisfactorily with them ; and the following morning at four o'clock, took the diligence for Bordeaux ; it rained hard until eight, when it cleared away.   Putting his head out of the vehicle, to take a

view of the country, he was astonished by the magnificent spectacle that burst upon his view. Far along
the horizon stretched the lofty peaks of the Pyrenees,
covered with snow and glittering in the sun ; while
brilliant, fleecy clouds were rolling away before the
wind, from the mountain sides ; beneath smiled the
verdant plain, cultivated like a garden, in renovated
loveliness, altogether forming a landscape of the most
surpassing grandeur and beauty. He gazed delighted
on the picture, till it gradually faded from his sight.
The road to Bordeaux was a very pleasant one,
through a fine level country. He spent three days in
this city.

The Bordeaux brandy is mild, and preferable in his
opinion to the cognac ; but the latter is stronger, and
preferred by the English. From Bordeaux he proceeded in a diligence to Pons. The scenery was picturesque and beautiful ; diversified with chateaux, some
of them castles — ancient strongholds of the nobility ;
others modern country residences, with fine gardens
and grounds, grape-vines, fruit-trees, and ornamental
forest trees.

The merchant, who was to furnish the brandy, resided
at Pons — an Irish house of long standing, which had
remained unmolested during the struggles of the Revolution. Mr. Jarvis called on the head of the firm to
inquire if they had heard from his vessel.

" Yes," he said, " but the brandy has to be brought
down the Charente in boats, and has not yet arrived."

He asked if his mate stated that he was ready to
receive the cargo ; and if his letter had been answered.

The merchant replied affirmatively, and showed the

letters. Mr. Jarvis begged him to write again, and
state the cause of the delay; he also wrote himself,
requesting his mate to preserve the correspondence,
and that probably he might be detained some days.

After doing all in his power to forward the business,
he again took the diligence for Saintes, another town
on the Charente, *en route* for the port where his ship
lay. A row of noble, stately elms, that looked as if a
century old, o'er-canopied the road, forming a beautiful
arcade for twenty miles, before they came to this town,
making a delightful drive. On arriving at the public-
house at Saintes, he ordered a good supper, for he was
both weary and hungry, and sat down to rest himself
while it was preparing. In a reasonable time the landlady and her maid-servant brought in an abundant and
smoking hot repast, which looked very inviting; but
just as they were about to partake of it, a sergeant with
four or five soldiers suddenly entered and demanded
the supper, saying that a party of military were quar-
tered near by, and he had been sent out in quest of
provisions.

There was a war at this time in La Vendée, and this
was a reinforcement. The landlord was very timid,
and seemed to think it was useless to resist the orders
of an officer of the military corps; but the woman, bold
as a lion, came forward with great volubility and an-
ger, declaring that he should not have it; that it had
been cooked for the passengers in the diligence; that it
was theirs, and he had no right to claim it. The officer replied that they were without provisions; that he
had orders to obtain some; and that he must seize
them. At this juncture Mr. Jarvis came forward to

interpose; for he foresaw that on the principle that " might makes right," the military would carry off the supper, and not at all relishing the idea of losing it, he thus addressed the officer, —

" Is this the way you treat a stranger? Is this your boasted liberty, of which we hear so much, thus rudely to take away the supper of a foreigner and an American — a nation with whom you are at peace? Can this be sanctioned in *La belle France?* "

The sergeant, abashed and astonished, gazed at the bold American.

The landlady now proposed to compromise the matter by a division of the viands. This was peaceably acceded to; and as there was an abundance of food on the table, the passengers had sufficient remaining to make a very comfortable meal. Mr. Jarvis often remarked that but for his intrepid remonstrance, everything would have been seized, leaving the passengers supperless.

The next day he pursued his journey to Charente, the small town at the mouth of the river where his vessel lay, about three miles from Rochelle.

Here he found two or three other American vessels, which had arrived before his, waiting for brandy, destined for London. One of the captains was a brother of an intimate friend of his in Boston, and feeling interested in his welfare from this circumstance, he advised him to get a certificate of the time he had first applied for the brandy, and also of the time when it was delivered; otherwise he might lose his demurrage. But being a young man, and not much acquainted with the forms of business, he thought these precautions quite unnecessary.

Mr. Jarvis was detained at this port forty days, though he wrote to the merchant several times to remonstrate against it.

While waiting at Charente, he purchased, for three dollars, a barrel of the wine of the province for his crew — a pleasant beverage, not quite as strong as cider. "Vin de grave" and "Sauterne" are also made in this part of France.

At last the kegs of brandy began to come down the river in boats, and he immediately wrote to the house in Pons for a certificate, testifying as to the time the first and last boats came down. It was duly forwarded, and then he obtained certificates from the custom-house, as to the time the vessel entered the port, when the cargo was put on board, and when she was cleared, taking these precautions, lest he might be implicated by the delay they had occasioned him. The ship was in perfect order for sea, and as soon as the last boat was unloaded, he sailed.

On his arrival in London, he heard that the merchant had failed, who had chartered his vessel. But although this house had made the contract, yet several gentlemen had engaged the brandy, who came on board requesting the delivery of their respective shares. Mr. Jarvis had gone to the city, but he left orders with his mate to retain a part belonging to each owner, their names being branded on the casks, fearing that he might have some trouble in obtaining the demurrage. The mate, however, finding that he could not easily separate them, refused to deliver any in the absence of his captain.

The owners were very willing to pay the freight, but

objected to the demurrage.   But Mr. Jarvis, as usual, stood his ground with great firmness and decision ; and, aided by Mr. Braddick, laid his claims and papers before commissioners appointed for such cases.   He asked Mr. Braddick if he should make a plea before them. He told him that he thought his papers would be sufficient.   They finally allowed him all that he demanded, except for the three days in London, after the mate refused to deliver the brandy.   His claims amounted to $4,598, *i. e.* nine hundred and fifty pounds sterling.

The care he had taken to obtain exact evidence of his detention in France, enabled him to furnish convincing proof that it was owing to no fault of his, but that the loss of time was wholly owing to the house in Pons.   There was no evading it, and he received full compensation.   Not so with the captains who had been at Charente with him, and had really lost more time. They would not follow *his* advice, though it had been very kindly intended, but trusted wholly to their logbooks, which were not deemed sufficient evidence ; and so they lost the whole of their demurrage, much to their chagrin and that of their employers.

One day as he was walking on the Exchange, Mr. Braddick directed his attention to a tall, erect, dignified gentleman, as Sir Francis Baring, an eminent banker, and the wealthiest merchant in London.

On closer observation, Mr. Jarvis noticed with surprise that his dress was almost shabby, neither in good taste not style.   His vest and small-clothes were much the worse for wear ; and his brown broadcloth coat had gilt buttons nearly as large as dollars, then quite *passé* in fashion. His outer man gave no indication of his wealth and standing, which was remarkable ; as gentlemen in those days were more punctilious in their dress than at the present time. But it plainly showed that his mind was too much engrossed, to think much of his appearance.

Having invested his funds in excellent Caraccas cocoa, and his ship being nearly ready for sea, he called quite early one morning upon Mr. Braddick, who with great eagerness asked when he should sail.

" To-morrow morning. Why do you ask ? "

" Because," said Mr. Braddick, " at about three this morning, I received intelligence that peace had been decided upon."

" But how can this be, when it is only a few weeks since it was announced in all the papers that your government had refused Napoleon's proposals for peace, and that the war was to be continued ? "

" I will tell you. Last night a council was in session till a late hour in the night, discussing this question. They finally concluded that it was advisable to make peace, and a message was immediately dispatched to acquaint the Messrs. Goldsmiths with this decision, calling them up in the night ; they sent to me about three this morning to announce the fact.[1]

---

[1] The Goldsmiths were the principal bankers of the government, and when Mr. Pitt found it necessary to raise a large sum of money to carry on the war, they undertook the loan on condition that they should be informed of any important changes that were to take place in the measures and policy of the government. They did not loan much money themselves, but various merchants and men of wealth contributed to it: one £10,000, another £20,000, a third £50,000, and so on, until the desired amount was made up. Mr. Braddick had loaned £10,000. Each stock-

You perceive, therefore," said Mr. Braddick, " that the sooner you leave London the better, as the price of cocoa will fall in Spain as soon as peace is declared."

" I have nothing to do but to have my vessel cleared at the custom-house."

" You can send your ship down to Gravesend, and have her cleared afterwards, joining her there; this will hasten your departure."

Mr. Jarvis went immediately to his vessel, gave the necessary orders, and inquired if they had bread enough; being answered affirmatively, he hastened back to Mr. Braddick, who accompanied him to the custom-house.

Here Mr. Jarvis was presented with a printed form, wherein he was to swear to his name, the name of his brig, where he was from, where bound, his cargo, etc., etc. The gist of the whole was that he was not to land his cargo in any part of France.

He began to read the paper with great attention, but Mr. Braddick told him that it would occupy too much time.

" But I do not like to take an oath without knowing what I am swearing to."

" It is a mere form," said Mr. Braddick; " a custom-house oath is thought nothing of."

It was found necessary to have the mate's testimony.

" I can go down and summon him, and be back in an hour."

---

holder was to be duly notified of any new movement in the governmental chess-board. *En passant*, Mr. Goldsmith entertained so high an opinion of Mr. Braddick's integrity and business talents, that he had placed a son of his in Mr. B.'s counting-house.

"No," Mr. Braddick said, "I will save you that trouble," and asked him to wait by a specified pillar until his return, when he *would provide a mate.*

In about fifteen minutes he returned with a respectable looking waterman, whose dress was similar to a sailor's. Mr. Braddick had explained to him what they wished him to do, and now introduced him to Mr. Jarvis, who told him his own name ; that of his mate, Solomon Norton, — reiterating it, to impress it on his mind ; the name of his vessel, that he had a cargo of cocoa, that he was from Boston, and bound to St. Sebastian, etc. To all which the waterman took an oath, with his hand on the Bible, though he had only Mr. Braddick's word for its truth. Mr. Jarvis was somewhat shocked by this proceeding, being so contrary to his principles of truth and honesty ; and after they left the custom-house he expressed his feelings to Mr. Braddick, who said it was a thing of very common occurrence when vessels were hastening out of port, and that no one attached any solemnity to a *custom-house oath,* for it was considered merely a *form.* Mr. Jarvis secretly thought it manifested a very corrupt state of society, but he merely turned to the waterman and asked him what compensation he should give him for his trouble. He replied that he owned three barges on the Thames, and all he asked of him was his custom.

"But I was never in London but once before, and shall probably never be here again. Please Mr. Braddick pay him what you think proper."

He gave him a crown, which was perfectly satisfactory.

Mr. Jarvis now took leave of his kind friend, Mr. Braddick, and hastened to overtake his vessel in a boat. He was safely on board, and they had proceeded a short distance in the channel, when his mate came to him with a complaint that there was no bread — the mice having eaten a hole in the bottom of the barrel, and spoilt the whole. He was obliged to put into a small town on the coast called Rye, and gave orders to the men that he sent ashore to get all the bread that they could obtain, and if there was none, to buy flour. They returned with a few dozen loaves of fresh bread and some flour. The former lasted the cabin table till they reached St. Sebastian, after a short voyage of ten days, and the flour being made into bread, and eaten new and warm, was considered a great luxury by the sailors.

He sold his cocoa very well, though not as high as before. He had given six guineas per cwt. avoirdupois, and sold it for fifty-eight dollars per one hundred lbs.

With the money he received for it, he purchased a cargo of iron, which is of an excellent quality in this part of Spain, and had made all his business arrangements, when a courier, as if half distracted, rode through St. Sebastian at full speed, crying " Peace, peace, peace ! " He was most fortunate to have disposed of his cocoa ere peace was proclaimed, for had anything detained him longer in London, or had there been any detention on his voyage, to delay the sale until after this proclamation, it would hardly have paid the cost of freight, so rapidly did the price fall. How greatly success in life depends upon perseverance, en-

ergy, and promptitude of action, guided by good sense
and judgment.

This series of remarkably successful voyages resulted from a combination of these qualities, though
his early training in mercantile affairs, and his thorough
knowledge of the subject, was a great aid undoubtedly
in planning them.

A cargo of butter coming in from Ireland, he purchased a quantity, sufficient with the iron he had previously bought to load his ship, and then sailed for
Lisbon. These articles not being in demand there, he
went to Cadiz, where they sold very well, especially
the iron. At Cadiz he made an advantageous sale of
his ship — that faithful companion of his many voyages !

Having now by the blessing of God acquired money
enough to clear himself from his liabilities, he remitted
most of it by bills of exchange on London, but secured
several hundred doubloons in leather belts about his
person, to provide for any emergency.

He took passage for New York with Captain Anderson, a Virginia merchant, who was owner of the ship,
and was an agreeable, gentlemanly man. A day or
two after he was at sea, Mr. Jarvis was threatened
with a return of inflammation in his eyes. He
thought that bleeding would benefit him, and tried
the bold experiment of taking blood himself, always
so difficult an operation at sea.

He opened a vein from which he bled a quart ere
it could be stanched, which caused him to faint.
The loss of so large a quantity of blood brought on
the jaundice. He craved acid drinks, but the cabin

had not been provided with fruit or many luxuries. But when he was about two thirds across the Atlantic, his wants were supplied by a kind Providence, for a ship came in sight, and he begged Captain Anderson to send a boat to inquire for fruit. She came from the West Indies, and it happened that there was on board an old acquaintance of Mr. Jarvis — Mr. Oliver of Boston, who very kindly let him have two dozen oranges out of his private stores; and the captain sold him a bottle of guava jelly.

These were not only agreeable articles of diet, but most efficient remedies, and he soon recovered.

Owing to contrary winds they had a tedious voyage of forty-eight days. Captain Anderson was very ignorant of nautical matters, and had gone out as captain in order to make a more profitable voyage. The management of the vessel devolved almost entirely upon the first mate, who although a good seaman, was deficient in the skill and judgment required to act efficiently as captain, which made him timid and undecided where prompt action was necessary.

At last, after this long passage, the welcome sight of Sandy Hook light-house greeted their eyes ; but just as bright anticipations of being soon on terra firma and with their friends, filled their hearts with joy, what should the mate do but put out to sea again, to the great surprise of all.

On being interrogated as to his motives, he replied, —

" I am afraid of running on Barnegat Shoals in the night."

Mr. Jarvis requested to see the charts, and after a careful examination, he told the mate that they were forty miles distant ; it was a clear coast, and there was

not the slightest danger in going directly in. But he
said he had "heard of a wreck upon these dangerous shoals," and his mind was so possessed with this
idea, that he was terrified lest they also should be
wrecked.

With the permission of Captain Anderson, Mr. Jarvis undertook to steer the ship in safety to land, and
about midnight they neared the light-house. Thinking there could be no farther trouble, he gave the mate
particular directions to keep the light-house in sight,
and retired to rest. But on rising early in the morning, what was his astonishment and vexation to find
they were again out to sea; and the light-house almost invisible. On demanding of the mate why he
had not followed his instructions, he found it was the
old bugbear — "running on shoals in the night." He
thought this too absurd, and represented to Captain
Anderson that there was every appearance of a northeast snow-storm, and unless they hastened into port
they would be unable to get in for several days.

Captain Anderson, glad to be relieved from the care
and responsibility, begged Mr. Jarvis to take the command, who readily assented, and gave orders to steer
directly for the light-house, which was promptly done.

To his great joy a pilot-boat soon came in sight.
They put up a signal for a pilot, who soon came on
board, and guided them safely beyond the light-house.
As the pilot was about to return to his boat, Mr. Jarvis inquired if he was going directly up to New York,
and being answered affirmatively, he asked if he could
accompany him. The pilot was willing. Captain Anderson, also sick of the ship, concluded to join them;

the baggage was put in, and by nine o'clock P. M. they were safely and comfortably established at a hotel, much to the satisfaction of both.

As Mr. Jarvis had predicted, a snow-storm came on in the night; but the ship came in next day, after beating about Sandy Hook light-house three days.

It was on his birthday, the 4th February, 1802, that he landed in New York.

He now completed the payment of the fourteen thousand dollars for which he had become liable, and which he had earned amid self-denials, hardships, labors, and perils such as few men could have endured or overcome. Was there not true heroism and nobility of soul in these five years of unremitting toil and exposure — of unwearied energy and action, for such an end.

How differently are failures managed at the present day, when creditors are frequently obliged to sacrifice a large amount of their property, if not the whole ; and sometimes the person failing contrives to have more property *after his failure* than *before !*

PART III.

—•—

CHAPTER IX.

CONSUL–GENERAL FOR PORTUGAL AND CHARGE
D'AFFAIRES AT LISBON.

HIS APPOINTMENT AT WASHINGTON AS CONSUL–GENERAL AND
CHARGE D'AFFAIRES. — MR. JEFFERSON AND MR. MADISON.

ON his arrival in Boston he made a final settlement
of all claims upon him, and was once more an independent man, ready to commence business for himself.

How sweet must have been his self-approval in the
accomplishment of his undertaking! His talents had
been improved to the utmost, and conscience whispered,
" Well done, good and faithful servant."

Most cordial and hearty were the welcomes and
congratulations of his father and friends on the ulti-
mate success that had crowned his labors, and his preservation through so many perils. He had long been
under the clouds of adversity, but they had a silver
lining, and now the sun again shone forth.

A few days after his return home, a friend informed
his father that he had just received a letter from Hon.
Josiah Quincy, then in Congress, stating " that William

Jarvis of Boston had been appointed consul to Lisbon; that the Senate unanimously confirmed the appointment on the 4th February, and he supposed it must be Dr. Jarvis' son, as he knew of no other William Jarvis in Boston."

Dr. Jarvis at dinner, communicated this intelligence to his son, who replied that while in Lisbon he had noticed that Mr. Jefferson stated in his message that any well-qualified citizen of the United States wishing for a consulate, then held by a foreigner, should, on making application, receive it. Mr. Bulkley, an English merchant, held the office of United States Consul at Lisbon, but was of no service whatever to American captains, not taking the trouble to exert himself in their behalf. Thinking he should like the situation, Mr. Jarvis wrote to his friend General Dearborn to that effect, but receiving no reply to his letter, he had thought no more about it. It is a remarkable coincidence that on his birthday, the 4th February, he landed on his native shore, terminating with almost unprecedented success his five years of hazard and hardship at sea, freed himself from all his liabilities, and on that *same birthday* was appointed to an eligible office in a mild and delightful country ! Had not his energy, integrity, and self-denial been blessed and rewarded ?

In two or three days Dr. Jarvis received an official communication from Mr. Madison, then Secretary of State, informing him of his son's appointment, by a unanimous vote of the Senate; but they were unacquainted with his present address, his letter being

9

dated in Europe, and would thank Dr. Jarvis to communicate to him the knowledge of his appointment.

In ten days Mr. Jarvis was in Washington to answer
the letter in person.

Travelling at that time — when it was seven days'
journey by stage from Boston to Washington — was
a very different affair from the celerity with which
people are now transported on the wings of steam,
from city to city.   On his arrival at the Capitol, he
learned that Mr. Jefferson wished him to act as chargé
d'affaires at Lisbon, having recalled Mr. William
Smith of South Carolina, who had been minister at
that court.

Mr. Jarvis called on General Smith of Maryland, a
Senator in Congress, with whom he was personally
acquainted, and conversed with him on the subject;
stating that he had applied for the consulship because
an Englishman held the office; and he thought from
his knowledge of mercantile affairs, that he could discharge the duties of that station to the satisfaction of
himself and countrymen.   But as he was a stranger to
diplomacy he felt incompetent to assume this responsibility.   General Smith argued, that from his early and
extensive acquaintance with commerce and his familiarity with foreign ports, he thought him really much
better qualified for the office than many professional
gentlemen who were appointed, but who were deficient
in information regarding the manners, customs, and
policy of foreign nations; and concluded by urging
him to accept the proffered honor.   Thus encouraged,
Mr. Jarvis waited upon Mr. Madison, and modestly
expressed the same sentiments that he had done to

General Smith. Mr. Madison very politely assured him that he had no doubts as to his ability to discharge the duties of both offices in a perfectly satisfactory manner, and begged him to oblige him by acting as chargé. In conclusion, he remarked that the treasury was then very low, and he would not fix upon a salary; but Mr. Jarvis should have a suitable and satisfactory remuneration for his services.

It is not amiss, however, here to state that he never did receive one dollar for his faithful and arduous services as chargé d'affaires, though he fulfilled all the duties of a minister, carrying on an extensive diplomatic correspondence with various ministers from the United States in Europe, and with his own government; and corresponding at great length with the Portuguese ministry, to effect measures of much importance to the United States; which, by his personal exertions and judicious negotiations, he succeeded in accomplishing. When he returned from Lisbon he found that the treasury was empty, and his country on the eve of a war with England — and he was too good a patriot to prefer his claims under such circumstances. In after years he always spoke of this circumstance with modesty and simplicity, assuming no merit for his conduct, but saying that as he had been prospered in his pecuniary affairs, while in Lisbon, he was satisfied; "and never afterwards called upon the United States for a cent." Thus he assiduously labored for *nine years* in his country's service, without compensation! Born in the midst of the Revolution, he was imbued with the patriotic spirit that characterized that period; and the welfare of his beloved country was always with

him a subject of intense interest. This disinterested
conduct stands out in bold relief, when contrasted with
the corruption and selfishness of so many officials at
the present day, when the highest offices and the
greatest emolument are sought after with eager competition.

Mr. Madison placed the correspondence of the two
preceding ministers at Lisbon, Mr. Humphreys and
Mr. Smith, in the hands of Mr. Jarvis, to impart some
insight into the relations between the United States
and Portugal, appropriating to his use a little private
room within the office of the Secretary of State, for
the examination of the letters. After devoting five or
six days to its careful perusal, he found that they had
attempted to carry measures, which he knew were
diametrically in opposition to the policy to which the
Portuguese government had pertinaciously adhered
for a century — that of uniformly protecting the products of her Brazilian colonies. Mr. Smith, very
naturally wishing to benefit southern commerce, had
constantly endeavored to persuade the Portuguese
government to admit rice and tobacco, notwithstanding
both these articles had been strictly prohibited; the
mother country thus securing to her colonies the
consumption of their rice and tobacco, though inferior
in quality to that of the United States. The latter
was never admitted with the consent of the government; but was sometimes smuggled in for rappee
snuff. And from Mr. Jarvis' knowledge of the jealous
care with which the mother country cherished her
colonies, he saw that to strive for their admission was
useless. He finally accepted the proffered office, think-

ing that he might, at least, be as useful in advancing
the interests of his countrymen as his predecessors had
been. Mr. Jefferson devoted the morning from nine
to eleven to executive business; and from eleven to one
he received calls from all classes of the community—a
levee without much ceremony or attention to dress.

Mr. Jarvis attended these levees frequently, to pay
his respects to the President, and enjoyed the privilege
of often conversing with him, which afforded him great
pleasure. He said that Mr. Jefferson's colloquial
powers were most remarkable. He was well informed
upon all subjects; and his conversation flowed on like
a smooth stream from a deep fountain of knowledge.
With a wonderful comprehensiveness of mind, and a
retentive memory, he could, with perfect ease, adapt
his discourse to the various people assembled at his
levees — never at a loss; at home on all subjects.
None were awed by any assumption of consequence
or superiority; all were charmed by the versatility of
his genius and his varied information. Social and
agreeable in his manners, he was very popular with the
people. Yet it was very remarkable that he could not
speak in public; he acknowledged that whenever he
attempted it, he felt oppressed, as if he had something
in his throat.

Mr. Madison, on the reverse, was dignified, a little
stiff in his manners, and not fluent in conversation;
but an able public speaker.

Mr. Jefferson was about six feet in height, erect,
with an intellectual countenance. He dressed plainly,
and somewhat carelessly, — the faithful discharge of
his duties, and the adornment of his mind with varied

knowledge, apparently superseding much attention to his outward appearance.

At one o'clock he rode on horseback an hour, for health and recreation. On one of these excursions, as he was about to turn his horse homeward, he met a rough-looking Virginian, mounted on a fine horse, with cloth leggins tied on above and below the knee over the stockings, then a common mode in Virginia when travelling on horseback.

He greeted Mr. Jefferson, with " A good day. Where are you going ? "

" To Washington."

The planter said he was also going there, and should be glad of his company. Mr. Jefferson civilly assented to the proposal, and they rode on together a short distance, when the planter, surveying Mr. Jefferson's horse attentively, remarked, —

" You have a very fine horse."

" Yes, it suits me very well."

" How do you like mine ? " said the Virginian.

" Very much," replied the President.

" Will you *swap ?* "

" No, I make it a rule never to exchange a horse that suits me."

The man stared in amazement, and then said, —

" Where are you from ? "

" Virginia."

" Well, you are the first Virginian I ever saw that would not swap horses ! "

The two horsemen now ascended a hill, commanding a view of Washington ; and the White House became a prominent object. The man inquired if he knew what building that was.

" Yes, the President's house."

" Do you know the President ? "

" Yes, I am intimately acquainted with him."

" What sort of a man is he ? "

" His friends esteem him highly ; his enemies condemn him."

The planter continuing his inquiries about the President, Mr. Jefferson remarked, —

" If you will go to his house with me, I will introduce you."

The man stared, supposing him in jest.

" No. I am quite in earnest."

The man still seemed a little doubtful as to his sincerity, thinking he could not expect such an honor ; but they continued to chat about the buildings in the city as they passed them, until they came to the White House, when Mr. Jefferson stopped. A servant was in immediate attendance to take his horse, held the stirrup, and treated him with the utmost deference.

When the planter witnessed these attentions, he suspected his mistake, and setting spurs to his horse, was out of sight in a moment, to the President's great amusement.

His self-possession and control over his passions was great ; so that he appeared perfectly calm, even when strongly moved. An anecdote is related in illustration of this, of a gentleman, who on his arrival from Madrid, went to him and preferred a complaint against a chargé in that city, upon whose conduct he dwelt with acrimony. It vexed Mr. Jefferson sorely that an officer of the United States should have acted in so injudicious and impolitic a manner ; but wishing to investigate the truth of the story, he listened politely, and then, without one word of comment, changed the conversation, by asking if he had a pleasant voyage. The gentleman took his leave unable to decide what impression he had made.

Mr. Jarvis returned to Boston, and sailed for Lisbon in a vessel owned by his friends the Gilmans, who had a cargo of coffee on board, and begged him to stop at Bordeaux, and dispose of it advantageously ; which he consented to do. They put into Bordeaux after a good voyage, but he found that coffee was so low, that he left it until it should command a better price. After leaving Bordeaux, they were becalmed, and obliged to lay off the shore. A gentleman on board said that the Chateau Margeau estate was in that vicinity, and proposed to Mr. Jarvis and the captain to land and accompany him to the chateau, saying that the present occupant was an acquaintance of his, who would treat them with some of the fine old wine which was so much celebrated. The captain at first declined, but as there was no prospect of a change of wind, he was finally persuaded to go, and they took a boat and went ashore. A short walk brought them to the stately old mansion, where they were hospitably received by Mr. Lynch. This fine old estate had belonged to a royalist, and during the Revolution it was confiscated and sold. It was purchased by Mr. Lynch, an Irish merchant of large property residing in Bordeaux. Some time after taking possession of it, he accidentally discovered that the wine-cellar doors were locked. A servant was dispatched to the steward of the old family, who lived two miles distant, to inquire for the keys — he had kept the keys though his master was no longer owner. He went with the servant, and with some difficulty opened the doors, for the lock had become rusty. It was found that the cellar was full of this highly esteemed claret wine, which takes its name from the chateau and the estate.

On estates where wine is made in large quantities, the wine-cellars have doors opening outward; through this the vintage for the year is carried in, and packed away, after which the door is built over solid with stone and mortar. The inside doors are strongly locked, and the wine is left to be mellowed by time. Owing to revolutionary changes, this wine had remained in the cellar for years, and when discovered by Mr. Lynch, it was a choice and rare liqueur. As there was more than he wished for his own consumption, he sold a considerable quantity to Napoleon, and persons of high rank, for a crown a bottle. He invited his guests to dine with him, and after dinner favored them with a bottle of this old wine.

On drawing the cork, the aroma resembled a bouquet of fragrant flowers. Mr. Jarvis said that he never, before or afterwards, tasted of any wine that compared with this. The three gentlemen took leave of their hospitable host in the afternoon, thanking him for his attentions, and returned to the vessel. A favorable wind arose toward night, which enabled them to pursue their voyage without further detention.

CHAPTER X.

CHARGÉ D'AFFAIRES AND CONSUL-GENERAL FOR PORTUGAL.

MR. JARVIS arrived in Lisbon on the 1st of August, 1802, and took lodgings at Mrs. Derbyshire's, where he had previously boarded when in Lisbon. Among other-gentlemen who boarded here, was Thomas Tomazina, who appeared like an old acquaintance, as he had formerly met him at this house. Tomazina was born in Portugal; his mother was a Portuguese, his father an Italian. He was a great linguist, speaking five languages with perfect ease — English, French, Spanish, Italian, and Portuguese. He said he spoke English the worst of either, yet he spoke this more correctly than do many Englishmen and Americans. He had been secretary of legation at Paris and London, and was at this time secretary to Don John de Almeida de Mello de Castro, the Minister of Foreign Affairs.[1]

In a foreign land, where only a strange language fell upon his ear, it was delightful to find one with whom he could freely converse in his native tongue, and they soon became intimate.

---

[1] Tomazina died a few years later, to Mr. Jarvis' deep regret, who attended his funeral, and bore an immense wax-candle in compliance with Portuguese customs.

Mr. Jarvis now commenced a fresh career in this new field of duty and responsibility, of labor and enterprise. It has been truly said, that "The boy is father of the man." And as in early life he had been faithful to his employers, and diligent in their service; in mature years, honest, upright, industrious, and attentive to his business; in misfortune enterprising, energetic, self-denying, and persevering; so in public life he manifested the same assiduity in promoting the best interests of his country and countrymen; the same integrity and activity in transacting their business; and a remarkable tact in doing the right thing at the right time. He was enabled to accomplish a vast amount of business during his nine years' residence in Lisbon, by system, punctuality, prompt attention, and close application, — to satisfy the multitude of sea captains that were constantly resorting to him, — to gain the approbation of his own government, — and to conciliate the good-will, esteem, and respect of the Portuguese, — the ministers at court as well as the business men with whom he was associated.

The next day after his arrival, agreeable to custom, he sent the following note to the Portuguese Cabinet: —

"To His Excellency Don John de Almeida de Mello de Castro, *His Royal Highness the Prince Regent's Minister and Secretary of State for the Foreign and War Departments:* —

"Sir, — I take the earliest opportunity to announce to your Excellency my arrival at this court; the Government of the United States of America by commission, bearing date the 4th of February, 1802, having appointed me consul for this and the adjacent ports.

"Permit me to request that you will appoint the day and hour which may be most convenient for my waiting upon your Excellency, to present my commission, and to pay my personal respects.

"I have the honor to be, etc., etc., etc.

"WILLIAM JARVIS.

"LISBON, *Aug.* 2, 1802."

On the 3d of August he wrote a long letter to Mr. Madison, in reply to one dated May 6th, in regard to American vessels seized in the Brazils, and upon the situation of our affairs with the powers of Barbary; .... also informing him of his safe arrival, and inclosing a copy of his note to the minister of foreign affairs. He closes the letter with, "I have, agreeably to your wishes, been particularly careful that Mr. Bulkley shall have no cause to complain of any want of delicacy on the part of my government, or myself, of which he appears to be fully sensible." ...

On the 10th of August he again writes at length to Mr. Madison on the state of affairs in Morocco, speaking of rumors regarding the Emperor's policy, etc.; then goes on to say, "On the 4th I received an answer to my official communication to the minister, who appointed the 8th for me to wait on him. He received me with politeness. I presented my commission, which the minister said should be immediately attended to; and then observed that his Royal Highness saw with much satisfaction the increasing commerce between the two countries, and that he had it in charge from his Royal Highness to assure the President of his friendly disposition towards the United States. I answered that the President was actuated by similar sentiments with these of his Royal Highness, for that I had been instructed to assure his Royal Highness' Minister of the satisfaction which the President took in the friendship and good understanding that had so long existed between the two countries; and which I should upon all occasions use my utmost endeavors to cultivate and extend. We had some conversation relative to the quarantine, as on the 4th an order was received by the health officers to make vessels coming from New York lay a few days. I informed his excellency of the regulations that had been adopted at home, which would prevent foreign nations from being in any sort of danger from our vessels; for if any disorder existed even of a suspicious nature, it would be inserted in the bills of health of all vessels coming from such place; and when the master came without bills of health, it was presumptive evidence that some disorder existed; but with *clear bills of health*, his excellency might be assured that no contagious disease existed at the place from which they came. He answered that notwithstanding these orders, the officers might be induced to grant clear bills of health when some disorder prevailed. I replied that our collectors were men of reputation, who would not risk the loss of character by doing such a thing; — much less the loss of office, which would be the certain consequence. That the disorder that had prevailed appeared to be only an epidemic, being entirely local. That the cargoes exported to this country could not receive it, etc. . . . . . That the instructions given to our collectors, his excellency might rest assured, would be rigidly adhered to, for we had suffered so much ourselves, that no reasoning, however plausible, nor any other consideration, would induce us to risk the health of other nations. At taking leave, I requested his excellency's permission to address him whenever necessary, which he politely granted. I shall wait a few days and see if any effect is produced by what passed concerning the quarantine, if not, I shall address him relative thereto." . . . .

The remainder of the letter is occupied with an account of the misunderstanding between General Lannes and the Portuguese Court, and states that General Lannes had requested passports, and was to leave Lisbon that afternoon. He speaks of dining out the day before in company with the French Consul, and receiving this information from him.

On the 5th August he addressed official letters to Wm. Kirkpatrick, Malaga; Joseph Yznardie, Cadiz; John Gavino, Gibraltar; Robert Montgomery, Alicante, American consuls at these places, informing them of his appointment, and in behalf of our government particularly requests them to "forward advices relative to the Barbary States; also concerning United States frigates and their several stations, and the latest advices concerning the state of the markets, which may be often serviceable to masters of vessels, who may wish to leave this port for a better market." . . . .

On the 9th of August he received his exequatur in due form, and entered upon the duties of his office.

He took a carriage and called upon the ministers composing the Portuguese Cabinet, and upon the various members of the " Corps Diplomatique," leaving a card at the door, which formal call was returned in the same manner, with the exception of two or three of the foreign consuls, who called in person.

Mr. Jarvis was Consul-General for Portugal, and there were American vice-consulates established at Figuera, Faro, Oporto, and St. Ubes.

He appointed M. Marcellina Sylva, who had acted in this capacity for Mr. Bulkley, vice-consul at Lisbon. He was a Portuguese, but understood English very well, which made his services valuable as an interpreter, and in the translation of papers.[1]

In Mr. Jarvis' correspondence there are copies of seven letters dated 12th August, 1802, namely, to Edward Baker and Charles F. Kruse, Esqrs., vice-consuls at Figuera and Faro. After informing them of his appointment, etc., he says, " Permit me to tender to you the office of vice-consul, which you now hold, upon the same conditions that you received it from Mr. Bulkley, as it is my determination not to change any of the officers under my jurisdiction that have given satisfaction to my predecessors."

To Bernard C. Brown and to Charles Liligreen, Esqrs., vice-consuls at Oporto and St. Ubes, to the same purport. To Hon. Charles Pinckney, Minister to

---

[1] Remarking that when on 'Change Mr. Sylva had always a greater or smaller number of pieces of clean white paper twisted through his button-holes, Mr. Jarvis, with surprise, inquired why he did it.

He replied, " To recollect the business for the day I have to transact."

" And how does this recall it ? "

" For every applicant I draw in a paper, and then remember the first, second, and third, and so on, until I get through." This is an amusing Portuguese custom.

Spain, at Madrid, he says, " I take the earliest opportunity to inform you of my appointment by the President," etc., etc., " and to offer my services to forward
any letters you may have for America, and to execute
any commands you may think proper to favor me
with," etc., etc.

To A. Murray, Commander of the United States
frigate *Constellation* stationed in the Mediterranean,
in answer to a letter addressed to Mr. Bulkley, he
writes a long and able letter upon the Barbary States,
alluding to the policy pursued by other nations toward
them ; to their recent seizure of an American vessel ;
to their barbarity and cruelty toward prisoners ; to
their hatred of Christians, etc., etc.

He alludes to the fact that England and France had
neglected to rescue the British and French prisoners
that had been captured by their corsairs. But goes
on to say, " While we have a navy commanded by
brave and enterprising officers, our countrymen in distress will neither want their interposition nor assistance,
much less their protection." In conclusion, he requests
Captain Murray to forward any " news concerning our
affairs with those nations ; and also with the station of
our navy, as it may oftentimes be serviceable to our
citizens bound up the Straits."

To the American consuls at Tangier and Algiers,
James Simpson and Richard O'Brien, Esqrs., he wrote
upon the same subjects. After informing Mr. Simpson that he had forwarded the dispatches that he had
inclosed to Mr. Bulkley to the government of the
United States, he says, " I am very glad you entertain
a hope of being able to settle our differences with the

Emperor of Morocco. . . . . In the mean time you will please favor me with what information you can, relative to the danger from the corsairs of that power," etc., etc.

To Mr. O'Brien, he acknowledges the receipt of three letters dated in May and June, directed to his predecessor, copies of which he had forwarded to the United States, and then says: "I am sorry to find by them that our affairs with the Powers of Barbary are in such an embarrassed situation ; and much more so, that the Tripolitans have captured an American vessel ; for every vessel they take will be an additional obstacle to peace, to say nothing of the sufferings of our fellow-citizens." He dwells upon the importance of making peace with them.

These official letters of the same date bear testimony to his untiring application to business and mental labor. The three last display much general information upon the politics and history of foreign nations.

"LISBON, 19th August, 1802.

" To the Provedor Mór of Health : —

" Sir, — I, the undersigned, Consul of the United States of America, have the honor to remit the inclosed petition of George Clarke, master of the " Antelope," with a translated copy of the orders of my government to the different Collectors of the United States, which I presume will so fully convince your Lordship that there is not the smallest danger of admitting vessels to an immediate entry, who have clear bills of health, that your Lordship will as soon as convenient give orders to raise the quarantine on the said vessel.

" With the greatest respect, I have the honor to be,

" Etc., etc., etc.,   WILLIAM JARVIS."[1]

---

[1] The Provedor favored him with no reply; but by calling upon him with his vice-consul, the vessel was cleared at last.

It would be uninteresting to enumerate all the various letters of Mr. Jarvis' extensive correspondence. His dispatches to Mr. Madison were sent by every vessel that sailed for America. In one sent the 22d of August, he congratulates Mr. Madison " upon the agreeable intelligence of the settlement of our differences with the Emperor of Morocco." He gives an account of clearing the " Antelope " from quarantine by visiting the health officer, and using the order that had been issued, his vice-consul Silva acting as interpreter. He also speaks of an order received at the custom-house from the Minister of the Interior, prohibiting the importation of cordage. On the 6th of September he again wrote Mr. Madison that, as he feared, the prohibition of cordage was only the forerunner of the prohibition of flour.

" Not being perfectly clear as to that part of the order relating to the consumption of flour, I sent to request an explanation, and received for answer that the consumption of all foreign flour after the 4th January next was *forbidden;* and what was then *on hand* must be *exported.* I am apprehensive that a repeal or modification of the order cannot be obtained, from the determination shown by this government in adhering to the prohibition of cordage, notwithstanding the exertions of the English and Russian ministers, which proved altogether unsuccessful, as I before informed you. . . . . But though I have my doubts whether they will grant any further favor, yet I will not lessen my exertions to try to obtain it."

Lisbon had heretofore afforded a very advantageous market for the surplus flour and corn of the United States; and the passage of this act would consequently inflict a great injury upon our commerce. The Portuguese government had admitted wheat, rye, barley, and corn; and whenever there was a scarcity of this commodity, flour also.

There were but three commercial houses in Lisbon at this time, where American business was done — that of Mr. Bulkley, an Englishman; Mr. Gould, from Ireland; and Mr. Dohrman, who was Consul-General from Holland. Mr. Jarvis thought that he would consult with these gentlemen upon a measure of so much importance to the commerce of the United States. He first called on Mr. Bulkley, who said that his son-in-law, Colonel Humphreys, had used every effort in his power to procure the free admission of flour, but in vain; and all attempts to prevent its prohibition now, would be utterly useless. He then visited Mr. Gould and Mr. Dohrman, but they also discouraged him, saying so many of the Portuguese nobility were interested in the windmills, that it would be unavailing to do anything about it.

"But," said the Chargé, "I am sent to this country to endeavor to promote measures beneficial to my countrymen, and surely you would not have me sit idly down, and make no attempt to carry this point?"

The coldness and indifference manifested by these gentlemen, aroused the lion within him, and only strengthened him in his determination to make strenuous exertions to effect the repeal. He gave the subject a thorough investigation, acquiring all the information within his reach, and then carefully prepared a memorial — a very able paper, a copy of which is still preserved. On the 9th September he dispatched it.

"To His Excellency Don John de Almeida de Mello de Castro, *His Royal Highness the Prince Regent's Minister and Secretary of State for the Foreign and War Departments, etc., etc., etc.:* —

" Sir, — It would be discovering a want of sensibility to the interests of my country, and with submission to the superior wisdom of his Royal Highness, the Prince Regent's ministers, to what I conceive for the advantage of this realm, if I remained silent relative to the order that was issued on the 4th inst., prohibiting the consumption and importation of foreign flour after the 4th January next. Therefore I must beg leave of your Excellency, to allow me to suggest such observations as occur to me on this subject. During my short residence here, I have not had an opportunity to become thoroughly acquainted with the state of agriculture in this kingdom, but have generally understood that more grain is not cultivated in the *best seasons*, than will supply the consumption of the inhabitants one half the year. In countries where this is the case, it is considered by the best writers the height of good policy to admit all kinds of breadstuffs freely."

Mr. Jarvis goes on to state in a clear and forcible manner, that much suffering to the people is likely to result from this law, in depriving them of a regular supply of bread; and that it would also greatly injure the commerce of the nation, as the United States would seek to exchange her flour for the wines of Spain, and the produce of other countries. His arguments were strong, and conclusively proved that the comfort of the people, and the commerce and revenue of the kingdom would be greatly increased by the admission of flour. Wheat is liable to injury in transportation, and " to use damaged wheat for flour, would endanger the health of the community," etc., etc., etc.

His friend Tomazina gave this memorial a favorable translation to the Minister, which added not a little to its weight.   He sent a copy of it to Mr. Madison on the 11th September.   He says : —

"Inclosed is a copy of the communication I made to the Minister on the subject, which I submit with the greatest diffidence to persons so eminent for abilities ; and must beg the indulgence of government towards it."

He goes on to discuss the grounds of the arguments that he used, in a way that shows he had thought much on political economy.   He states that doubts had arisen whether all the foreign flour in Lisbon after the 4th, was to be *exported* or *not*.

" I made inquiries of the Inspector-General, but after waiting upon his Excellency twice, I was referred to his representatives in the corn-market, who were as much divided in sentiment as the judge and administrator that I had previously consulted ; from which I conclude that the order was worded so ambiguously on purpose to *prevent* or *allow* the consumption, as there should be plenty or scarcity of grain on hand."

Mr. Jarvis waited several days, but receiving no reply from the Minister, addressed the following note to him, dated 30th September : —

" William Jarvis presents his most respectful compliments to his Excellency, Don João de Almeida de Mello de Castro, and is extremely sorry to be under the necessity of troubling his Excellency, but not being favored with an answer to the communication he had the honor to make the 9th inst., relative to the prohibition and consumption of flour on the 4th of January next, he must take the liberty to request his Excellency to favor him with a reply as soon as he conveniently can."

On the 1st October this note was inclosed to Mr. Madison, in a letter upon various subjects that demanded attention. On the 12th he again writes to Mr. Madison, and informs him that he had just received an answer to his note from the Minister, " by which you will see, sir, that they continue to adhere to the prohibition, but make no allusion to the consumption of what may be in the kingdom after the 4th January. . . . . This appears to be a studied omission, but I shall write to his Excellency to-day for an answer to that part, and remain silent as to admission until I am honored with some instructions from government." Mr. Jarvis begs Mr. Madison to write a memorial, as it would have " so much more weight and influence " than anything he could say. He says : —

" A gentleman whom I have conversed with on the subject, who has an opportunity of knowing the sentiments of some of the higher officers of this government, thinks that the only chance remaining for an admission, would be by holding out the idea of a duty being laid on our flour, equal to what is conceived to be the loss sustained, by its being manufactured abroad ; which, as it would afford a revenue to this government, it is likely would prevent their attending to the clamor about the mills, and would tend to quiet the owners of real estates, by assisting to keep up the price of grain. If the admission can be obtained, even on these terms, it appears to me it will prove advantageous to us."

He speaks of his success in liberating two American seamen " from the British sloop-of-war ' Cynthia,' who had been detained two years." In these letters he alludes also to his efforts to shorten the quarantine of vessels from healthy ports ; and to several cases in which he had succeeded.

On the 14th Mr. Jarvis again addressed a note to Don John de Almeida, expressing his extreme regret that they still adhere to the prohibition of flour, and begging him to honor him with a reply to his questions as to permitting the foreign flour in the kingdom after the 4th to be consumed.

In the remarkably short time (for a Portuguese Minister) of two days, he received a reply, in which he is politely informed " that the consumption of all the flour which may arrive before the 4th January next, will be freely allowed in this kingdom." . . . .

This was indeed a conquest over Portuguese policy and prejudice, and encouraged the Chargé in his efforts to obtain the more important concession of rescinding the prohibition of flour. He caused printed notices of this act to be circulated in Lisbon, and in various ports of the United States, for the benefit of his countrymen.

In his correspondence about this time, is a letter addressed to " —— Wright, Commander of his Majesty's sloop-of-war, ' Cynthia,' " to solicit the release of two American seamen who had been two years impressed. He concludes the letter by saying, —

" Their impressment and detention being contrary to the existing treaties and that harmony and good understanding subsisting between the two countries, I presume from the high sense of honor and justice which has ever distinguished the officers bearing his Majesty's commission, that you will have the goodness to order their discharge, and give them such prize money as they may be entitled to."

Through Mr. Jarvis' efforts these men were actually discharged, and received their certificates for pay and prize money. As they were without funds, with his active benevolence, he lent them sufficient to get home, running the risk of not being able to collect it in London. And this is but one of numerous cases in which, by his prompt and determined exertions, he succeeded in liberating American seamen who had been impressed by British vessels of war ; and then aided them with money.

He immediately wrote in their behalf to the American Consul at London, who was a friend of his father.

" LISBON, October 13, 1802.

TO GEORGE W. ERVING, ESQ., *American Consul at London :* —

" DEAR SIR, —. . . . Inclosed is an order for the wages and prize money due Stephen Mount and Ignatius Clark, who were impressed on board his Majesty's ship ' Cynthia,' the 29th September, 1800, and detained until the 11th inst., as per certificates annexed granted by the commander, etc., of said ship."

Mr. Jarvis solicits him to cause the money to be collected, " it really being an act of charity ; one of the poor fellows having a wife and two children in Boston, from whom he has been absent nearly three years." He begs Mr. Erving to let his secretary or a broker collect it.

" And when recovered please to remit the balance due Stephen Mount to the collector of the port of Boston, after deducting £8 18s 3½d, which I advanced him here ; and the balance due Ignatius Clark, to the collector of the port of Charleston, South Carolina, after deducting £5 4s 6d, which I advanced to him, and such charges as you may be at, I having given each of the men an order to each of these collectors, to pay them the money when they receive it."

It may be as well to say that Mr. Erving found it necessary that one of the men should "go in person to London ; he might go as a sailor ; and that the other must send a power of attorney, in order to secure their payment ; " consequently Mr. Jarvis was obliged to write several more letters on the subject to Charleston and Boston, giving him much additional trouble. He received another application, not long afterwards, for the release of two other seamen ; one of whom had been impressed five years. He addressed the following communication : —

"LISBON, *October* 12, 1802.
" *To the Commander of his Majesty's Sloop-of-War,* ' *Vansego* ' : —

" SIR, — I have the honor to acquaint you that an application has been made to me by Charles Woodland, who informs me that he is a native of Salem, in the State of Massachusetts, and was impressed into his Britannic Majesty's service about five years since ; and by John Martin, a native of Norfolk, in Virginia, whom the captain of an English transport sent on board the sloop-of-war ' Vansego,' under your command, in consequence of some dispute between them. The truth of which statements I have not had an opportunity of investigating. But from the high sense of honor and justice which is characteristic of the officers in his Majesty's service, I feel assured that if upon making the necessary inquiry their representations appear to be well founded, you will, sir, agreeable to the existing treaties between the two countries, release them and give them such certificates as are customary in his Majesty's navy, to enable them to obtain their prize money. I have the honor to be,

etc., etc.,   " WILLIAM JARVIS."

After the exchange of two or three more letters, Charles Woodland's statements were found to be true, and he was released and obtained his wages and prize money. But it could not be *proved* that John Martin was an American, and he was not discharged.

Mr. Jarvis became very solicitous about the prohibition of flour, as owing to long passages and stormy weather he received no instructions from Mr. Madison. From his friend Tomazina he learned that the ministry were divided upon the subject: two being in favor, two opposed to the admission, and one doubtful.

Don John de Almeida, Minister of State, etc., etc., and the Viscount de Anadia, Minister of the Marine, were in favor of it; Don Louis Pinta, Viscount Balsamão, Minister of the Interior, and Count Villaverde, were in opposition; and Don Vasconcellas, the Minister of Finance, was doubtful. It was said that the latter was very desirous of increasing the revenue of Portugal; could he therefore, be gained over, there would be a majority in favor of admission.

It was the 1st of January. In four days more the act of prohibition would take effect. Mr. Jarvis resolved to make one more attempt. He drew up a second memorial of ten folio pages, admirable for its strength of argument, and the extensive knowledge it displays of the policy pursued by various nations. It was addressed to Don John de Almeida, and dated January 3, 1803.

He commences by saying that he had forborne making further remarks on the subject, hoping to receive instructions from his government, but had been disappointed, etc., etc. " I deem it my duty not to let

the prohibition be carried into effect without offering
such observations as have since occurred.   . . . .
As a discussion was not entered into before, I hope
your Excellency will excuse my summing up, in as
concise a manner as possible, the grounds from which
my arguments were drawn." He discusses very fully
and clearly the probability of there being a scarcity of
breadstuffs in the nation, and the consequent distress
of the lower classes; shows how it will also affect
the proprietors of landed estates. Traces the policy
of England, France, and Holland, etc., etc., in regard
to the "admission of a plentiful supply of breadstuffs;" and shows how wealth and prosperity have
flowed into their kingdoms in consequence. In conclusion he suggests that a moderate duty of one crusade (which is a silver coin equal to sixty cents of
our currency), instead of the former duty of half a
crusade per barrel, would double the income received
from this branch of their commerce, without any additional expense, and thus half a million of crusades
might be added annually to the revenue of the kingdom, and an abundant supply of bread would at the
same time be secured.

This memorial was a success. It received the
approbation of Don de Almeida, who read it to the
Prince Regent, making comments in its favor. The
arguments had so much weight with the Prince, that
he viewed the subject in a more auspicious light, and
ordered an examination of the bread made from American flour, which proved to be of excellent quality.

Don Vasconcellas was so much pleased with the
idea of this addition to the revenue, that he joined the

two ministers in favor of admission, and the act of prohibition was repealed !

On the evening of the 6th of January, the day before the prohibition was to have gone into operation, Mr. Jarvis received an official communication from Don John de Almeida, very politely informing him that the Prince Regent had granted his petition; and that thereafter flour would be admitted with the moderate duty of only one crusade per barrel. To which document the royal signature and seal were affixed.

What a victory ! What a harvest of gratification and pleasure did he reap in this reward of his unflinching efforts to carry a measure for which he had negotiated five months. Deemed unattainable by the merchants ; his first memorial unanswered ; that a young man unacquainted with political life — by his unaided, undaunted exertions, by his strong arguments and able discussion of the question, — should have gained the ear of even royalty itself, in one of the most formal, ceremonious, and inaccessible courts of Europe, and effected the repeal of a law just to go into operation, was really a wounderful diplomatic achievement, for which we can hardly ascribe him too much credit.

It was considered of so much importance to the commercial interests of the United States, that when Mr. Jefferson was Minister to France, he had been particularly instructed to negotiate for the admission of flour into Portugal, and had held a correspondence on this subject with Don Louis de Pinta, then Portuguese Minister at the Court of France ; but this grandee was strongly opposed to it, being a large land-owner, and wishing to protect his own and other windmills in the country ; and Mr. Jefferson was reluctantly obliged to relinquish his attempts, convinced that they were useless.

Mr. Jarvis wrote a very polite note to Don Almeida, expressing his high appreciation of the favor his Royal Highness had conferred upon the citizens of the United States as well as on himself, — their representative in Portugal, — by rescinding this prohibition, and trusted the act would be conducive to the interests of both nations, etc., etc.

About the 1st of January an American captain had come into port with a cargo of flour. Mr. Jarvis knew that flour would fall as soon as it was proclaimed that it would be admitted with only a moderate duty of one crusade per barrel.

With his wonted thoughtful kindness, he sent for the captain the next morning, to ascertain if he had sold his cargo ; and if he had not, to advise him to do so without delay.

In answer to his inquiries, the captain informed Mr. Jarvis that he had sold it to Mr. Gould.

" Are you sure it is a settled bargain, not liable to be broken ? "

" Yes, sir ; Mr. Gould has bought it, and I am confident it is all settled. Why are you so particular about it ? "

" Because the prohibition of flour is repealed."

" Indeed ? " said the captain. " Mr. Gould said that it would never again be admitted."

" It has been, notwithstanding."

The captain hastened away to inform Mr. Gould of

this surprising intelligence, who could not credit it, but sent his head clerk directly to Mr. Jarvis, to ask what foundation he had for so improbable an assertion.

He told him that he had just received a communication to that effect from the Minister of Foreign Affairs.

O'Donohue, the clerk, returned with this answer to Mr. Gould, who was still incredulous, and came in person, and, in a hurried and agitated manner, made further inquiries.

Mr. Jarvis politely repeated what he had before told his clerk.

"But," said Mr. Gould, "I have recently had a conversation with Sarmienta, Don Louis de Pinta's secretary, and he assured me that flour would never again be admitted. There must be some mistake." Mr. Jarvis then handed him the official document he had received, pointing to the signature of Don de Almeida. He was not acquainted with his handwriting, and was unconvinced, until taking up the envelope, he saw the royal seal and arms of Portugal, when he dropped it, as if it had been burning wax, and precipitately left the office.

It appeared that he had been speculating largely in flour, assured by Sarmienta of its prohibition, buying it up at ten dollars per barrel, expecting to sell it at a large profit;—and now how great would be the fall! So much time, however, elapsed before the news reached the United States, and more was sent out, that the demand for flour continued, and his losses were not heavy.

All the foreign merchants were astonished when

they learned that through Mr. Jarvis' negotiations, *flour* was to be *admitted* at so moderate a duty.[1]

[1] I have omitted to mention an important letter, dated 2d October, to Peter C. Brooks of Boston, regarding the seizure of the " Aurora " and " Four Sisters," in the Brazils. He says: " From the want of success that had attended the applications of Messrs. Humphreys & Smith, at this court, it was necessary to adopt some other method. The trial has now gone through all the inferior courts of Lisbon, and a judge has been named to pass the final sentence."

CHAPTER XI.

THE expected birth of a prince in the royal household had been a topic of conversation for some weeks, and much gossip was in circulation as to the probabilities of a change of ministers after the christening, on account of the rumored return of General Lannes as Minister from France. But the prince was born, and no change took place. In a note addressed to Don de Almeida, dated 10th of January, 1803, after suitably acknowledging the receipt of his communication, Mr. Jarvis says : —

January, 1803.

"Permit me, Sir, to embrace this occasion to felicitate His Royal Highness, and his Royal Consort, on so happy an event, and to assure them that I most cordially participate in the joy that was experienced on the birth of an infant of such an illustrious family."

Mr. Jarvis was invited to attend the christening, with all the members of the " Corps Diplomatique." It was to be a grand reception, and of course a *court-dress* was *all essential*. For at a court, where dress and etiquette were deemed so important, even in this matter, he must do credit to the country he represented ; he therefore resolved that it should be in the height of good taste and propriety. Having ascertained that the American naval uniform was considered full official court-dress, he ordered a blue broadcloth coat, which was lined throughout with heavy yellow silk, turned over on the skirts, and embroidered on the collar and cuffs with gold cord. On the large gilt buttons was the American eagle. The vest was of rich yellow silk, heavily embroidered with gold cord, as were also the knee-bands of the yellow cassimere small-clothes. The stockings were white silk; and the shoes had large silver buckles. The ruffles on the bosom and wristbands of his shirt were broad, fine Brussels lace; a *"chapeau bras,"* with gilt tassels, under his arm; epaulets, and a dress sword or rapier, completed this handsome costume.

The Prince Regent and his family were at this time at their palace at Queluz,[1] three leagues from Lisbon.

On the appointed day Mr. Jarvis set out for the palace, accompanied by his vice-consul Silva, as interpreter, in a singular carriage, peculiar to Spain and Portugal — somewhat like an old-fashioned chaise, drawn by two horses, the driver mounted on one of them. It had windows on each side, and a boot with an iron frame and springs, which completely shut in the occupants, rendering it a close carriage; but at their pleasure the boot could be thrown back. They

---

[1] Another palace was at Mafra. Mafra was the name of a magnificent edifice, consisting of a church, royal palace, and monastery, situated about nineteen miles from Lisbon, and founded by John V. 1717. From its nature and magnitude it may be considered the Escurial of Portugal. It has a college and a library, supposed to contain 40,000 or 50,000 volumes. The gardens are very extensive, and stored with a variety of exotics, imported at great expense from Asia, Africa, and America.

had just entered one of the most thronged and public streets, when the bell, announcing the approach of the "Host," was heard.[1] The driver stopped the horses. Mr. Silva, a devout Catholic, threw back the boot, jumped out, and kneeled upon the sidewalk, leaving Mr. Jarvis in his showy national uniform exposed to the gaze of the multitude. He feared it would have the appearance of disrespect for the customs and religion of the country — where he was to act in a public capacity — to remain sitting in the carriage, before five hundred people, who were doing homage to the Host. And perhaps partly actuated by the spirit of the old proverb, which says, "When you are among the Romans, do as the Romans do," — he sprung out also, and kneeled on one knee; first spreading his white handkerchief on the wet stones, to save his stockings and small-clothes — for it had rained in the morning. It was no small discomfiture to remain several minutes in this position, on the damp pavement, with uncovered head, until the procession had passed. But this compliance with their religious ceremonies won the hearts of the Portuguese, gaining for him not a little favor, both at Court and with the clergy; for his dress was sufficiently singular to attract attention, and led to an inquiry as to who he was, and it soon went abroad that the American Chargé and Consul was a very good Catholic, or at least paid great respect to Catholic observances. Thus

---

[1] It may not be amiss, for the benefit of some readers, to explain that the *"Host"* is the sacred wafer, emblematic of the Body of Christ, which is often carried in a procession of priests. Catholics are required by the priests to fall on their knees while it passes, and foreigners to stand with their hats off.

an act, prompted by his innate politeness and regard for the faith of the people, eventually proved very advantageous to him.

When he arrived at the palace, he was ushered into an anteroom, where the diplomatic corps were already assembled. Among these, the most prominent for age and importance was the Pope's Nuncio, Monseigneur Galeppi, Archbishop of Nisibé. He was a man of extensive and profound information, with a very soft, gentle, and persuasive voice, and great colloquial powers, very winning manners, expressive of much interest in the person he addressed, rendering him altogether a most delightful companion. He was about five feet ten inches high, and dressed in the superbly rich robes of an archbishop. They afterwards met frequently, and a friendship was formed between them which continued through Mr. Jarvis' residence in Lisbon, and afforded him much pleasure. There was an agreeable interchange of notes and visits, to which the Archbishop's billets testify.[1]

Next in rank and honor was Lord Robert Fitzgerald, the English Minister Plenipotentiary. The Austrian Minister, M. Von Lebsetein, and the Russian Minister, were there; also the Russian Consul, Dubatchewskoy,

[1] *Copy of a note from the Archbishop of Nisibé, politely translated by General J. W. Phelps.*

"M. d'Araujo, Minister and Secretary of State of Foreign Affairs, etc., has just written from Mafra, to the Apostolic Nuncio, to inform the gentlemen of the Diplomatic Corps that as he is under the necessity of remaining at Mafra to-morrow, he will not be able to receive them at his residence, according to custom. The Apostolic Nuncio hastens to make known this fact to Mr. Jarvis, Chargé d'Affaires of the United States of America, and takes the occasion to renew to him the assurances of his perfect consideration. 6th August, 1806."

who was a wonderful linguist, speaking readily nine languages — Russian, German (he was educated in Germany), Spanish, Portuguese, Italian, French, English, Greek, and Arabic. Mr. Jarvis said that on the Exchange he had seen him converse with ease and fluency perhaps first with a German, then turn from him to an Italian or Spaniard and talk with equal readiness; and again with an Arab, or one of the Greek Islanders, without any apparent effort; never at a loss for a word, equally at home with all the representatives of these various nations. It was really wonderful. He spoke English remarkably well, enabling Mr. Jarvis to converse with him freely, and cultivate his acquaintance. The social disposition, refined, cultivated mind, and gentlemanly manners of Dubatchewskoy, soon won his esteem and friendship, and he became more intimate with him than with any other person in Lisbon, excepting Tomazina.

Jacob Dohrman, Consul-General from Holland, and Chargé d'Affaires, was a man worthy of all esteem; the most friendly intercourse grew up between him and Mr. Jarvis; many business letters were exchanged, and they frequently dined together.

After waiting some little time, the folding-doors were opened, and the Corps Diplomatique were introduced into the presence of the Prince Regent and his Court, the Pope's Nuncio taking precedence, being first in rank in Catholic countries, and the ministers and other members of the Corps following in pairs, according to their rank. Mr. Jarvis walked with Mr. Dohrman, and as they entered the spacious apartment he fixed his eye upon the stately Nuncio, to follow his example, and not infringe on the rules of Portuguese etiquette.   His quick observant eye noticed on the right hand of the door of entrance a vacant throne, elevated three steps above the floor.   The Prince with his retinue sat at the opposite end of the room.

On entering the presence of royalty, they all bowed low ; when they reached the centre of the apartment, they all bowed again ; and when immediately before the King, it was repeated.   On the presentation of a new member, a few words were exchanged.   The King, then Prince Regent, wore the Portuguese court-dress — a blue coat, and red small-clothes.   He was of the Braganza family, and rather a fine looking man, with an olive complexion, dark hair and eyes, oval face, expressive of good sense ; but his mouth was his worst feature — his under teeth and jaw projecting. His two sons were standing on each side of him.   The eldest, Pedro, resembled his father, and was a talented, amiable youth, who afterwards became Emperor of Brazil.   The second, Miguel, it was said, was like his mother in mind and person.   Even then there was something malign in his countenance ; and in after life, he became a traitor to his father, his brother, and his country.   The ladies of the Court were ranged on each side, in their peculiar court-dress — a high-necked close-fitting bodice, of thick, heavy, red silk, called " Padua Soie," the skirt of which only extended to the knee, and displayed a deep blue petticoat of the same fabric, richly embroidered with gold.   They usually wore jewels in their hair ; but sometimes a deep blue flower to match the skirt, and splendid necklaces, bracelets, and ear-rings.

When the Corps Diplomatique took their departure, they all made another obeisance, and, as it would be a great breach of propriety to turn their backs upon royalty, they stepped backwards to the door, making as many bows as on entering. Mr. Jarvis remembered the vacant throne and avoided it; but Mr. Dohrman, taking *less heed to his ways*, backed directly upon it, and stumbled. Looking up to see the effect upon the courtiers, Mr. Jarvis saw the nephew of the Marquis of Pomball stuffing his handkerchief into his mouth to prevent his laughing aloud. His comical appearance, and the idea of such a *faux-pas* in the presence of this dignified and ceremonious court, struck Mr. Jarvis as so ludicrous, that it was with great difficulty he restrained his risibles until he was out of the palace, when his mirth broke forth in uncontrollable bursts of laughter.[1]

---

[1] The following is a translated copy of an invitation to another christening from Don Araujo, in 1805:—

"PALACE OF QUELUZ, *the 26th July*, 1805.

"Yesterday, at about 11 o'clock of the night, the Princess of Brazil happily brought to light a robust infanta with all the good success that could be desired, and Her Royal Highness, as also the most serene Lady newly born, are in the best state which their circumstances can permit, which, full of the greatest joy, I have the satisfaction to participate to you, to whom at the same time I communicate that the Prince Regent, my master, will receive you in the palace, on so satisfactory an occasion, at one o'clock in the afternoon of the 28th instant.

"God preserve you many years.

"Your very certain and assured servant,

'ANTONIO DE ARAUJO DE AZEVEDO.

"Senor GUILHERME JARVIS".

[Another.]

"PALACE OF MAFRA, 23d *December*, 1806.

[After formally announcing the birth of another "fine female infanta," etc.,] "Her Royal Highness, considering the inconvenience the Diplomatic Corps will be under in a journey to Mafra on this happy event, defers their

In a letter to Mr. Madison he says, —

. . . . "From its long being a custom here, if any changes at Court were thought necessary, any promotions to be made, any royal favors granted near the time of the birth of a Prince, that they should be postponed till after the christening, the knowing ones had determined that the Ministry should be changed in consequence of General Lannes' affair. . . . . When to their sad disappointment, yesterday passed without any change in the Ministry ; the young Prince being christened the preceding day with uncommon splendor, owing to a rivalship taking place between the English Prince Augustus, and some of the first Portuguese nobility.   On the occasion there were a few marquises and counts created, and the Corps Diplomatique kissed the hands of the Prince. . . . . I assure you, sir, the people here are as ingenious in manufacturing news, as they are in the United States or in England . . . . though their speculations never meet the public eye in the various forms of newspaper paragraphs, owing to our having but *one weekly paper* in this kingdom, and that printed in this city under the immediate inspection of the Court." . . . .

reception till at another palace less distant. When the Royal orders are received, I will announce to you the day for that purpose.

" God preserve you for many years.

" Your very certain and assured servant,

"ANTONIO DE ARAUJO DE AZEVEDO."

The American Chargé d'Affaires had many invitations to Court on various occasions.

CHAPTER XII.

MANNERS AND CUSTOMS OF THE PORTUGUESE. — FRUITS
AND FLOWERS.

A FEW months after his arrival in Lisbon, Mr. Jarvis succeeded in hiring a new house on the Tagus, just completed. It was small but very convenient for business, being near the Exchange, and having a counting-house in the lower part. He had the whole house to himself, contrary to the customs of Portugal. The houses have no cellars, and the lower part is often used for a stable and carriage-house. What is called the first floor is occupied by people of the first rank, the second floor by people a degree less respectable, and the higher you ascend, the lower the station, until you reach the attic, which is inhabited by the lowest classes. One common stone staircase admits to her apartments the high-bred lady, attired in jewels and silks, and the poor fish-woman or mendicant, in coarse apparel or rags. These stairs are five or more feet wide, with an iron railing, and not over-clean. One large door of entrance admits horses, carriages, the rich and the poor. Most of the houses are five stories high. An anecdote is told of a young gentleman who saw a beautiful young girl in the street, whose grace and elegance he so much admired, that he ordered his servant, who was behind him, to follow her into the house and see where she lived, that he might pay his addresses to her.   On his return the master says impatiently, —

" You found her on the first floor ? "

" No, sir."

" On the second, then ? "

" No, sir."

In a passion he cries out, " At least, then, on the third."

" No, master, she lives on the fourth ! "

The master was in despair, for no *gentleman* could marry a woman residing on the *fourth* floor.

Mr. Jarvis hired two Portuguese men-servants — a cook and waiter.   The cook in Portugal acts an important part: receiving from his master at night his orders for the next day's dinner, and the money for the purchase thereof, he accounts for the expenditure the next night, squares his book, and takes a fresh supply for the following day's bill of fare ; for gentlemen never go to market.

Cows or goats were driven about the city to each customer's door, and as much milked as was desired ; rather a primitive mode, but insuring good milk. Singular as it may appear, swine were never sold dead, but were driven into the city in droves of one hundred or more.   Almost every family bought one.   A Gallego is hired to drive it home, who attaches a rope to the pig, and leads it along in this way.   Arrived at the purchaser's house, a fire of furze is kindled in the yard, and the porker is killed and placed over it to singe off the bristles, first on one side, then on the other.   If any part remains unsinged, it is pared off with a sharp knife.

The blood is saved for puddings, and then it is cut up and a portion salted, as in America.

"The Gallicians might be termed their hewers of wood and drawers of water. They are patient, industrious, and faithful to a proverb." They supply the citizens with water, which they carry in small wooden casks upon their backs, by means of straps and a pole ; and each day they replenish a stone jar in every family. There are many fountains in Lisbon, to which the Gallegos repair for water. "The police oblige them to fill their casks at night, and take them home to their lodgings, in case of fire. These laborers, who are from the province of Gallicia in Spain, and hence are called Gallegos, come to Portugal to earn a little money for their families, and it is said lay up about eighteen pence per week, from their hard labors."

No changes are made in Portugal from one generation to another. Should a foreigner object to this mode of furnishing families with water, they would be answered with a profound bow, in an expressive Portuguese phrase, "It is the custom." If you find fault with your cook's mode of dressing your meat or vegetables, he answers with a deferential inclination of the body, "It is the custom." Should you wish to send your waiter to market to procure some article the cook had neglected to buy, he makes a low obeisance and says, "It is not the custom ; the cook goes to market."

Their *customs* were as unalterable and binding as the laws of the Medes and Persians, and strangers were forced to submit to them. In the early part of the nineteenth century, their cart wheels, yokes, ploughs, saddles, and stirrups were of the most clumsy and primeval character, and gave one the impression that they had been in use since the days of the Romans.   The nobility did not patronize the fine arts ; and the sciences, useful arts, and mechanics were in their infancy.   This recalls the words of the poet —

" Souls are ripened in a northern clime."

For the bounties of nature which God had bestowed so liberally upon this nation, seemed to satisfy their wants, without being incited by stern necessity to any great mental exertion.

Fruits and flowers of various kinds abound.   The orange, lemon, pomegranate, shattuck, and apricot are easily cultivated ; and figs, olives, and grapes grow in the greatest abundance.

The geranium and myrtle grow spontaneously ; and the heliotrope flourishes in the open air, and is easily trained over the windows, as we do our woodbine, breathing its aromatic perfume into the apartments from its luxuriant flowers.

The climate is very favorable to wheat, oats, and barley, and large quantities of the former might be easily raised, if more attention were given to agriculture ; but at that time not half enough was cultivated for the supply of the kingdom.   It is usually sowed in October, before the rains commence.   There is no rain in summer; the earth becomes very dry, and cracks in wide fissures.   Winter is their rainy season, and lasts about four months.

The Portuguese, who are famous for proverbs, say, " *Never trust God in the winter.*"   By this they mean that though appearances for fair weather may be ever

so favorable, yet you may be overtaken by rain, therefore " go not abroad without your capote[1] and umbrella."
The morning may be perfectly bright and clear, when
suddenly a distinctly defined white cloud makes its
appearance just above the horizon, and before you are
aware of a change of weather, a violent shower is
pouring upon the earth, continuing an hour or two,
the heavens enveloped with dark clouds ; but with
equal abruptness they pass away, leaving bright sunshine and a cloudless sky.

They have no fire-places in their houses except in
the kitchen. Occasionally, when it is damp and chilly,
they put on their capotes, and have a copper brazier,
which will contain about half a peck of lighted charcoal,[2] placed in the centre of the room, around which
the family gather. Mr. Jarvis said that he had really
suffered from cold in winter for want of a fire-place or
stove, though it is one of the most equable and salubrious climates in the world, the mercury never rising
above 80°, or falling below 40°.

Fruits are abundant during nine months of the year,
In February the orange becomes eatable; in March
and April, better ; in May, very good ; in June, fine ;
and in July, delicious. Grapes commence in July, and
continue till October. The fig ripens in June, they
become more and more sweet and juicy till September.
In July and August apricots are in perfection, and are
exceedingly rich in flavor. The chestnut, which is

---

[1] The *Capote* is an outside garment, something like a cloak, with loose
sleeves, which can be worn with the arms through them or not, at the
wearer's pleasure.

[2] It is lighted in the open air, that the gas may escape.

about as large as a horse-chestnut, is boiled, and sold
in the market. During November, December, and
January nuts abound, fine English walnuts, almonds,
and filberts. Olives, too, are much used as we eat
them. A poor man can buy a breakfast of boiled
chestnuts, fruit, and a little sour wine for a few reis.
Partridges and ducks are in plenty; the latter are
very fine in the winter. Wine is made in October.
The " vin du pays " [1] from the native grape. Neatly
dressed women come in from the country with donkeys
loaded with panniers of fruit, which they arrange
tastefully for sale; they have flax wound round their
waists, and when not employed in selling fruit, they
spin it on a spindle held in the hand; this thread is
woven into cloth, which is very durable.

Mr. Jarvis was in the habit of walking for rest and
recreation an hour or two every evening, in the beautiful gardens of Lisbon, with his friend Tomazina, conversing on various subjects, and enjoying the loveliness
by which they were surrounded. The song of the
nightingale delighted them with its melody. Very
near the color of the bark of the tree, it conceals itself
from the curious gaze of its admiring auditor, and pours
forth its melodious, plaintive notes till midnight.

The orange-tree was cultivated with much care in all
the gardens, and to a great extent in that of the Inquisition. The bud, blossom, and ripe fruit are found
together on the same tree, which renders these orange-
groves extremely beautiful. The fragrance of the
flower makes the air redolent with perfumes. On one
occasion Mr. Jarvis, on entering a grove in the Queen's

---

[1] Wine of the country.

garden, became suddenly faint, so powerful was the aroma, and was obliged to hasten away to recover himself. But this was owing to being surrounded by them. On the smooth gravel walks of these gardens, at a little distance from the trees, the odors floating on the balmy air were most agreeable and refreshing.

CHAPTER XIII.

HIS PRIVATE COMMERCIAL AFFAIRS.

A few months after he went to Lisbon, Mr. Jarvis entered into a partnership with his old friends, Nicholas and Daniel Gilman of Boston, as commission merchants. The first year it was a new house, and no consignments were made to him until near its close, when a captain applied to him, saying that he had invested his all in a venture. Mr. Bulkeley would not dispose of it for him, and he was afraid he was a ruined man, and his wife and four children would be left destitute. Mr. Jarvis asked to whom his cargo had been consigned.

He replied, " To Mr. Bulkeley."

" Will he not sell it for you ? "

" No, sir, he said he could not."

" I don't wish to interfere with his business, therefore go to him again if you please, and tell him that if he will not undertake to sell your venture, the American Consul says he will try and do so."

He returned, saying that Mr. Bulkeley would be glad to be relieved from the trouble.

Having learned that tar and rosin were the principal commodities, and that the remainder of the venture consisted of gin and herring, Mr. Jarvis went to

an English ship-carpenter, and asked him to buy the
tar. He declined, saying he did not like American
tar ; it was dirty ; he preferred Swedish.

"But if you do not use some American tar, you
cannot expect American custom in repairing their
vessels."

After some further talk upon this subject, the carpenter said, —

"Well, it does not make much difference. What do
you ask ? "

"What do you pay for Swedish ? "

He named the price.

"I will sell this American lower, as you say it is
inferior," and stated what he would take.

"Very well, I will buy it."

"Captain —— has rosin ; do you want rosin ? "

"Yes, but I use Swedish."

"I know this to be superior to the Swedish ; it is
purer and better for your purpose."

"What is the price ? "

"What do you pay for Swedish ? "

"So much" (stating what it was).

"I shall ask the same, for it is quite as good."

"Very well, I will take it."

When Captain —— learned the success of this
negotiation, he was overjoyed, for it was fifty per cent.
higher than he had paid in the United States. Mr.
Jarvis told him the gin would be a difficult article to
dispose of, as Holland gin was used altogether ; but
asked the captain to let him taste of it. Finding it
remarkably good, he promised to do his best, and went
to an Irish dealer in liquors, and inquired if he wished

to purchase some gin. He said he did, and asked if it was good. The Consul told him it was excellent, and requested him to try it. He liked it very much, and paid so liberally, that the captain received a handsome profit. He then offered the herring, but at first the dealer declined taking them, saying he used only the Scotch.

" But," urged Mr. Jarvis, " examine these, they are equally good."

He did so, and was so well satisfied, that he paid the same that he did for Scotch ; making a clear profit of fifty per cent. on these also.

The captain was delighted, and could not find words to express his gratitude. He told all the American captains what a remarkable man their Consul was, who had sold his venture so advantageously, and thus saved his family from being impoverished.[1]

On his return to America, he continued to relate the account of the wonderful sales made by the American Consul, who thus acquired a high reputation among mercantile men for zeal and intelligence in the disposal of merchandise ; and the next year many American vessels were consigned to him, making his receipts by commissions $1500. His business steadily increased ; and after the French came to Portugal, the British merchants returned to England, and he transacted nearly the whole of the commission business, making the last year $20,000.

Mr. Jarvis never spoke of his acts of benevolence as if meriting encomium, but simply as kindnesses *due* to his fellow-men in difficulties.

[1] The captain paid Mr. Jarvis sixteen dollars for his trouble; his sole commission that year.

12

CHAPTER XIV.

QUARANTINE.

The long and tedious quarantine to which American vessels were subjected, had become extremely oppressive, and a great burden to commerce.

Mr. Jarvis had called several times on the head of the board of health, called in Portuguese " Guarda Mŏr da Sande," to assure him that the yellow fever had entirely subsided in the United States, and there was not the least danger in admitting vessels with clean bills of health. But he was a narrow-minded, ignorant old man, whose most lively emotion was a dread of this fever. Having no knowledge of geography, he supposed that all parts of the United States were subject to this disease; and talked of Boston and Charleston, New York and New Orleans, as if they were contiguous to each other.

When Mr. Jarvis made his appearance he would draw his *capote* around him and over his mouth, and shrink into the most remote corner of the room, permitting the Consul to stand by the door, apparently fearing to come in contact with an American, who *must of course* be infected with this dreaded disease. At the same time he would take snuff with unceasing industry, as if he thought he might thereby close his nostrils against contagion.

Finding it utterly useless to attempt to reason with such a man, and having made as fruitless an effort to convince and enlighten another higher health officer called " his lordship, the Provedor Mõr da Sande," he found that his only hope of redress would be in once more addressing a memorial to Don John de Almeida de Mello de Castro, etc., etc., etc. It was a very full and explicit statement of the facts in the case, and commenced as follows : — " While there was the shadow of danger to the subjects of his Royal Highness the Prince Regent from the free admission of vessels from any port in the United States, I avoided troubling your Excellency on the subject of the quarantine, in expectation that the moment it was known the disorder had subsided, a measure so oppressive to our commerce would be rescinded. But, to my regret, I find that a knowledge of the fact has not produced an effect so salutary. Instead of which the quarantine has lately been extended to vessels from Baltimore, and to the other ports of the United States.

" An acquaintance with the history of the epidemics that have afflicted some of our sea-ports for about nine years past, will make this step appear the more extraordinary, as the season of the year has arrived when the disorder totally disappears, it having in no instance appeared before midsummer, and as constantly subsided on the setting in of cold weather in the autumn. So invariably has this been the case, that by our State laws, vessels from the West Indies, where the same disorder rages with much more violence, are not obliged to perform quarantine after the 20th October, and I presume it will not be disputed that such laws would not be enacted by enlightened legislators, were they not certain that neither their own health nor that of their countrymen, would be exposed by the free admission of vessels after that season. . . . . The only time the disorder ever appeared in Europe, it was marked by the same character, subsiding as soon as the cool weather commenced in the fall." He goes on to say that American cargoes usually consisted of breadstuffs and staves, and salted provisions, never of any article that would receive the contagion.

' And from the crews there is certainly nothing to fear, for by the closest attention to the disorder, it is well ascertained that from the time the contagion is received, it never remains in the human body longer than six or seven days, or at longest ten days before the person is attacked; consequently there cannot be the smallest danger from persons who have been at sea thirty or forty days — the usual passage from America.

" In our own sufferings, feeling the necessity of taking every precaution to prevent our communicating the disorder to other nations, the Government of the United States gave strict and precise instructions to the collectors and naval officers of all our sea-ports, to issue BILLS OF HEALTH, in addition to those granted by the municipal officers of such port; and in every instance to let them be attended with the strictest adherence to truth.

" In expectation that a measure so liberal and humane would meet that attention from the enlightened policy of the governments of Europe, to which it was so justly entitled, I have taken the liberty to inclose

a translated copy of their instructions. ... . . Our
collectors and naval officers are all men of the most
respectable character, and hold their places entirely at
the will of the President. This must prevent suspi-
cion that they would make false representations in the
bills of health, by them granted, as it would only
expose them to public odium, and the loss of a lucra-
tive office. . . . . It is seldom that the disorder has
appeared in more than three of our sea-ports in one
season. . . . . Should the whole commerce of the
United States be subjected to an indiscriminate quarantine ?

"To prove to his Royal Highness' government that
these orders have been rigidly adhered to, and of
course that foreign nations have nothing to apprehend
from giving the most implicit attention to our *bills of
health*, I shall instance some facts that every health
officer at Belem is perfectly acquainted with. These
are that all the vessels which have arrived here, that
sailed from Philadelphia during part of August and all
September and October, were without these documents.
The epidemic having subsided in the beginning of
November, they were again granted ; and the last
vessel that arrived here, which sailed the early part of
that month, brought two, one of which was certified
by the Portuguese Vice-Consul. A measure so perfectly calculated to secure the health of the nations
with whom we have any intercourse, and which has
been strictly adhered to, ought to inspire such entire
confidence as to prevent any unnecessary embarrass-
ments and restraints upon our commerce.

"In addition to the just grounds of complaint, we
have from the difficulties to which our navigation has

been subjected in this port, for want of due faith being given to our bills of health, — by yesterday's post I received the inclosed copy of an order sent to Porto and Figuero relative to this quarantine. That part of it which orders vessels from the United States sent round to this port, to perform their quarantine, appears to me as unprecedented as it is unnecessary. . . . . There can be no necessity for an indiscriminate quarantine ; nor that they should experience the additional hardship of being forced round to this port, when it could be performed with equal safety to the nation at either of the others.

" From the high opinion I have of the justice of his Royal Highness' government, I feel confident that it will meet a remedy as prompt and effectual as a grievance so great so imminently requires, particularly at so inclement a season, on such a dangerous coast. And from the friendly and mutually beneficial intercourse that has so long subsisted between the inhabitants of this kingdom and the United States, and the harmony and good understanding that has so happily existed between the two governments, — which permit me to assure his Royal Highness that the President wishes to perpetuate,— I presume that my hopes will prove equally well founded, of his Royal Highness being pleased to give immediate orders that vessels from the United States shall no longer be subjected to quarantine. . . . .

" With the greatest consideration and respect, I have the honor to be,

" Your Excellency's, etc., etc., etc.

" WILLIAM JARVIS.

" LISBON, *Jan. 8th*, 1803."

Don Almeida replied to this memorial on the 10th, and on the 17th Mr. Jarvis dispatched another letter of four large folio pages.

" By your Excellency's communication I perceive that mine had not done away the apprehension of danger from the epidemic. . . . . I waited on your Excellency, in hopes to have had the honor of a personal interview; but being disappointed in this, I had the pleasure of some conversation with Señor de Morais, with whom I left the bills of health, brought by the last vessel from Philadelphia, which sailed the early part of November." . . . . He recapitulates his former arguments, and places the subject in a clear light, to convince the ministers that their excessive fears and precautions are groundless.

" The same phenomenon takes place in the torrid zone, including, I presume, the northern part of Brazil, it being a periodical disorder to which that climate is subject, and which commonly disappears after the autumnal equinox. In those countries, when it proves moderate, it is universally known under the name of the bilious fever ; and is precisely the same in all its symptoms, with the disorder known under that name, in this and all other warm countries. But when it prevails with such violence as to be contagious, it is called the West India camp or yellow fever. And it is generally confined to cities that are situated in low, marshy places, which have not the benefit of a free circulation of air ; or to camps, or hospitals that are not kept *clean*, and there the disorder rages with most violence. . . . . I feel sanguine that the evidence of such respectable, various, and unquestionable testimony

will convince his Royal Highness' government, that
the disorder subsided in Philadelphia early in November; and this is the only city in the United States
where it made its appearance last summer and fall.

"In a country so extensive as ours, an *indiscriminate* quarantine must always be unnecessary, the
disorder being altogether local. In fact, so entirely
has the infection been confined to cities where it has
prevailed, that the inhabitants two miles distant ever
felt themselves perfectly safe." . . . . Mr. Jarvis
alludes to the fact that the French government freely
admitted vessels with clean bills of health. "Talley-
rand having been in Philadelphia the two or three first
years that yellow fever prevailed, must have become
perfectly well acquainted with the disease."

He refers to a report of which Don Almeida had
spoken, "that a man had died on board a Portuguese
vessel, in a Spanish port, of this *disease;*" but on
investigation Mr. Jarvis says: "It had been satisfactorily ascertained that this man had killed himself by
excessive intoxication. . . . . I should not so soon
have troubled your Excellency again, had not one
vessel arrived from Alexandria, and two from Baltimore, all with clean bills of health, and the two last
certified by the Spanish Consul.

"In neither of these ports has the disorder prevailed this year, notwithstanding all three vessels are
put under quarantine.

"But as your Excellency seems so sensible of the
disadvantages of a suspended intercourse, now the
disorder has subsided, I must solicit your Excellency's
influence with his Royal Highness to give orders that
the quarantine may generally be raised." . . . .

The following day Mr. Jarvis wrote to Captains William Allen, Benjamin Shillaber, and John M. Cobb, masters of the vessels he had mentioned as being so unjustly subjected to quarantine, and informed them that he had made application to the Minister of Foreign Affairs in their behalf, and "that possibly it might induce them to shorten the term of their quarantine; but the alarm here is, at present, so great, that I have some doubts of it." He advises them, unless it is shortened, to leave that port, and go to Marseilles or elsewhere, and promises to assist them to do so.

"It appears to me that they have worked themselves up to such a pitch of apprehension, that the evidence of their own senses will hardly convince them that there is no danger."

On the 21st of January, he received a reply from Don Almeida to his second memorial, in which he assures him that the subject shall be investigated.

On the 22d, he addresses Don Almeida again, thanking him for his promise that he will attend to the grievance, and particularly drawing his attention to these three vessels, the cargoes of which being wheat, were in great danger of spoiling; he also incloses a letter from Marseilles, speaking of the high prices of grain, and a probable scarcity, "and an American newspaper, to show how slight was the disorder in Philadelphia, when our public officers refused to give clean bills of health," etc., etc.

On the 29th of January, he sent copies of his correspondence with Don Almeida to Mr. Madison, and very modestly stated what efforts he had made for the reduction of the quarantine, and his hope that it may

be raised ; and also alluded to his labors in regard to
the prohibition of flour. He says, " The great alarm
regarding yellow fever, which prevails in Spain, has
induced her to make her laws more stringent than
ever ; and the Portuguese have followed her example." He goes on to say : " To see the property of
my fellow-citizens falling a sacrifice to so unnecessary
a quarantine, has chagrined me beyond measure ; the
fears suggested in my last, relative to it, not only
being realized, but much extended, the order having
been general, and rigidly enforced. I have written
what my information or ingenuity could suggest on
the subject, but as yet without any effect. . . . . At
present we have the five vessels under quarantine
mentioned in my last dispatch, and two that I understand arrived last night."

On the same day, he writes a note to Don Almeida,
" acknowledging his high sense of the obligations he is
under to his Excellency for the orders he has given to
have the copies taken of the judicial proceedings in the
cases of the 'Aurora'[1] and 'Four Sisters.' " And
after going into the case at some length, he reverts to
the five vessels formerly mentioned, still undergoing
quarantine, and to the two just arrived, " both with
clean bills of health, and that of the latter having
the French Consul's certificate to it.

" Mr. Jarvis must notice that it is now nearly sixty
days since the first and last vessels sailed from the
United States, without the least sickness on board
them. . . . . The certainty he feels that an accurate

---

[1] Mr. Jarvis had had a laborious correspondence with the Minister of
Foreign Affairs, regarding this lawsuit.

investigation must have been in favor of his request, makes him confidently hope that his Excellency will grant his solicited influence with his Royal Highness, that those vessels may be admitted to immediate pratique, and that the quarantine may be raised."

His zealous and unremitting efforts were at last crowned with success. On the 8th of February, Don Almeida informed him that an order had been issued to raise the quarantine. The seven vessels in " durance vile " were immediately released from their ruinous detention, and he communicated the glad tidings to the United States.

On the 10th of February, he dispatched the following note to Don Almeida : —

" Mr. William Jarvis presents his most respectful compliments to his Excellency, Don John de Almeida, etc., etc. It would hardly be doing justice to his feelings not to say that the information his Excellency did him the honor to communicate in his note of the 8th instant, gave him great satisfaction, and he is confident his government will receive it with as much pleasure. The measure, he has no doubt, will prove equally agreeable to his countrymen ; and among other proofs, it will tend to inspire such confidence in the liberality, justice, and wisdom of his Royal Highness the Prince Regent's government, as to induce them more generally to frequent the ports of this kingdom, to the great increase of the exchange and consumption of the productions of the two countries, and a corresponding benefit to each nation.

" LISBON, 10th Feb. 1803."

"To the Collector of the Port of Petersburg, Virginia: —

"Lisbon, *9th Feb.*, 1803.

"I have the satisfaction to announce to my fellow-citizens that the importation of flour is no longer prohibited in this realm, his Royal Highness the Prince Regent of Portugal having granted unlimited permission for the introduction of foreign flour into this kingdom, paying a duty of sixty cents per barrel; and that vessels from the United States with clean bills of health, and whose crews are free from any sickness, shall no longer be subjected to quarantine."

On the 9th he sends dispatches to Mr. Madison. " .... To-day I received the inclosed letter of yesterday's date, informing me that orders were given to raise the quarantine. The vessels under quarantine were admitted to pratique the 7th inst., by an order of the 4th, with the precaution of discharging their grain through a spout; but this unnecessary expense will be avoided by this last order. It has given me a vast deal of trouble and vexation, and the rescinding it, proportionate pleasure.

" I was, however, much more pleased with the admission of flour again, it being a measure I did not anticipate.

"I shall pay particular attention to the instructions in your letter. .... It would require persons of your superior abilities to teach patience to those who have to do with this Court on some occasions; but latterly I have no complaint of this kind to make, my communications having been attended to with a promptness that almost anticipated my wishes."

Then follows a list of the dispatches, many of which

were duplicates of the correspondence with Don Almeida, sent by other vessels, regarding the admission of flour, reducing the quarantine, and the lawsuit in the case of the " Aurora," etc., etc.[1]

So long as the old " Guarda Mōr da Sande " retained his office, Mr. Jarvis feared that he would always be troublesome to American vessels. Could he therefore be displaced, and a younger and more intelligent man supersede him, and the Marquis of Pomball placed at the head of the health department, — called the " Royal Junta of Health," — he was confident that his regulations would be marked by justice, discrimina tion, and wisdom.

The Marquis of Pomball was a nobleman of liberal mind, extensive information, and enlarged views for the benefit of Portugal. He was the son of the old Marquis of Pomball — that eminent statesman, the most talented and illustrious man that Portugal ever produced. How to effect such a change was now the question.

It would require no little diplomacy, first to induce him to accept it, and then to have the narrow-minded " Guarda Mōr " removed. But difficulties never deterred Mr. Jarvis from doing his utmost to carry any measure that he thought beneficial to his countrymen. He sought an interview with the Marquis of Pomball, entered into conversation with him on the subject of the quarantine ; stated how greatly intercourse with other nations had been impeded by these oppressive

---

[1] The official correspondence with this eminent Minister, with his successor Don Araujo, Mr. Madison, and others high in authority, constitute several large folio volumes, which are in the possession of Mrs. Cutts.

acts, what an advantage it would be to Portugal could a wise and discreet man be placed at the head of the department of health. He then drew a ludicrous sketch of the terrors of the old " Guarda Mōr," which vividly exposed his incompetency.

The Marquis listened with much attention and interest; smiled at his description of the old health officer; perceived the evils, and thought they ought to be remedied.

Much encouraged by his ready concurrence, the American Chargé with much delicacy remarked that he had been informed that few noblemen in Portugal were so warmly interested in the welfare of the nation as his lordship. This compliment was graciously received, and with much tact and caution, he then suggested how greatly it would benefit the commerce of Portugal, if his Excellency would allow himself to be placed at the head of the " Royal Junta of Health," as he was confident that his liberality and wisdom would remedy these grievances. The Marquis, not at all displeased with the idea, said he was always glad to serve his country.

Mr. Jarvis now took his leave, and immediately wrote a very polite note to Don Almeida, stating that he had some interesting communications to make, relative to the quarantine, and sought the favor of an interview, which was granted. He opened the conversation by a warm and respectful acknowledgment of the great favor done to American commerce by the late order, — then described the excessive fears of the " Guarda Mōr da Sande," placing him in a ludicrous light, — then suggested that he was too old and ignorant to be a useful servant of the Prince, in so important a station.

Don Almeida admitted it: " But could a substitute be found to do better ? "

The Chargé replied, " Could the wise Marquis of Pomball be placed at the head of the health department, he would most ably and efficiently regulate all matters pertaining to the health of the nation, and could remove this superannuated officer."

" Yes, but I fear the Marquis will be unwilling to accept so troublesome a position."

The Chargé ventured to say that he was very desirous to improve the condition of his country, and that this motive might induce him to do so ; that he could employ subordinate officers to execute the business, and that it would only be necessary for him to instruct them how to act, and to regulate the quarantine, — that if the Prince Regent were pleased to offer it to him, the Marquis could take no offense, even if he chose to decline.

Don Almeida assented to these ideas, and said he would lay the subject before his Royal Highness.

Mr. Jarvis then expressed the pleasure he felt that Don Almeida took so favorable a view of the matter, and said he felt sure that such a change must be very advantageous to the nation.

Success again rewarded his exertions. The place was offered to the Marquis of Pomball and accepted ; the old incumbent removed, and a new board of health appointed, consisting of five members, of which the Marquis was President.

Mr. Jarvis took the earliest opportunity to pay his

respects to the Marquis after his appointment, who received him with much affability and kindness. The American Chargé said he congratulated the State that it had obtained the services of so wise and judicious a man as his Excellency; that his being placed at the head of the health department would cause great rejoicing in America, as it would prove so advantageous to her commerce; and he augured the happiest results to both nations from his administration.

He then suggested, with the utmost respect and deference, that if a committee from the board of health should visit the vessels the third day after their arrival, and found that the crew were all healthy, and came from a healthy port with clean bills of health, that he thought there could be no danger in admitting them. This was a bold reform; but it was finally carried into effect, to Mr. Jarvis' joy and the great relief of American vessels, which had a ruinous delay of six weeks reduced to three days.

Mr. Jarvis carefully improved these three days by requiring the captains to have their vessels and the sailors undergo a thorough cleaning, that everything might be " ship-shape, and Bristol fashion," when the inspection took place on the third day; which was really conducive to the health and comfort of the crews.

From this period he called frequently upon the Marquis, who always treated him with great kindness and urbanity.

That a young foreigner could have effected these changes by his single efforts, is truly surprising. We are told that faith removes mountains; allied to which is that indomitable energy, that never rests till the desired end is attained. Had he acted with less prudence and wisdom, or the least neglect of Portuguese etiquette, he might have defeated the whole.

The Marquis of Pomball was one of the highest and richest noblemen in Portugal ; and had it been directly proposed to him to accept the office, he would probably have felt insulted. But by arousing his patriotism with a representation of the injurious effects of the present system, not only to American vessels but to Portugal, he was strongly interested in having these evils remedied, and was willing to act himself, in order to effect a reform.

On the other hand, had he intimated to Don Almeida that he had conversed with the Marquis on the subject, he would have been jealous of foreign interference, and suspected some intrigue.

13

CHAPTER XV.

EVIL REPORTS.

WHILE Mr. Jarvis was thus faithfully laboring for the benefit of his countrymen, to relieve commerce of this burden, he was one day astonished by the abrupt entrance of a captain into his office, who, seeming to be in a passion, said, after walking about a few minutes, he did not think much of a man who took pains to shorten the quarantine of vessels consigned to *himself*, but neglected to make the same effort for those consigned to other mercantile houses. The charge was so false, that Mr. Jarvis could scarcely believe that any one would be audacious enough to make it, and cross-questioned the captain, to ascertain the author of such an assertion, who confessed that he had been so informed by Mr. G——, to whom his vessel was consigned. The Consul then took him into his private office, and requesting a clerk to bring his official letter-book, showed the captain the letters he had written to Don Almeida, to prove how earnestly he had labored for the reduction of the quarantine, and for the release of the five American vessels then in port. From his books it appeared that the only vessel consigned to him had been in seventeen days; while this captain's, which was consigned to Mr. G——, had been in but fourteen.

1804.

The captain, now entirely convinced that the Consul had been greatly wronged, apologized heartily for his rudeness. But determined to free his reputation from the slander, Mr. Jarvis sought an interview with Mr. G——, and found him in his counting-house, surrounded by four or five captains. Stating what the captain had said, he plainly asked him if he had made such an assertion. Mr. G—— at first affected astonishment, and inquired how he could have heard such a story. Mr. Jarvis pointed to the captain as his authority, who, boldly confronting Mr. G——, said : " You cannot have forgotten that you made this statement this very morning."

" If you did," said Mr. Jarvis, " you know it is utterly false. I leave you to settle that matter with Captain ——. Good-day, sir."

By thus openly facing his calumniator, he completely refuted the aspersions, in the presence of these masters of vessels. This and another anecdote show that even the most faithful and upright servants of the people, do not escape ill-will and misrepresentation.

A vessel from Boston was consigned to him with an unsalable cargo, and he directed the captain to go to Alicant, where he disposed of it to advantage, and made a handsome profit. About the same time a like cargo was sent to Messrs. Dohrman & Co., by Smith & Gorham of Boston. Mr. D.'s partner was an Englishman, who, for the sake of the profit, sold it, though at a sacrifice, and bought a return cargo, deducting commissions for both. S. & G. suffered a heavy loss by this transaction.

At this time there happened to be some difficulty between the corn market [1] and custom-house.

A day or two after the vessel returned to Boston, Mr. Daniel Gilman, walking on Change, was surprised to hear Mr. Jarvis — his friend and partner — censured for neglect of duty in settling difficulties in the corn market, etc., etc., thus impeding the sale of cargoes. Mr. Gilman said he was intimately acquainted with Mr. Jarvis, and to neglect any duty was so contrary to his character, that he could not believe it. He begged to see the letter alluded to. It was from Messrs. Dohrman & Co. to Smith & Gorham. Mr. Gilman requested the favor of copying it, which was politely granted, and he inclosed it to his friend. When Mr. Jarvis received it, he was indignant that such a calumny should be sent to so respectable a firm in his native city. In addition to which, the report might reach Mr. Jefferson and Mr. Madison, and injure him in their estimation. This would occasion him deep regret and mortification ; although, in truth, his exertions for the interests of his country and countrymen had been indefatigable.

He immediately called on his friend Dohrman and showed him the letter. With unfeigned surprise, he said he knew nothing about it, and summoning his partner, Mr. T——, sternly asked if he had written it. He hesitated and evaded a direct answer ; but Mr. D. requested him to bring the letter-book, and there was the identical letter, and the amount of com-

---

[1] The corn market regulated the prices of all provisions entered there for sale. These prices were hung up for inspection once a week.

missions received on the cargo. Mr. D. was exceed
ingly displeased, and asked Mr. T. how he could make
a statement that he knew was utterly without foundation.

He said he did not intend to convey such a meaning.
"It is the simple acceptation of your remarks," said
Mr. D., with severity.

The truth was, to cover his want of fidelity to the
interests of his consignor, Mr. T. had thus tried to put
the blame on the Consul for neglect of duty.

Mr. D. turned kindly to Mr. Jarvis, and asked what
he could do for him.

He replied that it was of great importance to keep
his reputation untarnished in America, and he would
be obliged if Mr. Dohrman would write a refutation.

To this Mr. D. cheerfully assented, and wrote a
certificate, saying that he had known the American
Consul since he first came to Lisbon; that he had
most faithfully discharged the duties of his office, and
had made unremitting efforts to induce the government
to admit flour, reduce the quarantine, and remove all
obstacles generally in the way of making voyages
profitable to ship-owners, etc., etc. He signed it, and
Mr. Jarvis, thanking him, cordially took his leave,
and inclosed it to Mr. Gilman.

It proved a great injury to Mr. T., for when his
conduct became known, no more vessels were consigned to them from Boston; whereas, the consignments to Mr. Jarvis were doubled. The vessel, too,
that he had advised to be sent to Alicant, regardless
of his own interest, and consulting only the good of

the owners, made a fine voyage, much to their satisfaction. His conduct stood out in bold relief, when
contrasted with that of Mr. T., and elevated him
proportionately in the esteem and confidence of his
fellow-citizens.

CHAPTER XVI.

A NEW HOUSE. — AN EARTHQUAKE.

A WEALTHY man owned a garden on the top of a hill which was fifty feet above the Tagus, and wishing to ornament it with a fish-pond, erected a high mansion of massive stone, the back being built up solid against the hill.   He had a flat roof, covered with water-proof cement — for which the Portuguese are remarkable, — which becomes as hard as stone when thoroughly dry.   It is probably the same as the old Roman cement, the art of composition being handed down from generation to generation. In this way he was enabled to convert the top of the house into a fish-pond for his garden.

1805.

Mr. Jarvis had watched the progress of the building, and hired it as soon as completed.   It was much more spacious than the one he had previously occupied, and exactly adapted to his business, being near the Exchange and Custom-house, and háving a large warehouse on the ground-floor, a convenient counting-room, and handsome apartments for a family — a large drawing-room, dining-room,[1] etc., etc.

It was near the " Praça do Commercio," or New

---

[1] The Consul uniformly hired the whole of every house that he occupied in Lisbon.

Square, which was six hundred and fifteen feet long, and five hundred and fifty broad. The Royal Exchange and Custom-house were on the north side of the square. The latter was a splendid building of white marble, originally built for a palace, but was thought to be too near the water, and appropriated to this use. It would contain about eight thousand people, and was often full. In the centre of the square was the equestrian statue, in bronze, of Joseph I., a fine work of art, designed and cast by Portuguese artists, under the auspices of the Marquis of Pomball.

On the side next the river was a handsome white marble balustrade. The square was paved with pebbles and fine sand, made level, which rendered it extremely hard and smooth.

"It commanded one of the most extensive prospects imaginable, of the spacious harbor — one of the finest in the world, which was constantly crowded with ships of various nations, fourteen hundred having been counted at one time — and of the broad Tagus, varying in width from two to nine miles, with its delightful banks, covered on one side with convents, churches, castles, and gardens, and on the other were picturesque mountains and high impending cliffs."

Altogether, it was a most refreshing and beautiful promenade.

Not long after his removal to this house, he invited several American sea-captains to dine with him. Dinner had been announced, and they had been seated at the table a few minutes, all in fine spirits, when suddenly the plates, knives, forks, glasses, and even the chairs and table, began to move about with violence. The first idea that occurred to Mr. Jarvis was that the fish-pond on the top of the house had given way. But the fearful cry of " Terra mota ! Terra mota ! O, Jesu ! O, Jesu ! " [1] arose in the street from the terrified inhabitants.

Mr. Jarvis explained the excitement to his alarmed guests, some of whom grew pale, and all rushed into the street, where multitudes of men, women, and children had already assembled. In every tone of despair and horror they were invoking Jesus, the Virgin, and the saints for protection, having in their fright fled from their houses, to seek shelter in the country, or in squares, thus to escape from the fall of buildings. Mr. Jarvis conducted his party to the Quintilla Square, which was not far distant, and contained four acres, the centre of which consequently would afford a safe refuge. Thither great numbers repaired. It was a fearful moment, and it is no wonder that the boldest hearts were awed. Soon, however, it ceased. Mr. Jarvis waited awhile, to see if there would be a second shock, but as there was none, he invited the gentlemen to return and finish their dinner, who, impatient to escape from the threatened calamity to the safety of their vessels, were reluctant to do so ; but being finally persuaded, the repast was quickly dispatched, and they hurried away. Thirty thousand people went into the country that afternoon, as it was generally believed there would be another shock twelve hours after the first. The Consul remained in his house, but kept watch until this time had expired, when, there being no repetition, he yielded himself up to sleep, sound and

[1] "The earth shakes! O, Jesus!"

refreshing. Very little injury was done in the city. This was the first earthquake of any note since the great earthquake of 1755, and it was the only one of consequence that Mr. Jarvis experienced while in Lisbon.

That of 1755 destroyed the old arsenal and a considerable portion of the city; twenty-four thousand inhabitants perished. The cathedral fell, burying an immense quantity of wealth in its ruins, and crushing great numbers, who had fled to it for refuge. More than one hundred palaces, churches, and convents were ruined, and the property of all kinds destroyed was incalculable. It commenced at the Exchange and Arsenal, and extended to the Quay de Soadres, about half a mile upon the Tagus, then turned an angle and went up through three streets, to the Square of the Inquisition, where it stopped. The elder Marquis of Pomball had the ground leveled, and built on the ruins three wide, handsome well-paved streets, with sidewalks, and fine commodious stone buildings on each side, three or four stories high — lower than is usual in Portugal.

" The new streets were a great improvement on the ancient, contracted lanes and unhealthy habitations, proving that the severest visitations of Divine Providence are often attended with manifold blessings."

Three of them ran from the Tagus to the Palace of the Inquisition, and were called in Portuguese after the articles sold in them, namely: Cloth Street, where only cotton, linen, and woolen fabrics were sold. Silversmith Street, where every description of silver plate was manufactured and for sale, tea services, dinner-services, candlesticks, spoons, etc., etc. The

Portuguese received a great deal of silver from the Brazils, and were very skillful in its workmanship. The third street was called Goldsmith Street, where splendid jewelry was exhibited. Some of the finest gems in the world were sent to the mother-country from the Brazils: magnificent diamonds, topazes, emeralds, and rubies; the topazes were especially large, brilliant, and abundant. The mode of acquiring diamonds was to permit any person who chose, to seek for them; but before they were allowed to quit the mines they were strictly searched and every diamond taken away, for which a moderate compensation was allowed them. The diamonds were then sifted through a coarse sieve, and the large ones that would not pass through were reserved for the king, and the smaller ones sold. In this way the king possessed an immense amount of diamonds.

CHAPTER XVII.

IMPRESSMENT OF AMERICAN SEAMEN.

THE British press-gang were constantly going about the streets of Lisbon and impressing American seamen, under pretense of their being English. British sailors often escaped from vessels of war, and secreted themselves on shore; a press-gang was immediately sent in pursuit, and if the missing man could not be found, they would impress an American seaman to supply his place, to the great sorrow of the poor fellow, and the great injury of masters of vessels. In this way large numbers had been impressed.

This unjust and cruel practice had been pursued from the time of Mr. Jarvis' coming to Lisbon, and indeed since 1794.

Mr. Bulkeley was an Englishman, and although acting as Consul for the United States, had been perfectly passive; and if the American captains applied to the Portuguese authorities for redress, they could not tell English from Americans, as both spoke the same language. When it was represented to them that the man in question had escaped from his majesty's service, they could not decide the question. And thus the American masters were forced to endure this gross violation of the rights of nations. It has already

been stated that Mr. Jarvis succeeded in releasing two
seamen a few weeks after his entering upon the duties
of his office, who had been detained two years on board
his majesty's sloop-of-war "Cynthia," and obtained
for them their wages and prize-money; and another
man who had been detained five years on board his
majesty's sloop-of-war "Vansego," also securing for
him his wages and prize-money.

The only man who applied to him and he failed to
rescue, was carried off to Gibraltar in the night. He
wrote to Mr. Simpson, the American Consul there,
but he was taken to India, and it was five years before
he returned to the United States.[1]

When cases were brought before Mr. Jarvis, he
frequently wrote to the British admiral, stating the
facts, and demanding the liberation of the seaman.
He found that a very respectful letter was sure to
receive a rude reply; but to an imperative and stern
one, the answer was very civil. He learned however that it was not the admiral who treated him
thus, but his secretary, a conceited, consequential up-
start, who thought it would add to his own importance
to treat others insolently; until it seemed probable
that his conduct might reach the ears of the admiral,
when he suddenly became very complaisant and obliging.

The American Chargé obtained one or two interviews with the admiral, but it was evident that he
secretly sanctioned practices that he was ashamed
openly to acknowledge. In one instance the press-
gang had boarded an American ship at midnight,

---

[1] Files of letters testify to the numerous applications he received.

under the plea that they had lost a sailor, claimed the
most able-bodied, and carried him off. As soon as Mr.
Jarvis heard of it, he wrote to the British admiral, and
to the new Minister of Foreign Affairs, Don Antonio
de Araujo de Azevedo, representing to them this great
wrong. He then took the captain and mate and went
on board the English vessel, identified the sailor, and
took him back to his own ship.

Finding it was a constant source of annoyance, and
a great grievance to his countrymen, and that there
was no other means of obtaining justice, he addressed
a memorial to Don Araujo de Azevedo, stating all the
circumstances, and the wrongs to which American
nautical men were subjected, and besought him to use
his influence with the Prince to extend the protection
of Portuguese law to American seamen ; and to forbid
the British press-gang from going about the streets of
Lisbon. He received a very polite reply from the
Minister, saying the subject should be investigated.
This promise was kept, and soon after he was informed that his statements were found to be correct,
and that an order had been issued, —

" That no press-gang should be allowed in Lisbon. That
in cases where it was necessary for the British to search for
their missing sailors, the Portuguese police might be called
to their aid ; but no press-gang should be permitted to enter
the city under any circumstances, and the seizure of American seamen was strictly forbidden."

This was the third important diplomatic act he had
accomplished for the good of his countrymen, by his
earnest, unwearied efforts, and a final appeal to the

highest powers of Portugal.   But he had more or less annoyance and vexation about the impressment of seamen until after the French took possession of Lisbon, as the English often evaded the law, by taking seamen from the ships, and rendering it necessary for him to appeal to the British admiral and to Don Araujo. This nobleman was enlightened and liberal, and possessed great worth of character.   He treated Mr. Jarvis in the most kind and courteous manner.

Besides the official correspondence, many private, friendly notes were exchanged between the American Chargé and the Minister of Foreign Affairs.[1]

The strict police of Junot, while Governor-general of Portugal, preserved perfect order in Lisbon, and the impressment of American seamen ceased.   But after his capitulation at Cintra (August 22, 1808), British troops were stationed in the city, and brawls and drunkenness were frequent among them.

The old trouble of impressment recommenced, under greatly aggravated circumstances ; for the Portuguese government was too weak to aid in suppressing it.   His correspondence shows that scarcely a week passed without one or more cases occurring, which obliged Mr. Jarvis to apply for redress to Vice-admiral Berkeley, commander-in-chief of the British naval forces on the Lisbon station.

---

[1] Don Araujo was truly a *noble* man. Wise, affable, and obliging, he laid aside much of the Portuguese ceremony and formality, and manifested a most friendly disposition towards the United States, and her representative, in complying with Mr. Jarvis' applications for the benefit of his countrymen. His letters to the Chargé are very numerous.

There are also various communications from the Marquis of Pomball, the Viscount de Anadia, Minister of Marine, and the Viscount de Balsamao regarding the quarantine, the impressment of American seamen, etc., etc., all expressing esteem and good-will.

There are letters dated 14th, 16th, and 18th July, 1809, appealing to the admiral to liberate several seamen taken from the American ship "General Eaton," by means of which he succeeded at last in obtaining an examination of their case by Sir Thomas Hardy.

It was an ever-recurring grievance; and to effect the release of the sailors, in which he almost invariably succeeded, Mr. Jarvis was compelled, with unflinching pertinacity, to write letter after letter to Admiral Berkeley, and often to make personal application, ere he succeeded in having them liberated from British vessels of war. His labor and energy in defending the rights of his countrymen, and redressing their wrongs were very great. As he apprised Mr. Jefferson and Mr. Madison of all that transpired, it was one cause that led to hostilities with England.

CHAPTER XVIII.

IMPAIRED HEALTH. — GUNNING ON THE KING'S HUNTING-GROUNDS.

MR. JARVIS was often obliged to sit up writing until one or two o'clock in the morning; and this close confinement at his desk, and intense application to business, impaired his health. His stand- 1805. ard of loyalty to his government was a very high one; and he conscientiously and zealously endeavored to act in such a manner as to prove himself worthy the confidence reposed in him by Mr. Jefferson and Mr. Madison.

Without emolument, he discharged the duties and bore the responsibilities of American Minister at the court of Portugal. He wrote Mr. Madison by every vessel going to the United States, often inclosing duplicates of his former dispatches, as the risk and uncertainty in the transmission of letters was much greater than in the present day of steamers and packets.

His letters were long; communicating not only his official transactions, but all the foreign news of interest. His memorials to the Minister of Foreign Affairs had also been frequent and lengthy, requiring much thought and study in the preparation, and a careful

14

observance of the Portuguese forms in addressing those of high rank.

He corresponded also, extensively, with various American ministers at foreign courts: as Mr. Charles Pinckney at Madrid, and afterwards with Mr. Monroe, who succeeded him; with Mr. G. W. Erving, at London, etc., also with the American consuls on the coasts of Spain and Africa, and with his own vice-consuls. In addition to which he carried on a correspondence, though a far less laborious one, in transacting his private business as commission merchant.

His folio letter-books, containing copies of his official and private letters, are evidences of his ability and industry, as well as of the unusual efforts he made to advance every measure conducive to the interests of his country.

But his mental energy was greater than his bodily strength. A pain in his side became so troublesome that he was obliged to consult a physician, who ordered exercise in the open air, and riding on horseback. He had been fond of field-sports in early life, and he thought that by combining amusement with exercise, it would prove more beneficial to his health.

Through the courtesy of the new Minister of Foreign Affairs, Don Araujo de Azevedo, the American Chargé received a permit from the Prince Regent to hunt in the king's hunting-grounds, which extended from the Tagus to Cintra, and were ten miles square. This was a great privilege, that had never been granted to a foreigner but once before, when it was given to an English Minister. It shows how high in favor the American Chargé had become at the Portuguese

Court. Some of these grounds abounded in partridges, others in ducks and plover. He purchased a saddle-horse, and rode out into the country every afternoon for an hour or two ; devoting the holidays, which were numerous, to gunning, as on these days no business could be transacted. On such occasions he rose at four o'clock, equipped himself in leather pants, and long water-proof boots (saturated with rosin, wax, and tallow), which were strapped on above the knee ; and provided with a roast chicken in his haversack, and a hunting-case, containing a knife, fork, and spoon, mounted and set out for the day's hunt. He frequently asked the Count de Bourmont, or the son of the Baron Viomenil to join him. They were French refugees, with whom he was on very friendly terms ; and being affable, agreeable, and good sportsmen, were pleasant companions.[1]

[1] From Count de Bourmont, on receiving a young pointer from Mr. Jarvis : —

" To MONSIEUR JARVIE, *Chargé d'Affaires des Etats Unis :* —

M. de Bourmont begs Mr. Jarvis to accept with his respectful compliments, a thousand thanks for the handsome dog which he has had the kindness to present to him. He will watch over his *education* with great care, and flatters himself that the time is not far distant when he will be serviceable at Barroca d'Alva. Madame de Bourmont charges me to thank Monsieur Jarvis for his kind souvenir, and to invite him to come and pass a day with us when his business permits. If he can come to-morrow, he will find some of her acquaintances, who would be charmed to meet him.

" 10*th March*, 1807."

From Madame de Bourmont : —

" Madame de Bourmont accepts with much pleasure the curious and pretty bird that Monsieur Jarvis had the goodness to present to her. In return she begs him to receive her thanks, her compliments of true friendship, and the assurance of her perfect esteem.

" BEAFILA, *Thursday Morning.* '

He had obtained permission for a friend to accompany him. When he wished to partake of the lunch provided, he usually sought out a peasant's cottage, and requested the favor of taking dinner in their house. "O, certainly, with pleasure ; we are honored by the stranger's company," was the prompt reply. On receiving the chicken, the woman spread a clean and very white cloth of her own manufacture on the table, and bringing from the garden a fine salad, placed it on the table with salt, oil, and vinegar, and the best bread she had, — sometimes white, sometimes brown ; the wine of the country, which is about as strong as cider ; and always fine fruit — grapes, figs, or oranges, doing all with alacrity and good-will.

Their morning sports had given them a keen appetite, and they partook of this repast with great zest. When about to depart, Mr. Jarvis offered to pay their hostess ; but "O, no," she would not take money ; " it is sufficient recompense that the foreign gentlemen have thought my house worthy to take refreshments in." He thanked her very cordially for her hospitality, but on going out contrived to slip a crusade or half dollar into a child's hand.

Most of the peasants have good gardens, and raise fruits, salads, and vegetables, especially carrots and onions, of which they are very fond. They keep fowls, which supply them with eggs and chickens. They raise a good many turkeys, which are driven alive in droves to market and sold ; one person preceding them scattering corn, another driving them. The turkey is as great a favorite in Lisbon as in New England ; no entertainment is considered complete without them. They are called "birds of Peru."

The Prince did not hunt himself, being too corpulent, and not fond of field-sports; and the game had increased so much in the royal hunting-grounds (Barroca d'Alva), that it became very troublesome to the neighboring peasantry, injuring their crops, and obliging them frequently to drive them off from the grain. They were very glad to have them killed.

The peasantry, both men and women, were industrious, honest, devout, simple in their manners, and very hospitable. The women's dress is of coarse cloth, but neat, and tastefully put on. Mr. Jarvis drew comparisons between the Portuguese peasantry and the lower classes in England, much in favor of the former. The Portuguese, sober, disinterested, kind, respectful; while in England he encountered a regular system of extorting fees, and more or less insolence. In the English hotels it was, "Don't forget boots;" "Don't forget the chambermaid;" "Don't forget the waiter," etc., etc. In the coaches, "Sir, don't forget the postilion, the coachman," etc.

The fish-market of Lisbon is a place of resort to the lower classes; but even here Mr. Jarvis never witnessed any quarreling, fighting, or swearing; and drunkenness was held in abhorrence. He never saw a Portuguese drunk but two or three times, and that after the arrival of the English under Wellington.

He had three fowling-pieces while in Lisbon. He sent to Mr. Braddick in London for one. The second was of the very best Spanish manufacture, made of mules' shoes, and cost $100. The third was Italian, light and very malleable.

In 1807 he purchased a fine, large, chestnut horse

of Mr. Bulkeley, which he had imported at the price
of one hundred guineas from Tattersalls', London.   It
was so high spirited that Mr. Bulkeley was afraid to
ride him, and bought a small black horse for his own
use, his groom mounted on the hunter behind, after
the English style.

He became a favorite with Mr. Jarvis, who rode
him every day, and brought him to America on his
return.   He was an excellent saddle-horse, and quick
in the harness.   In crossing the Connecticut River
once, with his eldest daughter, then a child of six or
seven years, the ice broke near the New Hampshire
shore, and the water came into the sleigh.   A moment
more all would have been borne down by the rapid
current; but this spirited animal made one brave
bound, and landed them safely on the shore.

CHAPTER XIX.

A ROBBERY.

AFTER the cares and fatigues of the day, and the close confinement of the counting-house, Mr. Jarvis, at this period, was in the habit of walking for an hour or two after tea upon the " Praça do Comercio." 1805.

Returning from his walk one evening about nine o'clock, he found his candle unsnuffed, and nearly burned to the socket. He called his servant for another; he did not make his appearance, and Mr. Jarvis went into the kitchen, but José was not there, and the old cook was sound asleep, his head resting upon the table. On being aroused after some effort, he could give no account of José, saying he was about the kitchen when he dropped asleep; perhaps he had gone out.

This José had been educated for a priest, but had left the church for some offense. He retained an affectation of priestly deportment, a demure, quiet manner, and hitherto had discharged his duties faithfully.

Mr. Jarvis took a candle and retired to his chamber, thinking no more of the matter, but soon missed a strong, heavy, iron-bound trunk, in which until recently, he had deposited bags of silver and gold ; now, however, it contained only private papers of value, American clothing, and one hundred pounds of powder and shot, which he had imported from London, and placed here for safe-keeping. Not long before he had purchased an iron chest or coffer, with a curious secret lock, in which he then kept his specie in the counting-house.[1] On going to his closet a new suit of clothes, sent home from the tailor's the day before, was missing ; also a new pair of boots and hat had disappeared. It was evident that he had been robbed. Recollecting his silver-plate in the dining-room, he looked into the sideboard where it was kept ; lo, it was all gone ! — tea-spoons, table-spoons, ladles, candlesticks, etc., etc. He next opened the drawer containing his table-linen, valuable long cloths and napkins that he had imported from England — not one left !

Some of his clerks coming in at this time, he sent them to notify the police at different stations of the robbery, and to offer them a reward of $100 for the arrest of the thief. Every effort was made to trace him, but in vain ; and about four o'clock A. M., worn out by fatigue, he retired to rest, thinking he must be resigned to the loss. He slept soundly, awoke later than usual, and was at breakfast, when suddenly a

---

[1] It was made by the blacksmiths in Lisbon, who are famous for such workmanship, of iron bars bolted together, the ends of the bolts clinched. It was exceedingly strong, — stronger than welded iron. The lock was remarkably ingenious, having two secrets, which years afterwards defied the penetration of one of the most skillful locksmiths in America. It cost $120. But he found this too small as his business increased, all payments being made in specie, and kept it especially for gold, buying a larger one of similar construction for silver, which he left in Lisbon on his return to the United States.

Gallego rushed into the room and fell on his knees before him, crying out in Portuguese, in an impassioned manner, —

" Pardon me, sir ; pardon me, sir."

Much astonished, Mr. Jarvis said, —

" Pardon you for what ? "

" O, pardon, pardon, senhor."

" For what shall I pardon you ? "

" For carrying off your trunk."

" Did you carry it off ? "

" Yes, sir."

" And the table-cloths and silver ? "

" Yes, sir ; and if you will promise to pardon me, I will tell you where they are."

Mr. Jarvis promised ; and he then explained how Joseph had hired him to come in the evening, take them to his house and there secrete them ; that José had removed the trunk, but the other things were still there ; and he would restore them in safety if the Consul would send for them. He was induced to make this confession, partly from fear of the police, partly from the arrest of José, and actuated in some degree from gratitude to Mr. Jarvis, who had sometimes employed him.

" Where are José and my trunk now ? "

" In the police court, sir, before the judge."

He then related the circumstances as follows. José, alarmed by the vigilant search of the police, had engaged the Gallego to take the trunk to the boats, intending to carry it up the river, but had been overtaken by the civil police, who, suspecting that the trunk contained contraband goods, arrested him.

He assured them that there was only his clothing in it.

They said, "If that is the case open it, and prove that you speak truly."

"But I have forgotten the keys."

"Then we must take possession of it."

"But I have several dollars; I will give them to you if you will allow me to keep it. I assure you there is nothing but clothes in it."

The police, after some deliberation, concluded to take the money and give up the trunk. But at this juncture who should come up but the military police, and inquired who they had under arrest.

They answered, "A man with a trunk, which he was about to put into a boat to go up the river, and we suspect it is full of contraband goods."

"Then it must be seized."

"But he has just promised to pay us seven dollars to release it."

The military police inquired if he had more money, and being answered in the negative, said in that case they must attach the trunk, and carry José to the police court to be examined by the judge.

When the Gallego had finished his narration, Mr. Jarvis dispatched one of his clerks with him for the table linen and silver, while he hastened to the police court.

He was convinced José had discovered that gold and silver were kept in this trunk, and ignorant of the removal, was tempted by so rich a prize to appropriate it to his own use, as well as the clothing, silver, etc., selecting the time when his master was walking as the most convenient season for his depredations ; probably having first drugged the honest old cook.

On arriving at the court, the first thing Mr. Jarvis saw was his trunk. The judge had just sent for a blacksmith to break it open, which would doubtless have been done had he been ten minutes later. He immediately informed the alcaldé or judge that it belonged to him, and had been stolen by his servant ; telling him who he was.

He replied that it was supposed to contain contraband goods.

" To convince you, sir, that this is a mistake, I will enumerate its contents, state how the letters are directed, and open it with my keys in your presence," which he accordingly did. One of the locks was a common, but strong one, the other a very curious padlock, which none but those initiated could open. Both instantly yielded to his keys. He then displayed the articles that he had described, and his letters, directed to " Mons. Guillaume Jarvis, Consul des États Unis."

This was proof positive, and would have convinced an honest man of his veracity. But no, Senhor Alcaldé chose to say that the law required him to detain such articles as evidence, probably intending to keep them as the perquisites of his office.

" But," said the Consul, " I have proved that the trunk belongs to me, by opening it with my keys ; and you see the address of the letters corresponds with the name I gave you. What further evidence is necessary ? "

Still Senhor Alcaldé alleged the law required its detention.

Recollecting a similar incident in " Gil Blas," where the judge took possession of the property, and the owner was unable to recover it, Mr. Jarvis was determined not to submit to such a fraud, but to make a strong effort for its rescue. Assuming an air of authority, he said, —

" Unless the trunk is immediately delivered to me, I shall complain of you, Senhor Alcaldé, to the Minister of Foreign Affairs, with whom I am personally acquainted."

This threat of exposure to one of the magnates at court, uttered so boldly, intimidated the alcaldé ; and he reluctantly resigned his prize.

Rejoicing in the recovery of his trunk, Mr. Jarvis began to look about him, when whom should he see, a little retired from observation, but master José ; and scanning him for a moment, he noticed that his sleeves were very long. Another scrutinizing glance disclosed to him his own new broadcloth coat. He went to him and said loud enough to be heard by the judge, —

" José, this is my coat ? "

With a very humble and penitent air he replied, —
" Si, Senhor." [1]

" And these are my pantaloons, boots, and hat ? "
" Si, Senhor."

Noticing that his shirt was unusually fine and clean, this also proved to be one of his own.

" My shirt, too ? "
" Si, Senhor."

" Where are your own clothes ? "

[1] " Yes, sir."

" I have them in a bundle."

" Go and put them on, and return mine."

He obeyed, and Mr. Jarvis then showing the judge his name written on a piece of paper by the tailor, and tacked to the lining, said, —

" On my entrance I informed you that I am the American Consul, gave you my name, and stated that the trunk had been stolen by my servant. This man, whom you arrested this morning with the trunk, is my servant; and in your presence he confesses that he has stolen my clothes. Here is the same name on the coat that you saw on the letters, which is strong corroborating evidence. You can need no further proof of his guilt."

There could be no doubt of it, and José was condemned to one year's imprisonment.

Mr. Jarvis employed two Gallegos to carry home the trunk and clothing, so that ere night he had recovered every article of which he had been robbed, which gave him no small satisfaction.

Six months afterwards, as he was passing the prison in which José was confined, he begged an alms of the Consul, which he freely gave him.

The prisons in Portugal are so horrible, that none could be so heartless as not to commiserate the condition of the prisoners. The greatest villains and those guilty of but small offenses are thrown into one filthy room, full of vermin, which will contain about fifty persons. When the prison becomes so full that it will hold no more, the oldest culprits are released, and those guilty of the greatest crimes sent to the galleys. The government only supplies prisoners with bread and water; their extra food is obtained by begging money of those passing by, which petitions are commonly granted. Thus every alleviation of their misery is derived from private charity.

CHAPTER XX.

CATALINI.

THIS celebrated singer was in Lisbon at the time of Mr. Jarvis' residence there, and whenever he attended the opera, her wonderful vocal powers were a source of unfailing delight. Her compass and sweetness of voice were astonishing: now rising higher and higher, keeping the house in breathless suspense ; then gradually descending, and again warbling forth melodious notes in rich variety. Her throat was very large, and dilated and · contracted perceptibly while she was singing.

When Mr. Jarvis wished to entertain the American captains for an evening, he frequently took them to hear Catalini, — sometimes doubting if they would appreciate her voice ; but they always listened with close attention, and seemed charmed by her performance, which he considered an evidence of her great ability.

Christientini, manager of the opera at Lisbon, heard of a young Italian girl who was a remarkable singer. He went to Italy, and finding the parents of the young Catalini poor, offered to give her $2,500 per year for five years if she would sing for him in the opera at Lisbon. Her parents accepted the proposal on condition that they should accompany and watch over her.

Christientini, who was a singer, and master of his profession, instructed the young genius in the rules of music. She soon attracted large audiences, and the teacher was eclipsed by his youthful pupil. At the expiration of the five years, she was offered a very high price to go to England; but Christientini doubled her salary, with the addition of one benefit a year. His *protégé* continued to receive thunders of applause, while he was coldly received. His mortification at last became so great that he could endure it no longer, and he returned to his native Italy, where he compensated himself for loss of fame by purchasing, from the fortune accumulated in Lisbon, an estate and marquisate, which gave him rank and honors, with which he was satisfied.

About this time a handsome French gentleman, of polished manners and agreeable address, appeared at one of the hotels in Lisbon, and represented that he was a French officer who had fought a duel with a superior officer. It proved to be Captain Valabrégue, who fell in love with Catalini, and sought her hand in marriage; and his proposals were finally accepted.

After her marriage, "from her concerts in Paris, her fame spread over all Europe. In London she had in the first year of her engagement a salary of $12,931, and in the following, of $17,241. Two concerts beside brought her $5,000 each." [1]

---

[1] Madame Junot speaks of Catalini as the "Prima Donna," and in her zenith at Lisbon in 1805 and 1806.

CHAPTER XXI.

M. MARCELLINO R. SILVA, VICE-CONSUL AT LISBON. — AT
FARO. — HIS IMPRISONMENT. — A SHIPWRECK.

M. SILVA, vice-consul at Lisbon, thinking it would
be for his advantage to enter into partnership with Mr.
Abreu, a merchant at Faro, requested Mr.
Jarvis to appoint him vice-consul for that port. 1806.

From his knowledge of English, and of Portuguese
forms in transacting business, he had been a most
valuable assistant, frequently acting as secretary, and
the Consul regretted to part with him, but complied
with his wishes.

At the end of the year, on settling accounts, it
proved that M. Silva had been a loser by the change ;
he therefore dissolved the partnership and returned to
Lisbon. Soon afterwards being imprisoned, he sent
to Mr. Jarvis for relief. The circumstances are related in the following letter : —

"To His EXCELLENCY DON ANTONIO DE ARAUJO DE AZEVEDO, *His
Royal Highness the Prince Regent's Minister and Secretary of State
for the Foreign and War Departments, etc., etc.:* —

" SIR, — Under the government of a Prince so deservedly
celebrated for justice and clemency, I little expected to be
obliged to trouble your Excellency with a complaint of a
most wanton outrage of these virtues.

15

" Yesterday morning at six o'clock the criminal judge of the le Moira prison entered the apartments of M. Rodriguez da Silva, vice-consul of the United States at Faro, in Algarva, with four police guards and some civil officers, took him out of his bed, seized his books, papers, and cash, and carried him to that prison, without allowing him to speak to any person.   So secretly was it done, that I did not hear of it till three o'clock, when I went to the prison to inquire the cause of so extraordinary a step.   I was informed that M. Silva was in the *dungeon!*   The prison-keeper could not tell me his crime, and the judge was not at home.   Upon repeating my visit this morning, I understood that M. Silva had just been taken into another apartment, and the judge was examining him.   When admitted to see him in presence of the judge, he told me that it was at the suit of Mr. Abreu, and was owing to a difference which had taken place in the adjustment of their copartnership accounts.   I then observed to the judge that I thought the laws of this realm would not justify such a measure ; and although a Portuguese subject, yet being the acknowledged vice-consul of the United States for Faro, he ought to be considered as under the protection of the laws of nations ; at least it entitled him to more consideration.   The judge acknowledged that he had read his patent (which your Excellency confirmed about a year since), and made some indistinct reply. I told him I should make an application to higher authority in behalf of the prisoner, and requested a copy of the alleged causes of his commitment.

" He answered in seeming confusion, that it was a secret, and he could not give it to me ; but if I would become responsible for the prisoner, he would deliver him up to me, with his books, papers, and cash.

" Upon my return to my house, Mr. Abreu called, and said it was at his and his partner's suit, that M. da Silva had been sent to prison." . . . .

Mr. Jarvis relates the details of the case, which briefly amounted to this : —

"A dispute had arisen in the settlement of their affairs, and M. Silva had requested that the difference might be left to arbitrators, who had examined the books, and said they were perfectly fair; the books were then returned to M. da Silva, a week since. The arbitrators, not proceeding so fast as Mr. Abreu wished, and fearing M. da Silva would leave Lisbon, he had taken this step."

Mr. Jarvis speaks of M. Silva's rights as a Portuguese citizen, and as an American officer, and then says : —

"I hope your Excellency will allow me to say that it appears to me a most wanton and cruel breach of the security and safety of foreign officers, which this government is so remarkable for treating with the respect, attention, and civility due to their station. . . . .

"That any person should be so transported by avarice or resentment, as to put a man of respectable standing in society, — lately his partner, — and whose honesty he does not pretend to impeach, into a dreary dungeon, for a difference of accounts, seems to me a monstrous dereliction of every sentiment of humanity! . . . . I am too well acquainted with the mercy, justice, and wisdom of his Royal Highness the Prince Regent, not to be satisfied that an immediate inquiry will be made into this affair, and that ample satisfaction will be afforded.

"With the highest consideration,

"I have the honor to be, etc., etc., etc.

"*July* 26*th*, 1806."

On the 9th August Mr. Jarvis received a letter

from M. da Silva, saying that the "Relação"[1] had decided in his favor.

In reply, he expresses the pleasure he feels at this decision, but says : —

"Had it been otherwise, I am satisfied that the affidavits, etc., that I had completed yesterday, would have induced his Royal Highness the Prince Regent, through the intervention of his Excellency Don Araujo, to give an order for your release and satisfaction." . . . .

On the same day he informs Don Araujo of this decision ; but on the 13th August is obliged to address him again : —

" . . . . I find the inveteracy of malice is never to be checked or satisfied. Not content with the unworthy treatment M. da Silva has already received, Mr. Abreu has embargoed the decision given in his favor, and of course renders the interference of your Excellency necessary."

Mr. Jarvis inclosed the affidavits, and again places the case in a clear and strong light before this just and wise Minister, by whose order da Silva was released, and his books, papers, and money restored to him.

In a very handsome note to Don Araujo, the Consul acknowledges his high appreciation of the great favor conferred upon him, by this humane and prompt attention to the wrongs of an injured man, etc., etc.

M. da Silva's gratitude knew no bounds. He begged to be restored to his former employment, and to be reinstated in the office of vice-consul at Lisbon. His petition was granted, as soon as an eligible situation could be found for the young man who had filled his place. He remained with his benefactor till he left Lisbon, zealously and faithfully discharging his duties.

_____
[1] Court.

About this period a vessel was cast away in a storm near the mouth of the Tagus. The crew escaped in the boats. Captain Cook, the master, reached Lisbon, and went to the Consul to inform him of his distressed situation. He was in his shirt and trousers, having lost everything. Mr. Jarvis gave him a suit of clothes, invited him to stay at his house, and treated him with great kindness and sympathy. In a few days a book-case, sideboard, and pair of card-tables that had been boxed up floated ashore with some other articles, and by Mr. Jarvis' advice, were put up at auction. Mr. Jarvis bought the card-tables, book-case, and sideboard, and retained them till his death; he particularly valued the two latter pieces of furniture. By these sales Captain Cook realized between one and two hundred dollars, which enabled him to return to the United States.

On the Consul's arrival in America, he was informed that Captain Cook, who resided in Salem, cherished the most lively gratitude towards him. While he, oblivious of his good deeds, had nearly forgotten the circumstance.

In December, 1806, Mr. Jarvis received a gift of a singular animal, called a bubabus, from some one returning from Africa, and very modestly begs Don Araujo " to do him the honor to accept it, to place among the curious animals at the Royal Palace at Belem."

CHAPTER XXII.

LORD ST. VINCENT AND HIS SQUADRON. — THE "CON-
STITUTION." — COMMODORE CAMPBELL. — A BALL ON
BOARD THE "CONSTITUTION."

Extracts from a letter to Mr. Madison : —

"Admiral Sir John Jervis, Earl of St. Vincent, came to Lisbon in command of a British squadron in August, 1806, and as Ambassador Extraordinary to this Court.

1806.

"On the first week, thousands of both sexes went on board to see his ship. They were treated with the greatest civility, and the ladies with the utmost gallantry, giving tea, coffee, chocolate, cold collations, etc. . . . . He has been extremely polite to everybody ; some persons have been in constant attendance to show the ship ; this has made him very popular among the Portuguese.

"A few days after his Lordship's arrival, he was joined by the Earl of Rosselyn, who had a separate commission as Envoy Extraordinary ; and at their first reception at Court they were received with great attention by the Prince, who, after the audience was over, introduced them to the Princess and their children, with whom they conversed an hour, and were most graciously treated.

"His Lordship has given several dinners on board the 'Hibernia,' to the Portuguese nobility ; and makes it a point to accept all their invitations. . . . . Two days since the Ministers of Foreign Affairs and of the Marine, Don

Araujo and the Viscount Anadia, were invited to dine with his Lordship, with six or eight noble ladies and noblemen."

All sorts of rumors were in circulation in regard to this squadron and embassy, producing much excitement in the public mind, but nothing definite was known.

" Some say that it has some relation to the negotiations now pending in Paris ; that the Emperor has determined, in case a peace is not concluded, to oblige this Court to *prohibit* the importation of British manufactures ; and if it refuses, to send an army to enforce it." [1]

Others thought that it was to form an alliance with the Portuguese government — the most probable supposition. Another report was that Napoleon was about to take possession of Lisbon, and that Lord St. Vincent had come to take the royal family and nobility to the Brazils with their property. Mr. Jarvis says that he has been more minute in relating these details, as they seem to be connected with the political events of the period.

Early in September the " Constitution," Commodore Campbell, put into Lisbon for repairs, having lost her anchor, and being otherwise damaged.

Mr. Jarvis invited the Commodore to make his house a home, which hospitable invitation was accepted. It was found that the frigate would have to undergo thorough repairs, and that her powder was damaged. That it might be restored, Mr. Jarvis applied to Don Araujo as follows : —

" William Jarvis, Consul and Chargé d'Affaires of the United States, offers his most respectful compliments to his

---

[1] Extracts from a later letter to Mr. Madison.

Excellency Don Antonio de Araujo de Azevedo, his Royal Highness the Prince Regent's Minister and Secretary of State for the Foreign and War Departments, etc., etc., and from the well known disposition which the government of his Royal Highness the Prince Regent has always discovered to oblige foreign powers, W. J. is encouraged to solicit the favor that permission may be given for sending the powder of the United States frigate ' Constitution ' (about 200 barrels), to the powder fabric, to be benefited and aired ; for apprehensions are entertained that it is somewhat injured, owing to the length of time that it has been confined in the magazine of the ship. The expenses attending the operation, Mr. Jarvis will with pleasure defray. He embraces this occasion to reiterate his sentiments of profound veneration for his Excellency.[1]

" LISBON, 16th September, 1806."

In a letter to Mr. Madison, dated 18th September, after discussing the causes of Lord St. Vincent's embassy, he says : —

" The ' Constitution ' has had her rigging stripped ; that which was bought in Cadiz, for the fore and mainmasts, is almost ready to go over head ; the mizzen mast rigging, which I have purchased here, will be ready in a day or two.   It

[1] From Don Araujo to the American Chargé d'Affaires : —

"The Prince Regent, my master, assenting to the requisition of your office, dated 16th inst., has been pleased to permit the portion of powder, belonging to the frigate ' Constitution,' to be benefited at the Royal Powder Fabrick, and for that purpose has desired to expedite the necessary orders to the Royal Junta of the Arsenals and of the army, in conformity with your said requisition; to whom I am ordered to communicate the same for your information.

"God preserve you many years.

"Your very certain and assured servant,

"ANTONIO DE ARAUJO DE AZEVEDO.

"PALACE OF MAFRA, 17th September, 1806."

appears that all her upper works want caulking. Commodore Campbell thinks several new sails will be necessary, lest she should be called out in winter service. The foremast is also found to be considerably rotted ; I hope a new one will not be wanted, as it will be attended with an enormous expense. Her repairs will probably be completed in three or four weeks." . . . . Mr. Jarvis says, — " Within a few days a press has been sent out to complete the Portuguese marine corps, and is still continued. I shall leave you to make your own comments on this."

Mr. Jarvis was obliged to write to the Minister of the Marine, the Viscount Anadia, to solicit permission to purchase an anchor at the royal arsenal, as none could be found elsewhere in Lisbon, of sufficient size.

Lord St. Vincent hearing of Mr. Jarvis, sent to him and requested an interview, thinking there must be a connection between them. Accompanied by Commodore Campbell he called upon the Admiral, and was much pleased with his noble, gentlemanly bearing ; and was struck by the resemblance between him and some of the Jarvis family ; especially to his uncle Leonard. The Admiral treated the Consul in the most friendly, pleasant manner, and said that when he entered the navy as a midshipman, he had spelled his name Jarvis ; but had been rallied by some of the officers for so doing, saying it was a corruption of the old Norman name Jervois, and they had induced him to change it ; but he had no doubt they sprung from the same ancestors, in which opinion Mr. Jarvis fully coincided. The Admiral afterwards invited Commodore Campbell and Mr. Jarvis to dine with him. The Commodore accepted, but the Consul declined. He admired Lord St. Vincent, but he had maintained the most cordial intercourse with the French officers,[1] and as France and England were at variance, he disliked the appearance of dining in amity on board one of his Majesty's ships of war. In addition to which, the impressment of American seamen had caused unceasing collision between him and the British navy, ever since he came to Lisbon.

The following very handsome note from Sir John Jervis expresses his regret : —

" Lord St. Vincent presents his compliments to Mr. Jarvis, and regrets exceedingly the cause which has deprived him of the honor of a visit, begging at the same time to assure Mr. Jarvis that it will afford him the highest satisfaction to show every attention in his power to the representative of the United States of America.

"' HIBERNIA,' 10th September, 1808."

After remaining about two months, Lord St. Vincent and his squadron left Lisbon, his abrupt departure producing almost as great a sensation as his arrival had done ; and a few weeks later the Earl of Rosselyn departed ; the object of their embassy having been enveloped in a veil of mystery.

When the " Constitution " was nearly ready for sea, Commodore Campbell wished to give a ball on board the frigate, and Mr. Jarvis being desirous to have it conducted in such a manner as to do honor to the naval officers of the United States, aided him

---

[1] Among these he was most intimate with Mr. Legoy, Junot's private secretary; Magendie, commander-in-chief of the navy; Count de Bourmont, the son of the Baron Viomenil, etc.; and they frequently dined with him.

essentially, especially in the invitations. They invited Don Almeida, Don Araujo, Viscount Anadia, the Marquis of Pomball, and several other Portuguese noblemen with their families; the Corps Diplomatique, including the Pope's Nuncio — Monsignore Galeppi, and several merchants with their families; among the latter were Mr. and Mrs. O'Niele.

The decks had been cleared and scrubbed clean, and an awning placed over the first deck for dancing. An elegant supper-table was prepared on the lower deck, ornamented with a variety of fruits and flowers. At the appointed hour the guests, including many ladies, assembled. Mr. O'Niele took Mr. Jarvis aside and asked him if fish had been provided for the entertainment, as it was Friday.

It had not occurred to them. What an oversight! What was to be done? They had meats in great abundance, game, etc., but no fish.

Mr. O'Niele suggested delaying the supper till a little past midnight, when a new day commenced. This plan was adopted. The Commodore had a fine band of music, and conversation, music, and dancing so agreeably occupied the time, that probably few noticed that the handsome repast was an hour later than was customary. The Nuncio pronounced grace, and all did ample justice to the viands, and seemed highly to enjoy the festivity. After supper the grandees departed, but the young people continued to dance until about three o'clock, when the company broke up. It was really a delightful occasion. Every one was in fine spirits, and it afforded the Commodore great pleasure.

CHAPTER XXIII.

GENERAL JUNOT. — EMBARKATION OF THE ROYAL
FAMILY. — THE FRENCH ARMY SUPPLIED WITH
FLOUR. — JUNOT'S CAPITULATION.

LANNES, though a brave general, was no statesman
or diplomatist. He was impetuous and passionate,
and had greatly offended the Portuguese by
his bluntness of manner and disregard of
their customs and court etiquette. Lord Robert Fitzgerald, the English Ambassador, and his lady,[1] had
become very obnoxious to Lannes ; the former by always
taking precedence of him, the latter by her prejudice
against the French, and open abuse of Napoleon ; and

1805-7-8.

[1] The following is an answer to an invitation, about this period, from
Lord Robert Fitzgerald and lady to Mr. Pinckney and Mr. Jarvis: —

"Mr. Jarvis presents his most respectful compliments to his Excellency
Lord Robert Fitzgerald and lady, and has the honor to acknowledge the
receipt of his lordship's polite note of yesterday; but not seeing Mr.
Pinckney until the evening, prevented an earlier reply. Mr. Pinckney
desired Mr. Jarvis to make his very respectful compliments to his lordship
and her ladyship, and to acquaint them, that as the ship in which he takes
his passage sails to-day, it would be out of his power to accept their polite
invitation; but Mr. Jarvis will with pleasure embrace the invitation to tea
this evening, and have the honor to pay his personal respects to Lord and
Lady Fitzgerald.

" *Tuesday Morning, November 19th, 1805.*"

" Lord Robert Fitzgerald presents his compliments to Mr. Jarvis, and
shall be very happy in having the honor of his company to tea, if he cannot have the pleasure of seeing him at dinner.

"*November 19th.*"

it was said that the French Minister privately requested to be recalled. Napoleon sent out General Junot in his place, who came to Lisbon with Madame Junot and his suite in April, 1805, and took possession of the spacious and beautiful mansion that Lannes had occupied, which was in the vicinity of the opera house and Tagus, and very near the house in which Mr. Jarvis then resided. Junot combined the talents of an able general and a statesman in an eminent degree. He was a fine-looking, tall, military man, with a noble countenance, good-humored, affable, and gentlemanly. He took great pains to conciliate the good-will of the Portuguese government; and by scrupulous attention to their etiquette, and deference to their customs, as well as by his upright character and courteous deportment, he won great favor at Court, and became deservedly popular.

In compliance with the wishes of Napoleon, Madame Junot gave splendid balls and entertainments, inviting the Portuguese nobility and Corps Diplomatique. She was very handsome, with an oval Italian face, bright hazel eyes, and much vivacity ; her dress was rich, tasteful, and elegant, and greatly excited the admiration of the Portuguese ladies.

Mr. Jarvis, as a member of the Corps Diplomatique, was invited to these assemblies, which were remarkably pleasant. He admired Junot, whose bearing toward him was kind and courteous.

Junot returned to Paris to attend Napoleon in some of his campaigns, which he preferred to being Ambassador at Lisbon. He came out the second time as General-in-Chief of Portugal in November, 1807.

Napoleon had decreed that the Braganzas should no longer reign in Portugal. For a few weeks they were incredulous, but too late found that he was in earnest, and that Junot was entering the kingdom with a large army.[1] Then all was bustle and dismay at Court; furniture, plate, jewels, and clothing were hastily packed and put on shipboard. But they were obliged to leave many valuables behind. An immense crowd assembled to witness the embarkation, for the Prince was much beloved by his people; and his departure occasioned them great sorrow and forebodings of evil.

The following extracts from a letter from Mr. Jarvis give the particulars of the Prince's departure.

"LISBON, 20*th November,* 1807,
"9 *o'clock,* A. M.

" To JAMES MADISON, ESQ. : —

" SIR, — At the moment I am writing this, the Portuguese squadron, consisting of eight line-of-battle ships, two frigates, and three or four smaller vessels, are under weigh. The Prince Regent and the whole royal family are on board; the Duke of Cardival, first prince of the blood; the Visconde Anadia and M. de Araujo, Ministers of Marine and Foreign Affairs; the Marquis of Pomball, and several others of the nobility; with a number of officers of government, servants, etc., etc. Few or no soldiers, except the

---

1 " The army under Junot arrived at Abrantes after a dangerous and tedious march along the banks of the Tagus, through the woody, mountainous, and barren Beira. Junot ordered the castle as well as the city, which he found ungarrisoned, to be placed in a state of defense; and in spite of the great fatigue of his troops, hastened to Lisbon, then occupied by 15,000 Portuguese soldiers, and inhabited by 350,000 souls. The quickness of his march, and the daring courage he displayed, induced Napoleon to make him Duke of Abrantes."

marine corps, have embarked. The preparations began the 24th, since which they have worked day and night to get on board. Everything relating to the embarkation has been in great confusion. Appearances seem to indicate that the government was taken by surprise; not even provisions for the ships' use were on board, but little bread prepared, so that they have been obliged to purchase flour; the vessels have gone away very short of salted provisions, and most of them not half manned. The Prince and nobility have had only time to take their most valuable movable effects, leaving their fortunes behind.

"On the 22d the Prince received notice that the French forces were entering Portugal, which caused him much alarm, and occasioned great perturbation at the palace.

"On the 24th a report reached the public of the Prince's intention to embark.

"That night a grand Council of State was called, and the next day orders were received at the arsenal to prepare the ships immediately.

"They also began to embark the Prince's effects, but the ministers and nobility delayed packing until the 25th. . . . . There are now several British line-of-battle ships in the offing, which it is supposed will accompany the Prince to the Brazils. . . . .

"It is reported that the value of the diamonds taken with the Prince is about one hundred millions of dollars, and that he took thirty millions of dollars in specie, plate,[1] etc., etc.

"It is just a fortnight to-day since the Marquis of Marialva went to France on an embassy with diamonds to the amount of upwards of a million of dollars, as a present to the Emperor.

"The advanced guard of the French army are expected

---

[1] In a subsequent letter Mr. Jarvis says, "I believe both estimates are very much overrated."

here to-night or to-morrow morning. Until the ships were actually under weigh, many well-informed persons thought the Prince would remain." . . . .

On the 30th November, when riding on horseback, Mr. Jarvis met the first detachment of French troops that entered the city. He observed that the commanding officer was talking in French to a Portuguese, whose bewildered and frightened manner indicated that he could not understand one word that was said, which induced the Consul to pause and relieve him. He found that the officer was inquiring the way to Belem, and gave the right direction ; for which he was politely thanked. The castle and batteries at Belem were strong defenses on the Tagus, four miles below Lisbon, and in case of attack by sea, effectually protected the city.

The Prince had issued an order that his people should submit without resistance to the French ; and Junot's army of 10,000 men marched peaceably into Lisbon, and took possession of all the forts, and garrisoned the city.

Mr. Jarvis thought that the Emperor's policy, in dethroning the Prince Regent, was very censurable, for the government would readily have paid tribute to Napoleon, and his authority would have been better secured than by the unjustifiable overthrow of this peaceful royal family.

Quintilla, the Farmer-General of Portugal, who was very rich, gave up his splendid new palace for the use of Junot and his staff, thinking it judicious to conciliate the French commander. He had intended to reserve some apartments for his own use, but Junot politely intimated that he should need the whole of it for his suite, and Quintilla was obliged to retire to his country seat, a little out of Lisbon.

These extracts from a letter from Mr. Jarvis to Mr. Madison give further details : —

"I have received official notice of the blockade of St. Ubes ; and the British fleet are still here, but a small part having accompanied the Prince. The embarkation was attended with the utmost haste and confusion, and the quays were filled with packages that could not be taken away. . . . .

"It is said that the Prince did not absolutely decide to leave the kingdom, until an article in a French paper was shown him, to the effect that the House of Braganza should become extinct in Europe. . . . . That the determination was sudden and unexpected may be inferred from the circumstance that the royal family, ministers, and nobility have left in their palaces all their rich and superb furniture, pictures, libraries, carriages, horses, and servants, so that several that I have been in are externally and internally precisely as when their former masters were here, but are occupied by French generals. In the Queen's palace there were found 60,000 crowns in silver coin, beside many of her valuable jewels. Everything remains perfectly quiet here, although commerce, manufactures, and agricultural industry are at an end. It is estimated that about 70,000 inhabitants have left the city and gone into the country."

Just before the events now related, Mr. Jarvis had removed to a spacious, handsome house near the Quintilla Palace, which had an immense warehouse on the ground floor. It contained at this time 5,000 barrels of flour, — indeed most of the flour that was in the city, for merchants were afraid to purchase. Bulkeley

16

and Gould had left Lisbon, and Dohrman, fearing it might be seized, would not run the risk. From his knowledge of Junot's character, Mr. Jarvis was confident that he could trust to his honor and integrity to respect the rights of an American officer, and had ventured to purchase this large amount.

Junot's Commissary, expecting to find it in the city, had neglected to provide flour. He came to Mr. Jarvis, and informing him that the French army stood in great need of a thousand barrels of flour, asked if he had any to sell, and at what price.

"Yes, General, I can supply you, if you will pay me $24 per barrel," was the reply.

"That is too high ; they sell it in the corn market for $18 per barrel." [1]

"True, but their prices do not affect me. I imported it myself, and it has been stored in my own warehouse, and has never been entered at the corn market ; and unless I receive the sum I have named, I cannot sell it to you."

"It is too much to give."

"It is my price."

"We have no money and no flour, and unless you sell it for less, I shall seize it."

"If you do, I shall immediately inform the United States government, and no more flour will be sent out, and in consequence your army will be starved."

At this the Commissary departed, and hastening to Junot told him that the American Consul would not sell them his flour ; and said he meant· to starve the French army.

---

[1] The corn market regulated all prices for the city. A sort of price-current was posted there weekly.

Junot sent for Mr. Jarvis.

He was ushered into an antechamber and politely requested to wait a few moments, as his Excellency was engaged. He entered into conversation with General Kellermann, with whom he was acquainted, and was soon informed that General Junot would be happy to see him, and met the person coming out with whom he had been occupied. When he entered the apartment, Junot greeted him very cordially in French, for their conversations were always sustained in this language; and when, as it sometimes happened, Mr. Jarvis was at a loss for a word, he supplied it with one in Portuguese.

"Ah! Monsieur Jarvie, how do you do? I hear you intend to starve the French army."

"Who could possibly have told your Excellency so false a story?"

"The Commissary told me you would not sell your flour to him, and said you should starve the army."

"O no, your Excellency; he has wholly misrepresented my words. I never had such an idea. I told him that I must be paid in money for my flour, and that my price was $24 per barrel, and when he threatened to seize it, I said that if he did I should immediately inform the United States government, and no more would be sent out; consequently the French army would be starved."

Junot laughed heartily, and then said, —

"But we have no money. Will you take Portuguese paper?"

"No, Monseigneur, I cannot."

"What then shall we do? We have no money and are in great need of flour."

" Your Excellency has issued an order to raise half a million of crusades ; I will wait till this levy is paid in, and I will take your parole that I shall then be paid."

" What ! prefer my parole to Portuguese paper ? "

" Yes, Monseigneur. I have had enough of Portuguese paper to convince me it is of no value ; but I know I can confide in your word of honor."

Junot laughed again, and then said, —

" *Je vous donne ma parole.*" [1]

" I am satisfied ; your Excellency shall have my flour."

Mr. Jarvis now took his leave, and in less than two hours one hundred and fifty barrels were delivered to the Commissary ; and during the time the French were in Lisbon, he furnished them with three thousand seven hundred barrels.

"LISBON, 21*st December*, 1807.

" To JAMES MADISON, ESQ. : —

" SIR, — . . . . About twenty-four hours after the squadron sailed, the first division of the French army, consisting of 6,000 men, reached here, and were marched toward the mouth of the Tagus, taking quiet possession of several of the forts ; and as the remainder of the army arrived, they occupied the others, and have garrisoned Lisbon, and all the strong places about it. A considerable body of Spanish troops have also marched in. Everything remained quiet until the 15th inst., when the French colors were hoisted instead of the Portuguese, which produced an excitement in the minds of the people, who became riotous, throwing stones and discharging pistols and guns at the French soldiers on guard, killing one, and wounding several

[1] I give you my parole.

others. The guard was called out, who fired on the mob; two or three were killed, and twenty or thirty sent to prison. It collected again next morning, but was immediately dispersed. Everything is now quiet. The Portuguese soldiery took no part with the people, and have since been put on the same pay as the French soldiers, which without rations is more than double. The French soldiery have been very orderly, and much credit is due General Junot for his moderation on that occasion, and for his general conduct since he took possession of Lisbon.

"When I made my official visit to his Excellency, he spoke to me about provisions, particularly about breadstuffs. I mentioned rice, and he said he would permit its entry, but desired me to address him in writing, as well as on the subject of our vessels which have been detained, in common with all others.

"I am informed to-day, by a gentleman high in office, that an order will be given immediately for the departure of our vessels, and for the admission of rice and tobacco also; and I have positive assurances that ere long, vessels with the produce of our country will be admitted. . . . .

"With entire respect, I have the honor to be, Sir,
"Your most obedient servant,
"WILLIAM JARVIS."

Mr. Jarvis' correspondence with Junot on these subjects was frequent, especially to obtain passports for vessels, and in their behalf in various ways.

In another letter to Mr. Madison he alludes to the British blockade of the port, and says, — "If continued, it will cause great distress for want of provisions."

In about three weeks, having ascertained that Junot's levy of five millions of crusades had been paid into the Treasury, he called on Monsieur Herman, Secretary of the Treasury, to present his claim, but did not succeed in obtaining an audience. He went again with no better success. " This will never do," thought Mr. Jarvis ; " I must apply at head-quarters ; " for he always found that this was the only way to effect his object.

He immediately wrote a very polite note to Junot, reminding him of his promise, and requesting him to appoint a day when it would be convenient for him to see him. Junot named the following day at four o'clock.

Mr. Jarvis was punctual to the hour, and was promptly admitted.

Junot was very affable, and when reminded of his parole, said, —

" Monsieur Jarvie shall be paid."

He sent for Monsieur Herman, and after the customary greetings said, —

" Monsieur Jarvie wishes to be paid for his flour."

" O yes, ere long," Monsieur Herman politely replied.

Mr. Jarvis knew that he could not trust him, and requested that he would do him the favor to fix upon a day.

" I have a great many demands to settle. I cannot now exactly, but will do so soon."

This was equivalent to an indefinite postponement ; and Mr. Jarvis again pressed his claim.

Junot now interposed, and said he might as well pay him the next day as at any other time. Herman was reluctant, but Junot insisted upon it.

" At what hour shall I wait upon you," said Mr. Jarvis.

" You can call at the office — but no, I may be out, you may call at my house at ten o'clock in the morning."

He did so, and received an order on the Treasury, which Herman said would be opened at one o'clock. He went at that time, it was not opened; he waited till two, still no one came; till three, and became apprehensive of some deception. At last he heard a presentation of arms, and knew that some French officer was approaching; then a second presentation as they ascended the second and third flights of stairs, when the door of the antechamber in which Mr. Jarvis was waiting was opened, and in came the Secretary of the Treasury.

" Ah, Monsieur Jarvis, I have kept you waiting; excuse me." He offered some apology.

Mr. Jarvis answered very civilly that he was not in haste; it was no consequence. They were about to pay him, when a clerk objected that there was no regular account.

He immediately presented the account, and said he could swear to its correctness. He wished that it might be carefully examined, and if any error were detected, he would give his parole that it should be rectified.

" Ah, oui." They paid him, and he never heard from them more.

He was obliged to take a small part in bonds; but they were perfectly good security, being signed by Luis de Vasconcellas and the Marquis of Pomball, two of the wealthiest noblemen in Portugal.

Mr. Jarvis was very much struck with the admirable discipline of the French army, — that wonderful army which had Napoleon for its moving spirit, and so many able generals as subordinates. One day as he was riding on horseback, he entered the square of the Inquisition, where two or three thousand men were on parade. The tinkling bell announced the approach of the Host. The order was given. In a moment the whole command were on one knee, and in passing the eye along the line, not the slightest irregularity could be observed. As the Host was borne along to the front, again the word was given, and every man rose up simultaneously, displaying the same wonderful regularity. It was a grand spectacle. The uniforms were very handsome, especially that of the hussars, — that of the officers being often richly embroidered.

A duty of sixty cents per barrel was imposed by the Portuguese government on every barrel of flour sold in the kingdom. Mr. Jarvis had not obtained from the French a certificate of the amount of flour with which he had supplied their army, and unless he did so, he was liable to be taxed for it by the officers in the corn market.

On the day that Junot evacuated Lisbon, at an early hour Mr. Jarvis ordered his horse and went to Magendie, " Commandant-en-Chef de la Marine," [1] to obtain such a certificate. The streets were full of Portuguese, gathered together in groups, and talking very earnestly. It had been rumored for several days that there would be a rising among them, and this

---

[1] Commander-in-Chief of the Navy of "S. M. I. et R."

seemed to indicate it. On arriving at the house he was ushered into an apartment where Magendie, his private secretary, and two or three other officers were at breakfast. Magendie rose and said very cordially, —

"Ah, Monsieur Jarvie, I am happy to see you; will you take a cup of coffee with us?" They were on very friendly terms.

He thanked him for his polite invitation, but had breakfasted; he came on business, and begged that he might not interrupt their meal or their conversation; he was in no haste, and would wait with pleasure.

Magendie and his friends had been discussing, with great warmth and animation, some disputed points regarding the battle of Marengo; they now resumed the argument with as much zeal and vivacity as if no dangers threatened them, sipping their coffee, and eating their breakfast very leisurely at the same time. When at last it was ended, Magendie turned to Mr. Jarvis and said, —

"What shall I have the pleasure to do for you to-day, Monsieur Jarvie?"

He explained to him the law of the corn market, and his liability to have the duty claimed on the 3,700 barrels flour with which he had supplied the French army, unless he could show that it was consumed by them.

"Ah, oui, oui; but what writing do you require?"

He explained, and Magendie told his secretary to write such a paper as Monsieur Jarvie should dictate, which he did, and then presented it to Magendie for his signature, who with great nonchalance glanced his eye over it, and signed it; then turning it over, directed it to the Alfandega or Governor of the Corn Market.

Mr. Jarvis thanked him, and rose to take his leave ; but as Magendie had just ordered his carriage and horses, the Consul thinking it very dangerous for him to go unattended, said, —

" You surely will not go to the arsenal without an escort ? Are you aware that it is rumored there will be a rising to-day among the populace ? "

" Ah, les coquins ! they will not dare to raise an insurrection," he answered with great vivacity, and in the most unconcerned manner.

" But you know most of your troops have left the city ; it might be quite a serious affair."

" Ah ! I don't care for them. I have duties at the arsenal that must be attended to. I have no fear of them."

Mr. Jarvis had always considered Magendie a man of courage, but this seemed to him so reckless, that he half suspected it was said for effect ; therefore, prompted by curiosity, he took another street, and entered the square about the arsenal at nearly the same time Magendie did. He was alighting from his carriage with perfect ease and unconcern, and the men were presenting arms, Magendie relaxing not a whit of the usual military discipline and etiquette. Mr. Jarvis, now perfectly satisfied that he was a brave man, and admiring his cool self-possession, turned his horse toward the corn market, where the certificate was accepted.

He afterwards supplied the English with 150 barrels of flour.

" When Wellington landed in Figueira at the mouth of the Mondego, he was joined by General

Spencer with 5,000 men, making his force 13,000 effective men, beside an army of Portuguese and Spanish insurgents, and marched toward Lisbon. Junot, having about 9,200 men, went out to meet him. On the 21st August the battle of Vimeira was fought, which was disastrous for the French.

" Had the Admiral of the Russian squadron, consisting of eight vessels of war, then anchored in the harbor, coöperated with Junot, he might have held Lisbon. The Admiral at first promised to do so, and then dishonorably broke his pledge to his ally (from whom he had received many favors). Added to this disaster, there were rumors of a secret insurrection against the French among the Portuguese, and Junot was obliged to capitulate." [1] Sir Hugh Dalrymple arriving, took command, and made the Convention of Cintra. The terms were most favorable for the French, who were to have sixty days to remove their troops and baggage to France, and were then to be again free to serve in the French army.

[1] See *Memoirs of the Duchess of Abrantes.*

CHAPTER XXIV.

HIS MARRIAGE.

MR. JARVIS had been so highly prospered in business, that he began to think of a union with Miss
1806- Mary Pepperrell Sparhawk, the young lady
1809. to whom he was engaged before his misfortunes. He had his own peculiar views on this subject, and had always resolved that he would not marry until he could provide for a wife all the comforts and elegances of life, to which she had been accustomed. In the summer of 1806 he renewed his suit in a frank and manly declaration of his continued preference, and an offer of his hand and heart, hoping she was disengaged. Ten years had now elapsed since the storms of adversity had separated them; but she had remained constant to her first and only attachment. She was too lovely and accomplished not to have been sought in marriage, but she had steadily refused every proposal. With the entire approbation of her friends, she accepted his offer in the simplicity of confiding affection. He was greatly rejoiced to find that her sentiments toward him were unchanged, and that she was willing to commit her happiness to his keeping; but new difficulties arose, which long delayed their union.

Mr. Jarvis was so situated that he could not leave his business to come to America to be married; and her friends were unwilling to permit her to go to him.

It was several months before this obstacle could be overcome; but the pertinacity with which he urged his suit, and pleaded with her to come and make him happy, and the arguments he used with her Uncle and Aunt Bartlett, and his father and mother (the latter also her aunt), ultimately prevailed over their scruples, tenderly as she was loved by them, and carefully as they guarded her happiness.

A long correspondence on this subject ensued.

The following is an extract from one of many letters, dated —

"LISBON, *December* 22, 1806."

After mentioning previous letters that he had written, and his disappointment in not hearing from her, he says : —

"Your letters would afford me as much solace as anything could for your absence; but I am awaiting your arrival with the utmost anxiety and solicitude. I cannot think, after what I have said, any further objections will exist in your mind, at least I am certain that none ought to exist.

"I pray you, if you have any consideration for my happiness, to come as early as possible. A state of suspense is of all things most irksome, even on ordinary occasions, but how much more so is it, when the object is the nearest thing to our hearts. That I love you with all the tenderness which so much goodness and virtue must inspire, in the bosom of a man who knows your worth, and has a heart to feel it, I hope you will not doubt. . . . . . I long for the indissoluble knot to be tied; I long for the right to call you *my wife*, —

that endearing name, — since you have consented to be mine. I long in fine for the sweet content which your sense, your benevolence, and virtues must secure to me. Then, my dear Mary, let me again beseech you not to delay longer." . . . .

That there was a long series of obstacles, this extract shows : —

"LISBON, *May* 22, 1807.

"After toiling all day and all the evening, I am commencing at a quarter before ten at night, to write a few lines to say that could I be gratified by your society, neither toils, vexations, nor any other circumstance would prove heavy. . . . . I am sometimes disposed to be altogether dissatisfied with my friends for not having provided you with a passage."

Nearly a year passed away before she went, for his father and her other guardians watched over her with such jealous care, that every plan Mr. Jarvis had suggested had been objected to.

Finally he sent out a vessel and arranged for his cousin, John Jarvis, to be her escort during the voyage. Her Aunt Bartlett engaged a respectable young woman for her attendant and companion. In November, 1807, she bade adieu to all the loved and loving friends who had cherished her from childhood, and accompanied by Mr. Jarvis and her attendant, set out in a stage-coach for Washington, to sail from Alexandria in the brig that was sent for her. By her journal it appears that they travelled through Connecticut, and were a week in going from Boston to New York.

The news of the sudden death of Dr. Charles

Jarvis reached her while in Washington, which was a great grief, not only for the loss she herself sustained, but from sympathy with her widowed aunt, to whom she wrote the most feeling letters, and with that only son, to whom she was to be the bearer of this afflicting intelligence. The voyage was a long and tedious one, and called forth all her fortitude and strength of mind. A sense of isolation would sometimes come over her, and nothing but her trust in God and steadfast affection could have sustained her. As they neared Lisbon, hope's rainbow visions swelled her heart with joy and thanksgiving, for O, the voyage was safely accomplished, and soon the warm welcome and tender kindness of her betrothed would make amends for all she had endured. But alas! no — unforeseen trials awaited her. The city was strictly blockaded by the English, and no vessel was permitted to enter the harbor. They were forced to put out to sea again, and steer for St. Lucar, a port in Spain near Cadiz. What a severe disappointment! Instead of receiving the immediate protection of her affianced husband, for whom she had braved the perils of the ocean, under circumstances so trying to woman's delicacy of feeling, she must depart without an interview. The wise man hath said, "Hope deferred maketh the heart sick," and to her, delicate in health, sensitive in spirit, of a retiring nature, and deeply attached to her friends, from whom she was now wholly separated, it must have been a great trial. She was now to be cast among utter strangers, in a foreign land. At San Lucar a quarantine of six weeks was imposed upon them, although the crew were perfectly healthy, and they came from a healthy port.

The following are extracts from Miss Sparhawk's letter, written on shipboard, to Mr. Jarvis : —

"SAN LUCAR, *February* 26, 1808.

"MY DEAR FRIEND : —

"I wrote you on the morning of the 23d ult., which was the morning of our arrival here, and also the day afterwards. I hope you have received one or both before this. In each of them I mentioned our having forty days' passage to this port, and also the painful event which preceded our departure from America. I wrote you immediately on receiving the intelligence, but could hear of no opportunity of sending it; though at the time and among strangers I needed the consolation and sympathy I *wished* to *impart*. . . . . The present is on every account an anxious state of suspense. . . . . I will only say there have been many moments that called for all my fortitude and resolution. . . . .

"On our arrival, Mr. Hackley encouraged me to think that in a few days I might have permission to become a resident in his family ; but to-day I have heard that if permitted to go on shore, we must take a house in the country ; but by that time, I am certain of it, I cannot but hope to see you — certainly to hear from you. Heaven grant that it may be the former.

"Since my last I have had the pleasure of reading a letter of yours to Mr. Meade, which he was kind enough to inclose to me in a note, as an assurance of your health, and he united with Mrs. Meade in offering to execute any commissions, and also in a polite invitation to visit them. With you it would be pleasant to accept their civility ; but till then, varying emotions will agitate the mind of

"Yours, with truth and affection,

"MARY P. SPARHAWK."

Through the intercession of the American Consul,

Mr. Hackley, she was allowed to take a cottage out of the city, with her attendant.

She heard several times from Mr. Jarvis, who had learned that the ship had been in the harbor of Lisbon and had proceeded to St. Lucar, as appears from his letter dated 20th February; and in one dated the 28th he speaks of requesting a passport of his Excellency, and of his impatience to join her, but unavoidable business and the sickness of his young friend, Mr. Charles Gilman, detained him.

In a long letter to Mr. Madison, he explains the situation of his betrothed, and says that he is extremely anxious to go for her, and is assured that Mr. M. will enter into his feelings, sympathize with a lady under such trying circumstances, and will approve of his absenting himself from his official duties, in such a cause, for a few days.

She submitted with patient endurance to this trying situation. At last he wrote as follows : —

"LISBON, 5th *March*, 1808.

"To-day, my dear Mary, I set away. My detention, which has been unavoidable, has caused me infinite pain. . . .

"I am determined to proceed to where you are, although I now do it under many disadvantages, and considerable hazard to my affairs, from the sickness of Mr. Gilman.[1] . . . .

"You, my lovely Mary, and my beloved father, and good mother, and Harriet,[2] have been the objects for whom I have toiled. The thoughts of one day being able to afford you comfort and add to your felicity, has lightened every toil, and almost endeared labor, hardship, and hazard.

---

[1] Charles F. Gilman, who died a few months later.
[2] An adopted niece of his step-mother.

17

Yes, I repeat it, I have lived more for my friends than for myself. I loved them, wished their happiness, and have linked my own entirely to theirs. . . . .

"In losing our father, we have lost much; but in our endeavors to do what his life has been devoted to, — the happiness of his friends, — we must try to lighten the sense of his loss, although never a tender remembrance of his virtues." . . . .

Mr. and Mrs. Hackley manifested the utmost kindness, courtesy, and sympathy for her, and at the end of a fortnight they succeeded in obtaining permission for her removal to their pleasant home. In this delightful family she was welcomed with cordial hospitality, and no pains were spared to make her happy.

Mrs. Hackley was a Randolph of Virginia. She was a superior woman; dignified, elegant, and intellectual, at the same time abounding in all womanly virtues. Miss Sparhawk was very lovely in mind and person: graceful, slender, with blue eyes and a fair complexion, high intellectual forehead, very long, fine, brown hair; amiable and pleasing manners, great sweetness of disposition, and a highly cultivated mind. She was very fond of children, and it is not surprising that she won the affection of parents and children, and soon became a great favorite with them.

Mr. Jarvis was obliged to go to St. Lucar by land, and the journey was performed on mules. The meeting between these long separated lovers must have been intensely interesting and affecting, and can be better imagined than described. Mr. Hackley, as American Consul, solemnized the marriage.

The eldest daughter, a child of ten years old, afterwards Mrs. Glass, related in after life that she had become so fond of Miss Sparhawk, that when Mr. Jarvis arrived, she was inconsolable, and said she did not like that Mr. Jarvis, who had come to take away her " beautiful Miss Sparhawk." To reconcile her, he begged her parents to let her go to Lisbon, and make them a long visit, which she did, passing some months with them. He also extended the invitation to Mr. and Mrs. Hackley, and a warm friendship subsisted between the families during his residence in Lisbon.

Mr. and Mrs. Jarvis, her companion,[1] Mr. John Jarvis, and the guide, went to Lisbon, mounted on mules, which was a tedious mode of travelling for a lady; but they reached that city in safety, and the bride was welcomed to a commodious house, provided with all that Mr. Jarvis could devise for her comfort and gratification.

In compliance with the laws of Portugal, on their arrival in Lisbon they were again married by a Catholic priest, and the ceremony was performed a third time by a Protestant clergyman, in conformity to the wishes of Mrs. Jarvis, who was a member of the Congregational Church. Three wedding-rings attested to the triple marriage.

Several of the merchants' ladies, and some of those of the Corps Diplomatique, called upon Mrs. Jarvis. Among the former was Mrs. O'Niele, a refined and cultivated woman, who became a warm friend, and was very kind and attentive to her. Mrs. O'Niele's father was a Swedish merchant, who married a noble

---

[1] She soon returned to America, being very homesick.

Portuguese lady.   Mr. O'Niele entered into partnership with the father, and married the daughter.   He
was vice-consul at St. Ubes under Mr. Jarvis, but
resided at Lisbon.   Mr. and Mrs. Jarvis were invited
to several splendid entertainments, one especially so,
given by General Junot.

It was universally the style for ladies to wear jewels,
and the Consul selected for his wife an elegant set of
topaz and pearls, consisting of a crescent, two stars,
ear-rings, with long topaz pendants, surrounded with
pearls, a superb necklace and bracelets, and a shell
comb, inlaid with topaz and pearls.   Some of the pearls
were very large, and the Brazilian topazes of uncommon size and brilliancy.[1]   Her dress was simple, in the
prevailing French style : an India muslin, gored very
much, over white satin, with a long train.[2]

But Mrs. Jarvis cared little for dress or the gay
world.   The affection of her husband and intimate
friends, books and home, were the jewels her loving
and intellectual spirit most prized.

She had a master to give her lessons in Portuguese,
and soon acquired sufficient knowledge of the language to enable her to converse with ease.

[1] Now in the possession of Mrs. Cutts, and of her sister Elizabeth's
daughter, Mrs. Mary W. Smith.

[2] A description of her dress at Junot's ball, — as a picture of the
costume of that period, — may be interesting to ladies: The skirt of the
dress was very narrow at top; wide, heavy embroidery passed down the
front breadth and round the train, which was a yard long. The sleeves
and waist were also embroidered, and very short and full, the latter not
over three inches long, and very low in the neck. Her long, fine hair was
arranged in braids, a Grecian coil, and curled in short ringlets about the
face. The crescent was worn on the top of the head, and the stars and
comb supported the braids. The white satin round-toed slippers had no
heels.

The Consul took much pleasure in showing objects of interest in Lisbon to his bride. Among these was the Church of St. Roque, which formerly belonged to the Jesuits, built of stone, the exterior plain, but magnificent within. Mrs. Jarvis has given a fine description of it in her journal. " The walls and ceilings exhibit some good pictures in fresco. A small chapel, dedicated to St. John the Baptist, is the most valuable for its size perhaps in Europe. Among the materials with which it is decorated are lapis lazuli, oriental granite, porphyry, amethyst, alabaster, verd-antique, coral, and Carrara marbles. The floor is of mosaic, with a centre ornament and border. The columns and front of the altar are of lapis lazuli ; the table of the altar is supported at the angles by cherubs of silver, and accompanied by two lofty candelabras of the same metal. The shafts of the columns are formed into striæ by fillets of gold." [1]

But the pictures by the best masters were most worthy of admiration. A head of the Virgin Mary, by Raphael, was especially beautiful, combining in a wonderful degree the expression of the mother's grief for the death of her son, with her hope and faith in his resurrection unto glory. Three splendid pictures, executed in mosaic, designed by Raphael, and second only to those in the Vatican, were masterpieces of art. One, over the altar, represented the baptism of our Saviour by John, who stands in the water, his feet seen distinctly beneath the ripples. Jesus has just arisen from the water, which is dripping from his hair and person, while a glory from the heavens is resting

Murphy's *Portugal.*

upon him. The whole scene — the heaven-illumined countenance of the " Beloved Son," the noble figure of John, the brilliancy of the water, sparkling as in sunshine, with precious stones, were executed with a truthfulness to nature truly astonishing.

On one side of the altar is the " Descent of the Holy Ghost " ; on the other is the " Annunciation." In the latter, Mary — meek, lovely, graceful — kneels with bowed head before the angel, receiving the announcement of the birth of Jesus. The angel's face was seraphic. The blue eyes, expressive of celestial sweetness, were formed of gems, and had the bright and lustrous appearance of living eyes.

" They were executed at Rome by the most eminent artists of that city, at the desire of King John V., who presented them to the Jesuits of St. Roque in 1751."

It was by especial favor of the Pope that " his most faithful majesty " the King of Portugal, was allowed to possess them.

The lowest estimate of the expense of these precious works of art was two millions of crusades.

The robes of the Archbishop, which were kept in the church and exhibited by the sacristan, were of rich brocade, heavy with gold embroidery.

A gentleman from Boston, who considered himself a connoisseur in painting, requested Mr. Jarvis to show him the mosaic pictures that had been so celebrated. Mr. Jarvis took him to St. Roque's. He gazed awhile intently at the pictures, which delighted him, and then said, —

" Now show me the mosaics."

" These are mosaics."

" O no, impossible ! I cannot believe it."

Mr. Jarvis called the sacristan, and requested him to bring the steps and a torch, the light in the chapel being dim, that he might examine them more closely, and directed his attention to one corner of the " Last Supper," in which some of the stones had been loosened by the earthquake of 1755. Mr. O——— was now convinced, but his astonishment and admiration were only increased, for he said it seemed incredible that stones could be united to form so beautiful and harmonious a whole. He abstracted for a relic one of the fragments of which it was composed, which was half an inch long, and one eighth of an inch wide.

Another wonder of art, which Mr. and Mrs. Jarvis viewed with admiration, was the Aqueduct, " which may justly be considered one of the most magnificent monuments of modern Europe ; and in point of magnitude is not inferior to any aqueduct of the ancients. That part of it a mile from Lisbon is an admirable structure, consisting of thirty-five arches, by which the water is conveyed over a deep valley, formed by two opposite mountains. The height of it in the most depressed part is 263 feet ; breadth of principal arch 107 feet; breadth of the piers of the principal arch each 28 feet; thickness of the piers in general 23 feet 8 inches. The arches on each side of the principal one diminish in breadth, as the piers whereon they rest decrease in height with the declivity of the hills." [1] There are two conduits, semicircular channels, thirteen inches in diameter, through which the

[1] Murphy's *Portugal.*

water is conveyed to the city. When one is out of order the other is used, but both are never used at a time. The water, which is cool and pure, comes from the mountains of Carnassus, fifteen miles from Lisbon.

Mr. Jarvis purchased a saddle-horse for his wife soon after her arrival (for the ladies in Lisbon never walk in the streets), that she might accompany him in his rides, which they both highly enjoyed. He frequently took her to retired baths on the Tagus, a little above the city. The water being salt, was equally conducive to health as sea-bathing.

There was a singular geological phenomenon at this place: the bank rose 200 feet above the level of the river; at the height of ten feet there was a strata of shells, exactly resembling those in the bed of the river, which extended an eighth of a mile. There was a similar strata at Villa Franca, fifteen miles further up the Tagus.

In one of their rides through Buenos Ayres,[1] an elevated beautiful spot in the environs of Lisbon, they saw on a card in the window of a house, " *To Let*," in Portuguese. They alighted, and went over the house. It had been built by an Englishman, who had left the city when it was taken possession of by the French. It was so comfortable and home-like, that Mr. Jarvis hired it, and they removed there. The parlor was twenty-four feet long, with apartments at each end, intended for sleeping rooms, having an open fire-place with a grate for coal in each, which was a luxury they highly prized, after having been constrained to warm their shivering frames wrapped in their capotes, over a

---

[1] In Portuguese " Boens Aires," good air.

copper basin of lighted charcoal, as was the uniform practice in all Portuguese houses. The stable too, instead of being underneath, was at a little distance from the house, another agreeable change. Verandas on three sides commanded fine views of the noble harbor and river as far as Belem ; with the " churches, convents, castles, villas, and gardens on the northwest side of the Tagus, and the picturesque scenery on the southeast, with its lofty mountains and high, impending cliffs."

Business was now very dull, and as Mr. Jarvis rode to his office every day, he could readily transact all there was to be done.

After the unceasing care, responsibility, and toils of many years, domestic happiness was very highly appreciated by him. About a year after their removal to Boens Aires, in May, 1809, their first child was born, who became a joy to both parents. From a boy Mr. Jarvis had been fond of children, and he was very happy in having a little one of his own. When only a few months old, he often took her on his horse and carried her through several streets, then sent her back by the servant, who had accompanied him for that purpose, though the transition sometimes occasioned a loud cry of disappointment.

As a token of friendship for Mrs. Jarvis, Mrs. O'Niele sent the baby a beautiful present of a glass house, in which was a wax doll, prettily dressed, and a nice cradle.[1]

---

[1] This house was about a foot long, and was so curiously executed, that I will attempt to enlighten " the *young folks :* " The roof and all were very neatly made of pieces of glass, cut in proper proportions, bound with narrow satin ribbon, pasted on the edges, and sewed together.

In the summer of 1809 the widow of Mr. Jarvis' father, and her niece, Miss H. H. Sparhawk, came to Lisbon, in compliance with most cordial invitations from Mr. and Mrs. Jarvis, who did everything in their power to promote the comfort and happiness of their mother. The baby soon became a great favorite.

As a pleasant excursion, Mrs. Jarvis took them in a carriage to Cintra, which is about sixteen miles from Lisbon — a picturesque, lovely spot, abounding in fruits and flowers. It has since become a place of resort in summer for the nobility.

The " rock of Cintra " is a mountain over 3,000 feet high, veiled with mists in the morning, but retaining a sunset glow long after the valleys become obscure in the twilight. Oranges, grapes, musk and water melons, and vegetables are cultivated in the greatest abundance in the valley of Cellares, near the village of Cintra, supplying in a great measure the markets of Lisbon.

One of the curiosities of this place is a convent or hermitage, built by monks of the Order of St. Francis, with twenty cells. It is dug out of the rocks, partly subterranean, partly above ground, and lined with layers of cork, from the bark of the cork oak, to keep it dry, from which it derives its name. These hermits live chiefly on fish, bread, and fruits, and are very strict in their rules.

There is a palace here, built by King Alfonso; a curious Moorish bath, always full of pure water ; and there are also several villas. " That great Christian hero of the sixteenth century, Don John de Castro, built a villa here, with beautiful gardens, which for diversity of prospect, surpasses any in the kingdom. The country on every side presents a wild assemblage of striking scenes : mountains and valleys interspersed with rock, wood, and water; little temples and grottoes are constructed in many parts of the gardens, the former furnished with altars, where Don John used often to pray, — a duty which he strictly observed whether in peace or war, for he justly considered that piety is not incompatible with true courage." [1]

In the autumn of 1809, an increase of business requiring the Consul to be nearer his office, he returned to the house near the Quintilla Palace, the warehouse of which he had retained while at Boens Aires. This was the most spacious and elegant residence that he occupied. Here he received his bride, and here they remained until they left Lisbon. The stucco ornaments of the ceiling in the " sala," or drawing-room, were very elegant, and it was handsomely painted in fresco with scenes from the heathen mythology.

A Russian ship-of-the-line had been anchored in Aldea Galego,[2] directly opposite Mr. Jarvis' residence at Boens Aires, which, being 200 feet above the Tagus, made the view a very commanding one. He was one night awakened about midnight by a bright light shining into his windows, which were glass doors, opening with hinges on the veranda. He started up and looked out. The Russian ship was on fire. He awoke his wife, and they gazed long at the magnificent spectacle. The cannon went off with a deep,

---

[1] Murphy's *Portugal.*
[2] The river widens into this bay just above Lisbon.

heavy booming; the fire burst out at the port-holes, ran up the masts, and then all over the deck; finally the cable burned off, and she drifted down the river, greatly endangering the British shipping. Boats were sent out, and she was stopped at Julien's Castle.[1]

This ship had been used by the French as a hospital, but there were then only a few Russians on board. It was supposed that it was set on fire by the English, for fear the French should take possession of her, though *they reported* that it took fire accidentally.

Mr. Jefferson and Mr. Madison sent to the Consul for two barrels of pure Lisbon wine, without brandy. He went to a wine merchant, and found this could only be obtained at a vintner's, twenty miles out of the city, where the wine was made. He purchased it and made a present of it to the President and Mr. Madison, who were very much gratified by the attention, and wrote very cordial and appreciative letters.

Mr. Madison in return presented the Consul with ten gallons of fine peach brandy, made on his plantation, which was ten years old, begging him to accept it as a gift from Mrs. Madison. He sent two gallons of this choice "liqueur" to the Nuncio, Mons. Galeppi, who was greatly pleased with it, and said it was one of the most highly flavored and richest cordials that he ever tasted.

The Consul also presented two gallons to Don

---

[1] The British had possession of Fort Bougie and St. Julien's Castle, — strong defenses built of stone on each side, at the mouth of the river. Junot's troops occupied Belem Castle while he was in Lisbon, which is four miles from that city and about the same distance from St. Julien's Castle.

Araujo. The following is his note of acknowledgment : —

" Don Araujo has the honor to present his best compliments to Mr. W. Jarvis; and it is with the utmost gratitude he accepts of the delicious peach brandy Mr. Jarvis was so good as to gratify him with, and the more so, as it is acknowledged as a mark of his benevolence and friendship.

" BELEM, *August* 15, 1807."

CHAPTER XXV.

MERINO SHEEP.

SPAIN probably contained the largest number of fine wooled sheep in the world, at the time of its 1809-1810. invasion by the French, the number being computed at six millions.

" Merino " means beyond sea; and it is supposed that they may have been introduced into Greece from Colchis, classic writers having celebrated its " golden fleece."

The conquering arms of the Romans probably transplanted them to Rome, and then to Spain, in their march of conquest.

This country, with its mountains and valleys and temperate climate, was peculiarly well adapted to the growth of sheep; and it was said they had been protected and cherished by the Spanish government for more than a thousand years.

The Moors had large flocks in the south of Spain, which, for a long period, were objects of their especial care.[1]

" The fine wooled sheep are divided into two classes: the transhumantes, or travelling sheep, and the estantes, or stationary sheep. The wool of the transhumantes is very

---

[1] Some have thought that these sheep were first introduced/ by the Moors.

much superior to that of the estantes, owing, undoubtedly, to the superior care and attention which is given to them. The transhumantes are owned in flocks from 5,000 to 30,000; the larger flocks are placed under the superintendence of a mayoral, who has the whole control over the flock, and annually accounts with the owner for the net income. Two shepherds, four dogs, and a pack-horse or mule are employed for every thousand sheep. The travelling sheep are divided into three classes, which take their names from the provinces where they are principally kept: namely, the Leonesa, which are by far the most numerous, and are universally esteemed the finest sheep in Spain; the Segovian, which are considered the next best, and the Sorian, which are deemed a little inferior to the latter.[1] The Leonesa are pastured in the summer on the mountains and hilly country of Leon and the two Castiles; and in the fall are driven into the plains of Spanish Estremadura to be pastured through the winter. Many of these flocks are driven two hundred miles from the summer to the winter pasture, and *vice versa*.

"The plains of Estremadura are subjected to an almost invariable drought from the latter part of April to the autumnal equinox. The rains commence about the 21st September, and continue to fall every two or three days in very heavy showers, till the latter part of March, when they gradually cease. In six or seven weeks after the first rain, from an apparently arid waste, these plains are covered with a beautiful coat of verdure, and so continue till April, as Fahrenheit's thermometer rarely falls below 40° at sunrise. In the mountainous regions, they have occasionally refreshing rains in the summer, which keep the pastures fresh and good."[2]

---

[1] The Consul never saw any of the two last classes.
[2] Extracts from a letter to L. D. Gregory, Esq., from Mr. Jarvis, January 31, 1844.

The flocks usually migrate in April to Castile and Leon, from the plains of Estremadura, and return in October. A road, four miles wide, is provided by law to furnish pasturage on the journey, the autumn rains causing the grass to grow luxuriantly, ere the sheep return to their winter quarters. The boundaries of the pastures are known to each shepherd, and are marked by stones. If a dog sees a sheep straying from its pasture, he walks leisurely along, heads the sheep, and makes him return to his flock. These "shepherd dogs," as they are called, are large, powerful animals, resembling the St. Bernard dogs, capable of seizing and mastering a wolf, to which the sheep are exposed in the mountains. The sagacity of these noble animals is truly astonishing.

The proprietors of the flocks always own lands in the mountains and in the plains, sufficient for both their summer and winter pastures. They are sheared in May, and the wool is sent to St. Andero and Bilboa for sale — the two nearest sea-ports to their summer pastures.

No one is allowed to export sheep out of the kingdom, under penalty of death.

In 1801 or 1802, Mr. Jefferson appointed Chancellor Livingston Minister to France, and he obtained from the Rambouillet flock three or four merinos, which he sent to New York, and put on one of his farms. This flock was obtained by the King of France from the King of Spain, and were undoubtedly pure blooded sheep when brought from Spain.

Colonel David Humphreys[1] had been Minister

---

[1] Colonel Humphreys was born near New Haven, Connecticut; was a

Plenipotentiary at the Court of Madrid since 1797, and was recalled by Mr. Jefferson in 1802. When about to leave the Court, the customary present of a certain number of bars of silver was offered to him, which he declined, duly acknowledging the high honor conferred upon him, it being contrary to the regulations of the United States ; but afterwards intimated that for the benefit of his country, he would accept some merino sheep. He was informed, that being against the laws of Spain, no order could be signed to that effect, but doubtless he might obtain some himself, and no notice would be taken of it.

Colonel Humphreys says : —

" I succeeded in getting a person of the most respectable character to deliver to me at Lisbon one hundred ; composed of seventy-five ewes and twenty-five rams, pure merinos, from one to two years old. They were conducted with proper passports across the country of Portugal by three Spanish shepherds, and escorted by a small guard of Portuguese soldiers. On the 10th April, 1802, they were embarked, and after a voyage of fifty days, twenty-one rams and seventy ewes were landed in Derby, Connecticut (nine having died on the passage), and were sent to my farm." [1]

The whole of the latter he retained in one flock, but

Colonel in the Revolutionary War; became aid to General Washington, and was a member of his family. Washington, when President, appointed him Minister to Lisbon, in 1790, where he married the second daughter of Mr. Bulkeley, the richest British merchant in. that city. In 1797, President J. Adams appointed him Minister Plenipotentiary to the Court of Madrid, and Hon. William Smith superseded him in Portugal. Both were recalled by Mr. Jefferson, and Mr. Jarvis succeeded Mr. Smith as Chargé d'Affaires in Lisbon, really acting as Minister. Charles Pinckney, Esq., of South Carolina, was appointed Minister Plenipotentiary to Spain.

[1] See *The Miscellaneous Works of Colonel D. Humphreys*, page 349, published in 1804.

18

a portion of the former were sold to farmers for the improvement of their stock. This was the first export to America.

When Mr. Jarvis heard that Mr. Humphreys had obtained these sheep, he was very desirous to procure some, and wrote to his correspondent in Spain to that effect, but in reply was informed that it was impossible. He possessed great facilities for acquiring information regarding Spanish affairs, and from his keen observation of events, availed himself of the first opportunity to obtain merinos, convinced that the introduction of this fine wooled breed into the United States would greatly increase her prosperity. Spain was in a most distracted state from civil dissensions and foreign aggression, at the time of Napoleon's first invasion, which, as Mr. Jarvis was informed, would enable him to purchase some of their jealously guarded flocks. He wrote to his friend, George W. Erving, Esq.; then Minister at Madrid, as follows : —

"LISBON, 13*th September*, 1809.

. . . [After speaking of the French invasion, he says] : —

" I have been informed that it is not now very difficult to obtain merino sheep for exportation. If it is not, I am sure that your patriotism will induce you to use your endeavors to obtain me one hundred, principally rams. The cost and expenses within any reasonable bounds, I should not mind. I should wish them shipped to Messrs. Cornelius Coolidge & Co., of Boston. They ought to be sent between decks, in a double-decked vessel, in small pens, with a shepherd or two, and a couple of extra sailors, careful, sober men, to take care of them. Plenty of forage, barley, and water, ought to be supplied for them. Be satisfied of their being true merino.

> " With entire respect, etc., etc., etc.,
>
> " WILLIAM JARVIS."

Through the intervention of Mr. Erving, in December, 1809, he purchased two hundred of the royal Escurial flock, by special favor. Sir Charles Stewart, of England, also bought two hundred, which were all that were sold of this flock. Consequently all the Escurials that ever came to the United States were these two hundred, sent by Mr. Jarvis.

His first shipment consisted of twelve sheep, which he instructed the merchant to whom they were consigned, not to sell for less than $150 a piece. When he received the letter inclosing an account of their sale, he was very busy, transacting business for several persons in his office, and glancing it hastily over, read that one sheep died on the passage, and the eleven sold for $1,500. He was much disappointed, and threw the letter into a drawer. When at leisure, on reperusal, he found that they had sold for ($15,000) fifteen thousand, to his great surprise and pleasure, which was far beyond his utmost expectation. This was one of the highest sales.

Twelve more of these sheep were sent to J. H. Hooe, a merchant at Alexandria, with directions to present a pair to ex-President Jefferson, and a pair to President Madison, and to sell the remainder, which orders were executed. Mr. Hooe writes: —

> " Chief Justice Cranch and Dr. Thornton, of Washington, bought three rams: one was sold to J. Threlkeld, Esq., for General Mason, of Analostan Island and himself one

to General Thompson Mason, of Virginia; one to Mr. Philips, of Delaware, and one I bought." [1]

Mr. Jefferson's went to Monticello ; Mr. Madison's to his residence at Montpelier ; they were thus spread through Virginia. Mr. Jarvis' idea was to have them distributed throughout the United States. This tribute of respect was very gratifying to Mr. Jefferson and Mr. Madison.

On Napoleon's second invasion, when his army under Joseph Bonaparte advanced toward Madrid, the Junta [2] fled to Badajos, and their finances being exhausted, it was suggested to this assembly that they might sell some of their confiscated sheep, which were feeding in thousands on the plains of Estremadura. They resorted to this measure. Mr. Jarvis was informed that a sale was to take place, by his correspondent, Don Juan Pablo Soler, a highly respectable merchant of Badajos, in June, 1810, and hastened to improve the opportunity.

Colonel John Downie, British Commissary-general, and a colonel in the Spanish army, possessed great advantages for the selection of sheep, being high in favor with the Junta. Four thousand of the Paular flock were bought and sent to England for the king ; and Colonel Downie and Mr. Jarvis purchased, in company, the rest, between three and four thousand. Of these, Mr. Jarvis took fourteen hundred, and Colonel Downie the remainder, which he sent to Scotland,

---

[1] A certificate, signed by Celestino de Cordova, dated 28th December, 1809, is preserved, stating these sheep to be " fine wooled trashumante merino, of the best caste of Spain."

[2] Junta — High Council of State.

his native country, with the exception of two or three hundred sold to come to the United States. This being the first sale, Mr. Jarvis must have had a better opportunity to obtain the " true trashumante merino sheep " from the best flocks, than any other American, and his sheep were undoubtedly the best sent to the United States.

They were bought of the Junta upon the express condition of their granting licenses to carry them out of the kingdom.

Certificate and Passport from the Secretary of the Junta.[1]

" I, Don Fermin Coronado, Honorary Paymaster of the Army, General of the Masterships of Military Orders, Rents, and Confiscation, *Secretary to the Governmental Junta* of the Province of Estremadura, in the Department of Real Estate, and its Commission of Subsistence, and the direction of Cabanas, etc., etc., etc. —

" Do hereby certify that the said Governmental Junta, by its decree of the 24th of the present month, has sold to Col. John Downie, Commissary of the British Army, two thousand eight hundred and fifteen ewes, eleven hundred and thirty males (3,945 in all) ; eighteen dogs, five shepherd ponies, and five mess kettles, all pertaining to the Cabana, confiscated from Don Manuel Godoy, called the *Paular flock*, and which are to have a free passage to Lisbon, or any other convenient port. And at the request of the said Commissary, I give this certificate at the city of Badajos, on the 25th of June, 1810.

" FERMIN CORONADO."

---

[1] General J. W. Phelps, the able Vermont officer, a scholar and a gentleman, has most obligingly translated these certificates from the Spanish.

"I, Don Pasqual Tenorio y Moscoso, Brigadier-general
of the Army, Pensioned Knight of the Royal and Distinguished Order of Carlos III., etc., etc., Groom of the Bed-
chamber to our Lord the King, Don Fernando VII., Consul
and General Agent of Commercial Affairs of Spain and
Portugal, and its dominions, etc., etc., certify that the fore-
going is the copy of a true, authentic, and original certificate, which has been exhibited to me by Colonel John
Downie, and with which it conforms. In evidence of which
I give this certificate, sealed with the royal seal of this
Consulate-general at Lisbon, this 12th day of July, 1810.

[Seal]   "PASQUAL TENORIO Y MOSCOSO."

*Passport from the Marquis of Romana, Captain-General of
the Spanish Armies.*

"I, Don Pedro Caro, y Sureda, Maza de Lisana, Cornel,
Luna de Aragon, Fontes, Carillo de Albornos, Roca, y Ruis,
Valero, Fortuny Togores, etc., etc., *Marquis of Romano*,
Visconde de Banaesa, Baron and Señor de las Villás de
Moxente, Novelda, y Castillo de la Mola, Casa y Estados de
Maza, of the kingdom of Valencia, Señor of the Cavallerias
of Lloro, and San Juan de Sonorrosa in the Island of Mal-
lorca, Grandee of Spain, Knight of the Grand Cross of the
distinguished Spanish Royal Order of Carlos III., Coun-
cilor of State to his Majesty, General of Engineers of the
Army of Fortifications and Frontiers, Perpetual Member
of the Supreme Council of War, Captain-general of the
Royal Armies, and of the Provinces of Old Castile, and of
the Kingdom of Leon, General-in-Chief of the Operations
of the Left, and President of the Royal Chancellors of Val-
ladolid, etc., etc., etc., [1]

"Do hereby grant a safe passport to Cipriano Garcia

[1] It is customary with the Spanish grandees thus to enumerate their
titles.

Elias, to take to Lisbon a flock from the sheep-farm del Paular, confiscated from Don Manuel Godoy, and sold by the Junta of this Province to the English Commissary-general, Don Juan Downie. The military and civil authorities along his route will put no hindrance in his way ; he is accompanied by four shepherds.

"All civil officers, therefore, subject to my jurisdiction, are directed — and all others are urgently requested — not to allow any impediment to his journey, but to give him all necessary assistance, in accordance with the royal service. Given at head-quarters, Badajos, the 25th day of June, 1810.

{ On the left of his name is engraved the royal arms of Spain, which is surmounted by a crown, and supported by cannon. }   " ROMANA."

Certificate of the Mayoral, Don José Alvarez y Suares.

" I, Don José Alvarez y Suares, Mayoral of the fine trashumante Leonesa Cabana, called the Paular, certify, that for ten years previous to the sale of this flock, I was its assistant mayoral, during which time it belonged to the Carthusian order, del Paular; that in the year 1796 it was sold by the said Carthusian order to Don Manuel de Godoy, Prince of Peace, in which year I entered upon the sole charge of it, and so remained for fourteen years, making in all twenty-four years, previous to the confiscation by the government of the property of the said Godoy, that I have had charge of it; and during all this time there has been no mixture of any other cabana with this; and that at this date, there has been sold by the Governmental Junta of the Province of Estremadura to John Downie, Colonel of the Royal Armies of Spain, and Commissary-general of the British Army, two thousand eight hundred and fifteen ewes, and eleven hundred and thirty-two males (in all 3,947), all

of the best quality and condition, from the said flock, this
cabana being the choicest and best of the kingdom, and its
wool being held in the highest estimation in foreign countries.
In evidence of which I give this certificate, at the good
Castle of Piedra, where the flock has been delivered, this
27th day of June, 1810.

"JOSE ALVAREZ Y SUARES."

" I also certify, that as mayoral of this cabana, I have
accompanied it to Lisbon, in accordance with directions from
the Junta of Estremadura; and in my presence, Colonel
Downie has delivered to Don Guillermo Jarvis, the number
of seven hundred and fifty ewes, and two hundred and fifty
males, making in all one thousand head of the same cabana
del Paular; and in truth of which I hereunto set my hand,
at the city of Lisbon, this 10th July, 1810.

"JOSE ALVAREZ Y SUARES."

Colonel Downie's Certificate.

" I do hereby certify upon honor that the one thousand
merino sheep stated in the annexed certificate, and which I
have this day sold to William Jarvis, Esq., American Consul
and Chargé at this Court of Lisbon, are the same sheep that
were placed at my disposition by the Supreme Junta of
Estremadura, and as well by the sacred assurance of the
said Junta, and that of his Excellency the Marquis of Romana (as is also stated in their passport, dated 24th June
last past, and that of the Secretary of the Junta), these
sheep are all really and *bona fide* of the breed of Paular, of
the cabana of the Prince of Peace, which are the most
valued in Spain.   Given under my hand and seal, at Lisbon, 10th July, 1810.

[Seal]

" JOHN DOWNIE,
" *Colonel Spanish Service, and*
"*Ex. N. Comy. General, British.*"

Certificate from the Spanish Consul at Lisbon.

" I, Don Pasqual Tenorio y Moscoso, Brigadier-general
of the Army, etc., etc., etc., Consul and General Agent of
Commercial Affairs of Spain in Portugal and its dominions,
etc., etc., do hereby certify that the preceding signature of
Don José Alvarez y Suares, is his own true signature, and
that he is a person of probity, who is entirely worthy of
credit in his statements, both judicial and extra-judicial, and
the signature of Colonel John Downie is also legitimate
and true, who, as a person of character and standing, is
worthy of credit. In evidence of which I hereto affix the
seal of this royal Consulate-general in Lisbon, this 12th
day of July, 1810.

[Seal] " PASQUAL TENORIO Y MOSCOSO."

The whole of the Paular cabana was driven to
Lisbon, and shipped from that city.

*Extract from a Letter of Instructions from Mr. Jarvis to H.
H. Green, an intelligent clerk in his counting-house, whom
he sent to take charge of the sheep on the journey, official
business requiring his presence in Lisbon.*

" Two men will leave here to-day to assist in conducting
the sheep from Spain to Lisbon. . . . . If the weather is
hot, order the men particularly only to drive them nights
and mornings, and allow them occasionally to drink, but
only temperately.

" If the feed on the road is bad, let them purchase straw
or fenno to feed them. They had better be divided into
two flocks. . . . . Should the danger from the armies be
great, drive faster, and always in by-roads, such as are
most difficult to cavalry. The Portuguese gazettes mention
that a considerable force has lately appeared in the neighborhood of Badajos. Should there be any of the enemy

stationed near there, the sheep had better be got out of
Spain in small parcels, say two hundred and fifty on one
road, and two hundred and fifty by another, the same day,
and the same number the next day, by different roads.
Engage as many pastores [1] as are necessary, and it is
hardly necessary to stand about a little more or less wages.
Tell Manoel he shall have from five to eight moidores [2]
extra, if the sheep come on in good order. We pray you
make all the dispatch possible.

"With respect, we remain, dear sir,

"Your most obedient servants,

"WILLIAM JARVIS & CO." [3]

"LISBON, 27th June, 1810."

The sheep were unmolested, and reached Lisbon in
safety.

Mr. Jarvis had read in a treatise on sheep that wool
was finer if they were kept short of food. When the
mayoral, Don José Alvarez y Suares, arrived, he expressed this idea to him, who said, with astonishment, —

"Sir, I have been mayoral twenty-four years, and
my father and grandfather were mayorals, each as
many or more years, and it is always found that sheep
do well on good feed, and very badly if half starved."

This was conclusive testimony.

Before the Paulars were exported from Lisbon,
Mr. Jarvis purchased four hundred more of Colonel
Downie.

The four first flocks in Spain which were sold by
the Junta were the PAULARS, AGUIRRES, NEGRETES,
and MONTARCOS.

---

[1] Pastores — shepherds.   [2] A gold coin worth six dollars.

[3] Mr. Jarvis was still in partnership with Messrs. Nicholas and Daniel
Gilman, in his commercial business.

" The Paulars were undoubtedly one of the handsomest flocks of Spain. The wool was close and compact, soft and silky, and the surface not so much covered with gum." [1]

This cabana was originally owned by the Carthusian friars of Paular, on the borders of Andalusia. These friars were an agricultural people, something like our Shakers, in their thrift and husbandry, who had paid great attention to horses and sheep. Their Andalusian horses were justly celebrated, for they had preserved in purity of blood the Arab breed, left by the Moors. After matins, the novitiates for the priesthood were required to devote the day to the superintendence of the laborers on the land, and the shepherds. They were the best agriculturists of Spain. The friars sold their cabana to Godoy, the Prince of Peace, when he came into power,[2] and when he was banished to Italy, this flock was confiscated by the Supreme Junta.

The *Aguirres* cabana, which had been owned by the Count of the same name, and was confiscated in consequence of his joining the French, had originally belonged to the Moors in Spain, and at their expulsion, was bought by the family of Aguirres. The wool in

---

[1] Extract from a letter from Mr. Jarvis to L. D. Gregory, Esq.

[2] Don Manuel de Godoy was the unprincipled favorite of King Charles IV. and his queen. By his handsome person, talents for music, and yet more by his intrigues, he rose so high in their favor that they bestowed upon him the highest titles and an enormous income, which, combined with his bad management of the public affairs, caused great disaffection among the nobility, and opened the way for the dominion of Napoleon. The title of "Prince of Peace" was given him in consequence of an alliance he pretended to make with the French in 1795.

England was known as the Muros flock, and was highly esteemed.[1]

These sheep had more wool about their faces and legs than either of the other flocks; the wool was more crimped than the Paulars, and less than the Negretes, and it was thick and soft; they were short-legged, round and broad bodied, with loose skins.

The *Negretes* were the tallest merinos in Spain, but were not handsomely formed; the wool was somewhat shorter than the Paular, and more loose, and inclined to double; and many of them were wooled on the face, and on the legs, down to their hoofs. All the loose-skinned sheep had large dewlaps.[2] The Negretes were previously owned by the Conde del Campo de Alange, who joined the French, and his flock also was confiscated. The bucks of these three flocks had large horns.

The *Montarcos*, which had been owned by the Count of Montarco, who also joined the French, bore considerable resemblance to the Escurials. These four flocks were moderately gummed. The *Guadaloupe* flock were rather larger in bone than the two preceding; about the same height, but not quite so handsomely formed. Their wool was thick and crimped; skins loose and doubling; faces and legs not materially different from the two latter flocks; but they were generally more gummed than either of the others.

The *Escurial* flock had formerly belonged to the

---

[1] One of the certificates states that "they were once the Imperial cabana of Charles V."

[2] This was not considered desirable in Spain, nor was it considered so by Mr. Jarvis.

crown, but when Philip II. built the Escurial Palace, he gave them as a source of revenue to the friars, whom he placed in a convent that was attached to the palace. They were about as tall as the Paulars, but rather more slight in their make; their wool was crimped, but not quite so thick as the Paular; nor were their skins so loose as the Negretes and Aguirres, nor had they so much wool on the face and legs.

Mr. Jarvis had thirty of the Negretes of the mayoral, and one hundred of Sir Charles Stewart, who purchased the entire flock, and sent the remainder to England. They were shipped from Lisbon.

Mr. Jarvis purchased 1,700 of the Aguirres flock, and the remainder was sold and sent to England. The Montarco flock was bought by a Spaniard and Portuguese, and about 2,700 were shipped to this country. Mr. Jarvis purchased about two hundred of them.

The following are some of the certificates; several have been lost.

The Montarcos.

" CONSULATE OF SPAIN, IN LISBON.

"I, Don Pasqual Tenorio y Moscoso, Brigadier-general of the Royal Army, etc., etc. (here follows the long list of titles), do hereby certify that Don Juan Pablo Soler, a subject of his Catholic Majesty, and a mer...ant of Badajos, residing in this city, has exhibited to me an original certificate, given and signed by Don Fermin Coronado, Honorary Paymaster of the Army, etc., etc., etc., Secretary of the Junta, etc., etc., etc., dated at Badajos on the 10th August, by which it appears that the said Junta did sell to Don Joaquin Guerra of Yelves, 6,023 fine wool trashumante sheep, from the confiscated flock of the Count Montarco, whose flock is among the best of Spain, its wool always having been held in high estimation in all markets, both domestic and foreign. And at the foot of the said document there is an indorsement of the following tenor and effect, namely : —

" ' I hereby declare that I have sold to Señor Don Juan Pablo Soler y Escardo, a part of the above-mentioned flock.

" ' JOSE JOAQUIN DE GUERRA.

" ' LISBON, *August 28th*, 1810.'

" Which signature I recognize to be true ; and having returned the original to the party who presented it, I give this certificate, sealed with the royal seal of this Consulate-general, and of my own coat of arms, at Lisbon, this 5th day September, 1810.

"PASQUAL TENORIO Y MOSCOSO."

Certificate of part of the Aguirres purchased by Mr. Jarvis.

" I, the undersigned, merchant of this city, certify on honor that I have sold to William Jarvis, Esq., Consul-general and Chargé d'Affaires of the United States, resident in Lisbon, six hundred and ninety-eight sheep of the true Trashumante Aguirres breed, being one of the most esteemed flocks in Spain, which said sheep were sold by the Junta of Badajos, and repurchased by me ; and that these sheep are well known by the goodness and fineness of their wool.

" JOHN FLETCHER.[1]

" ELVAS, *30th August*, 1810."

(Elvas is near Badajos.)

Mr. Jarvis purchased a thousand more Aguirres of the Junta, but there is only a *copy* of the original certificate preserved.[2]

[1] To this certificate is appended an authentication in Portuguese, with very elaborate signatures.

[2] This certificate states that the Aguirres cabana " proceeded from the Imperial cabana of Charles V." It is dated Badajos, 6th July, 1810.

He conversed with several sea-captains who had been in the habit of carrying live stock to the West Indies, and gained all the information in his power on this subject. He provided the sheep with an abundance of hay, barley, water, etc., and was careful not to put too many in one vessel, allowing them plenty of room and air, and gave the captain fifty cents, and the mate twenty-five cents, for every sheep that reached the United States in safety ; consequently he lost very few. He also employed shepherds, and bought two dogs to accompany the sheep.

Mr. Jarvis shipped to the United States fourteen hundred Paulars, seventeen hundred Aguirres, two hundred Escurials, one hundred and thirty Negretes, about two hundred Montarcos, making in all three thousand six hundred and thirty (3,630), more than all others put together ; and they were such sheep as could not have been obtained in Spain, had it not been for the invasion of the French, and the distracted state of the country resulting from that invasion.

"Of this number, about 100 were sent to Wiscasset and Portland, 1,100 to Boston and Newburyport, 1,500 to New York, 350 to Baltimore, 100 to Alexandria, and 200 to Norfolk and Richmond. Besides those which I shipped to the United States on my own account, there were about 300 Guadaloupes purchased by others, and from two to three hundred of the Paular flock sold by Colonel Downie, shipped to Boston ; and of the Montarco flock shipped by others, about 2,500 were sent to Boston, Providence, New York, Philadelphia, Baltimore, and Savannah. The Gaudaloupes, Paulars, and Montarcos, shipped to Boston by others, were for Gorham Parsons, Esq., General Sumner, Deacon Tiche-

ner, and E. H. Derby, Esq. All these sheep were shipped
in the latter part of 1809, during 1810, and early in 1811,
and were the only Leonesa trashumantes — if we include
Colonel Humphreys' and Chancellor Livingston's (which I
have no doubt were of the same stock) — that were ever
shipped to the United States. Badajos is but little over one
hundred miles from Lisbon, and all the sheep purchased
there and in that vicinity were shipped from Lisbon ; and
from my office as Consul, I was accurately acquainted with
all the shipments, as certificates of property always accompanied them." [1]

"I employed the Paular shepherds, who came with that
flock, to select three hundred sheep, which I shipped to
Newburyport. The half of these were Paulars, a fourth
Aguirres, one eighth Escurials ; the other eighth Montarcos
and Negretes. These I put on the farm in Weathersfield,
Vermont, and also had one hundred driven up, the remainder
of those I had shipped to Boston. In compliance with the
custom of Spain, I bred the respective flocks separately, till
1816 or 1817, when I mixed them together, and have so bred
my merinos ever since. In 1834 I found twenty or thirty
samples of the wool of the Paular flock that were sent me
from Spain to Lisbon, and by clipping from my sheep as many
samples, as they came to hand, I was satisfied that my flock
had improved, and ten or twelve wool-growers, who compared
them, were of the same opinion. Whether it was owing to
mixing the flocks together, or to a very careful selection of
my bucks, I cannot say ; but the fact is unquestionably so." [2]

" With the exception of eight or ten pure blood merino
ewes which I have sold within three or four years, and about

[1] Extract from Mr. Jarvis' letter to L. D. Gregory, Esq.
[2] Letter to L. D. Gregory, Esq., 1844.

fifty pure blood merino bucks, within about five years, I do not know, nor do I believe, that there is a pure blood merino in the United States besides those which I own. The reason for this is, that from 1825 to 1836, the rage for Saxony sheep was so great, that our wool-growers gave the preference to Saxony bucks, almost unexceptionably."[1]

The origin of the Saxony merino is this. An Elector of Saxony sent a present of a pair of handsome carriage horses to the King of Spain ; who, in return, gave him thirty of the royal merino sheep, which were carefully cherished for many years. It is thought, however, that they deteriorated in that country, becoming smaller, lighter in the fleece, and subject to that contagious disease in their feet, which was such a scourge to the farmers for years after their introduction to America. Deceived by the puffs and encomiums as to the fineness of the Saxony wool, and its superiority in the manufacture of delicate broadcloth, Mr. Jarvis was induced to attend the sale in Boston, in 1825, and to purchase a number, with their showy cards of pedigree, employing a Saxon shepherd to take care of them. But too soon, to his astonishment, the foot disease appeared among them, which the shepherd

---

[1] Mr. Cutts, who commenced farming in Vermont many years ago, but after the Saxony experiment had been tried, has now a flock of full blood merinos on his farm in Hartland, which have never been tainted with the Saxony blood, and are probably the most reliable of any now to be found, for purity of descent, from Mr. Jarvis' imported Spanish sheep. Avoiding excess of gum, Mr. C. has bred for real wool, and strength of constitution, rather than for gross weight of fleece; and it is conceded by some of the best breeders, that his flock yields the greatest amount of actual wool, at the least cost of keeping. His are among the few fine-wooled sheep that can be carried through the winter, in good order, without grain or any extra keeping.

19

affirmed was common in Saxony, and Mr. Jarvis deeply regretted that he had been lured into introducing them upon his farm.

From the first, he carefully preserved in purity of blood, without any admixture of Saxon, a considerable portion of his merinos, and he disposed of his Saxony sheep as fast as he could.

In September, 1810, General E. H. Derby, of Salem, came to Lisbon with a fine new brig, and solicited Mr. Jarvis to aid him in obtaining a large number of merino sheep.

Mr. Jarvis informed him that a friend of his, Mr. O'Niele, had one thousand Montarcos, which he had purchased of the Junta, and perhaps he would sell them. As General Derby was eager to see them, Mr. Jarvis accompanied him to Mr. O'Niele's house, and introduced him. The General purchased the whole lot, though at an advanced price. A few days afterwards, Mr. Jarvis found that he was putting up a platform between the decks, so that the sheep would be placed above each other, and very kindly explained to him why this would prove injurious, and probably fatal to many, and told him what course he had adopted in regard to his own; but the General thought he knew best, and most unfortunately for him disregarded the friendly advice.

Lisbon being blockaded at this time, no vessel was allowed to leave the harbor; and General Derby, in this new trouble, again applied to Mr. Jarvis for assistance. In the course of conversation he mentioned that his commission would soon expire. Mr. Jarvis thought that this might be turned to account, and finding that he had his uniform with him, recommended that he should put it on, and they would then, in due form, wait upon Don Miguel Pereira Forjas, Minister and Secretary of State for the Foreign and War Departments. They were so fortunate as to obtain an audience, and through the earnest intercessions of the American Consul and Chargé, Don Forjas seemed favorably disposed toward the General, but stated that a law had been passed that no vessel should leave the harbor, unless they were willing to take a family to Brazil. As he knew of one who wished to go to the Azores, and escape from the two contending armies, then occupying Portugal, he would permit General Derby to leave Lisbon, on condition that he should take the ten members of this noble family to Terceira. There being no alternative, the General consented, and landed them in safety on the island. He had adverse winds, and a long, tedious passage, and as Mr. Jarvis apprehended, nearly half the sheep died. When they landed in New York they were placed in very muddy yards, which caused the death of many more, so that in the spring the number for sale was reduced to two hundred and fifty, and these sold low. General Derby reserved one hundred and sixty or one hundred and eighty for himself, which he placed on his farm.

CHAPTER XXVI.

MASSÉNA'S INVASION OF PORTUGAL. — WELLINGTON'S
DEFENSES. — TORRES VEDRAS. — REMARKS ON NA-
POLEON'S INVASION OF SPAIN AND PORTUGAL.

EARLY in the winter of 1810, Masséna entered Portugal from Spain, with a formidable army of 80,000 veterans. Lord Wellington, with an inferior force of 18,000 British troops, and the remainder Portuguese and Spanish, upon whom little reliance could be placed, adopted the defensive plan.

1810.

He first fell back to Busaco, where he was attacked by the French, who were repulsed with mutual slaughter. Wellington then withdrew to his lines of defense around Lisbon, which had long been constructing, and extended from Torres Vedras to Cintra, a distance of twenty-eight miles, " bristling with six hundred pieces of artillery, and one hundred and fifty forts ; flanked with abattis and breastworks."

Torres Vedras was a remarkable natural formation, — a study for the geologist. There were masses of rock, thrown up in a conical shape from a plain, fifty feet high, and only a few rods apart. Here the soldiers were able to make intrenchments that were impregnable ; but on most of the lines there were no other fortifications than felled trees, the branches turned toward the enemy, and the earth thrown up about the roots, on the inside ; in some places the trees were small, and the barrier might have been easily surmounted.   Wellington's aim was to keep possession of Lisbon and the harbor ; he would thus have access to his shipping, and be abundantly supplied with provisions.   He seemed fully aware of the inferior strength of his forces, and unwilling to hazard an engagement. But he made up in vigilance what he lacked in strength.   No officer was allowed to come into Lisbon on any pretense ; every man was kept close at his post of duty, as if in hourly expectation of a surprise in some direction.   He made the most careful arrangements for instant retreat to the shipping, in case of defeat.   All the boats and transports were numbered, to correspond with the numbers and letters of the companies and regiments ; the numbers and letters illumined by night.   A large flag was elevated by day, on which the numbers of the regiments were inscribed.   At night, a huge rotary lantern was raised, displaying the numbers on each side in the same way, to avoid disorder.   For six weeks it was impossible to hire a boat to convey cargoes to and from vessels.

A son of Lord Hood came to Lisbon, soon after Junot's capitulation, and brought letters of introduction to Mr. Jarvis, who treated him with much kindness and hospitality, invited him frequently to dine, and extended the invitation to any of his friends that he would like to have accompany him.   He availed himself of this politeness, and often brought his friend Major Knight.   They were both agreeable, gentlemanly young men, and Major Knight was remarkably intelligent.

Should the French be victorious, and drive the English to their shipping, the port would be strictly blockaded, which would close commercial business, and prevent Mr. Jarvis' intended return to the United States with his family.

To ascertain the probabilities of such an event, he said one day to Major Knight; " I do not wish to pry into the secrets of your army, or to ask any impertinent questions, that as a man of honor you may find it difficult to answer ; but as I am situated, I should be very unwilling to be blockaded in this port by your fleet; and, therefore, it is a matter of great importance to me to ascertain what are the probabilities of your resisting the French army ? "

" All that I am at liberty to say," replied Major Knight, " is that in lines so much extended as ours, there must necessarily be some weak points."

This was sufficient.

Mr. Jarvis determined to make immediate preparations for his return to America. He bought a brig, and had it fitted up for the comfort and accommodation of his family; but before this was accomplished, there was a sudden abatement of vigilance in Lord Wellington's defenses. More or less of the officers were permitted to enter the city daily, and the men came in sometimes in squads of twenty or thirty.

From close observation of all that transpired at that period, Mr. Jarvis was convinced that Masséna must have been bribed, for with his powerful army of disciplined men, victory would have been almost certain, had he made a bold attack. But he was a second Duke of Marlboro' ; a brave and able general, but an avaricious man, and capable of this base treachery, if thereby he could increase his fortune. At the end of six months he withdrew his forces, under pretense of want of provisions. Napoleon never employed him again. When the Emperor retired to Elba, Masséna joined the Bourbons. He lost a very large sum by the failure of a bank in Paris, yet died immensely rich.

Mr. Jarvis had a high admiration for Napoleon, but thought he made a great mistake in attempting to conquer Spain and Portugal; that it was not only unjustifiable, but bad policy. The Portuguese government offered to pay him a tribute of $2,000,000 annually, if he would not invade their kingdom. The governments of Spain and Portugal were so weak, that as allies, they might easily have been controlled by able ministers. But he was ambitious to place one of his own family on every throne in Europe, England only excepted. When the French Consul at Lisbon, M. d'Ennerais,[1] heard of Napoleon's invasion of Spain, he expressed the deepest regret that his revered sovereign should have committed so great an error, saying the Spaniards, though proud and indolent, were very patriotic, and when their king and country were attacked, would defend them unto death. Their numerous mountains affording them shelter, no permanent victory could be secured. This prediction was verified. The Spanish nation rose against the invaders; appointed its Junta; sent out guerrilla parties,

[1] M. d'Ennerais had formerly been three years French Consul at Boston, and was a frequent guest at Dr. Jarvis'. He was afterwards appointed Consul at Madrid, and was then removed to Lisbon, when the old acquaintance between him and Mr. Jarvis was renewed.

who, when an opportunity offered, came down on the
French. When the French proved too strong, the
guerrillas retired to their mountain fastnesses; they
cut off supplies of provisions, and harassed the enemy
in every way, until, greatly diminished in numbers,
the French were obliged to quit the country. Through
Masséna's treachery, Portugal was lost. The large
body of forces sent into these kingdoms weakened
Napoleon's power, and strengthened his enemies. The
British became the powerful ally of Spain and Portugal, in opposition to him, and all Europe entered into
an alliance for his overthrow.

Mr. Jarvis often remarked that Sir Walter Scott's
history of the campaigns in Portugal and Spain was
full of errors. He read and re-read his novels many
times, with unabated interest, but thought " Scott's
Life of Napoleon " more of a *fiction* than his novels, —
he was so incorrect in many of his statements, and
took such an intensely *English* view of Napoleon's
character.

CHAPTER XXVII.

RETURN TO THE UNITED STATES. — FAREWELL TO
LISBON. — ARRIVAL IN BOSTON. — SENHOR PEREIRA.
— LETTER FROM MR. JEFFERSON. — INTERVIEW
WITH MR. MADISON.

In October, 1810, Mr. Jarvis embarked with all his
family for the United States, having made every
arrangement for their health and comfort.
His wife, being quite feeble, took with her two   1810.
Portuguese servants, and several goats were provided
for a supply of fresh milk.

Farewell now to Lisbon! its mild, balmy air, blue
and sunny skies, its orange groves, and olive and vine
clad hills, its picturesque scenery, noble river and harbor, — the finest in the world, not even surpassed by
the Bay of Naples.

More than nine years before, the American Consul,
with no costly outfit as Minister, entered Lisbon, an
unassuming private man.

He had won for himself the esteem and consideration of the Portuguese government and nobility; an
honorable standing as one of the diplomatic corps, —
respected by all, and enjoying the friendship of several
of its members; and earned a high reputation for
energy, integrity, and intelligence, in all his business
transactions.

His assiduity in discharging his duties as Consul and Chargé, and his devotion to the interests of his country and countrymen, could not have been surpassed.

They were favored with propitious gales, and had a short and pleasant voyage.   On arriving in Boston, he took lodgings at Mrs. Hatch's, near the Park Street Church, then one of the best boarding-houses in Boston ; the President of the Senate and Speaker of the House were boarding there.[1]

Many changes had taken place in the old family circle while he was abroad.   His father was no more ; his house occupied by strangers ; his uncles Leonard and Philip, and Aunt Mary, had removed to Maine with their families.   His Uncle Samuel had purchased a fine estate in Claremont, New Hampshire, in 1797, where he spent much of his time with his children, — his wife having died in 1794.

His Uncle Nathaniel and Mr. Russell were dead ; and his Aunt Russell resided with her adopted daughter, who had married Mr. Joseph Otis.   Mrs. Russell, and Mr. and Mrs. Benjamin Jarvis, were all that remained of his father's brothers and sisters.

About a week after their arrival, a Portuguese gentleman called one morning to see the Consul from

---

[1] At this time Miss Hannah Adams, who was a friend of Mrs. Hatch's, came to pass the day. Mr. Jarvis entertained a high respect for this learned lady, paid her particular attention, and in the evening offered to escort her home. They entered into conversation, and the Consul supposed she would tell him when they arrived at her lodgings in Hanover Street; but they walked on and on, until they reached the old North Church, when suspecting she must be oblivious of outward things, he asked her where her house was. Thus recalled, she looked about her, and found she had long since passed it, to her great astonishment, and they retraced their steps. One of many instances of her absence of mind.

Lisbon, who introduced himself as Senhor Charles Pereira.

He said that when the Prince Regent left Lisbon, he came to Boston; but he now wished to go to the Brazils, and an opportunity offered, as a vessel would sail in a few days; but he had no money to pay the passage of himself and family; that he had friends and funds in Brazil, but none here. He had applied to the Portuguese Consul, but he either could not or would not render him any assistance. He seemed to be in great trouble, which awakened Mr. Jarvis' sympathy, and he promised to accompany him to the ship the next day, and do all in his power to aid him.

On going aboard, he found that the master was Captain Sprague, upon whom he had conferred important favors when in Lisbon. They greeted each other cordially, and then Mr. Jarvis introduced Senhor Pereira, explained his situation, and begged Captain Sprague to give him a passage, as he stated that he had ample funds in Brazil. But Captain Sprague said he was only quarter owner, and had no right to incur the risk, without consulting the others, and was unwilling to assume the whole responsibility. Mr. Jarvis then asked Senhor Pereira if he had any property that he could put in Captain Sprague's hands for security, until he reached Rio Janeiro.

He replied that he had four large trunks containing clothing and valuables, and he would let him take two of them.

Captain Sprague consented to this, and the terms for the passage were then arranged. But Captain Sprague said he could only furnish for provisions the ship's stores, *i. e.*, hard bread and salt meat, etc.   Mr. Jarvis foresaw that this would be hard fare for a delicate lady and her children, and asked Mr. Pereira if he had anything he could sell to raise money.

"Yes, sir ; I have silver plate."

" If you will send some articles to me I will buy them of you."

He sent one dozen heavy table spoons, one dozen tea-spoons, two silver salvers, and a pair of candlesticks.   The Consul had them weighed, and they amounted to $150.

Senhor Pereira then informed him that he owed $100, and they must get along with fifty dollars' worth of provisions.

Much moved by his integrity and misfortunes, and fearing that his family would suffer, Mr. Jarvis said that if he would give him a bill of exchange on his banker in Rio, he would let him have $100 more for provisions.   This the poor gentleman gladly did, and was by this act of kindness enabled to provide all the comforts and necessaries that they required.   The vessel reached Brazil in safety, and Senhor Pereira honorably paid the captain for their passage, and his bill of exchange was duly honored.   Thus there was no pecuniary sacrifice, and the Consul had the satisfaction of having saved a fellow-man in a foreign country from great misfortunes.

Soon after his return, Mr. Jarvis received the following letter from Mr. Jefferson : —

"MONTICELLO, *December* 5, 1810.

" DEAR SIR, — Our newspapers received yesterday evening gave me the first information of your arrival in Boston, and I lose no time in congratulating you on it.

" While occupied in the government, the everlasting pres-
sure of business, which would not permit itself to be put off,
rendered it impossible to maintain correspondences, which
my warmest wishes would have led me to.

" I found it would be a sacrifice of duty to feeling, which,
therefore, I forbade myself; hence so many of your favors
remain unacknowledged. But I was not the less sensible of
their kind tenor, and the friendly spirit which dictated them.
I reserved myself, therefore, to make a general acknowledgment, when retired to a situation of leisure, which has been
delayed till now by the expectation of your present visit to
the United States. Permit me, therefore, now to return
you my thanks for the many marks of attention I received
from you, while in the administration; and the reiterated
proofs of your approbation and support. In an especial
manner, however, I must acknowledge your last favors, in
putting me on the list of those who were enabled to extend
the improvement of one of the most valuable races of our
domestic animals. The merinos are now safe with me here,
and good preparations made for their increase the ensuing
season; pursuing the spirit of the liberal donor, I consider
them as deposited with me for the general good, and divest-
ing myself of all views of gain, I propose to devote them
to the diffusion of the race through our State. As fast as
their increase shall permit, I shall send a pair to every
county in the State, in rotation, until the whole are possessed
of them. This object will be much accelerated by the great
shipments you have made of the same race, and the portion
of them offered for sale in this State. The expense and risk
you took on yourself by this measure, but especially the
promptitude with which you availed us of this single opportunity of transferring the rich possession to your own country, merits our general acknowledgments, and justifies our
wishes that you may be duly remunerated by advantageous

disposals of them here. Should this business, or any other circumstance, lead you to Richmond, I hope you will feel disposed to vary the route of your return. It will give you the view of a very different country from that through which you will pass to Richmond, and may give us the pleasure of seeing you here, and of possessing you some days. The passage of the mail-stage near us twice a week will facilitate this. You may remember some wines you were so kind as to procure for me in 1803 — Carras queira, Ocefras, etc. The first is now abroach, and is among the best wines I have ever had. It would be a great pleasure to give you proofs here how erroneous is the opinion of the Lisbon merchants, that the Termo wines will not keep unless fortified with brandy; and how injurious to the quality and estimation of those wines their brewing practices are. The Ocefras, with the age it has, has become also a fine wine; it did not promise this at first. Although sweet, it is not too much so, and is highly flavored. Come, however, and judge for yourself.

"So far my letter is merely private; but I cannot omit the duty I owed you in my late capacity, of bearing witness to your public services during my administration. The zeal and intelligence with which they were rendered, placed you preëminently among the faithful of the public servants; ever in unison with the measures of the administration, they gave to them all the effect which could be derived from your station, and frequent advantages for which we were indebted to your vigilance alone, and to the confidence which your good conduct had established with that government. This testimony is justly due to you. It is a tribute to truth which I render, with sincerity and gratification, and it is one which you had a right to expect from me. Accept with it, the assurances of my great esteem and consideration.

"THOMAS JEFFERSON."

Mr. Jarvis' respect for Mr. Jefferson as a statesman, a man of integrity, and of extensive acquirements, amounted almost to veneration, and these just encomiums must have afforded him the highest pleasure and satisfaction.

Business soon called him to Washington,[1] and he called on the President, Mr. Madison, who treated him with the utmost cordiality and attention, and invited him to dine. Several other gentlemen were asked to meet him, and after dinner, out of compliment to Mr. Jarvis, some of the wine that he had presented to Mr. Madison was produced, and the guests were requested to decide upon its kind and quality; some thought it Madeira, some one thing and some another; but they all agreed that it was very fine.

Mr. Madison finally informed them that it was a superior quality of pure Lisbon, without brandy, of which Mr. Jarvis had sent him a cask five years before. It had been carefully kept, and had improved by age.

Mrs. Madison presided at the President's table, with great dignity, elegance, and suavity. She was extremely polite and attentive to their guests; had a pleasant remark for every one, and was very popular. She seemed to have an intuitive insight into character, and adapted her conversation to each gentleman addressed.

In one of his first interviews with Mr. Jarvis, Mr. Madison had spoken with high appreciation of his services abroad, and alluded to the subject of compensation. The Consul replied that it was a great happi-

[1] To see Mr. Hooe regarding the sale of his sheep.

ness to him if he had been able, even in a small degree, to benefit his country, and aid the government; and that this was a sufficient remuneration.

He found that the United States was on the eve of a war with England, and that our national finances were still low; and, as he had been successful in business, — as he often in after years remarked, — he thought the government needed their funds more than he did.

His independence was a remarkable feature of his character. He sometimes observed that all the property he possessed was acquired solely by his own labors, and that he was not indebted to any one for any portion of it, not even to his father, who had lived in a handsome, hospitable style; but at his death, the income from his profession ceased, and the son, with delicacy and disinterestedness, secured to his step-mother all his father's estate.

CHAPTER XXVIII.

MRS. JARVIS REMOVES TO HAVERHILL. — BIRTH OF
THEIR SECOND DAUGHTER. — MRS. JARVIS' SICKNESS
AND DEATH.

MR. JARVIS had always been fond of rural pursuits,
and the high estimation in which landed property was
held in Europe, increased his wish to possess a   1811.
farm, well stocked with superior breeds of animals, and thereby improve the agriculture of his native
land.   In all his plans for the future, the good of his
country held a prominent place.

He had spent a portion of his early life so pleasantly in Virginia, that he thought of locating himself in that State.   As the selection of a plantation
would require that he should be absent some time,
his wife preferred to remove to Haverhill, where her
Uncle and Aunt Bartlett, and her cousins resided —
those dear, kind friends of her early life, to whom
she was so much attached.   Pleasant lodgings were
found at Mrs. Harrod's, and the Consul saw his wife
and child, his mother and her niece, with the Portuguese servants, comfortably established, and then went
south.

Mrs. Jarvis had loved her uncle and aunt as parents,
and her cousins as brothers and sisters; and this reunion must have afforded her great pleasure.   Most of

20

the daughters had grown up, and all were unremitting in their acts of kindness. It was a delightful family circle.

Mrs. Jarvis' complaints had for some time been consumptive, and the cold northern climate of New England seemed to develop the disease more rapidly. Some of her poetry, found among her private papers, shows that she felt her hold on life was very slender.

The last time that she ever left the house, she went to the church of which she had long been a member, to partake of the Lord's Supper, that sacred commemoration of her Saviour, which she so much prized.

Early in February her husband returned, and on the 22d another daughter was given them, named Elizabeth Bartlett, for her grandmother. For a time she seemed very comfortable, but she gradually declined; and early in April it was evident that she was failing. On the night of the 7th she was conscious that He who is the " Resurrection and the Life," was calling her to her eternal home; the bright promise, " Where I am, there ye shall also be," lighting up the passage " over the river."

As her last earthly acts, she wished that her children might be consecrated to God in baptism, and to receive the sacrament herself. Her pastor, the Rev. Mr. Dodge, was summoned, and he often remarked afterwards, that it was the most solemn experience of his life. That dying mother — those little ones on her bed, to be deprived of her tender maternal care in their infancy; but with heaven eyed faith, committed to *His care*, who watcheth over the little sparrow in its fall, and heareth the young raven's cry. Mr. Dodge made a solemn prayer, and she passed on.

" They saw not the angels who met her there;
The gates of the city they could not see;
But they knew she was safe on the further side,
Where all the ransomed and angels be."

Weeping and sorrowing friends were left behind; but she was blessed for evermore.

She was interred in the cemetery at Haverhill, near the remains of her mother, Elizabeth Bartlett, wife of Nathaniel Sparhawk, Esq.

Extracts from an obituary notice published in a Salem paper, written by Joseph E. Sprague, Esq., who knew her intimately, having married her cousin, Eliza Bartlett.

" Died, in Haverhill, on Sunday last, Mary Pepperrell Jarvis, wife of William Jarvis, Esq., late Consul at Lisbon. Aged 30 years."

. . . . " Perfectly unaffected and unassuming, she possessed an equanimity of mind which prosperity could not elate, nor adversity depress ; a benevolence of nature, which prevented her ever having a personal enemy. Regardless of herself, but alive to the misfortunes, sickness, and sorrows of her friends, so strong was her sympathy and affection, that with her utmost exertions, and entire devotion to their comfort and ease, she still thought she had done too little for them. Painting, the belles-lettres, and the study of several languages, — those acquirements which expand the heart and liberalize the mind, — engrossed all her leisure. . . . . Though greatly attached to reading, she suffered it not to interfere with domestic avocations, but without reluctance, cheerfully fulfilled every duty, in every station and relation in which she was placed. She was thoroughly read in the best English authors, often sitting up late at night to peruse them ; and her friends can witness how just were her observations, and how much taste and critical knowledge

she displayed, whenever she could be drawn from that retirement, which her unobtrusive modesty sought.   But the
study which most engrossed her attention, was the religion
of her Saviour; His precepts she diligently studied and
obeyed, and His religion she early professed. . . . . Returned to her native country to put in practice the benevolent purposes of her heart, that Being whose views are inscrutable to human eyes, has removed her to a higher sphere
of action, where we are confident she enjoys richer pleasures
than earth can yield, unclouded by pain, sickness, or care.
. . . . A stranger to terror, fear had no control over her.
The acute pangs of sickness, and dread certainty of approaching death, she met with perfect tranquillity and resignation; and as her life had been conspicuous for every Christian virtue, so in death, with her latest breath, she evinced
the complete triumph of Christianity over infidelity.

"J. E. S."

"ACROSTIC

TO MARY PEPPERRELL SPARHAWK, BY HER FRIEND AND COUSIN, SUSAN
SPARHAWK, JUST BEFORE HER DEPARTURE FOR LISBON.

" May's opening blossoms, gemmed with sparkling dew,
Appear less brilliant when your eyes I view.
Rareripes their velvet down in autumn boast,
Yet near your cheeks their glowing tints are lost.

" Possessed of every charm, how rare we find
Each excellence of person and of mind
Produced at once, and thus in one combined.
Propriety does o'er her acts preside,
Engaging sweetness, with good sense allied:
Rare though her form, by mental gifts outvied,
Regardless of her powers, she charms anew;
Enlarged her knowledge, though her years are few.
Lo! in her face beams bright intelligence,
Lovely content, and artless innocence.

" Sweet is her presence, grateful to the sight,
Pride of her family, her friends' delight.

Attentively polite she hears each call,
Replies with sweetness, though attacked by all.
How vain the attempt to draw her likeness here;
Ah! how successless does each line appear.
Words are but faint, what language can avail —
Know Mary's portrait, though the colors fail.   S. S."

Her father, Nathaniel Sparhawk, brother of young Sir William Pepperrell, who resided in England, and grandson of the hero of Louisburg, married his cousin, Miss Katie Sparhawk, daughter of Rev. John Sparhawk, of Salem, and was for many years a merchant in Salem.

Their children were, Nathaniel, William P., Eliza, Catherine, and Susan.

Mrs. Sparhawk died 1778, and in 1780 Mr. Sparhawk married Elizabeth Bartlett. She died in 1782, leaving an only daughter, *Mary Pepperrell*, who resided with her Grandmother Bartlett until her death, and then most of the time with her Uncle Bailey Bartlett.

ELIZA married Mr. Spooner, and died in 1802, leaving one daughter, who married Edward Jarvis, of Castine, Maine; now in California.

CATHERINE married Daniel Humphreys, of Portsmouth, and also died young, in 1805, leaving three orphans — Mary, Abby Atkinson, and Charles. They are now all dead.

SUSAN went to England in 1803, to attend her father in his sickness, and in a few months took the small-pox, which proved fatal.

These three talented and lovely ladies were only about thirty when they were "called up higher." Their sister Mary was with Mrs. Humphreys, who was a widow, at the time of her decease, and remained some time with the orphans, whom she tenderly cherished. Her health and spirits were deeply affected by these repeated bereavements, but were partially restored by the renewal of her betrothal in 1806, and going to Lisbon.

The letters from these sisters, which are remarkably well written, she treasured up. Susan left a volume of unpublished poems, which possess much merit.

The following lines, written after the death of her sister, Mrs. Eliza Spooner, are expressive of her sentiments of love and grief: —

"ON THE DEATH OF A SISTER.

"How has thy gentle spirit winged its way,
To milder regions of eternal day.
Where storms nor chilling blasts can e'er invade
Thy beauteous spring, nor make its blossoms fade.
Alternate joy and grief no more are thine,
And all is perfect harmony divine.
Sweet spirit! if your raptured soul can move,
A daughter's [1] anguish claims it from above.
Give her a taste of Heaven, while here below,
And point her hopes to what celestials know;
Thy sister, too, whom late thy friendship blessed,
Weeps o'er thy tomb, with heartfelt sorrow pressed.
O! who shall thy sweet tenderness supply,
That soothed her woes, and checked the rising sigh.
"M. P. S."

Their father, Mr. Sparhawk, went to England about 1790, and remained there until 1809, when he re-

---

[1] Mrs. Spooner had been a *protégé* of Miss Mary Jarvis, sister of Dr. C. Jarvis, and she was so solicitous to adopt her infant, that Miss Sparhawk finally consented.

turned home to the old Sparhawk Mansion in Kittery,[1] where his sons resided, and which was still furnished with his mother's once elegant furniture. He died in 1815, having outlived all his daughters, his sister, Mrs. Jarvis, and his brothers, excepting Sir William P.

[1] See Appendix B: Sparhawk family.

CHAPTER XXIX.

PURCHASE OF REAL ESTATE AT WEATHERSFIELD, VERMONT. — HIS REMOVAL THERE, ETC., ETC.

MR. SAMUEL G. JARVIS had bought the farm and mansion owned by Judge Kingsbury, in Claremont, 1811-1818. New Hampshire, one of the most picturesque and beautiful situations in the country, commanding a fine view of the Ascutney Mountain, and a varied and extensive landscape.[1]

The Consul had not found a plantation in Virginia that pleased him, and his uncle (S. G. Jarvis) and cousin, Dr. Leonard Jarvis, now urged him to look at an estate three miles distant from them, which was for sale in Weathersfield, Vermont, where the Connecticut River forms a bow. " The successive small plateaus, exhibiting the gradual subsidence of the river, which here must have formed nearly a circular lake, are most distinctly and wonderfully marked." Immense pines, the growth of centuries, had covered this rich alluvial soil. In its early settlement, a thriving village grew up, from its trade in lumber, called " the Bow,"

---

[1] When Mr. S. G. Jarvis removed to Claremont in 1797, one of his daughters accompanied him in a two-wheeled chaise; but the roads were almost impassable in some places. Afterwards, he and his daughters performed the journey on horseback several times, when they visited Boston.

or " Weathersfield Bow." Logs and sawed lumber were floated down the river, to Hartford, Connecticut.

The widow Haskell [1] and her sons, and Mr. Daniel Bowen, removed from Connecticut, and settled in the vicinity at an early period ; and Samuel Steele and Jonathan Nye were among the first settlers.

George Hubbard, a captain in the Revolution, owned about 600 acres in Weathersfield and Springfield, and in 1780 first built a log, and then a frame house (near what is now the ferry), which is still standing. [2]

Mr. George Lyman, a man of great enterprise and business capacity, bought several acres of Captain Hubbard, and erected the first frame house [3] and store in the village. Ere long two public houses, another store, several mechanics' shops, houses, and mills were built, and a lawyer and doctor sustained.

---

[1] Mrs. Haskell was a woman of undaunted energy and courage, and one of the pioneers, coming from Connecticut, up the river, on horseback in 1780, to find a farm and home. She selected and purchased some fine land, half a mile from the present village, and returned for her five sons, whom she had brought up in the Puritan faith. They all bought farms in Weathersfield, became members of the church, and firm supporters of religion, bringing up large families well. She lived and died in advanced years on her farm, as did *her son* John and *his son* John, a remarkable fact in our emigrating country. Captain Deane bought a farm adjoining the widow Haskell's, on the south side, where his son Barnabas Deane, Esq., a very respectable and capable man, lived until within a few years. He married a daughter of Dr. Frink, and they had several children, who are yet living. Dr. Frink lived in a house directly opposite Mr. Deane's. Mr. Deane's second wife was Miss Prentiss, who died in two or three years; his third wife has survived him. Gideon Haskell's farm was the next south of Mr. Deane's.

[2] The fine farm in which it is situated was bequeathed by the Consul to his grandsons, William and Samuel Dinsmoor, of Keene.

[3] This house is now owned by his grandchildren in New York, E. P. Wheeler, Esq., and his sister. The former has recently put it in thorough repair, retaining, as far as possible, its original style.

A few years before Mr. Jarvis came, nearly all the village had fallen into the hands of Mr. Francis Goodhue, including a tannery, bark, saw and grist mills, beside the rich meadows, and some small farms suitable for pastures.[1] It was sheltered on every side by high hills; a warm, sunny spot, over which the Ascutney, like a watchful sentinel, seemed ever to keep guard. The land was so fertile and valuable, the vicinage to his uncle and cousins so pleasant, that the Consul finally decided to locate himself here, and purchased the whole property of Mr. Goodhue, who established himself in Brattleboro'.[2] The Consul afterwards bought Mr. Steele's farm.

In the latter part of April Mr. Jarvis removed his family to Weathersfield, and with the assistance of Dr. Jarvis, who had some years experience in farming, all his animals were driven from Massachusetts, where they were landed, to Vermont: his selected merinos, Dutch cattle, Portuguese swine, goats, donkeys, English hunter, and the fine horses he had purchased in Virginia.

A Spanish shepherd accompanied the sheep, and the noble shepherd-dog "Coronel,"[3] and a favorite pointer, "Piniasco." The journey, performed on foot by these animals, was safely accomplished, though it occupied several days. The Consul planned to build a beauti-

---

[1] See Appendix F: Weathersfield Bow.

[2] See Appendix E: Joseph Danforth.

[3] This noble dog had long, curly white hair, with some black spots. A low man in the neighborhood, it was supposed, had attempted to steal sheep, for the dog always growled when he saw him. During the Consul's absence in Lisbon, poor Coronel was brutally killed by this man, and the handsome brown and white pointer was stolen, to the great sorrow of the Consul on his return.

ful villa on the hill opposite, with ornamental grounds on the declivity, and a fish-pond at the base, but finally relinquished the idea, and decided to reside in the brick house that Mr. Goodhue had occupied ; having a considerable addition made to render it convenient for a large family of workmen, and a dairy, and the front thoroughly repaired.

He then had barns and sheds erected for his sheep and cattle,[1] and enlarged and improved others at some distance for his horses.

All his arrangements were on a large scale for their comfort, yet there was no unnecessary expense. "Utility and comfort" now became his motto in everything. Coming from a large city, brilliant society, and court parade and etiquette, to the retirement of private country life, after the death of his wife, he erred, perhaps, in becoming too indifferent to appearances and adornment of every kind. His house, furniture, carriages, and dress were plain and simple, far removed from all ostentation. But his table and hospitalities were as liberal as ever, and his heart and hand were ever ready to assist young men commencing life, and to aid those in misfortune.

Mr. Jarvis next turned his attention to having the stumps, amounting to about 2,000, drawn from the plain on which the village was situated ; the lower interval was free from them, but the upper one was filled with the roots of giant pines. As soon as they were pulled out, which required much labor and expense, he had them placed in fences, which it was truly said would last a century. But some years elapsed before all the land was cleared.

---

[1] These were all whitewashed, which then was unusual.

When his little Elizabeth was about a year old he
went to Portsmouth, and had her brought to
1812.
Weathersfield.

At this time he very kindly invited his wife's half
brother, Nathaniel Sparhawk, to come and reside with
him. He was an upright, amiable man, but wanting
in energy ; not being educated for any regular calling,
owing to his father's false pride and aristocratic no-
tions. He assisted the Consul in his business, copied
his letters, and remained at Weathersfield until his
death, in 1830.

The Consul's step-mother, Mrs. Charles Jarvis, came
with him to his farm in Vermont. She left there in a
year or two, and returned to the home of her childhood at Kittery — the old " Sparhawk mansion," still
owned by herself and brother Nathaniel. He had
taken up his abode there, on his return from England,
in 1809, with his two sons. Her adopted daughter
and niece, Miss H. H. Sparhawk, was devoted to her
in her declining years, and rendered her every care
and attention that an own child could have done, until
her death, in 1815. Miss Sparhawk became her
heir.[1]

In 1813, Mr. Jarvis was very near losing his life.
On awaking one night, he thought he heard some one
in the house, and striking a light, without pausing to
reflect, he went all over it without slippers or stockings. He took a violent cold, which resulted in quinsy,
in so virulent a form as to defy the skill of his attendant physicians, Dr. Torrey, of Windsor, and Dr. Jarvis. Dr. Nathan Smith, of Hanover, was sent for.

[1] See Appendix A, B: Pepperrell and Sparhawk families.

On his arrival he found the case so critical that he sat up with him.   In the middle of the night the swelling in the throat had increased to such a degree that Mr. Jarvis was almost suffocated, and swooned.

Dr. Smith, with that presence of mind that characterizes great skill, instantly ordered a pitcher of cold water, and drawing the Consul by the shoulders over the side of the bed, dashed it violently into his face.

It occasioned a start, a struggle for breath, which broke the ulcer, and Mr. Jarvis was relieved.   He often afterwards remarked that he owed his life to Dr. Smith, for whom he entertained the highest respect.

By the " Georgia land speculation," Mr. Benjamin Jarvis (a younger brother of Dr. C. Jarvis) had recently lost most of his property.   The Consul, who was his favorite nephew, sympathizing with him in his misfortunes, invited Mr. and Mrs. B. Jarvis to Weathersfield.   The society of his uncle, who was a man of cultivated mind and extensive reading, afforded the Consul much pleasure.   His aunt, too, added to his happiness and comfort ; cheerful, pleasant, and energetic, she made it a pleasure and duty to preside over the household, for Miss Purcell, his housekeeper, had left Mr. Jarvis soon after his mother's departure.   To the two little motherless girls, their presence was a blessing ; and the kindness and affection of their uncle and aunt were among their earliest and happiest remembrances.

" Uncle Sam " now often came on horseback to spend the day with his brother and nephew, and was always a welcome guest ; for his kind heart, amusing stories, and an inexhaustible fund of humor, rendered him a favorite with old and young. It might truly be said of him, " He used to set the table in a roar."

His two sons, the Doctor and Russell (the latter a student at Dartmouth College), and his two lovely and accomplished daughters,[1] who had been educated in Boston, were then at home, and the families dined together regularly, at first twice, and afterwards once a week, alternately at Weathersfield and Claremont. These social visits were continued to the end of the Doctor's and Consul's lives, long after Mr. Samuel and Mr. Benjamin Jarvis had passed from earth.

[1] Mary and Helen. Susan Pierce, the eldest, married in 1804 Mr. John Jeffrey, afterwards for many years associated with his brother, Francis Jeffrey, in editing the *Edinburgh Review*. He purchased a pleasant place in Cornish, about four miles from her father's in Claremont. She was a talented, beautiful woman, warmly beloved by her husband, father, and brother L. On a visit to Boston, in 1806, she was taken sick and died. Her husband was inconsolable, and returned to Scotland. Their house was afterwards used for a boarding-school by Mrs. Seton, an English lady.

∵

CHAPTER XXX.

RETURN TO LISBON. — MUTINY ON SHIPBOARD. — BRITISH FRIGATES. — VOYAGE HOME.

BEFORE leaving Lisbon, Mr. Jarvis had taken his two principal clerks into partnership, and intrusted them with the business, leaving considerable 1813– capital in the mercantile house he had estab- 1815. lished. From accounts that reached him he was led to think that they were not managing judiciously, and requested a gentleman going out to make some inquiries ; but he merely took their statements, and reported that the concern was in a flourishing condition. But the Consul was privately informed to the contrary, by a most intelligent and trustworthy young relative of his wife, Edwin Bartlett, who was a clerk in the counting-house.[1]

He then employed Captain George Humphreys, nephew of the former Minister, Colonel D. Humphreys, possessing superior talents, to thoroughly investigate their affairs. His report was so unfavorable, that the Consul felt compelled to go out himself, though he left home with reluctance. He entered into part-

[1] Edwin Bartlett, Esq., recently deceased, universally honored and loved for his ability and many virtues. He went to Lisbon early in 1811, at the age of fourteen. By his remarkably wise and prosperous career, he became one of the merchant princes of our country.

nership with Dr. L. Jarvis, in part of his business, and gave him charge of his entire property, intrusting his children to the care of Mr. and Mrs. B. Jarvis.

To obtain a passage out was the next question. Crossing the Atlantic during the war with England was very dangerous, on account of British cruisers. But through the kindness of a friend in Salem, he soon heard of an opportunity. A fine brig had been taken a prize, and bought very low in Salem, by Captain Razor and others, who wished to send a cargo to Lisbon ; and to avoid detection, if overtaken by cruisers, they had employed a Spanish captain, a Portuguese mate and boatswain, Italian, Spanish, and Portuguese sailors, and hoisted Spanish colors. Captain Razor went himself to take charge of the vessel and cargo ; and Mr. Jarvis, and a young English gentleman, about eighteen, named Palmer, who wished to leave America on account of the war, took passage with him. Captain Razor had been in the British service, and was so strict a disciplinarian, that it was said of him that he was a lamb in his family, but on shipboard a roaring lion. The Spanish captain was indolent, and spent most of his time in smoking ; the mate, easy and ignorant. Not so the boatswain ; he had been in a Portuguese man-of-war, where the boatswain acts an important part, and was really capable ; but was a malevolent, bad character. The ship was not worked as well as Captain Razor had been accustomed to its being done in English vessels, which greatly irritated him ; and though the crew could not understand English, and he spoke neither Spanish nor Portuguese, yet they were offended by his angry manner and treatment, and the boatswain's malice was aroused.

Actuated partly by resentment, and yet more by daring and wickedness, he formed a plan to murder Captain Razor and his passengers, throw them overboard, take possession of the vessel, and assume the command. He so wrought upon the crew that they all joined him in the mutiny, except the Spanish captain; but it was providentially averted.

They had not been many days at sea when it was discovered that there were eight feet of water in the hold.

It was a fine ship, and Mr. Jarvis was sure that it was entirely owing to neglect, and expressed this opinion to Captain Razor, and to the captain in Spanish, saying that orders must be immediately given to have her pumped dry, or they should sink.

The order was given, but the boatswain refused to obey, and the others joined him. It was repeated; they stood immovable. Captain Razor was enraged, and threatened to beat them with a rope's end, etc., etc. Mr. Jarvis assured him that these threats were entirely useless; it was evident there was a combination among them, and they had mutinied.

Captain Razor and the Consul had each a fine pair of pistols; they now loaded them carefully, and put on their swords. Young Palmer having no arms, Mr. Jarvis gave him one of his pistols and a cutlass, making him promise to stand by him, and not fire unless he did; Captain Razor, too, was not to fire unless the Consul gave the signal.

He now said to the latter, "I can talk to them in Portuguese; if you will allow me to manage them, I

21

will endeavor to bring them to subjection." The danger was imminent, and Captain Razor gladly assented.

The three gentlemen now went to the quarter-deck, which was elevated three feet above the main-deck. In the mean time, the crew had armed themselves with cutlasses, and stood defiantly together, on the main-deck; but they could be shot down ere they could approach near enough to do any injury with their cutlasses.

Seeing their intended victims were determined to defend themselves to the utmost, and intimidated by their firearms, they stood irresolute, not daring to make an attack. Mr. Jarvis perceived that they were daunted, and addressing himself in Portuguese to the boatswain, whom he knew was the ringleader, he very sternly told him that unless he and the rest of the men immediately returned to their duty, he should, on his arrival in Lisbon, enter a complaint against them before the Minister of Marine, who was his friend; and his Excellency would have them arrested, and either put in prison, or sent to the galleys. The Lisbon prison and the galleys, were both fearful punishments, and greatly dreaded. The boatswain made no reply, and stood in dogged silence; but this threat seemed greatly to alarm the others.

Mr. Jarvis then spoke to them in both Portuguese and Spanish, and asked them if they wished to be drowned.

" No."

" Why then do you not pump ? "

One replied, " I will, if the others will."

While he had been aboard, he had frequently chatted

with one of the Portuguese sailors, who seemed to be a very clever fellow; he now spoke to him very pleasantly, and said, " Pedro,[1] will you not go and pump to save your own life, and all in the ship? "

He answered, " Yes; " and went promptly; the others followed, except the boatswain, who did not move.

Mr. Jarvis, in a severe, authoritative manner, told him that he deserved to be put in irons, and if he remained on the deck a moment longer, or even dared to come on deck through the day, he should be, and when they reached Lisbon he would deliver him over to the Portuguese authorities. His comrades had deserted him; Mr. Jarvis seemed determined to act as he spoke; discretion seemed the better part of valor, and he quickly went below.

The Consul, with Captain Razor's consent, now assumed the command of the ship; he kept the crew in subjection, and they worked the vessel well. But he, Captain Razor, and Mr. Palmer,[2] kept constantly

[1] This Pedro afterwards disclosed the whole plot to Mr. Jarvis in confidence.

[2] Young Palmer's history was a romantic one. His father, Colonel Palmer, was one day walking in the streets of Calcutta, when he heard such loud and piercing cries issuing from a house, that he entered, and found some British soldiers rudely maltreating two Hindoo ladies. He ordered them at their peril to leave the apartment, which they hurriedly did, ashamed of being detected by an officer in such disgraceful conduct, followed by Colonel Palmer. In the street he found some men belonging to his own regiment, and told them to keep a strict guard at the door, and permit no one to enter. He then returned to the ladies, and assured them they need feel no further apprehension, for his own men would protect them. He afterward visited the ladies several times; one of them cherished the most lively emotions of gratitude toward her deliverer, which ripened into an attachment; they were a high and rich Hindoo family, and he finally married her. This young man was their son. Colonel Palmer

armed during the rest of the voyage, and slept with
pistols under their pillows; they never went on deck
without each having a loaded pistol in his hand.   After
two or three days the boatswain returned to his duties,
and they reached Lisbon in safety, fortunately escap-
ing all cruisers.   Mr. Jarvis' firmness, presence of
mind, and courage, saved them.

He found his affairs in Lisbon in a very bad condition.   His partners had been most injudicious in
their management.   They had been excellent clerks,
but manifested a great want of prudence and judgment when they became the acting partners of the
house.

He had much trouble and vexation in adjusting
and settling their complicated business, and month
after month elapsed ere he could close the concern, in
which they had sunk many thousand dollars.

M. Silva was delighted to see his friend and benefactor; and Mr. Jarvis would have enjoyed his return
to Lisbon, and the meeting with many of his old
acquaintances, but for these harassing cares, and his
solicitude about his children.   The first letters that he
received informed him that his aunt's father, Mr. Hall,
of Dorchester, had been severely injured by a fall, and
sent for Mr. and Mrs. Jarvis, and that Dr. Jarvis had

wished to have him educated in America, and a vessel coming from Boston, owned by Messrs. H—— & E——, offered a favorable opportunity to
place him under the protection of these gentlemen, and have them send
him to the best schools. He had nearly finished his collegiate course at
the opening of the war, when his father wished him to go to England, but
no vessels now went there. At Lisbon he could easily take a packet to
London. Young Palmer was therefore placed under Captain Razor's care.
He finally reached London without further disasters.

removed the children, with their Portuguese attendant, to Claremont.[1]

The Consul wrote the Doctor and Mr. Sparhawk
by every vessel, giving minute directions regarding his
business; and also about his children's health, clothing,
etc., and he often in after years spoke of the satisfaction and pleasure Mr. Sparhawk's letters in reply
afforded him, by detailing all the little incidents that
were taking place in his family and on the farm, during his protracted absence.

He was detained until October, when he wrote to
John Quincy Adams to inquire if he could obtain a
passage in one of the cartels that ran every few weeks
from Holland to the United States, should he travel
there by land. Mr. Adams — then Commissioner at
Ghent with H. Clay and J. Russell, for the negotiation
of a peace with Great Britain — replied that the next
cartel would go in a week, too soon for the Consul's
accommodation, much to his regret.

A few days afterwards a captain called upon him,
and said, —

" Do you not recollect me ? "

" No. I cannot recall your countenance."

" Don't you remember a cabin . boy that Captain
Tom Coffin engaged for you, whom you thought too
small, and he said you must not judge of his capacity
by his size ? "

" O, yes ! "

" I am he, sir."

---

[1] It was a lonely winter for the children, " Uncle Sam " and his daughters being in Boston. But the Doctor was very kind to them, and carried
the eldest carefully through the whooping-cough. Their uncle and aunt
returned in the spring.

They shook hands, and were glad to meet. He had been steady, honest, and persevering; was now master of a vessel, and was well married in Philadelphia. He had entered Lisbon in a fog, unperceived by two cruisers that were sailing about near the mouth of the river. Hearing that the former Consul, his old master, Mr. Jarvis, was in the city, he had sought an interview.

His schooner was new, unusually large, well finished, fast sailing, and handsomely painted. "A real beauty," as one of the sailors said.

The Consul immediately engaged a passage, improving this opportunity to return to the United States, as did many other Americans who had been long detained in Lisbon. Among these was Captain Curwen, master of a privateer. He had taken an English merchantman, and put part of his crew on board to man her,[1] but both vessels were afterwards captured and carried into Lisbon.

There was also a young gentleman from Philadelphia, and fifty seamen, who engaged a passage with Captain Butler. Part of these were the sailors that Captain Curwen had put on board the merchantman, who would have been impressed but for the interference of Mr. Jarvis, among whom was William Rowe.

---

[1] William Rowe, aged seventy-four, one of these seamen who was put on board the merchantman, is now at Weathersfield, September 1, 1867. He came here on foot about a week ago, in the evening, having walked fifteen miles that day. As he seated himself in the kitchen, he said, "I thought I must come once more before I died, to visit the Consul's home." He says through the exertions of Mr. Jarvis he escaped impressment, when carried a prisoner into Lisbon. That he has been in many ports, but never found a consul so active, kind, and efficient in aiding distressed seamen.

Some were impressed sailors, who refused to fight against their countrymen, and were to be exchanged.

In anticipation of the danger of being taken prisoner, Mr. Jarvis converted what money he would be likely to need into doubloons, sewed them in a leather belt, and secured it about his person. When the preparations for sea were nearly completed, the mate, William Bodley, of Providence, a minister's son, informed Mr. Jarvis that there were but five or six pipes of water put on board, which he knew was insufficient, and there was not nearly enough bread for so many men. He was reluctant to speak to Captain Butler on the subject, as he would deem it impertinent; but he thought Mr. Jarvis, who was his first employer, and so long Consul at this port, could do so with propriety. Greatly astonished, he replied that he would see Captain Butler without delay, and thanked him for the information.

He went immediately to the Captain, and asked how much bread and water he had provided for the voyage.

He replied, " Six pipes and —— barrels of bread."

" Is it possible that is all for seventy-two persons ? Why, it is only enough for your own crew of twelve men ! "

" The American Consul said he thought it would be sufficient, sir."

" Then I will go and talk with him."

The acting consul was a very agreeable and gentlemanly young man, but ignorant of nautical affairs. Mr. Jarvis asked him if he had been correctly informed regarding the amount of bread and water he had considered necessary for seventy-two men.

He said, " Yes, I supposed it would be as much as they would require."

" Have you never read the law of the United States on this subject, which forbids any vessel to go to sea without a certain quantity of bread and water for every soul, and this is not one third as much as the law directs. Be pleased to examine this statute, and you will be convinced of your error."

Ten more pipes of water were sent on board, and several additional barrels of bread, which Mr. Jarvis still thought insufficient; but Captain Butler said, " O, she sails so fast that we shall be in the United States in eighteen or twenty days."

" But you may have adverse winds."

" In that case we cannot exceed twenty-five days."

Captain Curwen said he thought there was bread and water enough for thirty days. After arguing the matter a little longer, Mr. Jarvis was obliged to yield his judgment to their confidence.

Two fast sailing British frigates in the harbor, had kept an eye on the schooner, and probably ascertaining that Captain Butler had sold his cargo at a great profit, concluded she must have considerable specie on board, and seemed determined to make a prize of her; for no sooner did Captain Butler get her in sailing trim, than they stationed themselves near by, undoubtedly with a view to her pursuit and capture, as soon as she was beyond the protection of the Portuguese government. She was anchored at Belem Castle. One morning a Portuguese boat came alongside, from which a man came on board and walked about the vessel, observing her closely; as he lowered himself back into the boat he said to his companion, " We will take her a prize as soon as she gets out to sea."

" It so happened that Bodley, the mate, overheard him, and catching up a large white-oak stick, gave him a heavy blow on the hand which held on by the gunwale, saying, " If you do, you shall not have that hand to fight against us."

It was the lieutenant of the frigate disguised.

Every day Mr. Jarvis came down in a boat from Lisbon, to see if the frigates had gone ; but no, there they lay, maintaining a vigilant watch — a severe trial to his patience.

This lasted about a week, when apparently wearied out by the caution of their opponent, or tired of inaction, they moved some way up the river.

" Now," said Mr. Jarvis, to Captain Butler, " loosen your sails as if to dry them, raise the anchor, and let us try and get away unperceived ; if we have but two or three hours start of her, I think we can escape."

" I think so, too ; at any rate we will try it, for I am tired enough of this delay."

This was rapidly done, but on using the spy-glass, lo ! there was one of the frigates unfurling sails, evidently with the intention of pursuit ; their removal was a mere stratagem. It was contrary to the laws of Portugal for a vessel of war to pursue a merchantman under twenty-four hours. Mr. Jarvis went to the officer in command at the castle, told him of their intention to sail, and of their danger of being captured by the English frigates, and begged him to enforce their laws, and not permit them to pass the castle, which he promised to do ; and M. Silva, who had accompanied Mr. Jarvis, remained at the castle to see that they kept their word. Captain Butler sailed, and down came one of the frigates. A gun was fired from the castle. It was not regarded. Then another, which did some damage. It was returned. Then a third, which carried away the foretop-gallant-mast. The commander of the frigate, now highly incensed, fired again at the castle, and some of the stones in the wall came tumbling down, greatly alarming M. Silva, who was watching with deep interest the fate of his friend.

The Portuguese were so much under subjection to the English, that they dared take no further steps to detain the frigate, and in a few minutes the brig narrowly escaped having her mainmast cut down by a cannon ball aimed at her.

" We shall have a broadside upon us next," said Mr. Jarvis ; " our only safety, Captain Butler, is in returning to the castle, anchoring there, and placing ourselves under the protection of the Portuguese," which they immediately did.

" They seem so resolved upon our capture, that I think they will attempt to board us in the night, and my advice is, that all the men be armed, and kept on deck ready for action."

Captain Butler mustered all hands on deck, and armed them with cutlasses, boarding-pikes, pistols, and muskets. It was a wise precaution, for about midnight two boats, full of armed men, were seen approaching them from the frigate, probably expecting to find them off their guard and asleep, and intending to board and take possession, undiscovered by the Portuguese authorities. The large number of armed men on deck made a formidable appearance, and the boats moved leisurely up the river, without any evidence of hostile purpose, which deceived Captain Butler, who thought they were afraid to attack a vessel so well manned and armed, and would not return ; but Mr. Jarvis, better acquainted with their wiles, said they only meant to lull their apprehensions, and would return when they thought the crew off their guard.

This prediction was verified, for in about an hour they were seen slowly returning, making directly up to the schooner. The Consul advised Captain Butler to tell them, in a bold, determined manner, what would be their reception if they attempted to board. As soon as they were near enough, in a clear, strong voice, he said they had sixty-five men, all well armed, who would resist unto death ; that they were greatly superior in numbers, and that whoever attempted to board would be instantly cut down.

The boats' crew seemed daunted by his resolution and courage ; their forty men were hardly a match for those on the schooner, and they slunk quietly back to the frigate, which soon raised anchor and went down the river out of sight.

" Now," said the Consul, " by appointing a watch I think we may venture to get some sleep."

The next morning the frigates were just discernible out at sea, beyond the mouth of the river, moving to and fro, where they continued a few days, and then disappeared. Mr. Jarvis and Captain Butler took repeated observations, and the former went to the top of the Rock of Lisbon, which commanded a view out to sea of twenty miles, but they were not to be seen ; he espied a small sail-boat coming from the north, and proposed to Captain Butler to take a boat, and inquire if they had seen the frigates, which they did, but no vessel had been seen. In the afternoon he saw a fishing-boat coming from the south, round St. Julien's Fortress, and made similar inquiries, and received a similar reply.

" Now is our time to escape," said Mr. Jarvis.

Captain Butler gave his orders, and never were orders obeyed with more alacrity. The wind had been variable, with occasional showers ; the next day it died away, and a dense fog arose, obscuring all objects, and when about twenty-four hours' sail from Lisbon, they were becalmed for two or three days, a grievous disappointment to all. At last the wind changed, and came out from the northwest, dispersing the mist, and a ship was seen in the far horizon. A sailor was sent to the mast-head to make her out, who reported it Swedish or Norwegian. Captain Butler said that he never saw a Swedish or Norwegian vessel with such a breadth of canvas, and taking his spy-glass, what should she prove, but their old enemy, one of the English frigates, coming straight down upon them, and they were steering directly towards her. Captain Butler instantly changed his course, but the wind favored the frigate most. On, on she came, approaching so near that the men could be seen walking on the deck, and their employments, the copper bottom, gunwale, and port-holes became distinctly visible with a glass. Every moment a broadside was expected ; but secure of their prey, they probably thought the shot would be more destructive as they came nearer.

Was there, then, no hope? Were they, after all their caution, to become prisoners of war? This seemed their inevitable fate.

It was now about twelve o'clock, and the passengers were summoned to dinner. Captain Butler remained on deck.

" This will be our last dinner under American colors," said Mr. Jarvis, as he and Captain Curwen went below.

Their hearts were too heavy to feel any appetite, and they returned in fifteen minutes. But as if by a special Providence, the wind had come round into the north, very strong, — the most favorable quarter for them. On using the telescope, Mr. Jarvis exclaimed, " I do not think she has neared us."

" Then, with God's help, she shall not," cried the Captain, and gave orders to have every inch of canvas spread. The men worked with a will; the sails were unusually large, and when they were all unfurled, she took all the wind, and flew like a bird over the water.

The frigate in pursuit looked like a cloud of sails, but she was much heavier, and not as well adapted for speed as the schooner, which gained perceptibly. Soon the men and copper bottom became invisible, and as the sun went down, only the top-sails were seen on the edge of the horizon. They heard the distant report of a cannon, probably a signal to the other frigate. How mercifully a kind heavenly Father had saved them from a foe so bent on their capture. It was with a thankfulness and sense of relief that they had not known for many days, that they laid down to rest that night.[1]

[1] Mr. Jarvis took an intense interest in Cooper's *Pilot*, for his graphic

The wind continued favorable for a few days, then was variable and contrary. A gale followed, blowing with fearful violence. The vessel rolled from side to side, and was thrown on her beam ends. Their danger was imminent; but all were calm and composed, except a dissipated youth, who had been placed under Captain Butler's care, with a view to his reformation. He was greatly terrified, and began to confess his sins, and cry if God would only spare his life he would reform, and no longer grieve and vex his father. When Mr. Jarvis, greatly wearied, was about to lie down at nine o'clock, he besought him to sit up, for they should certainly sink. He told him there was One above who ruled the storm, and the danger would be the same, and threw himself on to his berth.

About midnight Captain Butler was heard speaking cheerily to his sailors, and they knew the peril was past. Soon he came in and told them that the gale had subsided, causing great rejoicings. Forgetful of all his promises of amendment, this young man, when he neared land, began to talk of his dissolute courses, and when reminded of his good resolutions, he answered, " O, then I thought I should die ! "

They had been at sea but a few days, when Mr. Jarvis, noticing that the sailors were very profuse in the use of water, told Captain Butler that he ought to put them all on an allowance, or their supply would fail.[1]

descriptions vividly recalled these and other nautical scenes of his own experience.

[1] Captain Butler understood the management of a vessel, but was inexperienced in providing for so many men. Mr Rowe says he only allowed the *seamen* two figs the alternate day, and that he was passionate and unfeeling toward his men. That they all owed their lives to the Consul.

One gallon apiece per day was at first ordered; then two quarts, and finally the last eight days it was reduced to one pint, and four ounces bread one day, and six ounces figs the next. They had plenty of salt provisions, but were afraid to eat them, as it increased their thirst. Mr. Jarvis always took books to sea; now he thought it most prudent to economize his strength, and neither read nor walked much, though he felt perfectly well.[1] They were seventy-two days at sea, and at last entered Delaware Bay in the night, and ran upon some shoals. In the morning it was found they were near the coast, and the boat put Mr. Jarvis, Captain Curwen, Captain Butler, and two others on shore at a small town. They went to a public house, and ordered a dinner, of which they partook with a relish that only half-starved men can know. They ate the whole of a large turkey weighing twelve pounds, and picked the bones. They finally reached New York in January, 1815, and from there Mr. Jarvis proceeded to Boston and Salem. He was sitting with Hon. Stephen White, transacting some business in the latter town, when a courier from Boston rushed through the streets, crying " Peace ! peace ! " The bells began to ring, a crowd assembled, and Mr. White abruptly left the Consul, to participate in the universal joy.

Our glorious victories on the lakes had so changed the aspect of the war, that the British government

---

[1] Mr. Rowe remarked the Consul had a florid complexion, and was an uncommonly healthy, fine-looking man when they left Lisbon; but he lost his color, and looked so pale and thin, and walked so feebly, that it was sad to witness the change.

were glad to make conciliatory negotiations, and a peace had been concluded.

It was with a thankful heart that Mr. Jarvis returned home, after an absence of fourteen months. All his friends were delighted to see him. So long a time had elapsed since any tidings had reached them, that serious apprehensions were felt that he had died or been taken prisoner. To his children his coming home was a jubilee. When he left them they were too young to understand that he would be long absent; but they had sadly missed their dear father, who was father, mother, and companion to them. Overjoyed to see him once more, they hoped he would never again leave them.[1]

[1] Mr. Rowe spent two winters at the old homestead, receiving liberal aid in money and clothing from the Consul, not long before his death.

CHAPTER XXXI.

DEATH OF MR. B. JARVIS. — DANGEROUS SICKNESS OF
THE CONSUL. — SARATOGA. — FAILURE OF CROPS.
— HIS MARRIAGE. — DEATH OF MR. SAMUEL G.
JARVIS. — HIS COUSINS. — IMPAIRED EYE-SIGHT. —
HIS CHILDREN.

IN February, 1816, his uncle Benjamin died after a short illness, and his wife soon afterwards went to her father's, in Dorchester. 1816–1818.

About the time of her departure, Mr. Jarvis took a severe cold at a town meeting, which resulted in rheumatic fever, and he endured the most excruciating pain. He had the best medical advice and attendance, but a good nurse could not be obtained for many weeks, and he suffered for the most common articles of diet, especially good bread. He was confined to his bed for three or four months. It was the cold summer of 1816.

In the latter part of June he was advised to try the waters of Saratoga. He was lifted over the stairs, and placed on a bed in his own carriage, and was a week in performing the journey of a hundred miles, he was obliged to ride so slowly.[1] Fortunately he was able

[1] There were then no public conveyances across the Green Mountains. Mr. Jarvis took his children, a respectable nurse, and of course a man to drive and attend upon him.

22

to secure a good room on the first floor, at the hotel kept by Mr. Holmes.

The waters proved so salutary, that in a few days he could walk with crutches, and in a month with a cane.

There were several very intelligent, pleasant people boarding here; and after his long confinement, it was a most agreeable change; he enjoyed the drives, too, to the lake, Ballston, etc., etc.

Saratoga was then a small village, containing only a few houses, Chancellor Walworth's being the handsomest. There were two boarding-houses, "Holmes' Hotel," and "Congress Hall;" and three noted springs, "Congress," "Flat Rock," and "High Rock." The present ornamental grounds near the first spring had been recently cleared, and were full of stumps and half-burned trees.

At the end of six weeks Mr. Jarvis returned home, restored to health.

About this time Miss Edgeworth's stories for children, and "Practical Education," by Richard Lovell Edgeworth, attracted much attention in the literary world.

Mr. Jarvis purchased these works, reading the former to his little girls, much to their delight; and adopting many of Mr. Edgeworth's suggestions, commenced teaching them by regular lessons, and still more by his conversation.[1]

Frosts in each month, partially destroyed the crops

[1] He found time to continue these instructions until 1818, when he employed a governess; but the two eldest daughters were wholly educated at home. He took much pains with their spelling, writing, and reading aloud, little foreseeing that he was preparing them to fulfill the important duty of reading and writing for him, after his eye-sight became impaired.

of grain on the hills of Vermont, in this cold summer of 1816. But the Consul's farm being sheltered and warm, suffered but little, and his granary became the store-house for the hill towns. Sympathizing with the people in their sufferings, he did not set a high price on the corn, but sold it reasonably, frequently agreeing to wait for payment, or take it in work in haying. The high lands being two or three weeks more backward than his sunny meadows, the farmers could work for him without neglecting their own hay, and he paid liberally for labor in haying and harvesting.[1]

On his return from Saratoga to his lonely house, no longer cheered by the presence of his uncle and aunt, — after the extreme suffering he endured through his tedious illness, he began to think seriously of a second marriage, for he greatly felt the want of a companion for himself, and a mother for his children.

His preferences led him to select a cousin of his wife, Miss Ann Bailey Bartlett, eldest daughter of Hon. Bailey Bartlett, as the lady of his choice, whose excellence of character was well known to him. With the intention of proffering her his hand and heart, he went to her father's, in Haverhill, Massachusetts, in January, 1817, and during this visit the engagement was formed.

His little Mary and Elizabeth, whom he had taken with him, were overjoyed when they were informed that " Cousin Ann " was to be their mamma.

---

1 One of the neighbors made a ballad upon this, comparing the Consul to " Egypt's Lord," and winding up with, —

> " And then agreed to take his pay
> In stout days' work in making hay.
> God speed his plough and bless his store,
> Then when we want we can have more."

Their mother had been loved like a sister, and her children were treated with the utmost kindness and attention by her cousins. Eight daughters and three sons were then at home, and order, elegance, and happiness reigned in this delightful family, which seemed like an elysium to the children, so secluded had been their lives.

Hon. B. Bartlett commenced life as an importing merchant, in Haverhill, Massachusetts, the same business in which his father had been engaged. He married Miss Peggy Leonard White, a beautiful young lady, and they occupied the same house in which his father had resided, making considerable additions to it. It was situated on the banks of the Merrimac, with a southern aspect, on the site of the house where the Johnsons lived, when taken captive by the Indians. Two of Mr. Johnson's children were saved by being secreted by a faithful domestic, under a tub in the cellar. The daughter thus rescued married Dr. Bailey, in the British navy, and was the grandmother of Hon. B. Bartlett.

This old family mansion was built of brick, three stories high, with gable windows in the third story, and a balcony; it was painted straw color; a luxuriant woodbine nearly covered the front, hanging in graceful festoons.

" Living in the most interesting period of the Revolution, Mr. Bartlett early mingled in political life. He was one of the earliest and most intimate friends of the venerable John Adams, and a fellow-boarder with him and Samuel Adams, in Philadelphia, on the 4th July, 1776. He was present in the yard of Congress Hall, when the Declaration of Inde-

pendence was first proclaimed. In 1783, he represented the
town of Haverhill in the House of Representatives, and in
1789, the County of Essex in the Senate. In 1797 he was
elected a member of Congress of the United States, and
held the office four years. He was the chosen companion
of the lamented Chief Justice Parker, between whom the
warmest and most cordial friendship continued to exist, until
the death of the Judge. He was a member of the last
Congress held in Philadelphia, and the first which met at
Washington.

" On the 1st July, 1789, he was appointed High Sheriff
of Essex County. Governor Hancock presented him the
commission in person, and stated to him that he did it with
peculiar pleasure, as it was the only nomination during his
administration that met the unanimous concurrence of his
Council. He held this office forty years, until his death, in
1830.

" He was kind and indulgent almost to a fault, and his
purse often paid the exactions of an unfeeling creditor,
rather than imprison a poor debtor. In all cases of difficulty he was firm, fearless, immovable. Such was the public life of this amiable, honest, faithful, unostentatious public servant. But the brightest traits of his character cannot
be known to the world. To see that, they should see the
family he has reared, trained, and stamped with his own
similitude, who never knew an angry passion, or a selfish
feeling. He had fifteen children ; two died in infancy,
eleven survived him.

" His leisure hours were devoted to reading, horticulture,
and mechanics. He had a large garden which he cultivated with great skill and care, and supplied his family
abundantly with a variety of fine fruit and vegetables. The
beautiful work-table, boxes, etc., that he made of nice wood
and ivory, etc., for his wife and daughters, testify to his

industry and ingenuity, and afforded him pleasure and recreation." [1]

Mr. Jarvis and Miss Bartlett were married in May, 1817, but the wedding was a very quiet one, only the near relatives and friends being present, owing to the recent death of a lovely sister, Eliza, wife of Joseph E. Sprague, Esq., of Salem, and the ill health of their mother, Mrs. Bartlett. Immediately after the dinner they sat out on their journey to Vermont, in his carriage, accompanied by her sister Catherine.[2] This short journey was attended with several mishaps, which, though not very agreeable at the time, occasioned much merriment in the retrospect. On arriving at Lebanon, the second day, after dark, a surly landlady refused to accommodate them for the night, and on turning from the door and the glare of light, unacquainted with the road, they were suddenly upset over a bank six or eight feet high, and ladies, children, wedding-cake, oranges, "great trunk, little trunk, bandbox, and basket," etc., etc., were thrown out.

Mr. Jarvis instantly stopped the horses, and the ground being sandy, no one was injured. A man, with apparent kindness, brought a lantern, and assisted in picking up the miscellaneous articles, and directed them to another public-house near by, where they were made very comfortable. As this *obliging* man left the room after everything was brought in, and he had been liberally rewarded for his trouble, what should the children descry but the tassels of "Mamma's"

---

[1] From an obituary notice of Hon B. Bartlett.

[2] Mrs. Jarvis was highly favored in always enjoying the companionship of one of her sisters, until they were all married in the course of years.

missing reticule, containing some valuable articles, hanging out of his pocket, but too late for its recovery; and it was afterwards discovered that he had appropriated several other things. The next day, within six miles of Weathersfield, in a pouring rain, off rolled one of the back wheels, letting the carriage down; but most happily this accident occurred near Captain and Mrs. Ingersoll's, in Windsor, old friends of Mrs. Jarvis, from Salem, who received the wet and weary travellers with the utmost kindness and hospitality, and prevailed upon them to remain to dinner. They reached home late in the afternoon.

A new and happy era in the Consul's life commenced with his second marriage. It was a most wise and judicious choice, and he could not have selected a lady better qualified to fulfill the duties that devolved upon her as wife, mother, mistress of a very large family, and of a house everywhere showing the want of a lady's care, which was soon wonderfully transformed by her experience and skill. Many and great were the difficulties she had to encounter; but by energy, industry, order, and admirable government over her domestics, she was enabled to overcome them all. Their hospitable, well-ordered mansion, soon became a resort for their friends and relatives in the vicinity and at a distance, much to the Consul's enjoyment, who now realized his anticipations of domestic happiness in the country.

General Lewis R. Morris and lady, who owned a beautiful place on the Connecticut, in Springfield, four miles distant, were the first to call on Mrs. Jarvis, and to welcome her to Vermont, by an invitation to tea.

The gentlemen had been intimate, and a friendship now commenced between the families, which continued through life.

"General Morris was born in Wall Street, New York. His father was Richard Morris, who was a Judge of Admiralty before the Revolution, and after the establishment of our independence, became Chief Justice of the State of New York. Lewis R. was intended for the bar, but the breaking out of the Revolution changed his plans. He entered the army at the age of seventeen, as ensign (or second lieutenant), and continued through the war in various positions. Was at one time aid to General Schuyler, and was aid to General Clinton, with the rank of Major, when the British evacuated New York. His reminiscences of the war were extremely interesting.

"Under the Confederation he became first Secretary in the office of Foreign Affairs, under Judge Livingston. He subsequently settled in Vermont, and cleared the fine meadow land on the Connecticut, where he resided the remainder of his life, erecting a large handsome house for the period. He was Marshal of the State, and took the first census of Vermont. Was a member of Congress two or three terms, and contemporary with Hon. B. Bartlett, in Congress. By absenting himself from the House, he gave the vote of the State to Jefferson, and thus secured his election, after a long struggle. Not having been elected on party grounds, and his State at that time having a majority for Jefferson, and his colleague being a strong Jefferson man, with the full approbation of his political associates in Congress, he decided to take this step." [1]

His first wife was Miss Olcutt, of Westminster, who died young, leaving one son; the General afterwards

---

[1] From a sketch of his life by his son, Gouverneur Morris.

married Miss Ellen Hunt, daughter of Governor Hunt, of Vernon, Vermont, who had four sons and one daughter.

There was a pleasant society of cultivated people in Windsor, and the Ingersolls, Dunhams, Everetts, Townsends, Leveretts, Greens, Thomases,[1] Dr. Torrey, etc., etc., soon called on Mrs. Jarvis, and social visits were frequently exchanged. Mr. Jarvis occasionally made dinner-parties for them, and Dr. Torrey, and two or three other gentlemen, were in the habit of dining with the Consul every other Saturday for years. In two or three months after her marriage, Mrs. Jarvis received long visits of several weeks from the Consul's aunts, Russell and her sister, Mary Jarvis, Miss Elizabeth Spooner, Mrs. Benjamin Jarvis, and other relatives. Mrs. Jarvis also had the pleasure of visits from her parents, and some of her brothers and sisters. The weekly dinners, with " Uncle Sam's " family, at Weathersfield and Claremont, were kept up, and Mary and Helen were frequent guests, passing many days at a time with " Cousin Ann." All this company was extremely pleasant ; but with only green untaught girls in her kitchen,[2] and a large number of workmen to be provided for,[3] it caused the mistress of

1 Mrs. Thomas, from Newburyport, was an early acquaintance of Mrs. Jarvis.

2 Mrs. Jarvis' discipline over her domestics was remarkable; for she not only instructed and trained them in the exact discharge of their respective duties, but she won their respect and made them happy. Many of them lived with her for years, until they were married; some five, some seven, some twelve years. Respectable farmers' daughters sought the situation, and she was always able to secure good girls.

8 Before the days of mowing machines, the Consul generally employed thirty men in haying and harvesting.

the family great care and labor, and was a trying experience of Vermont life. For years their house was filled with friends in summer.

When President Monroe made his tour through New England, in 1817, an ovation was prepared for him in Windsor, and the Consul was requested to lend a very large and beautiful gray horse that he had reared, for the President to ride in the procession, with which request he complied. The Consul took his family to Windsor to be present at the festivities. The ladies assembled to welcome the President, and watched with great interest for his appearance. When the procession came in view, all eyes were intently fixed on the gentleman on the noble gray, and handkerchiefs were waved from the windows as he passed. But lo, what was their mortification to learn that the President rode on a *bay horse !* [1] The music and guns causing the young gray to shy, he had exchanged horses with his younger and more active Secretary. But at a levee in the evening, all the ladies had the pleasure of seeing and shaking hands with the *President*.

In June, 1818, another daughter was added to the family, much to the joy of all, and none were more delighted than the elder sisters, who considered her their especial little darling, and preferred her to their dolls. She was named Anne Eliza.

In August of this summer Mr. Samuel G. Jarvis died, in advanced years, and his grandson, Samuel G. Jarvis, then an infant, was baptized by Rev. Mr. Howe, Rector of the Church in West Claremont, at the time of the funeral.

---

[1] Also belonging to the Consul.

"Dr. Leonard Jarvis studied medicine with his uncle, Dr. Charles J., and commenced practice in Claremont when his father removed there, in 1797. He was a successful and eminent practitioner, and particularly skillful in surgery; for he was not only a thorough anatomist, but was aided by great mechanical ingenuity and force of will. To his clear and comprehensive intellect, and sympathy and feeling for his patients, he owed his professional success. He was equally distinguished as a scientific and practical farmer, and after he came into possession of his father's real estate, he retired from the practice of medicine, except as a consulting physician, and devoted himself more to agriculture, and raising fine wooled sheep. He was an extensive reader of English and French literature. His mind was highly artistic, strongly characterized by perception of beauty in nature and art. Through his varied information, clear and rapid thought, and facility of expression, he had great power in conversation and argument. He was very hospitable and courteous in his manners."

The Doctor married Miss Clarissa Draper, of Claremont. She was handsome, sprightly, and pleasing; a most faithful and excellent wife, energetic and untiring in her industry. Their children were, Susan Pierce, Samuel Gardner, Leonard, Russell, and William. The latter died in infancy.

In 1818 the Doctor's brother, Russell, having completed his law studies with his cousin, William C. Jarvis, of Pittsfield, Massachusetts, opened an office in Claremont village.

After the death of their father, his sisters, Mary and

Helen, joined him, and they hired a convenient, pleasant house, built by Judge Ellis — a delightful home, where their friends were ever welcome.

In 1820, Russell married Miss Caroline Dana, of Chelsea, Vermont, a beautiful, accomplished girl, with whom he fell in love while she was attending Colonel Dunham's school, in Windsor. After his marriage, his sisters boarded with Colonel and Mrs. Dunham for several years.

Mrs. Dunham was a sister of Professor Hedge, of Cambridge; a superior woman, sensible, dignified, and benevolent. The Colonel's boarding-school was a very popular one, and his handsome, tasteful residence and grounds added much to the happiness of his pupils.

Mrs. Russell Jarvis died in two or three years, leaving a daughter, named for herself, who was adopted by her grandparents Dana, to fill the place of their beloved and only daughter. Russell removed to Boston, and afterwards married Miss Eliza Cordis.

Dr. Jarvis made great improvements in the house his father left him, adding a long dining-room for dinner parties, or a social dance; a snug breakfast-room, removing the large old-fashioned chimneys, making a fish-pond, and two fountains in front, and surrounding it with a hedge, mountain ashes, roses, snow-berries, etc., etc., etc., and extending the piazza all round. The majestic elms that Judge Kingsbury set out, formed a beautiful arcade over the fountains.[1]

In December, 1819, Mr. Jarvis, in adjusting a microscope in the evening for his children, strained his eyes. A cold which he took next day caused a

[1] See Appendix C: Jarvis family.

violent inflammation in them, and he was confined to a darkened room for three months, wearing a shade and green glasses constantly. Drs. Torrey and Jarvis were assiduous in their attentions; but medicine, blisters, and eye-washes afforded little or no relief, for the pain and tenderness continued. Loud reading was the only alleviation of this almost intolerable suffering and confinement.[1] As the spring opened, his health improved, but his eyes were so weak, that he was never again able to read, or to write more than a short letter. His wife, children, or some friend performed for him these labors of love to the end of his life. All his memorials to Congress, articles for the papers, letters, etc., etc., were written by dictation.

The fourth daughter, named Harriet Bartlett, after a beloved sister of Mrs. Jarvis, recently deceased, was born in February of this sad winter. She was a remarkably fine, intelligent child, and became a universal favorite.

Their first boy was born in August, 1821, an event that caused the greatest pleasure to their friends, who were desirous that they should have a son to sustain the name and family. When Dr. Torrey, the family physician, expressed this sentiment to Mr. Jarvis, he replied, "I have always been perfectly satisfied with girls, and thankful when they were sent to me."

This son, named Charles, for his grandfather, in-

---

[1] Scott's Novels, then so very popular, Mrs. Opie's and Miss Edgeworth's tales, reviews, papers, and many volumes of history, including Robertson's *Charles V.* and *America*, were listened to with close attention; his eldest daughters, and their cousin and teacher, Miss Humphreys, reading alternately from morning until he retired at night.

herited his loyalty and patriotism, and became the stay and staff of his father in old age, a blessing to his family, a benefactor to the community, and in the late war a Christian hero in the cause of his country, in whose service his life was sacrificed.

CHAPTER XXXII.

PECUNIARY TROUBLES OF THE FARMERS, AND THE
CONSUL'S READY ASSISTANCE. — HIS UNWEARIED
EFFORTS FOR THE ENCOURAGEMENT OF AGRICUL-
TURE AND MANUFACTURES.

THERE was a great scarcity of money for many
years after the war. The farmers were often troubled
to settle their store accounts, and as they were   1816–
not always able to pay as promptly as the   1850.
banks required, they applied to Mr. Jarvis. To accommodate those in the vicinity, he commenced loan-
ing money to them, at first small sums on notes. But
as he never charged over the lawful interest of six per ·
cent., and allowed them to keep the money as long as
the interest was regularly paid, he received applications more extensively, and on a larger scale, and took
mortgages of land for security. This mode of lending
money caused him a great deal of business labor, and
occupied a great deal of time to the end of his life.

He was influenced by benevolence in this matter,
wishing to benefit the agriculturists by long credits.
It was surprising how widely the community availed
themselves of this privilege. For many years, in the
winter season, there were often from five to ten per-

sons during the day in his parlor, paying interest, borrowing money, etc., etc.[1]

The Revolutionary times, in which Mr. Jarvis was born, seemed to have imbued his soul with disinterested patriotism.

On his return from Europe he began to devote much time and thought to the welfare of his country, which had been impoverished by the war. Manufactures were in their infancy, and agriculture in a very rude state. He had diffused the fine wooled merinos as widely as he could through the United States, and he now offered them for sale at so low a price, that all the farmers could afford to purchase them. He had been deeply impressed in Portugal by the ruinous effects of sending all her money out of the kingdom to pay for foreign manufactures, and even for breadstuffs. England was the workshop of the world, amassing wealth from manufacturing all kinds of goods and wares, and receiving in return the gold and silver of other nations. The United States had heretofore been dependent on England, for a great proportion of her goods. Since the beginning of the war we had made some feeble attempts at home manufactures. Wool was spun and wove in families, and dyed and fulled at small mills about the country; and spinning and weaving wool and flax were regular employments in every farmer's family. Mr. Jarvis now resolved that for the sake of encouraging American manufactures, he would use none other, sacrificing

[1] Unwilling to separate himself from his family, his business was always transacted in their presence, and in later years he often required their assistance

appearances to the good of his country. He had a
portion of his own wool made into yarn, flannel, and
fulled cloth, which he used for winter sheets, and
clothing for himself and children ; for their summer
wear he bought the cottons and ginghams, coarse
though durable, made at the State Prison, in Windsor.
The leather tanned in his tannery, which was of superior quality, he sold to the Farwells, of Claremont,
who manufactured well-made boots and shoes extensively, and supplied the adjacent towns.

He wrote articles for the papers, and to members of
Congress, to endeavor to draw the attention of the
people to the encouragement and protection of agriculture and manufactures, and to place the subject in
its true light before them ; and labored unremittingly
in this cause during the remainder of his life.

Niles, in his " Register," [1] Matthew Carey, and himself, began to write upon the protection of American
agriculture and manufactures about the same time,
without acquaintance or concert. Mr. Carey was
Irish by birth, and commenced life as a printer in
Philadelphia. He was a man of fine talents, and resembled Dr. Franklin in character.

He saw that the prosperity of England was in a
great measure owing to the fostering care of the government over her agricultural and manufacturing interests ; and giving his whole heart to his adopted
country, devoted himself with untiring zeal to the improvement of her condition.

In 1816 Mr. Carey commenced writing little pam-
phlets on this subject, which were widely circulated

---

[1] Niles' *Register.*

throughout the Union, showing that by encouraging the manufacturers and mechanics, they would open a home market for the wool and other produce of the farmer, and for the cotton, rice, tobacco, sugar, and turpentine, of the South, thus benefiting all portions of the community. They exerted a great influence over the South, by opening the eyes of the Southern people to what was for their own interest, and most conducive to the prosperity of the nation.

Mr. Carey labored more assiduously than any other person in advocating these measures, and died in the harness in 18—, having spent $10,000 in this cause, and in efforts to carry a protective tariff.

Henry Clay was another able supporter of home industry, commencing his labors about the same period. Mr. Jarvis highly appreciated him as an eloquent, talented, upright advocate of this cause. Not only an honest *man*, but an honest *politician*.

Charles Rich, Rollin C. Mallory, and Horace Everett, members of Congress from Vermont, were active coadjutors in "the American system." C. Rich had given much attention to the rearing of merino sheep, and was deeply interested in the matter. Mr. Mallory was distinguished for sound good sense, judgment, and talent, and was indefatigable in his labors for a protective tariff.[1] He effected a great deal by private conversation. He gained Virginia by saying that she sent more tobacco and corn North than to any other place.

[1] Mr. Jarvis at one period owned a large part of a woolen manufactory on the Quechee River, at Quechee Village, and out of regard to his friend Mallory, he called it the " Mallory Woolen Company."

A member from Virginia, after listening to the speech, went to him and said it was all "*a trick.*" He calmly replied that if he would examine the Treasury Reports, he would be satisfied of the truth of his statements. The Virginian did so; became convinced of the correctness of the assertion, enlisted on the side of protection, and gained all the members from Virginia over, so that the State went for a protective tariff. Mr. Jarvis reposed great confidence in Mr. Mallory, and corresponded regularly with him.

In 1823 the Consul prepared a very able memorial to Congress, giving a sketch of the policy and history of England in protecting her home industry for the last five hundred years.

Perhaps none of his writings possessed more merit than this memorial. He bestowed much time and thought upon it; the arguments were strong and conclusive, displaying great research, and his extensive knowledge of the subject both in past and present times.[1]

It was signed by a large number of Vermonters. He forwarded two copies to the Vermont delegation, and one to Henry Clay.

It had great weight in Congress; a most beneficial tariff was passed, and under its healthful influence the farmer and manufacturer began to thrive, and manufactories were extensively established.

The following letter to a member of Congress was written soon after the memorial was dispatched : —

"HAVERHILL, MASS., *February* 15, 1823.

"DEAR SIR, — Your favor of the 27th ultimo was re-

---

[1] See Appendix G: Extracts from this memorial in it.

ceived by me yesterday at this place. . . . . When in Boston and Salem, where I have been with my family on a visit, I was often assailed by the merchants as one of the warm supporters of the tariff bill, and my views on the subject appear to be equally objectionable in Washington. . . . It must be recollected that I voluntarily left a respectable office in Europe — in the execution of which, I believe, I gave perfect satisfaction to our government, and general satisfaction to our countrymen — and a very profitable mercantile business, to pursue what I then conceived, and still believe, to be a great object of national utility — cultivating the breed of merinos, and the general improvement of our native sheep; and it is probable that this will be my steady pursuit to the end of my life, unless the object I have in view should be defeated by some mistaken act of policy on the part of Congress.

"These remarks I have taken the liberty to make to satisfy you that I am a sincere well-wisher to the agricultural interests of our country, and equally so to the manufacturing, as its principal support. The whole history of Modern Europe proves that the agricultural and manufacturing interests have constituted the chief wealth and strength of nations, and that under ordinary circumstances, the commerce of most nations has emanated from, and been supported by, these two branches of national industry. . . . .

"I trust that the good sense of Congress will show itself in the passage of some law, however difficult in its details, to secure to our manufacturing class of citizens a sale of their goods in our home market, at a fair profit, notwithstanding the competition of foreign manufactures. . . . . A system that has been advocated by a Franklin, a Jefferson, a Madison, and all the most enlightened men of all parties in our country; and the advantages of which have been so fully tested in Europe by the experience of ages, and the great prosperity which has resulted to every nation who have practiced upon the restrictive system, ought to embolden Congress to proceed with confidence in pursuit of this object, in defiance of the clamor arising from local feeling, narrow prejudices, and self-interested views."

The following extract is from an article published in the " Republican and Yeoman," edited by Mr. Simeon Ide, of Windsor, whose political views and firm consistent conduct won the cordial esteem of the Consul.

" To Mr. C. C. Cambreleng, Member of Congress from the City of New York : —

. . . . " You stated that the bill to protect woolen manufactures ought to be denominated, 'a bill to enable farmers to sell their wool;' in this you are correct, and I must give you the credit of seeing more than you intended others should see. It is emphatically, a bill to enable the farmers of the Western, Middle, and Eastern States to *sell their wool.* This body, who constitute the bone and muscle of the nation; this body, who consume by far the greatest part of our foreign importations, and consequently pay the greatest portion of the revenue to the general government, as well as the bulk of the taxes to the State governments ; this body, upon which devolves the defense of the nation in time of war, and its strength and security at all times, is now in a more distressed condition than any other portion of the community, except the woolen manufacturers, who may aptly be compared to the spinal marrow. . . . .

" More than half the farmers of the Union are directly or indirectly interested in the success of that bill, and a property not much short of a hundred millions of dollars is involved in it, and yet these are to be sacrificed, unfeelingly sacrificed, to enable the city of New York to monopolize the woolen trade of England. . . . .

"It is the farmers, manufacturers, and mechanics, who are the working bees of the hive; it is those who constitute the wealth of nations. . . . .

"If you possess any talent for calculation, you will find out by the unerring result of numbers, whether it is most advantageous to supply a nation's wants from her own workshops, and to grow the raw material to furnish the manufacturer, and thus infuse into the body politic comfort, health, and strength, or by purchasing those comforts of foreign nations, to encourage and render prosperous *their* agriculture and *their* manufactures, at the expense of the consuming nation, and thus by degrees to exhaust its resources. Again you will also discover whether a nation will be a gainer by the sacrifice of eighty millions dollars of property, which actively employs many thousands of her most useful citizens, and in its ramifications diffuses its benefits through the whole community, and which, at simple interest, would add about five millions annually to the national stock; but which, by the industry and active ingenuity of those who are using the eighty millions, would undoubtedly add more than double this sum yearly to it. Or whether it is best to sacrifice this capital and compound accumulation, to the temporary advantage of an additional revenue of one or two millions of dollars, more or less, and which revenue must soon fail for want of means to pay for the manufactures upon which it is levied. . . . .

"I do not mean to have it understood that the farmers have any objection to our merchants being protected. So far from it, they are decidedly of opinion that every interest of our country ought to be protected, thoroughly protected; but they mean to have it as decidedly understood, that they will not patiently submit to the sacrifice of the agricultural and manufacturing interests of our country, to enrich a foreign rival, nor to gratify the foreign prejudices of some, and mistaken views and local interests of others, particularly at the South.

"A PRACTICAL FARMER.

"*December*, 1826."

HARRISBURG CONVENTION.

In 1827 Mr. Jarvis was appointed a delegate to attend the Harrisburg Convention, which was organized for the discussion of a protective tariff, and he was so deeply interested in this subject, that he accepted. He found that a great diversity of opinion existed among the members regarding duties; some wishing to impose a high duty on one manufacture, some on another, and that unless there could be some concert of action, nothing would be effected.

He therefore made a short speech, and moved that all the members interested in any particular manufacture, should meet together in committees, and agree upon the lowest duty that would be sufficient to protect their respective branches.

The motion was carried; the committees met, and the second day the reports were brought in.

Mr. Jarvis moved that each chairman read his report, which was acceded to.

Although some of the duties were rather high, yet with modifications, they all passed; and in this way the various manufacturers — woolen, cotton, iron, etc., etc. — were satisfied, and a very beneficial tariff for the Union obtained.

Mr. Jarvis had to labor as hard to convince the wool-growers that they did not require a high duty on wool, to benefit them, as he did to persuade the merchants to consent to a high duty on foreign manufactured woolens and cottons.

Mr. Francis Granger, of New York, was very much opposed to the admission of wool at a low duty, thinking there should be high duties to protect the farmers from foreign competition ; he said that he had been so instructed by his constituents, and that he should act according to their wishes.

Mr. Jarvis listened to his remarks, and then replied that it cost England more to raise sheep than it did us. Our pasture land was worth but from two to five dollars per acre, while in England it was worth from twenty to forty dollars ; consequently we could afford to sell wool cheaper. On the reverse, labor was much higher in this country than in England, therefore the manufacturer needed protection. If they flourished, they would open a market for the wool-grower, and pay them prices affording a good profit. England has pursued this policy for the last five hundred years, but she is opposed to our imitating her example, as it would be prejudicial to her interests.

Mr. Jarvis was appointed one of a committee to draw up a petition to Congress. Matthew Carey expected to have been named, and had a memorial prepared. He considered it a great slight that he had been left out, and felt it so deeply that he was about to leave Harrisburg. On learning this, Mr. Jarvis immediately called upon him, spoke of the importance of the measures he had so long and so ably advocated, and in support of which they were now assembled ; of the great consequence of his laboring there in the cause. Should he abruptly leave the Convention, and suffer it to go abroad that they had split among themselves, and that he — the prime leader in the support of protection — had deserted, it might defeat the labors of years. Mr. Carey was so mollified, that he consented to remain another day, and promised to inform Mr. Jarvis should he then decide to go.

An active friend of the cause from New York was also much disappointed that another gentleman of much respectability in Connecticut was placed on the committee instead of himself.

The Consul now called upon the Connecticut gentleman, told him of Mr. Carey's disappointment, and that of the other member, and proposed to resign in favor of Mr. Carey, if he would do the same for the New York member.

A ready assent was given, and Mr. Jarvis then laid the whole matter before the President of the Convention, — a plain, sound, sensible man, — and informed him of his intention of declining, as it was really a mistake that Matthew Carey had not been nominated, he had been so zealous a supporter of the cause, and was so well known to the public.

The President said that if that was the case, it was not too late to rectify it; that when Mr. Jarvis declined, Mr. Carey could be nominated, and with regret expressed that he had not been named before, on account of his well-known public services. The changes were effected, much to the satisfaction of all parties, and harmony was restored.

When the committee met it was found that both Mr. Carey and the New York gentleman had memorials prepared; that of the former was excellent in its practical details. Each thought their own deserving of preference. In this dilemma, Mr. Jarvis proposed that the theoretical part of one, and the practical details of the other, be united. This idea was favorably received, and was adopted. It was an able exposition of the subject, was presented to Congress, and the tariff that was drawn up and passed in consequence, gave the great impetus to manufactures in 1828, 1829, 1830, and 1831.

Mr. Jarvis was very happy to meet and converse with Henry Clay at this time, for whom he entertained a high respect and admiration, and who was afterward his favorite candidate for the Presidency — the strong, talented, eloquent champion of the "American system."

He also formed an agreeable acquaintance with Abbott Lawrence, who subsequently remarked that Mr. Jarvis then made a convert of him to the cause of American manufactures; he acted up to his convictions by investing a portion of his capital in the manufactories of Massachusetts — " Lawrence " bearing the name of its founder.

Mr. James Perkins, of Boston, had established a manufactory for nice broadcloth, on Black River, in Weathersfield, in about 1824. The village was called Perkinsville. On his return from Harrisburg, Mr. Jarvis sent some of his best merino wool to this place, and had it made into fine black broadcloth. He presented Henry Clay with a full pattern for a suit of clothes, as a testimony of respect, and as a specimen of the degree of perfection which Vermont manufactures had attained.[1]

---

[1] Mr. Clay's letter of acknowledgment is still preserved.

The fashionable world were slow to believe that good cloth could be made in America. Mr. Shepherd, of Northampton, Massachusetts, made superior superfine broadcloth of Saxony wool, some of which he marked " Saxony wool, England," and his name. Another part of it he marked " Saxony wool, American," with his name, and sent it to New York. That marked ENGLAND sold readily for eight dollars per yard; that marked American could scarcely be disposed of at four dollars.

The Consul took a warm interest in all elections, endeavoring to ascertain who were the most suitable men for office, who would be most faithful to the best interests of the people and the country, and exerted all his energies to have them elected, supporting them in the papers, and sometimes canvassing the county.[1] He was often importuned in later years to accept offices himself: to be Governor, Senator, member of Congress, etc., but steadily refused, acknowledging the honor they did him. His public duties in Lisbon had been so arduous, and he had so deeply and conscientiously felt the responsibility, that he could never again be drawn from private life ; but by his influence in writing and conversation, he hoped as effectually to serve the State.

He took a very active part in the election of John Quincy Adams. During the session of the legislature, he went to Montpelier to call a Convention for

[1] Mark Richards and William C. Bradley, of Westminster, Hiland Hall, of Bennington, William Slade and Senator Phelps, of Middlebury, Senators Prentiss and Upham, of Montpelier, Solomon Foote, of Rutland, Jacob Collamer, of Woodstock, Justin S. Morrill, etc., etc., were among his favorite candidates, besides those already named as efficient supporters of the tariff.

his nomination. A member of Congress, H. Olin, whom he met there, feared the State would not go for Adams — but he was a very timid man.

Mr. Jarvis then requested two young men, one of whom was his friend, J. Cutler, to converse with each member of the House and Senate separately, and ascertain their sentiments. They did so, and found that three fourths of them were in favor of Adams.

The opposition party were to hold a meeting that evening in the House of Representatives. He went to see his friend and ally, E. P. Walton, Esq., inquired if Montpelier would support Adams, and was answered affirmatively. Would they permit a political meeting to be held in the church? Mr. Walton thought they would; they went together and obtained permission to use it; had handbills printed, announcing that a Convention would be held at a certain time. Several of the prominent men of the State were at Montpelier at this time, among whom were Judge Hutchinson, of Woodstock, and Horace Everett, member of Congress, of Windsor.

They, and several others, made speeches. There was a large number present, and the resolutions that Mr. Jarvis had prepared, were carried by an overwhelming majority.

The State went for Adams at this election, and in 1828.

He had supported C. P. Van Ness for Governor. When his gubernatorial term expired, Mr. Van Ness wished to go to Congress as Senator, and sought the Consul's influence, calling upon him with his talented, elegant lady, and afterwards, in several letters, pledged himself to support Adams, if elected Senator. General Jackson gained the election.

The ambition of Van Ness was stronger than his principles, and he went over to that party, thereby breaking his pledges, and ruining his reputation in Vermont. He was rewarded by an appointment as Minister to Spain, with an outfit of nine thousand dollars, and a salary of nine thousand dollars. Mrs. Van Ness, who was a noble-minded woman, died, and he married a Spanish lady.

In the great presidential campaign for William Henry Harrison, Mr. Jarvis enlisted in his support with the utmost zeal and energy ; writing, making addresses, and with liberal hand defraying the expenses of talented speakers, in awakening the people to the importance of the election.

The distress that had pervaded all classes of the community from 1835, convinced the people that a change of men and measures was needed, and they manifested an almost unprecedented enthusiasm in Harrison's election.

It was a great rally of the Whig party. A mass meeting was called at Windsor, Vermont, on the 4th of July, and Mr. Jarvis was to deliver the principal address. At an early hour in the morning long processions were formed, bearing flags and banners, with appropriate mottoes, from all the towns for many miles around ; and the valley of the Connecticut rang with cheers and shouts for " Tippecanoe, and Tyler too."

As one instance, well remembered, Mr. Cutts, of Hartland, sent a large wagon drawn by four beautiful gray horses. On the heads of each were small red flags, on which was inscribed in large white letters, *Tip, Tyler, Tariff, Trade.* In the centre of the wagon was a large white banner, with *The Farmers are coming*, on one side. On the other, *Protection to American Industry*, in large black letters. It was principally filled with workmen, who had no conveyances of their own. Many thousands had assembled by eleven o'clock. The Consul's address was a very able one, abounding with strong arguments, cutting satire, and ridicule,[1] and was received with enthusiastic cheering by the multitude. It occupied nearly two hours, yet they listened to it with unabated interest.

The Consul was followed by several eloquent speakers, among whom was Mr. Cutts; but their speeches were necessarily short.

Such a concourse of people was never before or since gathered together in Windsor, and it showed how heartily the people were interested in the struggle.

Harrison was elected, but how soon the joy of the people was changed to mourning by his untimely death! None but the Allseeing Eye knows why the hopes of the people were so soon crushed.

Mr. Jarvis was afterward an earnest advocate for the election of Henry Clay and Zachary Taylor; and his interest in the affairs of his country continued undiminished during his life.

Extracts from a Memorial to Congress in 1842.

" *To the Honorable the Senate and House of Representatives of the United States :* —

" A numerous meeting of delegates from the several towns in Windsor County, in the State of Vermont, held at

---

[1] This address was published in pamphlet form, and widely circulated.

Woodstock on the 15th day of March, 1842, beg leave to lay before the representatives of the people in Congress assembled, their complaints touching the present condition of the industrious classes of this community. . . . .

" Every branch of industry throughout our country is in a paralyzed state, and the distress of the people is far greater than was ever known in our country since the Revolutionary War, and the six subsequent years. In a time of profound peace, when Providence has showered abundance on our land, such a state of things is an anomaly in the history of mankind. . . . . Your memorialists are plain, practical men, who entertain the highest opinion of the knowledge and ability congregated within the walls of the Capitol ; yet we do not forget that we are citizens of the United States, and that your honorable body are chosen by the people to promote the general welfare. . . . .

" The disordered state of the currency is undoubtedly one of the prominent causes ; . . . . and another of equal magnitude, and perhaps more permanent in its effect, is the very large amount of foreign goods imported into our country, which depresses our home industry, and leaves over the amount of all our exports, a balance of many millions of dollars annually against us, which balance must be paid in gold or silver. The whole history of modern Europe has clearly demonstrated, that every nation in that quarter of the globe, whose imports have exceeded their exports for any number of years, has become impoverished, and weakness and degradation in the scale of nations have followed. On the reverse, those nations who have wisely protected the industry of their subjects, and thus enabled them to *export* annually a larger amount than they *import*, have become wealthy, vigorous, and powerful.

" England, with a soil and climate far inferior to Portugal, Spain, and Italy, affords an example of the prosperity and power to which a nation can attain by a wise and steady policy, affording protection and encouragement to every branch of her industry; and the three other countries named, with a superior climate and soil, offer as striking examples of national prostration, by pursuing an opposite policy.

"Yet we find many men, who are so charmed with the plausible theory of free trade, that they contemn the light of experience, for the pursuit of that bubble. . . . . A clear-sighted government, that has a perfect knowledge of the laws of trade, and which understands the interests of the nation, and steadily pursues them in all commercial negotiations, will obtain an advantage over a nation which has less knowledge of its true interests, — or one, — which, influenced by chimerical theories and visionary abstractions, is from year to year changing its policy.

"The English government is certainly entitled to the praise of having vigilantly, jealously, and steadily encouraged every branch of national industry. Whether the administration has been in the hands of Jacobites or Cromwellites, Tory or Whig, etc., the protection of the national industry against the rivalry of foreign nations, has never been lost sight of or neglected; until this perseverance has brought their manufactures to such a degree of perfection as to defy foreign competition. . . . .

"With thirty to forty millions of dollars worth of manufactures sent to us yearly from Great Britain, there are also sent for our instruction many magazines, quarterlies, newspapers, Parliamentary reports, etc., all lauding this doctrine of *free trade*.

"But how do they practice upon it at home?

"Every description of foreign manufactures that competes with her own, are either prohibited, or met with prohibitory duties. She will not take from us wheat, corn, rye, barley, nor oats, unless her population is in a starving condition, because our breadstuffs compete with her agricultural labor. She will not take from us the products of our fisheries, because it would compete with her own fisheries. She will not take from us any description of lumber, although she grows none at home, because it competes with the lumber of Canada. She takes from us our tobacco, by paying a duty and excise of three shillings and two pence, or three shillings and three pence per pound. She takes our rice, by paying fifteen shillings sterling per hundred duty. . . . . In fine, she will not take from us any article — the products of our soil, of our forests, of our mines, or our fisheries, — with the solitary exception of our raw cotton, a material which is all essential to her cotton manufactories, a branch of her industry which has amounted to from thirty to forty millions sterling a year, and which supports some hundreds of thousands of her population. She now appears uneasy at this large expenditure for this article, and is straining every nerve to encourage the cultivation of it in her East India possessions, so as to render herself independent of foreign nations for this raw material."

Mr. Jarvis speaks of her probable success in raising cotton, as it is a native of Hindostan; and of her cultivating opium and indigo in Hindostan, that she may avoid expenditures for these articles, and by exporting opium to China increase her revenues.

" We have had some examples in our own history of the effects upon our interests, by the free-trade policy. . . . . From 1783 to 1789, the trade of the thirteen old States was perfectly free to the whole world. The result was, that Great Britain filled every section of our country with her manufactures, of wool, of cotton, of linen, of leather, of iron, of brass, copper, and glass; and in four years she

24

swept from our country every round dollar, and every piece of gold, until there was not coin enough left to pay the people's taxes; and in addition, our merchants in every State were largely indebted to the merchants of England.

"Virginia and other Southern States had nothing left them but dollars cut into quarters, and pistareens cut into bits and half bits, for a currency; and although in the cutting process about twenty per cent. was extracted, — we suppose to pay the operators for this new species of coinage, — yet, as the only currency which could be kept amongst them, the people were glad to receive it, at its nominal value of five cents for a half bit, ten cents for a bit, and the four parts of the dollar as quarters.

"The debts to England finally accumulated to such an extent, that the Legislature of Virginia deemed itself compelled to pass a law to prevent lands being attached and sold under execution. . . . .

"Permit me to advert to the case of a foreign nation. In 1704, England made a treaty with the Portuguese government, commonly called the 'Methuen Treaty,' by which England was allowed to export to that kingdom all kinds of her manufactures at a lower duty than they were admitted from other nations, and in return allowed the importation of Portuguese wines into Great Britain at a lower duty than was laid on French wines."

He goes on to say, with an appearance of reciprocity, the advantages were all on the side of England, securing to her the exclusive supply of Portugal and her Brazilian possessions, with all the manufactures of wool, cotton, linen, iron, steel, and brass, and some of leather and tin, which destroyed the few manufactures that Portugal then had.

In payment, England received wine, salt, and fruit

from Portugal, and a large part of the gold, and the hides, tallow, horns, raw cotton, dye and furniture woods, etc., etc., shipped from the Brazils to the mother country. The effects were to increase the wealth of British subjects, while those of Portugal became poor.

"England would have remained as poor and feeble as she was at the Norman, the Saxon, the Danish, and the Roman conquests, had not that able monarch, Edward III., thought that by encouraging and protecting the industry of his subjects, he should increase their wealth, and add to the strength and power of his realm. His successors pursued the same wise policy, and that sagacious sovereign, Elizabeth, matured and systematized it. Every sea, every island, and every country on the globe, now witnesses or feels the effects of it. . . . .

"In France, the celebrated Tully and Colbert deemed it the first duty of a statesman to encourage the agricultural and manufacturing industry of that nation, and the surest way to add to the power of the kingdom, was to increase the wealth and prosperity of their subjects.

"Some of us are old men, and we well recollect that one of the strongest arguments made use of in favor of forming a Federal Constitution, was, that it would afford protection to the agricultural and mechanical industry of our country, against the depressing rivalry, skill, and capital of foreign nations. . . . . In General Hamilton's celebrated report, the encouragement of manufactures and mechanic arts was recommended, as highly necessary to promote the general welfare. . . . . Every administration, from that of General Washington to that of General Jackson inclusive (our first seven Presidents), has recommended this course as the surest source of national wealth, and to render us independent of foreign nations."

The tariff of 1828 had been so much altered during the administration of Van Buren, that it no longer afforded protection to the manufacturer and agriculturist. This second memorial exerted much influence in Congress, and the tariff was greatly improved in consequence of its strong arguments. But in Polk's administration it was again changed, to the deep injury of the home industry of the country.

Extracts from a Letter to Henry Watson, Esq.

"WEATHERSFIELD, 15*th June*, 1843.

"My dear Sir, — It is refreshing after so many years' silence, to receive a letter from an old friend, with whom I have fought shoulder to shoulder, in the cause of American industry. The more I have examined this cause, and witnessed its beneficial effects upon the prosperity of our country, as well as upon all others which have perseveringly encouraged and protected their own industry against foreign rivalry, the more satisfied I am that it is the only sure road to the wealth, power, and prosperity of nations.

"The *statesman*, with far-seeing penetration, adapts his measures to promote the durable advantage of his country. The *politician* is a man of expedients, looking but little beyond the present, and trusts to cunning management and address to carry his points."

He goes on to show that England has always advocated *free trade* for other nations, but has scrupulously avoided *practicing* upon this principle.

"From 1824 to 1834, our country gradually advanced in wealth, all branches of industry being in a prosperous condition. From 1834 to 1840 the reverse was the case."

CHAPTER XXXIII.

HIS CHILDREN ; BIRTHS, DEATHS, MARRIAGES, ETC., ETC.

Children of William Jarvis and Mary Pepperrell Sparhawk.

Mary Pepperrell Sparhawk, born in Lisbon, May 21, 1809.

Elizabeth Bartlett, born in Haverhill, Massachusetts, February 22, 1811.

Children of William Jarvis and Ann Bailey Bartlett.[1]

Anne Eliza, born in Weathersfield, June 30, 1818.

Harriet Bartlett, February 8, 1820.

Charles, August 21, 1821.

William, March 9, 1823.

Thomas Jefferson, September 4, 1824.

Margaret and Sarah, twins, July 20, 1826.

Catherine, March 16, 1830.

(She died at six weeks, in April.)

Catherine Leonard, December 25, 1831.

Louise Bailey, May 27, 1835.

William, a fair, gentle, affectionate child, died in August, 1825, when two and a half years old. A delicate flower, that bloomed for a little while, and was then transplanted to —

> " Warmer love and brighter skies."

[1] All born in Weathersfield.

This first death in the family group of children, occasioned heartfelt grief to all.

Little Thomas was so sick when his brother died, that by the advice of the physicians, Mr. Jarvis took him and all the family to Nahant for sea air. Anne, Harriet, and Charles were also sick, having the whooping-cough.

At a later period, by the earnest request of the family, the Consul changed the name of Thomas Jefferson to William.

In September, 1829, Mary P. S. married Hampden Cutts, Counselor-at-law in Portsmouth, New Hampshire.[1] In November, 1833, they removed to Hartland, Vermont, in compliance with her father's wishes, to improve a fine estate there, where they remained until after his death.

The Consul was so much attached to country life and agricultural pursuits, that it would have pleased him if all his children could have had the same tastes, and settled upon his farms. Mr. Cutts was very fond of his profession, and did not expect to give up the practice of it, but soon found that he could not be farmer and lawyer at the same time.

It was not without regret that he left the spacious house, built by his father and mother, just out of Portsmouth, with its fine grounds, filled with rare fruit, and a large circle of his early friends.[2]

---

[1] Rev. Mr. Converse was the officiating clergyman on this occasion. For fifty years he was pastor of the Congregational Church at the centre of the town, situated on a high hill four miles from the river, long the only church in Weathersfield. He was a graduate of Harvard College; a deep student, an earnest Christian, a gentleman in mind and manners, and was universally respected by all.

[2] The fruit in this place, which had been cultivated with much care by

In February, 1833, Elizabeth B. married David Everett Wheeler, Counselor-at-law in New York. She died in July, 1848, leaving two children — Everett Pepperrell and Mary H. She was a lady of great talents and acquirements. When not more than six years old, she read with interest books that would be thought beyond her comprehension.[1] Brought up in retirement, — with few playmates, — reading became her amusement and happiness. She had read or skimmed over most of the books in her father's extensive library before she was ten. When eleven, while on a visit in Haverhill, she read the whole of the " Arabian Nights " in about a week, ensconced in the window-seat of the pleasant, old-fashioned nursery, where Cousin Lizzie Sprague, Mary and Louisa Bartlett, and sister Mary, were merrily playing ; but she enjoyed these marvelous stories more than games, though she was very fond of these young friends. It was an elegant edition, with engravings, afterward presented to her by her mother's younger brother, Charles L. Bartlett.

On her return home she related them to her sister and the juveniles of the family, with the greatest accuracy of detail, much to their entertainment. Her

his father, was so remarkably delicious, that I cannot forbear speaking of it. There were the finest cherries — imperial, carnation, black and white hearts, Harrison and black mazards; rich juicy Jargonel, Sickles, St. Michael's and Bergamot pears, and a great variety of apples.

[1] As an instance of this, at a dinner party, when the cloth was removed, she left the table, and seated herself on the floor by the lower book-case, — a favorite spot of hers, — and was soon intently reading an article in the *Edinburgh Review;* when coming to a word that she did not understand, she took the book to her father, and very simply asked its meaning, as he always required her to do, unmindful of the company, who were very much surprised and amused.

memory was wonderful. She learned her lessons with great facility, and as she grew older, the amount of poetry she committed with ease was surprising. She could repeat pages of Moore's, Byron's, Gray's, and Campbell's poems, and a good deal of Shakespeare; Scott's poetry and novels were as familiar to her as household words, and she was constantly making quotations from them in common conversation with her companions.[1]

Her head was large and intellectual; her complexion clear and white, with a tinge of rose in her cheeks; her deep blue eyes were fringed with long silken lashes; her hands were small and delicate; her voice, rich, sweet, and melodious; her ear quick and accurate.

She retained a tune after hearing it once, and was ever warbling some beautiful air, frequently setting her favorite pieces of poetry to music. She was warm and durable in her attachments, noble and dignified in her bearing, and was said to resemble her mother.

When her father injured his eyes in 1820, she was only nine years old, and from that time she read aloud in turn to him. After she was twelve, she became his favorite amanuensis, because she wrote so correctly and rapidly after dictation.

Possessing great concentration of mind, she caught and rapidly transcribed her father's ideas. She usually kept a small edition of "Watts on the Mind," or a French Testament, in her pocket, to study in the

---

[1] Her treasures of knowledge were increased by reading to her father, but as he was not fond of poetry, her brilliant imagination resorted to it for recreation.

pauses, while her father was thinking and composing his sentences. Two thirds of his memorials to Congress, letters to the Vermont delegation, and articles for the newspapers, were written by her before her sister Mary's marriage ; and for three years afterwards, until she also was married, nearly all the reading and writing devolved upon her. She read so much aloud at this time, that it caused a complaint in her throat, and her eyes were weakened by being overtaxed.[1]

She injured her eyes yet more by using them too soon after the birth of her first infant ; and they gradually became more impaired, until a year before her death, when she almost wholly lost her sight. She was never well from the infancy of her youngest daughter ; an insidious disease, that baffled the skill of her physicians, preyed upon, and finally terminated her life. She lost her three first children, which was a great grief to her.

Complaining of weariness one day, she laid down to sleep, and awoke — in Heaven. What a joy ! to be summoned by her dear Lord to that world of unspeakable blessedness, where her noble soul, disencumbered from its frail tenement of flesh, that had occasioned her so much suffering, could commune with kindred spirits, the great, and good, and wise, in her Heavenly Father's mansions.

> " In a region lovelier far
> Than sages paint or poets sing;
> Brighter than summer glories are,
> And softer than the tints of spring."

Her attendant, thinking she slept too long, went to her, and found the earthly casket cold, white, beau-

---

[1] Ann, Harriet, and Charles were absent at school.

tiful as a marble statue, a smile of joy still on the lips.

Her reverence for God, and faith in the Lord Jesus, were deep and earnest, and she became a member of the Episcopal Church not long after her marriage.

She had a high appreciation of the beauty and sublimity of the Scriptures, especially of the Book of Job and the Psalms, and read them with great fervor.

Anne Eliza and *Harriet Bartlett* were partly educated by a governess at home, and partly at an excellent boarding-school at Windsor, kept by Miss Green, where they had many advantages.

Harriet was married in August, 1843, to Rev. J. De Forest Richards, then settled over the Congregational Church in Charlestown, New Hampshire.

Her father purchased for her the handsome and commodious house built by Mr. Horace Hall of that town, with the grounds. Her intimate friends, Miss Helen Wardner, of Windsor, now Mrs. William M. Evarts, of New York, and her cousin, Harriet B. Sprague, now Mrs. Judge Terry, of Rochester, New York, were bridesmaids.

Anne married Hon. Samuel Dinsmoor, of Keene, New Hampshire, September, 1844. Their friends and relatives being numerous, her invitations were very extensive, for she was social, and a great favorite with all. Never before did the old mansion accommodate so many guests, and several of the family were lodged at the neighbors.

The parlors were tastefully decorated with a profusion of beautiful, fragrant flowers, filling the air with perfumes, which came from Boston, and were presented by Mr. Dinsmoor to his bride.

The marriage ceremony was performed in the evening. One of the groomsmen was Chief Justice Parker, a friend of Mr. Dinsmoor; and Anne's sisters, Margaret and Sarah, were bridesmaids — lovely young girls of eighteen, attired in full white muslins, floating gracefully around them.

When did a bride ever think so little of herself and so much of her friends? When was there a wedding with so little stiffness and ceremony, and so much hearty sociality and enjoyment?

There was present, indeed, a bright galaxy of beauty and fashion. Mrs. William Dinsmoor, with her intellectual and Grecian face, and classic braids crowned with myrtle. Miss E. A. Hall, pretty and charming as a fresh rosebud; the stylish, agreeable, and brilliant sisters, Mrs. Hale and Mrs. Adams. Miss Caroline Dana Jarvis, of New York, talented and graceful, and many others; these being only some of the stars of the first magnitude.

There was music, and a social dance later in the evening, concluding with an elegant supper, and joy and gladness reigned in every heart.

At the height of prosperity, admired and esteemed by numerous friends, soon after her husband was elected Governor of New Hampshire, she died suddenly, July 17, 1849, universally lamented, leaving two sons, William Jarvis and Samuel.

She possessed a rare combination of womanly virtues. A most exemplary daughter and sister; a loving, faithful wife and mother; industrious, persevering, looking well to the ways of her household; genial, sensible, agreeable in conversation; dressing uniformly at home and abroad with taste and elegance ; she was the light and joy of home, and an ornament to society.

It seemed mysterious that one so useful, so much beloved, so happy herself, so essential to the happiness of her husband and children, should have been called from earth.

But thanks be to God for the revelation of a glorious immortality, through our Lord Jesus Christ.

CHARLES, the eldest son, received his first instructions from a teacher at home, a pious, sensible lady, a cousin of his mother. At nine years he was placed under the tuition of Solomon Foote, Esq., a young lawyer of great promise, who had recently opened a seminary for boys at Castleton.

This was our late respected Senator in Congress. Charles boarded with his former teacher, who had married Judge Meacham, and she carefully instilled religious principles at this early period.

Mr. Foote says of him, —

" He was remarkably studious, and attentive to the regulations of the seminary ; regular in his habits, thoughtful, sedate, and even grave for one so young. He manifested thus early in life those noble, generous, and manly qualities, which so highly distinguished him in mature years."

From Castleton he went to Exeter Academy, where he applied himself assiduously to his studies, reading works of useful knowledge for recreation, in addition.

He was joined by his brother William while at Exeter. Though unlike in their characters and temperaments, they were strongly attached to each other, and always harmonized.

In 1835, at fourteen, he entered the Vermont University at Burlington. Rev. John Wheeler was then President, whose warm interest and esteem he soon won, by his rectitude of character and attention to his studies.

His classmate, Professor W. G. T. Shedd, says of him : [1] —

" He was the youngest of our class in years, but remarkably self-poised. This used to strike me as a noticeable characteristic in him, and it was one that all observed ; so much so, that notwithstanding his extreme youth, his unusual moderation and strength of understanding secured for him the title of ' old Roman.' And the title was well maintained through all his college course. Though not, as afterwards, under the influence of strictly religious principles and experiences, his bearing and demeanor were marked by gravity and sobriety, in what is usually the most erratic and dangerous period in life. He was far less than most of us the creature of youthful impulses ; and as I look back upon him, after the lapse of thirty years, I see in him a more solid basis for a strong, firm character, than is usually found in youth.

" His scholarship corresponded with his natural traits. I do not remember that he showed decided predilections for any one branch of study, or remarkable superiority in any one ; but he was a sound, faithful student in the curriculum.

" There was great evenness and symmetry in his intellectual development, and he left college without any of those one-sided, exorbitant tendencies, which so often mar collegiate education.

" His social character was of a piece with his intellectual. A true, honest friend, he made no excuses, and never be-

[1] From a letter addressed to Mrs. H. B. J. Richards, after his death.

came embroiled with others. And yet he possessed high spirit, and great independence of feeling. Had he been less manly and noble in his temper, he would have been likely to have fallen into collision with others; but his evident transparency, and freedom from jealousy and all sinister motives, carried him through college with as much popularity as ever fell to the lot of a student, and with more respect than falls to the lot of most."

His classmate, chum, and intimate friend, Charles P. Marsh, writing of him, says : —

" Charles was most highly respected and beloved by all his classmates and acquaintances in college. He was never known to do an unworthy act, and no college rule or regulation was ever once wantonly violated by him, during his whole four years' course.

" His college duties were ever seasonably and fully performed. He scorned all ' college tricks,' and his influence and acts were ever on the side of order and rightful authority. He had a nice sense of honor, and scorned a mean act in another, as much as he would scorn to perpetrate one himself.

" The world is better by reason of his having lived in it. His influence and example will leave their impression behind him for many, many years; and religion itself has received an impulse by reason of his bold advocacy of its doctrines."

He then relates the following incident in their college life : —

" In the spring of 1838, after the monetary crash of 1837, I one day received a letter from home, informing me of my father's inability to furnish me with money to meet my bills, and that I should probably have to leave college, at least temporarily. Charles was with me, as usual, as I opened and read my letter, on my way to our room at the college. Observing that I was sober, and little inclined to talk, he inquired of me once or twice what the trouble was. At length I told him, and handed him the letter. He perused it, and I think felt as badly for me as I did for myself. His warm, kind heart, and all his feelings were at once in sympathy with me. I could hardly resume my evening studies; the prospect of leaving my class and college, tinged all my feelings with sadness. I told Charles when we went to bed that I should have to leave soon; I might as well go in a few days, and I thought I would at once seek for a position to keep school in a Southern State, and perhaps in a year or two I could come back and finish out my college course. He did not say much, but evidently felt pained at the sudden change in my prospects. I kept along with my studies for the next few days, wishing for advice, but not knowing where to seek it.

"In about a week, he seemed suddenly to become elated by something he was perusing in a letter just received. He handed it to me and desired me to read it. It was from his father, in reference mainly to myself. It seemed that Charles had written to him about my being compelled to leave college for want of money, and in reply he told me that I should do no such thing; that I should not want for money, and either in that letter, or one soon after, there was a check for me for ninety dollars. Once or twice after this I received help from the same source, and when, after leaving college, I paid Mr. Jarvis the money, he declined taking any interest. . . . . .

"Unknown and unsolicited by me, all this was done by Charles, in the natural outgushing kindness of his heart, and from that pure friendship which he ever seemed to entertain for me."

He graduated in August, 1839. The following autumn or winter he commenced the study of law in the office of Hon. Leverett Saltonstall and Judge Joshua Ward, in Salem, both gentlemen of high standing, and eminent for their legal ability.

They became much attached to him, and Mr. Saltonstall said that he was one of the most diligent and promising students he ever had.

He entered the Law School in Cambridge in 1840. He entertained a high respect and admiration for the varied learning and brilliant talents of Judge Story, who was then a professor.

In December, 1841, his father summoned him home on account of the dangerous illness of his brother William.

William [1] had grown up a cheerful, kind, affectionate, and genial youth, the darling of his parents, and beloved by all who knew him. He was frank, confiding, and truthful. While at Exeter Academy he was taken sick, but partially recovered, and came home, though far from well. A few weeks afterward, at Christmas, when all the family were assembled together, he took a severe cold and died, in a week, of pneumonia, January 1, 1842, aged seventeen. This unexpected blow was a terrible shock to his parents, who were completely overcome by this dispensation of Providence. Mr. Jarvis' fortitude and self-control seemed prostrated, and his grief and regret at the loss of this precious son were most poignant. Mrs. Jarvis fainted away when her loved one passed from earth, and her sorrow was no less deep; but to

---

[1] First named Thomas Jefferson.

behold the strong man thus bowed down, was a mournful spectacle.

The funeral was delayed until the return of his brother Charles.

Owing to some delay of mails, in those days of stage-coach travelling, the letters did not reach him till too late. He hastened home on their reception, but learned the sad tidings of William's death on the road from his brother-in-law, who had set out to summon him.

Anguish filled his soul, and he passed the whole night in affecting lamentations and bursts of grief, frequently exclaiming, " My God! my God! why hast Thou taken my brother from me? "

This affliction exerted an influence over his whole future life. His religious sensibilities were quickened, and his heart flowed out with almost feminine tenderness in sympathy with the sick and the afflicted.

His future was now changed. He had been preparing himself for the bar, and his hopes and aspirations had been centered in his profession. But his father, then seventy-two years of age, needed a son to relieve him of the great amount of business he had to transact. William was to have remained at home with him. It now became necessary that Charles should do so.

Few knew how great a sacrifice it was to him; but with the firmness and self-denial, for which he was so remarkable, he obeyed the call of duty.

His father did not at first foresee that this was incompatible with the practice of law, and wished him to complete his course of study; he consequently returned to the Law School in January, and graduated August, 1842. He then spent several months in the office of one of the leading lawyers of Windsor, to make himself familiar with the laws of Vermont, and was admitted to the bar at Woodstock, May, 1843. From this period to the death of his father, his whole life was consecrated to him. Patiently, quietly, with unwavering regularity, he was ever at his post of duty, faithful to each trust reposed in him.

One after another the elder sisters, who had successively read aloud and written after dictation for their father, were married, and this labor of love now devolved in a great measure upon the son, although assisted by his mother and two younger sisters. Every evening he devoted to reading aloud to him; first the numerous papers of the day, then his periodicals, and then various works of history, biography, and travels. As increasing years added to his father's infirmities the son's duties became more and more arduous. From a sacred sense of duty he never left him, but for a very short time, feeling that his services were indispensable; and though often urged by parents and sisters to take more recreation, yet when prevailed upon to take an excursion of pleasure to New York or Boston, or to attend some social party, he usually hastened back earlier than he was expected.

He rose at four or five o'clock in the morning, to see that the workmen set about their appointed work, and then secured time to read two or three chapters in the Bible before breakfast.

In the temperance reform that awakened so much interest in the country in 1844–45, he took an active interest, and joined the Society, and from that time till his death he strictly kept his pledge. Neither raillery, nor the example of companions that he loved, nor the hospitable habits of his family at social dinners and festive occasions, could induce him even to take a glass of wine, so firm and inflexible were his principles, his adherence to what he thought right.

He kept the Sabbath with equal strictness, practically making it the Lord's day. When not at church, he spent most of his time in his own chamber in prayer, meditation, and religious reading, especially the Bible, which he held in great reverence.

He had a large class of young men in the Sunday-school, and contributed liberally to the support of preaching the gospel, both at home and in missions. Though so remarkably consistent a Christian, he was a very humble one, and this deterred him from becoming a member of the Church till March, 1859, when he made an open profession of his faith in Christ by taking the Lord's Supper, much to his comfort and joy.

His father regularly retired at nine, and Charles improved an hour after that time in the study of law or medicine, with his usual unwearied industry.

In 1846–47 he was much out of health, and spent the winter in Philadelphia, under the care of an eminent physician, Dr. Pancoast, who said of him that he would have made an excellent doctor. He attended a course of medical lectures in his leisure, and the knowledge thus acquired, brought into action by his kind and feeling heart, rendered him a judicious counselor, as well as a tender nurse in sickness, and his friends were often blessed by his kind ministrations in severe illness.

He became imbued with his father's interest in history, and with his ardent love for his country, and its republican institutions. By his varied reading, he acquired a vast amount of information, and was continually storing up in his mind the opinions and sentiments of the wise and good.

Margaret and *Sarah* were placed under the judicious instruction of Miss Mary C. Green, who had left Windsor, and opened a boarding-school in Burlington. They afterward attended Mrs. Fiske's boarding-school in Keene.

Margaret died two years before Mrs. Dinsmoor, July 7, 1847, after a short illness, in the bloom of youth, and rich in promise of a useful life. Ere afflictions or trials had dimmed her fresh, bright spirit, she was removed —

> " To that home on high,
>   Where sorrow enters never;
>   Where friendship cannot die,
>   And love will live forever."

Her death caused her twin sister Sarah, her inseparable companion, the most acute anguish. Hoping that change of scene might mitigate her grief, her father prevailed upon her to go with her brother Charles to Burlington, where she had many schoolmates and friends, and thence to Niagara.[1]

---

[1] Dr. Leonard Jarvis died in February, 1848, in the seventy-fourth year of his age. A large number of relatives, friends, and townsmen attended his funeral. Rev. Mr. Smith, Rector of the Episcopal Church in West Claremont, officiated. He was interred in a cemetery on his farm, that he had himself inclosed, where his father and sisters reposed, a beautiful

In October, 1848, Sarah married her second cousin, Dr. Samuel G. Jarvis, of Claremont. Her father had a commodious house built for her in West Claremont, a beautiful situation owned by the Doctor, with a fine view of Sugar River, and a lawn and noble elms in front.[1]

She died July 3, 1855, after a tedious illness, through which her tenderly attached husband, parents, and sisters, watched her with deep solicitude, her sister Kate being entirely devoted to her. An earnest Christian, her soul was lighted up with peace and joy, ere the corruptible put on incorruption.

She was an irreparable loss to her husband and two little sons, William and Leonard. A large circle of friends and acquaintances in Claremont, who had been unremitting in their sympathy and attentions during her sickness, felt that they lost in her a warm-hearted, sincere, and generous friend. Her remains were interred at the side of her beloved sister Margaret, in the cemetery at Weathersfield.

Catherine Leonard and *Louise Bailey*, when quite young, received instruction from a governess at home, and were some years at Mrs. Sedgwick's celebrated school for young ladies in Lenox, where they finished their education. In July, 1860, after the death of her father, Catherine married Leavitt Hunt, Esq., who was educated in Europe. He was major in the late

place, commanding a varied and picturesque view of the Connecticut, up to Windsor, and of the Ascutney. Bierdstadt painted a much-admired landscape from this spot.

[1] It was on the site of the house owned by Hon. Sanford Kingsbury, after he sold his former residence to the Doctor's grandfather, Samuel G. Jarvis.

war, and distinguished himself in the service as aid to General Heintzelman.

They went abroad immediately after the wedding, accompanied by their sisters, Miss Hunt and Miss L. B. Jarvis.

Of his twelve children, the Consul outlived seven; and seven bright, interesting grandchildren died before him : —

Elizabeth Bartlett Jarvis Cutts, 5 months.
Hampden Cutts, 3 years.
Mary Pepperrell Carter Cutts, 5 years.
William Jarvis Cutts, 14½ years.
Mary Elizabeth Wheeler, 2½ years.
William Jarvis Richards, 5 years.
Anne Bartlett Richards, 9 years.

CHAPTER XXXIV.

THANKSGIVING DAY.

THE Consul's children and grandchildren grew up around him, and cheered his advancing years. Thanksgiving Day had for a long time been a season of great festivity in his household; when the different families of children and grandchildren assembled about the dear and revered head of the family, and were welcomed with his cordial greetings, benevolent smiles, and noble hospitality, which made all hearts happy.

Dr. Leonard Jarvis, and all his family, were invariably invited to the Thanksgiving party.

The children rejoiced in the return of this day, esteeming themselves especially privileged. One parlor, and a long table, loaded with duplicates of the good things at their seniors' table, were appropriated to them, at one end of which sat Uncle Charles, at the other, one of their aunts.

O, did anything ever equal grandma's dinners? Her roast turkeys and chickens, cranberry sauce, chicken pies, other pies in great variety, and above all, her rich plum-puddings! Through the open door, into the dining-room, their papas and ·mammas were seen seated at another long table, over which grandpapa presides, carving, helping, conversing merrily, and watchful over every guest, ever and anon sending messages to the juveniles, to inquire if they are abundantly supplied with good things, — a sun, whose genial brightness gladdened all.

With the old-fashioned dessert of large, shining apples, various nuts, dates, raisins, and sherry, came the toasts. The sons-in-law and other gentlemen were successively called upon; pleasantries were exchanged, and merriment reigned. In the evening grandpapa was delighted to promote the gladsome games of the young folks, and how the merry voices and peals of laughter rang through the dear, old, paternal mansion.

What fun the children had! What a jubilee it was to them! How reluctant they were to separate and say good-night!

And how can the house contain so many? That is a mystery! But grandmamma and aunts, with warm hearts and sagacious heads, have planned it all. There is a resting-place for everybody, and before midnight all are in their places; the " India-rubber " house being opened to its utmost capacity, and several chambers at the neighbors being brought into requisition.

What a merry-making it has been, and how the children wish that Thanksgiving Day would come oftener. It is confidently rumored that " Cousin Doctor " will have a family gathering at Christmas. Yes, it certainly is to be, and there will be a repetition of these grand times of reunion, feasting, and frolicking. Then came the breakfast, abounding in good cheer and merriment, — Thanksgiving dinner No. 2, — and then most of the guests departed; some of the children from a distance lingering a few days, to prolong the pleasure of being once more beneath the paternal roof.

" O, days departed never to return, how pleasing the remembrance ! "

O, that loving hearts might oftener meet, and longer dwell together !

But can we doubt that in the great assembly of the just made perfect, where there is fruition of all that is good, lovely, and beautiful, the dear ones of earth will be reunited, never more to separate?

CHAPTER XXXV.

CONCLUSION.

CROWNED with prosperity, honor, long life, and numerous friends, this wise, benevolent, and great man must at last close his earthly career. His mind continued strong and vigorous, his wonderful memory unimpaired, until he was eighty-nine, when he was suddenly attacked with a slight paralytic shock, in April, 1859. This weakened him; he partially lost the use of his lower limbs. His mind was somewhat impaired, and from this time he kept his chamber until his death. He seemed to rally a little in the summer, and rode out several times. But in October he was suddenly attacked with great pain, and the evil day came. His devoted, faithful wife and son, his four daughters, and three of his wife's sisters, were with him, to minister to his wants, and soothe and comfort him in his last hours.

He knew them all, and had a word of kindness and affection for each, though greatly distressed. He died October 21, 1859.

O, how much he was missed, and what a void it occasioned in that household!

No longer will his warm, generous hospitality welcome us to his home.

No more his cheerful, genial spirit shed a radiance around the table, over which he so courteously presided, — a true gentleman of the old school.

No more his entertaining, instructive conversation, enriched by his inexhaustible stores of knowledge and his tenacious memory, delight us by his fireside, where his chair is now vacant.

The mind that so long labored for the welfare of his country and the good of his children, is at rest, and the place that once knew him will know him no more.

The poor and sick miss his liberal hand, ready sympathy, and assistance ; those in want of pecuniary aid, his long credits and low interest ; and his country, one of her most disinterested, faithful, and zealous patriots, sparing neither time, labor, nor money in her service.

The funeral was a very large one. Many of his friends and relatives from a distance, as well as those in the vicinity, assembled together to pay their last tribute of respect.

A granite monument, durable as the everlasting hills, commemorates the spot where his body reposes.

On a beautiful white marble tablet is inscribed an epitaph that he wrote for himself.

Above the inscription are sheaves of wheat, and a wreath of oak leaves and ivy, elegantly carved. On the other side is a merino sheep in bass-relief.[1]

[1] This tablet, executed by J. Carew, of Boston, is a fine specimen of his artistic taste and skill.

WILLIAM JARVIS,

SON OF DR. CHARLES JARVIS,

BORN IN BOSTON, THE 4TH FEBRUARY, 1770.

DIED 21ST OCTOBER, 1859.

He was Consul at Lisbon, and acting Chargé d'Affaires of the United States for Portugal, from 1802 to 1811. To have served nine years in a difficult situation, under such able Presidents as Thomas Jefferson and James Madison, is alone a sufficient eulogy on his fidelity and capacity. He was the first large importer from Spain, and distributer through the Union, of that useful animal, the merino, which greatly contributed to lay the foundation of the woolen manufactures in this country.

His early life was checkered by the vicissitudes of fortune ; but by industry, perseverance, intelligence, and good faith, he made himself independent, and spent his latter years in tranquil retirement, amidst a numerous family; his last aspiration of affection being gratified, by laying his bones in peace amidst those whom he loved in life.

BIOGRAPHICAL SKETCH OF MAJOR CHARLES JARVIS.

AFTER the death of his father, a great amount of business devolved upon him, and he frequently sat up half the night to attend to it.

His widowed mother and sisters looked to him to fill the place of the revered husband and parent they had lost.

After the estate (with the assistance of the other executors, his brothers-in-law) was settled, he devoted his energies to remodeling and beautifying the old family mansion, in order to increase its comfort and convenience for his mother and friends.

When the rebellion broke out, his deep religious convictions, and ardent patriotism, were enlisted in the cause of his country.

As his pastor says of him : —

" From earliest childhood he had been taught by precept and example to revere the Constitution under which the nation had so greatly prospered; taught also the imperious duty of obedience to wholesome laws. When he saw the government assailed, the Union in danger, ... and the superstructure reared by the labors and sacrifices of the fathers threatened with destruction, his spirit was roused."

He had contributed liberally to aid the cause, but he began to feel that he must do more; that personal sacrifices must be made.

In March, 1862, after careful consideration of the subject, he believed that duty called for *personal* devotion to his country's service, and entered the army.

To his aged mother and sisters this was a great calamity. They tried to dissuade him from his purpose, telling him his duties to his family exempted him from such a sacrifice. He replied to one who urged this upon him, "I had rather be a martyr for my country, than remain at home in ease. . . . . Remember the Puritans, how their lives were risked to sustain their principles."

To another, who said, "Have you really made this matter a subject of prayer?" he answered, —

"Do you suppose that the resolution I have taken is anything but the result of prayer?"

He raised a company for the Ninth Regiment Vermont Volunteers, and was elected Captain.

Sad and bitter was the parting between him and his much loved mother. A presentiment took possession of her mind that his life would be sacrificed in the cause of his country.

The fate of the gallant Vermont Ninth is well known: first subjected to a tedious march from Washington to Alexandria, in a burning July sun, through some mistake, then ordered back the second day, causing much unnecessary suffering; many, overcome by the heat, dropped down by the wayside. They were then ordered to Winchester, where by night and day they performed the most arduous labors in erecting fortifications, producing much sickness, and leaving no time for drilling.

These defenses, erected with such a sacrifice of health and life to the heavily taxed men, were finally abandoned to the enemy, and the troops were ordered to Harper's Ferry, leaving four hundred sick at the hospital at Winchester. By the base treachery of Colonel Miles, they were here betrayed to the enemy. Colonel Stannard suspected foul play, but could not save them. He was peremptorily ordered by Colonel Miles to send back to the enemy seven Virginians, whom he called paroled prisoners, but which were undoubtedly spies.

On the following morning the attack was made, on weak points that Colonel Stannard had unavailingly pointed out as indefensible. On the approach of the enemy, Colonel Miles, pretending he could not defend the place, ordered the flag to be taken down, and was immediately shot by a cannon-ball, as if the retributive justice of God followed the traitor.

One regiment of cavalry bravely put spurs to their horses and escaped. But alas for the infantry! Twelve regiments, including the noble Vermont Ninth, were made prisoners, and were afterward paroled in the strictest manner; they were ordered to Chicago, where they endured great privations. Cast into the cattle-pens of the fair-ground, provisions at first scarce, and afterward of a very bad quality, owing to frauds of the contractors, they would have been in danger of starvation, had it not been for the benevolence of the New England people of Chicago. Ankle deep in mud, with no protection from the inclemency of the weather; for several weeks they endured all manner of bodily hardships, which were at last mitigated by their removal to Fort Douglas.

Their mental sufferings were also very great. Humiliated by their base betrayal; thirsting to aid their country; ready, if need be, to lay down their lives in her service; but to be deprived of every comfort, and remain in this paralyzed condition, useless to their country and their friends — absentees from their homes, — was galling to their spirit in the extreme, and trying to their patriotism. It is no wonder that some privates deserted, and that disaffection was creeping in among the remainder.

It was more fatal to health and morals than the most severe engagement. Two of the Ohio regiments were insubordinate; many were arrested, and a court-martial was held for some weeks, in which Captain Jarvis sat during the whole session.

Ere the commencement of cold weather, he clothed his company at his own expense, they being very needy, waiting till pay-day came round for reimbursement.

In the winter the Lieutenant-colonel was sick, and the Colonel was in Washington, endeavoring to effect an exchange, and most of the care and responsibility devolved upon Captain Jarvis.

Six New York regiments had been exchanged in the autumn, and finally all were removed but an Illinois regiment and the unfortunate Vermont Ninth. Friends had written to Washington, and to the Governor and Legislature of Vermont, to intercede in their behalf, but the long-hoped for exchange was not effected till March. Just as they were rejoicing at the prospect of removal, four thousand Arkansas Post prisoners, dirty, ignorant, sick, and ragged, were sent to Camp Douglas, and these regiments were obliged to become their guard. Though a great disappointment, it was preferable to inaction, and a new spirit was aroused among the men.

Toward spring, in compliance with his mother's earnest entreaties that he would come home, if but for one day, Captain Jarvis had obtained leave of absence for twenty days; but some new duty arose to detain him, and when afterwards leave of absence for ten days was granted, the arrival of these prisoners again deprived the mother and son of the much desired meeting.

In May the prisoners were ordered to Yorktown, in Virginia, and were divided into two bodies, the Vermont Ninth being their escort, and Captain Jarvis took the command of one division. In July some officers were to be sent

North on military duties, and Major Jarvis, who had been recently promoted, obtained permission to go.[1]

The thanksgiving and joy of his mother and sisters in once more beholding his noble face and form in health and safety, can be better imagined than described. What a world of love, not bounded by earth or time!

"Heaven born, and destined to the skies again."

His return was indeed a season of jubilee, not only for his family and friends, but for those in his employment and his neighbors. What a "welcome home" from all did he receive!

He remained in Vermont three or four weeks, and late in August went to Long Island, Boston Harbor, to take charge of Vermont conscripts. His mother and one of his sisters accompanied him to Boston, that they might occasionally have the pleasure of an interview with him, while he was stationed at this place.

The following beautiful letter to his sister, Mary P. S. Cutts, was elicited by the death of a darling son, early in September: —

"HEAD-QUARTERS, VERMONT DETACHMENT,
"LONG ISLAND, BOSTON HARBOR, *September* 17, 1863.

"MY DEAR SISTER, — I learn by a letter from Kate of your great affliction in the loss of dear Charley.

"It makes my heart ache to try to realize that he, so manly, so ingenuous and promising a youth, just breaking into manhood, and winning such favor from all who knew him, is no more on earth.

"If to me so trying, then how must it be to you, dear

1 The train was late, and for four hours his mother awaited its arrival, unwilling to go away, lest she should not be there to welcome him. It came at last. The moment the son's eye beheld her, supported by one of her daughters, he sprang over the steps at a bound, and clasping her in his arms, exclaimed, "O, mother!" expressing such deep love and tenderness, such a sense of trials and hardships endured since they parted.

26

sister, and his father, and you all? The heart only can know its own bitterness; but yet we must not weep as those that have no hope. Whose hand is it that deals these blows so deadly to our earthly hopes? The Lord gave and the Lord hath taken away; and still, though with broken hearts, let us join with His ancient servant in owning that the name of the Lord is blessed.

" ' Though He slay me, yet will I trust Him.'

" What a comfort, my dear sister, when all mortal consolations seem so inadequate, that there is One who has wept over such afflictions, and is touched with the feeling of our infirmities, who yet has power to bind up the brokenhearted, and is a God of consolation.

" You know that throne of Grace, and may you still prove the exhaustless supplies of mercy and comfort that a compassionate Saviour has for His suffering children.

" I should be glad to be with you now, but my duties will preclude it for the present. To-morrow I send off a detachment for the 4th Regiment. . . . .

" But I must close with my deepest sympathy for you all.

" Yours, affectionately,

" CHARLES JARVIS."

Early in October he rejoined his regiment, and then came the sad, sad parting with his mother, which was so heart-rending to both that he could scarcely tear himself away, and three times returned to repeat his farewell. But he had made every arrangement for her comfort and happiness, winning a promise from two of her sisters that they would pass the winter with her.

On his arrival at Yorktown he found that the regiment had suffered greatly from sickness, and with his usual promptitude of action, he made vigorous efforts to have the sick sent to hospitals at the North, and the rest removed to Newbern, North Carolina. To his sister, Mrs. Cutts, he wrote again on hearing of the sickness of two other children and grandchildren : —

" YORKTOWN, *October* 18, 1863.

" . . . . How constantly are we impressed with the sense of our mortality, and yet we are told to believe we have a God who pities us, if we fear Him, as a father pities his children. How comforting and how real are such promises! We could not have a more vivid illustration of His care and grace, than by viewing Him in the first of human relations.

" I, too, have had my sorrows; to come back and find our regiment so prostrated by malaria. We have had two hundred and sixty out of less than four hundred on the sick list, but have sent off to Fortress Monroe some one hundred, to be transferred to the hospital at Brattleboro' for treatment. We hoped to go to Newbern, North Carolina, but the order has been suspended, though I hope not indefinitely, as removal would improve the men. Newbern has the name of a healthy place. . . . . We have lost twelve among our best men. . . . . May God deliver us and guide us in all our trials. We must acknowledge His wonderful interposition in our national affairs, and may He speedily bring us as a people to a sense of our dependence on His righteousness and mercy for blessings. May Christ's kingdom, with its good will and peace to man, come, and the whole earth soon know its Lord. . . . .

" With kindest remembrances,
" Your affectionate brother,
" CHARLES JARVIS."

The regiment was removed to Newbern, and stationed at Newport Barracks, about thirty miles distant. Ever mindful of the happiness of the men, he privately provided refreshments for the regiment on Thanksgiving Day, intending that the giver should remain unknown; but as an intimate friend remarked, it was very easy for them to discover their thoughtful benefactor, as he had frequently done the same thing before.

Depredations having been committed on loyal citizens beyond the lines, by some Union cavalry, and especially by "one mounted on a gray horse," Colonel Ripley, commanding the post, unable to identify the guilty party, directed Major Jarvis to proceed at nine o'clock, December 1, 1863, with a cavalry escort of all the gray horses in the command, to a house beyond the cavalry outposts, to investigate the affair, identify the plunderer by the aid of the citizens, and return.

On this expedition he was mortally wounded by a rebel, who aimed at him from behind a tree.

As he was falling from his horse, two of his men, Caspar Lewis and John Henry, came to his assistance.

Lewis says, " Henry struck the rebel, whose name was Staunton, from behind, with the back of his sabre, ordering him to surrender. He yielded, and we tied his hands. I asked the Major what we should do with the prisoner; whether I should shoot him or take him along. He answered, ' He is a soldier; take him prisoner.' Assisted by Henry and I, the Major rode half a mile, though suffering great pain, and then being unable to proceed further, we procured a cart, lifted him carefully into it, and took him to the house of the nearest planter. I carried the intelligence to the camp, and did not return."

THE CHAPLAIN'S LETTER. — REV. MR. DICKINSON.

"NEWPORT BARRACKS, *December* 25, 1863.
" *To the Mother, Sisters, and Relatives of the late Major Jarvis:* —

" . . . . I have enjoyed the acquaintance of Major Jarvis with much pleasure, ever since we came out from home; but since his promotion to the office he has so honorably filled for the last six months, our acquaintance has been quite intimate. He extended to me the invitation at once to become his comrade and tent-mate, since which time we have eat, drank, slept, and prayed together.

"It was our custom to read the Scriptures, and pray together every night before retiring to rest, and I have never seen a minister of the Gospel that enjoyed such seasons of devotion more than he did.

"Agreeably to my request, he conducted these devotions one half of the time. He often made comments on the choice passages of Scripture that we read, and seemed *alive* both in the service of his country and his God. I deeply feel the death of this cheerful comrade and faithful Christian, and realize that the Lord, in His Providence, has come very near me.

"He has been my counselor amid all my trials as Chaplain, and I shall never find another that can fill his place. He always took part in our social meetings, and was accustomed to visit the hospital with me, when I went to read and pray with the sick and dying soldiers.

"As I went to the grave to perform the funeral rites of poor soldiers that had died far from home and friends, I had only to extend to him an invitation to accompany me, and inform him of the hour of burial, and he could always find time, amid all his duties, to pay his last respects to the departed. The Sabbath before his death, he attended divine service with me at Newport Village, about one mile from camp, at which time I preached to the citizens of the place, and some of our own regiment that went with us. That Sunday evening we walked from our tent to the prayer meeting together.

"In the record I here make, it will be seen that he improved and enjoyed the very last opportunities that were afforded him in this world, both for social as well as public worship, which was but a short time before the sad event that occasioned his death. He always took a great interest in preaching and in the Scriptures, which I read from time to time, often during the week calling up the instructions of the Sabbath. He always bore some part in our social meetings, either by prayer, or remarks to the men, and generally by both.

"It is universally understood (and I am sorry to say that I fear it is *too* true), that many temperance men, and even men appearing to be religious at home, by their connection with the army, become lax in their principles. It affords me pleasure, not merely for your sake, but for the sake of the Gospel I labor to promote, to say here, that amid the temptations and vices of camp life, he remained firm in his principles, and correct in his habits.

"Indeed, he seemed in reference to morality and religion, to remain as immovable as the mountains. I regard it almost folly to write this to those who know his firmness of character as you all know it; but I would that the Church and the world might know that the power of the Gospel and the grace of God are not vainly bestowed.

"When the afflicting tidings reached the camp of the Major's being badly wounded, I rode directly out to him, with the Colonel, Surgeon, etc., and the Hospital Steward, Squiers,[1] who was much attached to the Major. I found him in pain, suffering much nearly all the time, but he bore his sufferings with great fortitude.

"His pulse was feeble, his extremities inclined to coldness. He asked me of my welfare, and inquired for Sergeant Hooker, who had been very sick with pneumonia, and we were much interested for his life. He conversed but little, being in constant pain.

[1] An intelligent young man, who, when he first enlisted, served as clerk to Captain Jarvis, and was afterward steward.

"He had been taken to the house of a wealthy planter. They were in favor of the Confederate government, but were very kind, and did all in their power to promote the comfort of the Major. He lay on a mattress before an open fire-place, his feet to the fire, in an elegantly furnished parlor. Colonel Ripley, who had rode on a fleet horse and reached the house at the same time the Major did, had taken his head in his lap on a pillow, and was bathing it with camphor. But as soon as he grew a little more easy, the Colonel felt it his duty to go back to his post, and he and the Quartermaster bade him good-night, expressing a hope that he would be able to come into camp early in the morning.

"The Major had requested Squiers to stay with him, and I told him as they took leave of him, that I had come to remain all night. He thanked me kindly. I read one of the Psalms with him, and bowed in prayer by his side. I then informed him that his situation was one of danger, to which he assented with great calmness. . . . . I looked upon him as one who had faithfully attended to life's duties in his days of health and strength, and when the hour of death drew near, he was fully prepared to go. . . . .

"The pain he suffered was very great. About an hour before his death he said he thought it was all over with him. . . . .

"Squiers sat by him and held his hand; he appeared to be easier, as if asleep, and at half-past ten breathed his last peacefully, without a struggle or a groan."

A Christian hero was crowned with glory! The world lost in him a noble Christian man, the regiment a father.

They procured a wagon, and carried him carefully into camp, which they reached about half-past three A. M.

Not a man in the regiment had lain down to sleep, and there was not a dry eye among them, when they knew they had lost their kindest friend. Colonel Ripley and the other officers said he was, in truth, a *Father* to the regiment.

A metallic coffin was immediately obtained from Newbern; he was placed in it, clad in his military dress, and looked as if in peaceful slumber when he reached his family.

Captains Bartlett and Kilbourne, with about twelve non-commissioned officers and privates, were sent by Colonel Ripley as an escort with the remains. A young man, worthy of record for his trustworthiness and faithfulness, H. R. French, of Waitsfield, watched by his coffin through the whole journey.

A telegram from Captain Bartlett, at Springfield, to Major Austine,[1] first brought the tidings of this great calamity to his sister in Brattleboro', who, after sending it along the wires to his mother, had the mournful satisfaction of going on to Weathersfield in the same train with her brother. Captains Bartlett[2] and Kilbourne manifested the deepest feeling and sympathy, and related all the particulars of their friend's death.

O, the grief that burst from that stricken mother's heart, when she first met her daughter, and listened to the sorrowful narration.

And when an hour later, the coffin, draped with the flag for which he had laid down his life, was borne in military procession into the home he had so much loved, and which would never again be cheered by his presence, no wonder that thy anguish is poured forth afresh, O desolate and widowed mother! for thy first-born and only son, the staff

---

[1] Mrs. Cutts fully appreciated the delicate kindness with which Major Austine communicated this heart-rending intelligence.

[2] Captain Bartlett, a most excellent young man, was promoted to fill Major Jarvis' place. But he died six months afterward.

and comfort of thy declining years, has been taken from thee ! But God's will be done.

The escort had hoped to attend the funeral of their revered Major, and Colonel Stowell,[1] receiving a telegram from Captain Bartlett, came across the Green Mountains to pay this last tribute of respect to the memory of his lamented friend. Mrs. Jarvis had her hospitable house opened for their accommodation, and they were treated with the utmost kindness and attention ; but she felt that she could not consign the loved form of her son to the dust, ere *his* sisters and *her* brothers and sisters could be assembled. Rev. Mr. Kimball, her pastor and brother-in-law, held a solemn religious service in the parlor in the evening, the escort and all the family being present, making a consoling prayer, and reading selections from the Scriptures. They left for their several homes in Vermont the next day, after dinner, hoping to return to the funeral on Sunday ; but only Colonel Stowell and family, and Captain Bartlett were able to do so.

It seemed as if the spirit of the departed rested on the household, diffusing peace and hope, lifting the soul from the mournful present to the eternal blessedness into which he had entered.

Telegrams had been immediately dispatched to his sisters in Cincinnati and in New York, and to the near relatives and friends, and seldom are so many assembled as hastened to pay their last tribute of love and respect, and to sympathize with the bereaved mother.

On Sunday, though very stormy, and the travelling bad, neighbors and acquaintances came in large numbers to attend his funeral in the church. Rev. Mr. Kimball

---

[1] Colonel Stowell was the first Lieutenant-colonel of the Vermont Ninth; was with them through their trials, but resigned from ill health ere they left Chicago.

preached a just and excellent sermon. In a dreary storm of rain and sleet he was borne to his last resting-place, followed by sad and mournful hearts.

But he is not dead. His example, his character, his principles, his memory, yet live in this world, and his spirit has entered those celestial mansions our Lord hath gone before us to prepare.

He has been greeted with those blissful words, " Come, good and faithful servant, enter into the joy of thy Lord."

The noble, disinterested Christian patriot, exemplary in every duty, has been crowned with glory, honor, and immortality.

An elegant white marble sarcophagus marks his last resting-place on earth.[1]

On the top, exquisitely carved, is a cross and sword, entwined with ivy. Upon these lies a crown or wreath of laurel and oak leaves.

One end is draped with our national flag, the Stars and Stripes distinctly visible; and the blade of the sword, which is partly covered by it, is well defined beneath its folds.

On the front, in raised letters, in German text, is

" MAJOR CHARLES JARVIS."

On the back are the dates of his birth and death, and this inscription : —

" He took up his sword as a cross in the cause of his country and his God."

On one end, —

" I had rather be a martyr for my country, than remain at home in ease."

---

[1] For the finished execution of this marble structure, we are indebted to the artistic genius of J. Carew, Boston.

On the other end, —

" For me to live is Christ, to die is gain."

CONCLUSION, BY HON. WILLIAM C. BRADLEY.[1]

" Thus far, and perhaps not without bias, has been sketched by the hands of tender affection, the life of one who never sought notoriety, and was the more esteemed and even beloved, the more he was known and understood.

" But the sketch has failed of its object, if it has not left on the mind of the reader the impression that he who was its subject, — while he showed but few elements of what is usually termed *greatness*, was wonderfully possessed of what is better, — a sincere and well-balanced mind, and all those useful qualities which go to constitute goodness.

" Having come of a good family, and belonging to a somewhat conspicuous branch of that family, of which branch he was the last male shoot, he might exhibit neither the surpassing eloquence of his grandsire, the Revolutionary patriot, nor the irrepressive energy, far-seeing wisdom, great colloquial talents, and hospitality of his father, the Consul-farmer; yet he, in his own way, maintained their distinction. A most devoted son, a kind and affectionate brother, a worthy equal, not rival, of his fellows, choice in the selection of his friends; but having chosen, generous, delicate, and faithful in his intercourse. Surrounded by almost every phase of religious belief, he, with perfect single-mindedness, passed into the fold of the

[1] My late venerable friend favored me with this conclusion, at eighty-two years of age, after reading this sketch of my brother's life. He was an able and distinguished member of the bar in Windham County, was member of Congress for several years from Vermont, and became the intimate friend of John Quincy Adams, Henry Clay, etc., etc. His memory was remarkable, and his interesting and agreeable conversation abounded in anecdotes of the eminent men of that period, with whom he was personally acquainted. An accomplished gentleman, his varied attainments shed an attractive halo around him in advanced life.

old New England faith, and thenceforth the conscientiousness which marked his previous life became absorbed in devotion to the will of his Master. Of his patriotism, courage, and humanity, he gave ample proof, when he voluntarily surrendered unusual advantages of domestic life, and impelled by the exigencies of duty, took upon himself the manifold labors, hardships, and dangers of the nation's soldier. And when at last the enemy, who from ambush had purposely inflicted his death-wound, became his captive, whose doom was placed at his disposal, he not only repelled all temptations to revenge, but ordered him to be kindly treated like other prisoners. A character like this does not belong to the great public, which is unworthy of it, but belongs rather to every sincere individual, who is seeking for the example of what is honest, just, and true.

"May he here find it in the life and characteristics of Major Charles Jarvis."

Extract from Professor W. G. T. Shedd's letter to Mrs. Richards, dated Lexington Avenue, New York, January 13, 1864.

" . . . . I saw him last in the spring of 1862, upon his return from a visit to Washington and the army. Our conversation was rapid and earnest, as we had much to say. I was impressed with the high moral view which he was ardently taking of the war, and although he said nothing that indicated such a purpose, I thought it highly probable that his convictions would ultimately carry him into the field. When I heard that he had devoted his life to the support of the Union and the Constitution, I was not surprised. And when I heard of his death, I felt that no more valuable sacrifice of individual life had been made during the whole contest. He had no mercenary motives to urge him onward. All his worldly interests were against the decision.

" But he laid down his life, not from patriotism merely, but from religion. It was a whole burnt-offering. He died in the prime of manhood, with a Christian hope, leaving a high example behind him, and tender, tearful memories in the hearts of all who knew him. To us short-sighted mortals, it seems mysterious, that a world so full of pretense, and so greatly needing men of position and sincere native qualities, and Christian men, whose religion is a sober and deep conviction of the whole mind and heart, should be so often and so prematurely deprived of them." . . . .

Resolutions of the Ninth Vermont.

" *Whereas*, It having pleased an all-wise Providence to remove from us our esteemed friend and brother, Major Charles Jarvis, who fell mortally wounded in an encounter with the enemy, near Cedar Point, North Carolina, December 1, 1863, therefore —

" *Resolved*, That in the loss of Major Jarvis the regiment has lost a valuable officer, the State one of her most honored and worthy sons; the country, a man of eminent zeal and patriotism, and the world a consistent Christian.

" *Resolved*, That the deceased was distinguished alike for gallantry as a soldier, his affability as a companion, and his kindness as a friend; that he was faithful in the discharge of every duty, and ever watchful of the interests and happiness of both officers and men.

" *Resolved*, That we tender our sympathies and condolence to the friends and relatives of the deceased; commending and pointing them to the God of battles for consolation and support; while with them we mourn his loss we recognize the hand of divine Providence in this dispensation, and bow in humiliation to His will.

" *Resolved*, That the officers of this regiment, as a token of respect to his memory, wear the usual badge of mourning for thirty days.

"*Resolved*, That copies of these resolutions be sent to the family of the deceased, and to the " Vermont Journal " for publication.

" V. G. BARNEY,
"Lieutenant-colonel 9th Vermont Regiment.
" J. O. LIVINGSTON, *Secretary.*

" NEWPORT BARRACKS, *December 3, 1863.*"

Proceedings of the Windsor County Court, Woodstock, December 12, 1863.

. . . . (3d Resolution.) " *Resolved*, That we will ever cherish, with sincere respect, the memory of our departed friend and brother ; that in him we recognize all the nobler qualities that adorn the man ; public spirited and charitable in every good work ; to the unfortunate and poor, kind and generous ; that as a neighbor and townsman, he was beloved and respected ; and as a citizen, he was universally honored and esteemed ; as a volunteer soldier in the army of his country, he was ever at his post of duty, never shirking his full share of responsibility, nor avoiding the necessary dangers incident to his duties as a soldier. With a heart that ever beat with affectionate warmth for his friends and kindred, its pulsations were no less warm for his country, and his country's just cause, in this the day of her trial. We mourn his untimely death with most sincere sorrow, and bow with humble resignation to the sad dispensation of divine Providence.

" *Resolved*, That we tender to the mother of the departed, and to his surviving sisters and kindred, our sincere sympathies, in this day of great grief and calamity. And while they mourn the loss of a warm and tender-hearted son and brother, we also mourn the departure of a brave and sincere patriot.

"*Resolved*, That the Clerk of the Court communicate to Mrs. Jarvis, the mother of the deceased, the proceedings of this bar, at this time, and that she be furnished by him with a copy of these resolutions.

"NORMAN WILLIAMS, *Clerk*.

"WOODSTOCK, *December* 12, 1863."

Similar resolutions were passed at a meeting of the citizens of Weathersfield, offered by Hon. William M. Pingry.

DEATH OF MRS. ANN BAILEY JARVIS.

SINCE this work has been in press, the beloved mother has gone to meet her son, her husband, and all the dear ones gone up before, in the assembly of the just made perfect in Heaven.

In October she had an attack of paralysis, and summoned her sisters and daughters around her, thinking her end was approaching. She had sweet words of love and kindness for each, and was calm and peaceful, resting on the good Shepherd. But she rallied; and though feeble, with occasional turns of suffering, was quite comfortable until January, when she dropped into a deep sleep, soothed by the thought of a heavenly Father's watchful care, and awoke in His presence, unencumbered by the earthly tabernacle, January 12, 1869. She was eighty-one, and retained her faculties perfectly. Her eye-sight and hearing were unimpaired.

Her son-in-law, Dr. S. G. Jarvis, was her physician, and as assiduously devoted to her as an own son could be. She was patient and grateful for all attentions, during her illness, and it was a privilege to minister to her wants. She said one day, as we were around her bed rendering some assistance, "I never knew any one to have so much done for them. Were I a *queen*, I could not receive more kindness and attention."

And was she not a queen in her own household, over which she presided so wisely and judiciously; ever dignified and polite, just and true? How well her domestics were disciplined, the workmen provided for, and how admirably everything was regulated!

As I look back through the vista of years, how surprising appear the many garments she made so nicely and beautifully with her own hands for her husband and children, and the knitting she accomplished evenings. What care and attention she gave to the wants of her husband, as his bodily infirmities increased.

With what dispatch her morning avocations were performed; and handsomely dressed, she was seated in the parlor with her husband at eleven o'clock, a companion for him, ready to read the papers, (and she read aloud remarkably well, though her voice was not strong enough to read long at a time), play a game of backgammon, or receive their guests. Precisely at one a nice and abundant dinner was always on the table.

It was the Consul's principal meal,[1] and his tastes were scrupulously attended to, though he would never be consulted about it.

They seldom dined without one or more guests, as any friend who had called about that hour, or persons coming on business, were invited to their hospitable table.

She rose early to set all the wheels of the household in motion, to the end of her life.

She was a model of neatness, industry, and order — of all womanly virtues; and was greatly beloved and respected for her many noble and estimable qualities of heart and mind. Exemplifying Solomon's virtuous woman: —

"The heart of her husband doth safely trust in her; she

---

[1] He took nothing but tea and dry toast, morning and evening, excepting one boiled egg for breakfast.

will do him good, and not evil, all the days of her life. She is like the merchant's ships. She bringeth her food from afar. She worketh willingly with her hands. She reacheth forth her hands to the needy. . . . . Her children rise up and call her blessed," etc.

A respected minister thus writes : —

" She has gone before you into God's higher home, and yet, with your grief for the loss, is blended a larger joy in the thought of the grateful and pleasant memory of the goodly life, of the new member of the *upper household,* who has made a place *vacant here.* The thought of her will abide with you, a thought to grow in joy, with the advance of the years, as the vista of what remains to you of earthly life grows shorter, and the hour of the great realization draws near."

27

APPENDIX.

—◆—

A. — A SKETCH OF THE PEPPERRELL FAMILY.[1]

THE elder William Pepperrell came to the Isle of Shoals, from Tavistock Parish, near Plymouth, in Devon, at twenty-one. He invested his little stock of cash in fishing-boats and equipments, and let them to others on shares; and the fish, when cured, were sold to merchants for the Southern and European markets. Being highly prospered, in five years he removed to Pascataqua, Maine, now Kittery Point, in 1680, and married Margery Bray, the only daughter of John Bray, who, with his wife, left Plymouth, England, for the free enjoyment of their religious opinions; purchased land at Pascataqua, where the old Pepperrell mansion now stands, and spent a long life here in ship and boat building.

This was a very profitable business, and he extended it on a large scale. Mr. Bray gave his son-in-law the site for a house, on which young Pepperrell erected a very comfortable and good one for the period. Here all his children were born, and here he lived fifty-five years, till his death (at the age of eighty), a most useful and exemplary life.

As early as 1699, Rev. John Newmarch was employed

[1] Principally from Parsons' *Life of Sir William.*

at Kittery Point by the year, and was allowed a parsonage. In 1714 a church was organized. William Pepperrell and wife headed the list of communicants, after the minister, and were the main pillars in the church. Most of their eight children[1] became members. Sir William, not till his father's death in 1734. Rev. J. Newmarch continued sole pastor till 1751, when Rev. B. Stevens was ordained his colleague, and continued in the ministry till his death, in 1791. Consequently these two faithful and able men were ministers in this church for nearly one hundred years.

William P. was a Colonel in the war of thirteen years with the Indians, and for many years Judge of Common Pleas; and his son William, while a minor, served as Clerk of the Court. Andrew was at first in partnership with his father, and resided at Newcastle; at his death, William was taken into the house, and the firm changed from William Pepperrell & Son to *William Pepperrells*. The Pepperrells built and sent many ships to the West India Islands, laden with lumber, fish, oil, and live stock, to exchange for cargoes of West India produce for home consumption, and later sent cargoes to Portugal, France, and England. But a much larger amount of business was done in the fisheries. They sometimes had more than one hundred vessels at a time on the Grand Banks and at other places. They dealt in lumber, naval stores, fish,

---

[1] The children of William and Margery Pepperrell were, Andrew, Mary, Margery, Joanna, Miriam, William, Dorothy, Jane. Mary married Hon. John Frost, and had sixteen children; second husband, Rev. B. Colman, D. D.; third, Rev. B. Prescott, of Danvers, Massachusetts. Margery married Pelatiah Whitmore, and had four children; second husband, E. Gunnison, Judge of Common Pleas, of Kittery. Joanna married Dr. G. Jackson; six daughters. Miriam married Andrew Tyler, merchant, of Boston; five children. Dorothy married A, Watkins; two children; second husband, Hon. Joseph Newmarch. Jane married B. Clark; two children; second husband, William Tyler, of Boston brother of Andrew.

and provisions; extended their sphere of business, and
for some years were the largest merchants on the Pascataqua, or even in New England, and in a little more than
half a century amassed a princely fortune. With all their
vastly extended and diversified commerce, it should be
mentioned to their credit, that they never imported *slaves*
from *Africa.* They greatly enlarged their estate by the
purchase of an extensive tract of land, part of the present
townships of Saco and Scarboro, containing valuable mill-
privileges. The ascendency which the Pepperrell firm
enjoyed over any mercantile house in New England, gave
it a large agency in the transaction of pecuniary affairs of
the Province in the mother-country. This branch of business was conducted by the younger Pepperrell, and brought
him into an intimate acquaintance with the public men of
Boston; and this, while it cultivated courtly manners, and
an easy address, for which he became distinguished, introduced him into the best society, and favored his advance-
ment in military and political life. No sooner had he
passed through his minority, than he was appointed Justice
of the Peace, and Captain of a company of cavalry; and
was soon promoted.

Among the families of distinction in Boston to whom
young Pepperrell was presented, was that of *Grove Hirst,*
an opulent merchant, whose wife was the daughter of
Judge Sewall, of the Supreme Court. Here he met their
daughter, Mary Hirst, and afterwards had frequent interviews with her at the house of her uncle, Rev. Samuel
Moody, of York. He won her affections, and they were
married in 1723, when he was twenty-seven.[1]

---

[1] He made an addition to his father's house, giving it a stately appearance, and here the happy couple lived. In later years the walls were
hung with mirrors and paintings; his sideboard loaded with silver; his
park stocked with deer; he kept a costly equipage, and retinue of servants,

At the age of thirty, he was made Colonel, which placed him in command of all the militia of Maine. About the same time he was appointed representative for Kittery, and next year a member of the Board of Councilors, which appointment was renewed thirty-two successive years, until his death; during eighteen years he served as President of the Board. In 1730, Governor Belcher appointed him Chief Justice of the Court of Common Pleas. Colonel Pepperrell and his lady now passed much of their time in Boston: he in the General Court, and in mercantile pursuits; she, with her children. She had been highly educated in Boston, and was well qualified to direct their instruction. Elizabeth and Andrew received the best education the Province afforded. Elizabeth attended the. best schools there, residing much of her time in the families of the Hirsts and Sewalls. Andrew was also a frequent inmate, while fitting for college, which he entered in 1741. Naturally kind and affectionate, comely in person, and graceful in manners, he was the idol of his parents, and won the esteem and favor of a large circle of friends and acquaintances among the *élite* of Boston. He graduated at Harvard at nineteen, with distinguished honors, and soon afterwards (1744) became copartner with his father.

Lady Elizabeth, having completed her education, returned home to requite with filial duties and affection the care of her devoted parents.

Few, if any, belles of her day possessed equal attractions. An heiress of rare accomplishments and winning manners, daughter of a distinguished merchant, high in official station; above all, a lady of sound religious principles, and abounding in Christian graces, she was truly "a

and a splendid barge; and from his high position, he entertained many distinguished guests in the most hospitable and elegant style.

gem of the first water." Many were the admirers who clustered around her. A young merchant of Boston, Nathaniel Sparhawk, at last gained her affections, and they were married in 1742. He opened a mercantile house in Kittery, and her father built and furnished for her a handsome mansion, with a long avenue of trees; still standing, and known as the Sparhawk House. She became a member of the church in 1741.

In 1744, Sir William was appointed by Governor Shirley of Massachusetts, Commander-in-chief and Lieutenant-general of the provincial forces in the expedition against Louisburg. Louisburg was situated on the island of Cape Breton, and was an important stronghold of the French. The walls were forty feet high, and six feet thick, which, with other fortifications, had cost six millions of dollars, and it was deemed impregnable. After a siege of six weeks, in which General Pepperrell displayed bravery, wisdom, and prudence, in an eminent degree, Louisburg surrendered.

The successful issue of this expedition was hailed with great rejoicing in England, as well as in the Provinces; and for his gallant and efficient services, General Pepperrell was created a Baronet by George II., and a Colonel in the regular army. He received the most complimentary letters from the Duke of Newcastle, Governor Shirley, etc., etc. A series of ovations awaited him on his arrival in Boston (1st June, 1746, about a year after the conquest of Louisburg), and in all the towns through which he passed *en route* to Portsmouth and Kittery. Most happy was his reunion with his family after an absence of eighteen months.

In 1749 he visited London on public business. His companion in arms and friend, Admiral Sir Peter Warren, who commanded the British fleet at the siege of

Louisburg, hastened to meet him. They were soon presented at court, where King George II. gave Sir William a cordial reception, and bestowed high encomiums on his services at the siege. The Prince Regent, Lord Halifax, and other noblemen, sought many interviews with him, and bestowed upon him many civilities. The Lord Mayor caused a massive dinner service of plate to be raised, and presented as a token of respect for his military services.

The *hero of Louisburg* was made a guest at the tables of the nobility, and was an object of universal interest among the people. All this was highly gratifying. He visited Sir Peter Warren and lady, at their seat in Westbury, and remained in England a year.

He had high ambition for his only son, the object of his fondest anticipations, but his hopes were suddenly crushed. In February, 1751, he was attacked with typhoid fever; the best medical aid proved unavailing. His afflicted parents, believing that "the prayer of the righteous availeth much," sought the prayers of all the clergy in the neighboring parishes, and sent a special messenger to Boston to seek the intercessions of four eminent divines in their son's behalf. But it was otherwise ordered. He died after ten days' illness. Sir William's letters to Sir Peter Warren and lady, Governor Wentworth, etc., etc., evince his deep grief, and earnest, submissive piety.

· The siege of Louisburg had subjected him to hardships and privations, which laid the foundation of rheumatism; and this finally terminated his useful and eventful life, July, 1759, in the sixty-third year of his age. Few were blessed with a stronger constitution of body, and his mind was equally firm. Difficulties and dangers served only as occasions to draw forth his resolution, boldness, and intrepidity. He was humane, forbearing, and forgiving. His manners were engaging and elegant. He had a high relish for the innocent and refined pleasures of society; was the delight of his friends, and the life and spirit of every company.

His funeral obsequies were attended by a vast concourse. The drooping flags on both shores of the Pascataqua, the solemn knell from neighboring churches, the responsive minute-guns from all the batteries, and the mournful rumbling of muffled drums, announced that a great and good man had gone — the old hero of Louisburg.[1]

His funeral discourse, delivered by Rev. Dr. Stevens, was published by Lady Pepperrell, and a copy sent to each member of the House and Council. Many copies are still preserved. Lady Pepperrell caused an elegant and convenient house to be erected near that of her daughter and the church. Blessed by the filial love and dutiful attentions of her children, Colonel and Mrs. Sparhawk, and her grandchildren; happy in the ministrations of her friend and pastor, Rev. Dr. Stevens, and enjoying the resources of literature; here she lived thirty years, until her decease in 1789.

Sir William, it was said, could travel from Pascataqua to Saco River, nearly thirty miles, on his own soil; and his possessions were large in Scarboro, Elliot, Berwick, Newington, Portsmouth, Hampton, and Hubbardston. In Saco alone he owned five thousand five hundred acres, including the site of that populous town, and its factories.[2]

He left Lady Pepperrell all his furniture, carriages,

[1] After the death of his father, Sir William sent to England for the marble structure that he placed over his tomb, which still remains and marks the spot where the Pepperrells rest.

[2] When the land in Saco was sold after its confiscation in 1779, Thomas Cutts, who had served a clerkship in Sir William's counting-house, purchased a mill-lot, and a large portion of the Pepperrell lands. He was the youngest son of Hon. R. Cutts, of Cutts' Island, and removed to Saco at twenty-two, where he amassed the largest fortune in Maine next after Sir William's.

horses, etc., etc., and *half* his *real estate during her life.* To his daughter, all his real estate in the parishes of York and Berwick, and the *income* of the *other half* of his real estate. At *their decease,* he gives portions of his landed property to each of his grandchildren. But the great bulk of it, including his Saco lands, was left to his fourth grandson, William, as residuary legatee, whom he had adopted after his son's death, as heir to his title and estate, on condition of his changing his name to Pepperrell, and all his plate, all his portraits of his friends, his watch, and the sword presented by Sir Peter Warren.[1]

This immense estate was acquired by Colonel Pepperrell and his son, Sir William, by industry, perseverance, wisdom, and discretion, in the management of their affairs, and by the conscientious discharge of their duties to their families, the public, and their God. The uncommon executive ability, uprightness, and urbanity of Sir William, won for him the highest offices and honors in the gift of the government.

But how true it is that "riches take wings," etc. Sir William suffered some pecuniary losses by his patriotism in going to Louisburg. His grandsons, William, Samuel H., and Andrew, joined the loyalists in the time of the Revolution, and this large landed property was confiscated by the United States government in 1779.

B. — SPARHAWK FAMILY.

NATHANIEL SPARHAWK came to this country from Essex, England, with his wife and son, Nathaniel, in 1640. He was an educated man, and held several offices of trust in the new colony. He died at Cambridge in 1650. His only son married a Miss Newman, daughter of a clergy-

---

[1] This sword is now in the possession of Colonel Russell Jarvis, of Claremont. It was presented to his father by Mrs. Dr. Charles Jarvis.

man in Rehoboth, Massachusetts; settled in Cambridge, and had three sons — Nathaniel, John, and Samuel. These names have been handed down in every generation since.

John graduated at Harvard in 1689, and was first pastor over a Congregational Church in Bristol, Rhode Island, erected in 1690. (It was rebuilt in 1770; the present edifice in 1857.) He died at forty-six, in 1718. "A true servant of God, and a diligent minister of the Gospel; he was greatly loved and respected by his people, and his death was lamented for many years." His wife was a Miss Hemans, and they had two sons, John and Nathaniel.

She afterward married Jonathan Waldo, Esq., a wealthy merchant of Boston, who educated *her* two sons.

His son, Samuel Waldo, by a former wife, was highly educated, and had great advantages from foreign travel, having crossed the ocean fifteen times. He was for many years one of the Board of Councilors, in Boston, with Sir William Pepperrell, and was largely concerned with him in mercantile affairs. His only daughter was engaged to Andrew Pepperrell for two or three years, and finally married Mr. Thomas Flucker, much to her father's disappointment. John Sparhawk was settled in the ministry at Salem, and left many descendants.[1] Nathaniel entered

[1] After his decease, his eldest son, John, removed to Kittery, with his widowed mother and sisters, and went into business with his uncle, Colonel Sparhawk. He afterwards went to Portsmouth, and married Abigail King, granddaughter of Governor Vaughn, an exemplary Christian lady. At the close of the Revolutionary War, his cousin, Sir William Pepperrell, sent for him to go to England, and state before the High Court of Admiralty the losses which he had sustained by the confiscation of his estate; which evidence proved a great advantage to the Baronet, and was most satisfactory to him.

On the death of Colonel Sparhawk, his widow and her mother, Lady Pepperrell, who highly esteemed Mr. J. Sparhawk for his integrity and worth of character, intrusted their business to his care, and he collected their rents and dividends, had the oversight of their real estate, etc.

He became a prominent man in Portsmouth, and was Speaker of the

into a commercial house as partner with Benjamin Colman, of Boston. In 1742 he married Lady Elizabeth Pepperrell, and removed to Kittery, where he opened a counting-house, the partnership with Mr. Colman continuing many years.

Sir William built a handsome house for his daughter, and furnished it in a style of elegance unusual in the colonies. After the English fashion, the bed and window-curtains were of red, blue, yellow, etc., damask, and each chamber was designated accordingly.

Colonel Sparhawk was a tall, fine-looking man, with polished and elegant manners, a cultivated mind, and exemplary in his private life. They were a happy couple, and had five children — Nathaniel, William Pepperrell, Andrew, Samuel Hirst, and Mary Pepperrell. Their eldest son was only sixteen years at the death of his grandfather, Sir William Pepperrell, in 1759.

Colonel Sparhawk became a man of influence, holding many public offices, and was a member of the Board of Councilors several years before the Revolution. At its outbreak he was thought to favor it. An officer awoke him in the night, demanding his "boats for the King's service."

To which he replied, " Certainly."

The officer then said, "The boats are not to be found."

Colonel Sparhawk answered, "I saw them there at eight o'clock, and some one must have taken them away."

The truth was, he had sent his servants at nine o'clock to sink them, to prevent their being used for the king.

After his death the State of Massachusetts allowed his widow, for her right to the lands, devised to her by her father (Sir William Pepperrell), $30,000.

Their son, William P., married Elizabeth, daughter of

House of Representatives. He died at forty-five, leaving three sons: George King, Samuel (a man of rare excellence and virtue), and Thomas.

Hon. Isaac Royall, of Medford, a strong Tory, whose principles exerted so much influence over his son-in-law, that he also joined the king's party ; as did also his brothers Samuel H. and Andrew. They all went to England, young Sir William taking his rich plate and personal property, bequeathed by his grandfather; all three brothers were proscribed.

Andrew, a fine man, died in 1783, without children. Samuel Hirst, in 1787, leaving one daughter, Harriet Hirst, who has been frequently spoken of. Nathaniel went to England after his father's death, lived in the style of a nobleman, and spent most of his share of his grandfather's estate, leaving his two sons, Nathaniel and William, without professions and without property.

Young Sir William's lady died at Halifax, on her voyage to England. Their children were, Elizabeth Royal, who married Rev. Henry Hutton, and had ten children : Mary Hirst McIntosh, married Sir William Congreve; she died without issue : Harriet, married Sir Charles Thomas Palmer, and had six children : William, died young.

The name of Pepperrell has become extinct since the death of Sir William, in 1816; but his descendants are yet numerous in England, and many of them have Pepperrell for a middle name. All are highly educated, and in high stations.

Lady Pepperell, the relict of the hero of Louisburg, died at Kittery in 1789, and Colonel Sparhawk did not long survive her.

His widow was greatly afflicted by his death. She had lost her mother and husband, and was now alone in the old family mansion. Although an earnest Christian, she became so much depressed, that her daughter, Mrs. Jarvis, prevailed upon her to make her a visit in Boston, and then she was persuaded not to return, but to reside there.[1]

[1] Two faithful old family servants, Cæsar and Phillis, unwilling to be

Much of Madam Sparhawk's time was now devoted to works of charity; walking in the footsteps of her Master, she literally fed the hungry and clothed the naked. So that the Consul, who knew her when he was a young man in Boston, said he had never met with so consistent and exemplary a Christian; so cheerful, amiable, and benevolent. She died in Boston in 1797. The old homestead was retained in the family. Nathaniel, the eldest son, returned to it in 1809, and the only daughter, Mrs. Jarvis, in 1813. Here both ended their earthly career in 1815.

Madam Sparhawk had preserved about thirty of her father's portraits of his family and friends.

After Mr. Nathaniel Sparhawk's decease, the place was sold, and the pictures were widely scattered. Mr. James Sheafe, a wealthy merchant of Portsmouth, had aided him in his pecuniary affairs, which, by his long residence in England, had become much embarrassed; and after his death, Mr. Sheafe and his lady were very kind to his sons Nathaniel and William, who, in return, presented several of the portraits to them. Mr. George King Sparhawk, who also rendered efficient assistance to these relatives, received from them some of the most valuable. Among these were full-length portraits of Colonel and Madam Sparhawk, finely painted, I think by Copley, now in the possession of Charles Sparhawk, Esq.,[1] of Conway, New Hampshire. Soon after her marriage, Mrs. M. P. S. Cutts was indebted to the kindness of her kinsman, Colonel George Sparhawk,[1] for a very valuable old painting of Louisburg, while in the possession of the French, said to be the only picture of Louisburg extant. Also for one of

separated from their loved mistress, followed her to Boston, and remained with her and Mrs. Doctor Jarvis until their death. Their greatest happiness was expatiating on the various incidents and former grandeur of the Pepperrell family. Aunt Phillis had taken care of Mrs. Jarvis when a baby.

[1] Sons of Mr. G. K. Sparhawk.

Sir William Pepperell, the elder, and for a good portrait of Governor Belcher, the warm friend of Sir William.

When Mrs. Cutts went to Portsmouth in 1829, Mrs. James Sheafe very courteously presented her with a portrait of young Sir William Pepperrell, executed in England, in fine preservation. Just before the decease of this superior lady, in 1864, she presented another, yet more valuable, of the hero of Louisburg, in the full-dress of that period, while he was in England in 1750, taken by an eminent artist. Dr. Parsons has a fine steel engraving from this portrait, in his life of Sir William Pepperell.

The portrait of Sir William Pepperrell, received from Colonel Sparhawk, Mrs. Cutts gave to her sister, Mrs. David Everett Wheeler, of New York, in 1836. And Miss H. H. Sparhawk presented Mrs. Wheeler with a very superior painting of Lady Pepperrell, both of which Mr. Wheeler had cleaned and handsomely framed. Miss Sparhawk also gave Mrs. Cutts a portrait of Madam Sparhawk, by Copley, in crayon. A beautiful miniature of this excellent lady was bequeathed to her cousin, Mrs. Cutts, by Miss Abby Humphreys, at her decease in 1866.

Mrs. Mary Wheeler Smith, wife of Rev. C. Smith, of New York, has an elegant little silver box, in the cover of which is a fine miniature of Mrs. Royall; on the bottom is this inscription, " The gift of General Royall's lady to Mrs. Elizabeth Sparhawk."

The only descendants of Sir William Pepperrell now in the United States are, Mrs. Elizabeth Spooner Jarvis and her children, in California; Everett Pepperrell Wheeler, Esq.; his sister, Mrs. Mary Wheeler Smith, of New York, and their children ; Mrs. Mary Pepperrell Sparhawk Cutts, and her children and grandchildren, and Miss Harriet Hirst Sparhawk, now eighty-three years old, whose mind is still vigorous, corresponding with her friends, and writing a small, neat hand.

C. — JARVIS FAMILY.

LEONARD JARVIS and Sarah Scott had sixteen children. Seven lived to grow up, namely: Leonard, Betsy Stelle, Sarah Russell, Charles, Edward, Susan Gibbs, and Joseph R.

By the "Georgia land speculation," he lost most of his fortune, and went with his family to settle a body of land on the Penobscot, which he owned there, and died at seventy-three. His eldest son, Leonard, graduated at Harvard College. He was a man of high culture and taste; went abroad in early life, and made a fine collection of pictures, which, in after years, were destroyed by fire, as well as his elegant residence in Surry, Maine. He was twice elected member of Congress from Maine, and was appointed United States Navy Agent for the State of Massachusetts.

Charles was appointed by the State of Maine Colonel of the troops to defend the rights of the United States against England, in relation to the Eastern boundary. Died in 1860.

Edward married Miss E. Spooner; resided many years in Castine, Maine, and they and their children are now in California.

Joseph Russell entered the navy. He married Miss Mary Otis, of Boston. He was a Commodore in the service, and is now in Illinois with his wife and two children. He was a brave and able officer.

Betsy Stelle married Mr. Carr, and had two lovely, accomplished daughters. They are in Geneva, Illinois.

Sarah R. married Mr. Whiting, and had two sons, one of whom is in the army, the other is in Castine, Maine.

Susan G. went to Illinois with her sisters, and is unmarried.

SAMUEL GARDINER, the second son, had five children, who lived to mature years, that have been already mentioned.

Susan Pierce married John Jeffrey, Esq., and died without children in 1806.

Dr. Leonard married Miss C. Draper. Children: Susan Pierce, Samuel Gardner, Leonard, Russell, and William; the latter died in infancy.

Susan Pierce married Joseph Thornton Adams, Esq., and they had four children: Jeffrey, Leonard, Susan J., and Ellen Derby. The sons, two fine promising young men, one a physician, the other in the navy, died in early manhood.

Dr. Samuel G. has been spoken of in this memoir.

Leonard lost his life in California.

Russell married Miss Lucretia Pierce Rice, of New York. They have had two children, Anna Ladd and Russell. The former, a fine, intelligent child, has been recalled by the great Giver.

Mary, who was remarkably social, agreeable, and well informed, died in 1827, in Boston, warmly beloved by many friends.

Helen married Guy Hunter, Esq., and also died in Boston, leaving no children.

Russell married Caroline Dana. Their only daughter, Caroline D., married John H. Uhl, Esq., a merchant in New York, and they have two children. Russell's second wife and two lovely children were lost in Long Island Sound, in the burning of the "Lexington." Russell died in 1853, in New York.

NATHANIEL (fourth brother of Leonard) died at fifty-eight, leaving two children, William C. and Susan, who married Mr. Cushing, of Providence, Rhode Island. William C. studied law, married a young lady in Pittsfield, Massachusetts, established himself in that town, and became an eminent lawyer. He was for several years Speaker of the House of Representatives. He had no descendants, and died in 1836.

Susan, Mrs. Cushing, was sensible, witty, practical, and interesting. She left four sons and one daughter, who are widely scattered. She died in Providence.

The Consul's aunts, Mrs. Leonard Jarvis and Mrs. Russell, died within a few days of each other, in February, 1836, in Ellsworth, Maine. "Aunt Mary" died in Surry, Maine, February, 1826.

D. — THE CUTTS FAMILY.

In the early settlement of the country there was so much association between the Pepperell, Sparhawk, and Cutts families, that I cannot refrain from a short outline of their history.

Three younger brothers of an old family, John, Richard, and Robert Cutts, emigrated from Ackesden, Essex County, England, to this country prior to 1646. Their father's estate, Grondale Manor, belonged to the eldest son by entail, and these young men obtained large grants of land in and near what is now Portsmouth, New Hampshire, and came to seek their fortunes in America. Their friend, the renowned John Hampden, was to have accompanied them, but he was prevented from doing so.

John and Richard owned tracts of land on Pascataqua River, and in 1660 were the largest landholders in Portsmouth. Robert owned Cutts' Island, and a tract of land in Kittery. John was the first President of New Hampshire. The General Assembly held in that State, was convened by President Cutts, in Portsmouth, in 1679. Richard died in 1675, leaving a large property to his wife and children, and John in 1681, bequeathing a valuable estate to his son John. According to some accounts, he left his wife Ursula a farm on the west side of the Pascataqua, a retired but

28

picturesque situation, about two miles from Portsmouth, which she cultivated with taste and skill, and adorned with beautiful and rare flowers, brought from England. But in 1694 she was surprised, and cruelly murdered by the Indians, who, being unable to remove her rings, cut off her hands, and also her long, fine hair, with the scalp. Other writers [1] state that the Lady Ursula Cutts was the sister of John, Richard, and Robert. That she inherited a fortune from her mother, and was attached to an officer — a Colonel in the army. But her father objected to their union, wishing her to marry a nobleman. He was ordered with his regiment abroad, on foreign service, and she determined to come to America with her brothers.

After her father's death, the Colonel sailed for Boston, and they were to have been married, but as she sat in the open air awaiting the coming of her betrothed, she was barbarously killed by the Indians, and his anticipated joy was converted into horror, when on his arrival soon afterwards, he beheld her mangled body. He returned to England. This is the most romantic tradition, but may not be the true one.

Robert settled on Cutts' Island. It was afterwards connected with the main-land by a drawbridge, which was taken up every evening for the safety of the inhabitants, and let down in the morning, to permit the workmen to attend to their duties on the estate in Kittery. His son Richard succeeded to this landed property. Madam Wood gives a glowing description of the style of living and family, of Hon. Richard Cutts, grandson of Robert.[2] As a picture of the times, I venture to make a few extracts : —

[1] Madam Wood, of Kennebunk, Maine, whose grandmother was an orphan niece of Hon. Richard Cutts, of Cutts' Island (who resided in his family), and Mrs. Eliza Buckminster Lee, granddaughter of Rev. Dr. Stevens, of Kittery.

[2] A letter addressed to J. Wingate Thornton, Esq., of Boston, grandson of Hon. Thomas Cutts, of Saco.

. . . . " They kept thirty cows, and large flocks of sheep. The spacious, old-fashioned, comfortable house had a dining-room that would accommodate fifty or sixty guests. The mantels of the immense fire-places were adorned with colored glass, and silver branches for candles. The floor was daily scrubbed with wax, and was polished like a mahogany table. The six dozen pewter plates, and their attendant dishes, bore upon the edge the crest of the family, and were kept bright as silver. The walls were covered with paintings and work, executed by the daughters, who were sent to the best schools, and taught beside the solid branches, music, dancing, and embroidery. When at home, one day in every week was devoted to the manufacture of cake and pastry, in which they attained great skill. They also assisted in spinning and in the dairy, etc., etc., which last was under the careful supervision of Mrs. Cutts. They kept a pleasure boat, and each young lady had a horse and side-saddle of her own. They had a chaplain, and an apartment called the chapel, in which they had services on Sunday, and prayers every morning and evening. On Christmas, Easter, and Good Friday, they attended the Episcopal Church in Portsmouth. . . . .

" Once every year they gave a grand entertainment. Just before my grandmother's marriage, there was an unusually splendid one. It was the middle of June.

" The lawn had been rendered smooth for dancing, and the gravel walks, leading from the landing to the house, which were bordered with box, had been put in fine order. A barber came at sunrise to dress the hair of all the ladies and gentlemen in the family.

" The Major was arrayed in brown velvet, laced with gold, and in a wig of great dimensions, well powdered. Madam Cutts, in black damask, a lawn cap and hood, a white and silver stomacher, cuffs, with double lace ruffles, velvet shoes and blue silk stockings, with silver clocks.

"The daughters and granddaughters in rich brocades and yellow satins. Old General Atkinson was dressed in scarlet velvet, and his wife in crimson velvet, trimmed with silver. Governor Vaughn, whose mother was a Cutts, wore blue velvet, and his lady and daughters white damask and velvet, etc., etc. All the ladies wore high-heeled shoes, paste buckles, and gay silk stockings, with lofty head-gear, from which descended lappets of lace.

"The guests arrived at eleven o'clock A. M., and musicians were stationed at the landing to welcome them with 'God save the King,' etc.

"Upon entering the drawing-room, they were entertained with cake and sack. After sitting a *proper time*, they walked about the island, had a little excursion upon the water, danced upon the green, and were then summoned to dinner.

"A large barbecued pig stood in state at one end of the table, and boiled chickens, hams, and tongues at the other, flanked with ducks and a variety of fish, caught that morning. From the centre of the table rose a snowy pyramid — a silver tub that would hold four gallons, — filled with pancakes, rising from its polished sides, covered with powdered sugar. Just below was a floating island, representing a ship in the sea.

"Pastries of various kinds, generous plum-puddings, custards, jellies, fruits, wines, and cordials, crowned the repast. A large bowl of punch had been handed round to every guest, who did justice to it, in the early part of the entertainment. Everything was the product of the Island, but the sugar, wines, spirits, and lemons.

"After sitting two hours at the table, chocolate and tea were served on the green before the door, and then with an abundance of ceremonious bows and courtesies, the company bade adieu to their hospitable entertainers."

This is a sketch of a dinner-party one hundred and thirty or one hundred and forty years ago.

Major Richard Cutts (whose family has just been described) was with Sir William Pepperrell in the expedition against Louisburg, being a Major in one of the York regiments.

His children were Samuel, b. Dec., 1726. Foxwell Curtis, b. 1730, graduated at Harvard College, 1747; m. Mary, a sister of Gen. Goodwin, of Berwick, Maine. Richard, of Cutts' Island, b. 1732; m. Sarah, dau. of John Frost, Esq., of Kittery. Edward, m. Miss Welsh, of Boston; one son, Edward. Thomas, b. 1736. Mary, b. 1734; m. Charles Chauncey, Esq., of Boston, son of Rev. Dr. Chauncey. She died at twenty-four years of age, greatly beloved for her many virtues. Margaret, m. William Vaughan, Esq., of Portsmouth.

Samuel served a clerkship in the counting-house of Colonel Nathaniel Sparhawk; was afterward an eminent merchant in Portsmouth, and married Anna, daughter of Edward Holyoke, President of Harvard College. He was President of the Council before the Revolution. They were both highly esteemed for their superior minds and characters. Their children were Edward, Eliza Eppes, Samuel, Charles, Priscilla, Hampden, Anna Holyoke, George, and Sydney.

Samuel Hampden, Anna H., George, and Sydney, died unmarried. Edward was a merchant of high standing in Portsmouth; married Mary, daughter of Nathaniel Carter, Esq., of Newburyport, a large importing merchant, and a most estimable man. Of their seven children, only Hampden and Mary survive.

Charles was a graduate of Harvard College, a member of the bar, Speaker of the House of Representatives of New Hampshire, a member of Congress from that State, and for many years Secretary of the United States Senate. He married Lucy Henry Southall, a niece of Mrs. Madison, and a descendant of Patrick Henry. Children, Samuel H., Stephen, and Martha H.

Thomas, youngest son of Hon. Richard, a distinguished merchant in Saco, was senator in the Massachusetts Legislature. He married Elizabeth, daughter of D. Scammon, Esq. Children, Mary, Thomas, Sarah, Richard. Richard graduated at Harvard College in 1790, and visited Europe. On his return, he was elected to Congress, in 1801.

John Quincy Adams says of him: " Descended from one of the most ancient families in New England, and inheriting that inextinguishable love of freedom, — the peculiar characteristic of the English Pilgrims, — he gave a firm and efficient support to the administrations of Jefferson and Madison for six successive Congresses, until 1813, when he was appointed Superintendent General of military supplies." . . . .

In 1804 he married Anna Paine, sister of Mrs. Madison. Of their six children, three lived to mature years, Madison, Richard D., and Mary. Madison, now deceased, left two children, the lovely and beautiful Mrs. Douglas, and Madison, who was aid to General Burnside in the late war. General Richard D. married a daughter of Mr. Hackley, United States Consul at Cadiz, a lady of elegant deportment and great worth. General C. resides in Washington, and has long been a member of the United States Corps of Civil Engineers, and employed in the coast survey. For his efficient and loyal services he received the appointment of General in the late war.

E. — JOSEPH DANFORTH.

JOSEPH DANFORTH, now eighty-four, the oldest resident at the " Bow," and one of the oldest in the town, six feet in height, and naturally of strong and athletic frame, was but four years old when he came there with his parents in 1788. Joseph Danforth, Sr., was for several years extensively engaged in making potash, near what is now called "the Eddy." At this place all the boats that passed up and down the river, and the rafts, were moored. Potash, in the early settlement of the country, was one of the most important products in trade, being sent down the river in exchange for groceries, English goods, cutlery, etc., etc.

These potash works were afterwards taken down, and others more carefully built near the tannery and curriers' shop, on land which now forms part of the garden belonging to the house the Consul gave his daughter Harriet and her husband, Rev. J. D. F. Richards. Mr. and Mrs. Danforth had several children born at the "Bow," where they both spent the remainder of their lives. Joseph Danforth, Jr., married Margaret Bryant, of Weathersfield, and for many years plied a freight-boat between that place and Hartford, Connecticut. When Mr. Good-hue sold his real estate to the Consul, Mr. Danforth took his effects to Brattleboro' in his boat, on condition that he should be supplied with a load from there to Hartford, and this load was furnished by Deacon Holbrook, who then carried on an extensive business. Mr. Goodhue purchased a large tract of land in Brattleboro', on which he built several houses, a part of which is still in possession of his descendants.

F. — WEATHERSFIELD BOW.

Mr. REUBEN HATCH came from Norwich, and bought the large brick house built by a Mr. Jennison, a store, and considerable other property. He had a large family of sons and daughters. Jonas Cutting, who was afterward a Colonel in the War of 1812, owned a farm and brick house [1]

[1] Clark Tolles now owns this house and farm.

about a mile from the village, and had also a large family
Samuel Steele had several children, and the Haskells were
numerous ; so that the school, which was well conducted,
had sometimes seventy pupils.   There were so many young
people, that balls were frequent in the winter at the public
house owned by Mr. Hatch, and they had occasional gath-
erings or parties.

Mrs. George Hubbard, at the " Ferry," was an excellent
matron of the old school, looking well to the ways of her
household, and here " the young folks " often assembled.
Mr. Hatch bought Mr. George Lyman's house, tavern, and
store, and Mr. Lyman removed to Hartford, Connecticut.
In 1801 or 1802, Mr. Francis Goodhue bought all Mr.
Hatch's property, excepting the Lyman House, and a
small store, which he gave to his son-in-law, Darius Jones,
and his daughter.   Mr. Hatch then returned to Norwich.
Mr. Nye's house was a very good, convenient one, on the
hill above the tannery, a story and a half high.   Mr. Nye
sold it, with his farm, to the Consul, and Russell Mason
and his wife hired it of him for fifteen or twenty years.
She was a lovely Christian character, and he was an excellent gardener, painter, etc., but intemperance became his
ruin.   Mrs. Mason was universally esteemed, and her
house was a pattern of neatness and order.   They had
two daughters.   Harriet married a Sprague, Melinda a
Marcy.   All are dead.   The Nye House has lately been
pulled down.   The wheelwright shop has been converted
into a house on the Steele Farm, now owned by the Consul's daughter, Louise.

The blacksmith's shop, shoe-shop, Jones' store, potash
works, three or four houses, and the grist, saw, and bark
mills, are all taken down.   But a stone church, and two or
three new houses, have been erected ; among them one
owned by Mr. Danforth, in which his daughter keeps the
post-office.

G. — MEMORIAL WRITTEN BY MR. JARVIS IN 1827.[1]

" *To the Honorable the Senate and House of Representatives of the United States of America, in Congress assembled :* —

" WE, the undersigned wool-growers and woolen manufacturers, citizens of the United States, residing within the State of Vermont, deem it a duty, which we owe to ourselves, and to our country, respectfully to represent to your honorable body, that we are perfectly satisfied, partly from the statistical and historical records of modern Europe, and partly from the personal observation of many of us, that the great prosperity and power to which several European nations have attained, were primarily owing to their extensive manufactures ; and that the flourishing state of the manufactures in the most prosperous nations, particularly that of Great Britain, has been altogether owing to the *fostering care* and *uniform protection* which that government has given to them for nearly five centuries past.

. . . . "As American citizens, we are mortified to be under the necessity of saying that we have been disappointed in our expectations of receiving that legislative aid which was so essential to protect our manufactures, upon whose success depends the success of the wool-growers, and directly or indirectly, the great mass of the farming interest. The necessities of our country during the late war, requiring a large supply of woolen goods, caused thousands of our citizens readily to embark their fortunes in establishments for manufacturing wool, to supply its wants. After its expiration, being disappointed of the protection, which they had anticipated government would bestow upon them, great destruction of the property of all classes of persons, connected with this branch of in-

---

[1] This memorial was not found until this volume was nearly printed, and is consequently inserted in the Appendix.

dustry, ensued. For, from the total neglect of the manufacturing interests, except that of cotton, from the close of the war until 1820, our country was *inundated* with *British fabrics*, to the annihilation of our manufactures of almost every description.

Next to the manufacturers, none suffered more severely than the breeders of sheep; and the breeding of these invaluable animals, whose fleeces we had confidently expected would have proved a solid and profitable staple to the Eastern, Middle, and Western States, *retrograded* more rapidly than they had *advanced* from 1811 to 1815." . . . .

Mr. Jarvis then speaks of the "frauds committed on our revenue, by British agents in this country, by invoicing their goods far below their real cost, and our country has again been deluged with British goods, which has nearly put a stop to our manufacturing establishments, and left such of our farmers as were not compelled to sell their wool at a great sacrifice, with their last clip on their hands. And your memorialists are fully persuaded, that if Congress, in its great wisdom, and patriotic attention to the welfare of the community, does not immediately afford some further protection to the woolen manufactures, that a scene of bankruptcy and ruin, much more widely spread than that which took place from 1818 to 1820, must inevitably follow; which, so far as they have the means of estimating, will occasion a total loss to the country of over fifty millions of dollars of active property, and the irretrievable destruction of this most useful and necessary branch of American industry.

"The history of all civilized nations proves the great importance which has been attached to both of these branches of industry. The present prosperous situation of many of the States of modern Europe, and the miserable condition of others, incontrovertibly prove the truth of our assertion, not to quote the opinions and statistical calculations of the ablest writers for several centuries past.

" As it relates to wool, England has for many centuries given great attention to the extension and amelioration of her flocks, until, if some of their best writers are to be relied upon, they have increased in the United Kingdom to the enormous number of forty millions of sheep, and their annual clip of wool amounts to one hundred and forty million pounds weight.

" About sixty years ago the Saxons, being in an impoverished state, from the effects of the Seven Years' War, as a national resource, introduced merino sheep from Spain, to ameliorate their native breeds; and by the steady attention and great encouragement which the electoral government gave to this object, it was crowned with the most complete success. That wise government was no less attentive to her woolen manufactures, and the result has been, that instead of Saxony's being dependent upon foreigners for several kinds of woolen goods, she now manufactures enough to supply her own wants, and to vend a considerable surplus to other countries, in addition to annually exporting large quantities of the finest wool now grown in Europe; and she has now become more prosperous than any other portion of the German dominions. France, likewise, since 1787, has given great attention to the improving of her breeds of sheep, by the introduction of the Spanish merino; and the various governments of that country — since that period — have steadily kept this object in view, and have placed several of the national farms under the superintendence of scientific agriculturists, to accomplish so beneficial a measure. Sixteen years' experience has incontestably proved to us, that our country is as well adapted to the breeding of fine-wooled sheep, as either Spain or Saxony, or perhaps any other in the world.

" We will now appeal to the history of Spain, to show the effect which manufactures have upon the prosperity of nations. About three centuries ago, Spain was one of the most flourishing kingdoms of Europe. The bigotry of Philip III. expelled the Moors from Spain, and with them, the manufacturing industry of the country. South America and the mines, becoming the principal object of that government's attention, internal industry was almost totally neglected. The consequence was, that the precious metals, which flowed into the mother country from her American possessions, were sent to her more industrious neighbors, to pay for the various manufactures which they furnished her until the improvident inattention of that government to the improvement of her natural resources, has reduced one of the finest countries on the globe — in point of soil and climate — to a state of want and wretchedness, that has no parallel in the history of the civilized world. An equally salutary lesson may be drawn from the histories of Portugal and Italy. . . . . England, perhaps, affords the most striking example which is recorded on the page of history, of the astonishing prosperity to which a nation can attain by a wise encouragement of manufactures. We believe the first legal protection that ever was given to manufactures, was by a law of Edward III., in 1337; and from this beginning commenced a systematic encouragement of every branch of manufactures, which has continued to the present time. . . . . To her manufactures may fairly be ascribed the extension of her commerce, and her improvement in agriculture ; and to their united influence, her wealth and her naval and military strength, which, in our own times, have set at defiance and finally overthrown the most gigantic military power the world ever saw. What a contrast does she now present, compared with what she was, when exclusively an agricultural people. Conquered successively by the Romans, the Saxons, the Danes, and the Normans; until the establishment of manufactures, even the most of their Norman masters, for want of money, could with difficulty keep an army in the field six months together, for credit they had none. But we need not look abroad for examples to prove the injurious effects upon the welfare of nations, occasioned by a dependence upon foreigners for those kinds of manufactures necessary to their comfort, for we apprehend that the history of our own country affords some pretty conclusive ones. To go no further back than the late war, we might ask if much of the embarrassment, which our government experienced in conducting it, did not arise out of the difficulty of obtaining *clothing* and other *manufactured articles*, necessary for the supply of the army. Was it not humiliating to us, as a nation, that for want of a few thousand blankets, to fulfill our treaty stipulations with the Indians, a high executive officer was obliged to recommend a deviation from a system of policy, which had been adopted by Congress, to enable us to obtain them from foreigners?

"So dependent were we upon foreign nations, for almost every manufactured article of comfort and convenience, that at the very time Great Britain was waging an almost vandal war upon our country, we were furnishing her with the sinews for its support, by our great consumption of her high-wrought fabrics. In what manner has Great Britain paid for the immense amount of our funded debt, and United States bank stock, held in that kingdom, and which renders us indirectly tributary to her?

"The answer is easy. Her agents and our merchants have remitted it to them in payment for the very great quantities of her manufactured goods which we annually consume. . . . . The vast mind of Napoleon soon became sensible that the manufactures of England were the inexhaustible mines from whence she derived her wealth, and this was the origin of his ' Continental system,' or, in other words, his system for the prohibition of British manufactures from the Continent of Europe. This system, the very monarchs who were leagued with Great Britain to accomplish the downfall of that great man, have one after another been obliged to adopt, to protect the internal industry of their respective kingdoms from being paralyzed by the overwhelming capital and great skill of the British manufacturers, and to prevent their internal resources being drawn by degrees into Great Britain." . . . .

Mr. Jarvis discusses the question of the revenue being injured by a *protective system ;* but proves that without immediate protection, many thousands of our citizens will be reduced to a state of poverty and want.

" How such a state of things can benefit the revenue, we confess we cannot perceive. . . . . It is an axiom in political economy, that *consumption* always keeps pace with the *means of purchasing.*"

He then speaks at some length of the frauds on the revenue practiced by British agents, in selling their goods at auction, after passing them through the custom-house with false invoices, to the great injury of merchants and manufacturers. Then, with a thorough knowledge of the subject, points out the best mode of fixing the duties on foreign goods, in order to protect the manufacturer, and to guard against these enormous frauds on our revenue. . . . . Parliamentary speakers advocate *free trade ;* " but while we consume from *twenty* to *thirty millions* of her *high-wrought goods,* England systematically *refuses* to receive in return any of the *products of our country.*" [1]

1 This memorial occupied seventeen pages of foolscap, and I have been obliged to omit several pages.

EXTRACTS OF LETTERS FROM SEVERAL GENTLEMEN ON THE PUBLICATION OF THIS MEMOIR.

———◆———

From HON. E. P. WALTON, *of Montpelier.*[1]

. . . . "Your materials are rich and varied, embracing periods of time in the history of Europe and America that are hardly excelled in interest by any other era, unless it be the late rebellion, and embracing many men who yet live in the memories of their countrymen. . . . . . I remember your father, too, as a leader in political conventions, and better than this, I remember one ' élite day ' in my life, a good part of which was spent in an interview with him in the old homestead, when I bore him a commission as Senator of the United States, and vainly attempted to prevail upon him to accept it.

"I knew my father's high estimation of him, and Governor Paine's, but that interview satisfied me that if your father had been placed in the Senate long enough to be a match for his contemporaries in *experience*, he would have been esteemed as one of the giants of the nation.

"Respectfully yours,

"E. P. WALTON.

"MONTPELIER, *March* 9, 1868."

From FREDERICK BILLINGS, ESQ., *of New York, formerly from Woodstock, Vermont.*

. . . . "It must have been to you a labor of love. His quiet life so many years on his great farm, kept him away from the eyes of the people, and there is the more need that the story of his life should be told. No one could do it so well as you, and I anticipate the publication of the book with great pleasure. 'Consul Jarvis' was always to me a great man; and as I think of it, it seems almost wrong that he should have spent so many of his ripest and best years on that farm, in that region of Vermont. He was so wise and far-seeing in his views of public affairs, so full of learning, and so able to instruct and guide, it is a pity he was not in all his years in a wider field. It is a loss. . . . .

"With kindest regards to Mr. Cutts,

"Yours very sincerely,

"FREDERICK BILLINGS.[2]

"NEW YORK, *May* 26, 1868."

[1] For several years member of Congress, and son of the Consul's friend, who so long edited the *Montpelier Watchman*, a strong, firm advocate of Republican principles.

[2] Mr. Billings was a distinguished member of the bar in San Francisco for many years.

From CHARLES P. MARSH, Esq., *of Woodstock.*

"MY DEAR MRS. CUTTS, — . . . . In my opinion, we have never had in Vermont a man whose life furnishes so many incidents for an entertaining, useful biography, as that of your distinguished father, and I am glad it has been undertaken by one, whom I believe has the ability to do justice to the subject. . . . .

"I remain your friend and obedient servant,

"CHARLES P. MARSH.

"WOODSTOCK, *May* 25, 1868."

From COLONEL D. CRAWFORD, *of Putney.*

. . . . "I have attended political and tariff conventions with your honored father, listened to his sound remarks, and read with deep interest many newspaper articles from his pen. I need not tell you I esteemed him one of the best and most useful men in the State. . . . .

"Respectfully yours,

"D. CRAWFORD."

From JUDGE J. W. COLBURN, *of Springfield.*

. . . . "For the last twenty years of his life I felt intimately acquainted with your honored father. He was a marked man, a tower of intellectual strength. He had no *superior* in our State, and but *few equals* in our whole country. I often enjoyed the hospitality of his friendly mansion, and have often remarked that among all my acquaintance, none possessed the varied and extensive intelligence upon all subjects, that he did. His conversational powers were brilliant, his topics always interesting, and many were the hours I enjoyed, and much information did I obtain, in listening to his talk about old times, old subjects, and old countries, as well as things more modern, and of our own country. He was a man of wonderful energy, of the strictest integrity, and might have enjoyed the highest honors within the gift of our State, if he would have permitted it, but this he steadfastly declined. His example to the community around him was good; for a rich man he was economical, and none of lesser means were ever led into any species of extravagance by copying from him.

"I am glad you have undertaken the task of giving us a memoriam of his life and virtues; . . . . for such a man should not be left to rest in the silent grave, with none of the living to speak for him to the rising generation. I am glad, too, that you are to notice the tragic end of your lamented brother, the late MAJOR CHARLES JARVIS, who was killed in North Carolina, in the late rebellion. An honester heart, a nobler, purer mind, never existed in this frail mortal tenement, than he possessed. He esteemed it a duty to serve his country in her calamity; but I felt sorry to have him leave our neighborhood, and when I looked upon his remains, dressed in his uniform, covered by the Stars and Stripes, on that wet and dreary Sabbath, I could not repress the involuntary tears. It was so sad to see a young and promising man, the hope and stay of an aged mother, the idol of sisters, cut down by the ruthless hand of an unjust and cruel war! But such are the inscrutable ways of Providence. My respects to your husband.

"Your friend,

"J. W. COLBURN.

"MOUNT VALE FARM, *July* 19, 1868."

From L. C. WHITE, ESQ., *of New York, formerly of Windsor.*

. . . . "There are few men whom I looked up to with that degree of esteem and veneration with which I regarded your father. His kind words and friendly counsels to me in my younger days, when just starting in a business life, I shall never forget, and his genial manners and pleasant face are still fresh in my recollections.

"Very respectfully yours,

"L. C. WHITE.

"*April* 22, 1868."

From Mr. N. B. PIERCE, *of Cavendish.*

. . . . "None could say aught against your late honored father; no poor man that had ever lived by him, unless the fault was theirs. I know that he was always down on any one that speculated in bread-stuffs. As an instance, I relate this affair which happened in 1836, I think, when flour was high. A Mr. S——, of Chester, was speculating in flour. He came to your father with a note signed by a rich man of Chester for $2,000. Your father did not know S—— but by reputation. He said to him, 'I suspect you are the man that is speculating in bread-stuffs.' He replied affirmatively. 'You cannot have my money for this purpose. If any of your neighbors want money for any other use, I can let them have it; but no man shall have money of me to speculate in flour.'

"This happened while I lived at the 'Bow.' Where can we find a man who lived in those days, that had any amount of money to lend, who would not take *unlawful interest*. But your honored father never did. . . . . . I feel much interest in your book.

"Yours truly,

"N. B. PIERCE.

"*April* 24, 1868."

Extract from an article in the "Rutland Herald." By HON. HENRY CLARK.

. . . . "This volume will present a feature of the lives of the men of Vermont, who have helped to give our Commonwealth the fame it has justly earned as an intelligent agricultural community, and place upon record the services of one of her foremost citizens, whose life was marked for its strict integrity, liberal hospitality, great acquisition of knowledge, wonderful memory, remarkable colloquial powers, and disinterested patriotism. . . . . Consul Jarvis' field of labor was far wider than the limits of

29

his own State. He was the intimate friend and correspondent of some of the most distinguished men of his time in all sections of the country, and his views were often sought upon various public questions of national importance, and his influence oftentimes decided the course of action to be pursued.

" He was the correspondent of Henry Clay and Rollin C. Mallory, from 1820 to 1830, and many of their opinions and arguments upon the tariff during that period were made under his advice and assistance. Much of the correspondence between Clay, Mallory, and Jarvis, from 1820 to 1831, is in the possession of the writer of this article, which bears ample testimony of the valuable services rendered by Consul Jarvis to the cause of AMERICAN INDUSTRY."

From the "Montpelier Journal." By HON. E. P. WALTON.

" Many of our readers will doubtless be glad to learn that a volume, entitled ' The Life and Times of Hon. William Jarvis,' has been prepared by Mrs. Mary P. S. Cutts, and is soon to be issued from the press by one of the most eminent publishing houses in America. . . . .

" Had Mr. Jarvis done nothing but introduce the best sheep of Europe to America, he would justly be ranked as a national benefactor. For this, Vermont especially is greatly indebted to him. Fifty years ago, our farmers were not swift to accept costly improvements. They were then struggling with the difficulties of new openings in the wilderness. . . . . But this is not all the claim Mr. Jarvis has upon the gratitude of the State and of the nation. The production of fine wool in America was of little importance, indeed of doubtful utility, if American farmers were merely to export it, and compete in the markets of England with the nearer European producers of the same material.

" If Mr. Jarvis had been an intelligent farmer only, he might think himself well repaid by improving his own and his neighbors' flocks; but he was really a *statesman* of the broadest views, and in the front rank of American statesmen at that day.

" He foresaw that the introduction of fine wool was to make America the competitor of England in its manufacture, and not in wool alone, but in every material essential to the independence of the nation, and to gain a fair field for competition in the commerce of the world. I doubt if any American was better skilled in political economy or in the political history of the leading nations of the world. . . . .

" Mr. Jarvis was an earnest and influential advocate of what was known as ' the American system.' He had no high position, from which to address the public, as did Clay and Mallory, and many other distinguished men; but by his pen, through the press, and by correspondence, he both instructed the people, and moved men who were masters of public positions, and who for many years controlled the policy of the nation. With

Mr. Jarvis it was a short step from wool to manufactures, and with Governor Paine, from manufactures to the railroad. Both were pioneers in their way and day. . . . .

"My knowledge of Mr. Jarvis, little as it is, and my better knowledge of others since, who have a national reputation, has given me a strong impression that if he had received the same positions and opportunities, he would have taken rank with the giants of the land, such as those among whom his youth and early manhood were passed, when the foundations of the nation were laid, — men, who in vision beheld its future grandeur, and discovered the way to it.

"I fancy that in all the details of agriculture, manufactures, and commerce, he was as skillful as the late Senator Simmons, of Rhode Island, and probably in a wider field, embracing politics, history, and international law; that he was as practical as Senator Wilson, and a more logical and forcible speaker; and I know there was that in him not possessed by these eminent men, and rarely possessed by any, which gave the impression of a Titanic power of will, and courage, and intellect, that no modesty of the man could possibly conceal. Among historical men, I fancy Cromwell must have had it; among living men, I remember only one who impressed me in the same way; it is Thaddeus Stevens.

"E. P. W."